Personages
of
Pride & Prejudice

Personages
of
Pride & Prejudice

Charlotte Collins, "Maria Lucas," and *Caroline Bingley*

JENNIFER BECTON

A WHITELEY PRESS BOOK

A WHITELEY PRESS BOOK

ISBN-13: 978-0615595122
ISBN-10: 061559512X

Printed in the United States of America.

Cover: *Lady Morgan*, portrait by René Théodore Berthon, held in the National Gallery of Ireland. (Image in public domain.) *Woman with a Fan* by Hamilton Hamilton. (PD-US: Image in the public domain.)

OTHER WORKS BY JENNIFER BECTON

THE SOUTHERN FRAUD THRILLER SERIES
Writing as J. W. Becton

Absolute Liability
Death Benefits
"Cancellation Notice": A Southern Fraud Short Story

❧ ❧

✎ Contents ✎

Charlotte Collins

A Continuation of Jane Austen's *Pride and Prejudice*

For

Octavia Clark Becton

I consider everybody as having a right
to marry once in their lives for love, if they can.

᪥ Jane Austen ᪥

✑ Prologue ✑

1818

The sun shone on the day of the Reverend Mr. Collins's funeral, and Charlotte knew that her husband would have questioned the wisdom of the Almighty for allowing such fine weather on the burial day of one of the church's devoted servants.

As the exceedingly devout rector of Hunsford, near Westerham, Kent, Mr. Collins had always preferred to conduct a funeral in dour weather, which he felt appropriately matched the solemnity of the occasion. A light drizzle was an additional benefit, for it forced mourners to wear heavy attire despite the season. In his estimation, a funeral was a weighty thing, and no lightness or warmth of any kind was to be tolerated. So he would have been properly horrified by the impious gaiety of his own funeral day.

Fortunately, in his extinguished state, he would not have to tolerate the day's infernal light, for he had already departed the earthly realm for the kingdom of heaven. Should he take exception to the fine weather, he could discuss it with the Almighty face to face.

And he probably would.

Charlotte, however, had seen to every earthly detail; her husband was attired in his most expensive suit, mourners had remained constantly beside his body, and she was seeing to his legal affairs. But the weather was out of her control.

Now, Charlotte stood in the doorway of Hunsford parsonage and watched the funeral procession begin its morbid journey as the unseasonably warm wind caused leaves of vibrant red, orange, and yellow to rustle on their perches and blew her somber-hued skirts, revealing more ankle than was strictly proper. Sun glinted off the hearse that bore her husband's coffin, highlighting the buckles on the horse's harness as he trotted briskly away from the house despite the driver's attempts to slow him to a more sedate gait. The mourners maintained a more dignified pace. Among those men who

1

followed the coffin were her father, who genuinely mourned the loss of his son-in-law; Mr. Darcy, who did not mourn him at all; and a host of parishioners, whose grief fell somewhere between the two.

She watched as the procession disappeared down the drive, loath to return inside where the drawn drapes blocked out nearly all light. Even so, she fancied that her wretched light-swallowing bombazine mourning attire darkened the room still further.

She nodded to her companions, family and friends who were also clad in black gowns, gloves, and scarves. Like the men who escorted Mr. Collins's body to his final resting place, they too had gathered to grieve for a gentleman whom few had liked well enough to hold five minute's conversation.

As his widow, Charlotte felt a measure of sorrow at Mr. Collins's death; he had been her nearly constant companion these seven years. But she had not been in love with him. She could hardly even claim to have liked him.

Of course, Mr. Collins had not been in love with her either. Their marriage had not been his choice. The commandment for him to wed had come from on high: from his patroness, the Lady Catherine de Bourgh herself. And so, he had taken himself to visit his cousins, the Bennets, with the intention of securing a wife *en famille*. Upon discovering Mr. Collins's mission and the absolute revulsion of his intended fiancée—her dear friend Elizabeth Bennet—Charlotte had pursued him, quite literally.

Under the guise of easing Elizabeth's burden, she had put herself into Mr. Collins's path at social events and absorbed his conversation in private.

In truth, Charlotte had wooed him.

And when she spied him coming down the lane to Lucas Lodge, her family home, ostensibly to propose, she had rushed to meet him quite by chance so that he would not lose his nerve. Nearly seven-and-twenty, Charlotte was nigh on becoming a spinster and an encumbrance to her family, and marriage was the only option available to an educated woman of small fortune. And as a practical woman, Charlotte had seized the opportunity available to her, meager though it was.

Yet, somehow she and Mr. Collins had served each other well. Charlotte had removed herself as a burden to her parents and gained a comfortable home of her own, and Mr. Collins had pleased his patroness, lifting him in her esteem. And as long as they avoided each other most of the time, their marriage was quite pleasing.

In the early days, Mr. Collins had actually served as a somewhat tolerable companion, but after the death of their only child, Margaret, a beautiful dark-eyed replica of Charlotte who had not survived even the first year of her life, the couple had become even more disconnected, merely existing in the same household. Mr. Collins had sequestered himself with his sermons, fawned over the number of windows in Lady Catherine's home, and consumed all the biscuits in the parsonage before Charlotte had ever had the opportunity to eat one.

Skirting the company of assembled ladies, Charlotte disappeared into the kitchen where she discovered her childhood friend Elizabeth Darcy, the very woman who had spurned Mr. Collins. She had traveled with her husband from Pemberley, their grand estate in Derbyshire, to attend.

Elizabeth appeared unsure of words appropriate for the situation, but she offered her a sympathetic smile.

Charlotte broke the silence for her. "I am pleased that you have come." She gestured to a chair that was tucked beneath her small kitchen table. "Have a seat in here away from the others and talk with me."

Elizabeth sat while Charlotte produced a tin of biscuits and set them on the table between them. They both selected a treat and ate in silence until Elizabeth found her voice.

"My dear Charlotte, I am sorry for your current circumstances."

Charlotte smiled. "My current circumstances must not be so negative, for they have brought you to my kitchen, and I have missed you, Eliza."

She and Elizabeth had always been good friends, but Elizabeth had disapproved of her decision to marry Mr. Collins. And Mr. Darcy found him absolutely intolerable. Consequently, they had seen little of each other over the intervening years, and the separation had caused a certain level of detachment in their friendship.

"Tell me, Charlotte, for I have heard nothing of the particulars of what has transpired: What has happened to take Mr. Collins away so unexpectedly?"

"A carriage accident. He was walking to Rosings Park to pay his daily compliments to Lady Catherine and was struck by a runaway mule wagon."

"A mule wagon?"

"Certainly, if it had been his choice of the means by which to meet his demise, he would have chosen a vehicle of quality pulled by a perfectly matched team of horses."

"Indeed!" Elizabeth said.

"But we may not always choose our circumstances."

Elizabeth sobered and met Charlotte's eyes. "No, we may not. Sometimes society—and transportation—makes demands of us that we must do our best to meet. You, Charlotte, have always exceeded the demands of society, even if I have not approved of your choices. And now you have a new set of circumstances with which to deal, and I hope that happier choices will be available to you."

Tears welled in Charlotte's eyes. She had hoped for happier choices too. But with the death of her husband, her protection and place in society had also vanished. She was alone, without daughter and husband, without home. Those circumstances merited her mourning, if the loss of her husband's company did not.

"Perhaps one day *I* shall meet with another Mr. Collins."

"Do not even joke about the possibility, my dear friend, for I believe you have done your time in purgatory. It is time for you to experience the heaven that a marriage of true minds can be. I consider everybody as having a right to marry once in their lives for love, if they can."

Charlotte envied her friend's felicity in marriage, and though her example had taught her that romantic love existed, she had no plans to pursue it herself. Her sole aim was to secure what money she could from Mr. Collins's estate and create a small, but comfortable, home for herself.

"I thank you for your kindness. If I cannot manage happiness in my choices, then I will have to make the best of those indifferent choices that are before me."

"As you have always done."

Elizabeth fell silent, and at length, Charlotte nodded in the direction of the sitting room and said, "But now, I fear, I must do my duty to the assembled company." She had balked at calling them guests, for that denoted people who had been invited for pleasure. Those in the sitting room appeared anything but pleased. In fact, they appeared quite ready to depart, and Charlotte could not blame them.

Upon entering the room, her younger sister Maria Lucas came to her side and touched her arm briefly. It was the most meaningful gesture her flighty sister could manage. And her mother, now swaying under the effects of ill health, lurched to her feet and wobbled alongside. They managed to encircle her, and Charlotte wished they would have kept their seats.

Her mother pressed her hand in hers. "Oh my dear daughter, whatever shall you do now? For we cannot possibly afford you."

Charlotte understood well her worries. A woman alone was at a disadvantage in society. And Charlotte was now truly alone.

But she produced what she hoped was a comforting smile for her mother. "All will be well, Mama. Pray, take your seat and do not be concerned about my future. Worry does no good."

Charlotte restrained a wry smile. Indeed, it would do no good for her mother to waste feeble energies on concern for her. She was concerned enough for herself, but only decisive action would remedy her situation, and at the moment, she was rendered ineffective by duty.

Even now, she wished she could be about the business of securing her independence, of talking to her husband's solicitor. Alas, she must fulfill her final obligation to Mr. Collins, though in her heart, she wished that the mourners would depart.

Why had any of them come? The scene was utterly nonsensical. No one lamented the death of the gentleman to whom she had been married, except perhaps Lady Catherine, and she could not even be put upon to visit the parsonage.

Perhaps they had come simply to verify that Mr. Collins had well and truly departed for the mansions of heaven, which undoubtedly had as many fine windows as Rosings Park, and to ensure that he would never again bore them with his tedious conversation.

৯৯ One ৯৯

1820

"Do not tell me that you intend to spend the rest of your days in this dreadful sitting room, Charlotte," Maria said, settling herself on the faded upholstered chair beside the fireplace with a flounce.

Charlotte set aside the letter she had been writing to her cousin Mary Emerson in London, abandoned the writing desk, and walked to the settee, knowing all too well that she would be unable to complete her correspondence now that her sister had joined her. In lieu of paper and quill, she picked up a cup and saucer from the mismatched tea set on the tray beside the settee. The cup was empty. She felt the pot; it had gone cold. Such a bother.

She rang the bell for beverage reinforcements, lowered herself to the settee, and regarded the room. She had to admit that it was rather dreadful, the furniture worn, and the rented cottage small, but at least she had such comforts, and two servants as well.

"I do intend to sit here in this room, for, despite its faults, I find it rather pleasant."

Indeed, it was the loveliest room in her cottage. Two comfortable chairs with curving wooden arms flanked a cream-colored settee, which had probably been white at one time. The seating area was situated in front of a modest but cheery hearth, and an old writing desk was tucked between two windows, facing south and opening toward an herb garden. As the sun made its course through the sky each day, it brightened the room and nurtured the plants outside and the occupants inside.

"How dull." Maria, who obviously did not feel nurtured by the small room, practical furnishings, or the sunlight, clucked her tongue as she glanced around her.

"I much prefer the quiet life, and now that Mr. Collins has gone to his reward, I feel that I deserve mine. I shall enjoy my little home and meager income, and I shall live out my days as a very eccentric old widow."

"Old? Bah! You are but five-and-thirty years old, and that is not so very aged." Maria leaned forward. "You must get out into society again."

Charlotte reclined against the settee. "Must I?"

"Indeed, sister, for you have worn your widow's weeds far longer than required, and you of all people deserve a happy existence after living with such an odious man as Mr. Collins."

Charlotte smiled at her sister, wishing for her sake that the world worked in such a manner, that people actually received that which they deserved, and knowing it never would. Maria had reached her early twenties and remained unmarried, but still she retained the hopefulness and innocence of youth.

Foolish girl, Charlotte thought as she studied her sister. Maria's blond hair had slipped its pins and now the loose strands glinted in the firelight. Without so much as checking her own coiffure, Charlotte knew that her dark hair remained neat and precise. She was never anything but neat and precise.

Maria blew a wisp of hair out of her face. "And it would fit in with my plans."

Charlotte narrowed her eyes. This certainly did not bode well, and she meant to interrogate her sister immediately, but before she could demand an explanation, the door opened, and Edward entered balancing a tray of fresh tea things.

Edward Effingham. His name was grander than his intelligence. And even if his family had managed to retain its fortune, he would not have married well. Edward was her housekeeper's son, a young man of fourteen years with thin strawberry blond hair and a body as sturdy as a fence post. A good servant, he tended to many household duties, but his mind seemed to be caught somewhere in early childhood.

He walked into the room with slow, metered steps and placed the tray on the table as though he carried royal porcelain and not chipped pieces from Charlotte's old set.

He made a deep bow and rather than exiting the room unobtrusively, he said, "Mama told me to make certain that your tea is properly set for you, Mrs. Collins. She told me not to open my mouth and speak a word to you, but I cannot know if the tray pleases you without asking, can I?"

Charlotte cast a cursory glance at the teapot and fresh cups. "Everything is as it should be. Thank you, Edward."

He grinned in relief and exited the room without remembering to take the old tea tray with him. The door closed with a click behind him as he returned to Mrs. Eff in the kitchen. Charlotte turned her attention back to her sister. She had been watching Edward's departure as well.

"He's forgotten the old tea tray," Maria said. "He is not the brightest lad, is he?"

"No, but he is kind, and that often makes up for mental facility." Moreover, Charlotte was grateful for her servants. Her family had been unable to afford much household help, and so she, Maria, and her other siblings had often been required to prepare meals or beat rugs. She certainly did not desire a return to household chores. She added, "Besides, he and Mrs. Eff have released me from most of the kitchen drudgery."

"It *is* nice to live in a home in which I am not required to cook." Maria's face had turned wistful, reminding Charlotte that something was amiss. "I wish to have servants of my own one day."

"Yes, now, tell me of these plans to which you have so subtly alluded."

"I know that my visit was intended to endure only a few months, but…" Here Maria paused dramatically and mustered a pouty expression. Trouble was certainly afoot. "I had hoped that I might come to reside with you here in Westerham. Mama and Papa are ever so feeble, and they have made arrangements for our brothers and sisters. I am the only child who was to remain at home. However, they will never again make proper chaperones, and I shall have no hope of meeting a gentleman suitable for marriage unless I can move about in society. I am virtually an old maid, you know."

Charlotte poured two fresh cups of tea and considered her sister's situation. Their parents' health had continued to decline, leaving Maria without the benefit of society during the prime of her young life. She had not had the opportunity to experience the exuberance of youthful courtship. Or its disappointments.

Indeed, Charlotte had never experienced love as such and had doubted its very existence until she had too late seen the evidence of it. Now, she believed that it was a rare commodity. "Better to be an old maid than unhappily married."

Maria's expression soured briefly. "Even you are not convinced of the truthfulness of that statement. Confess. You have always believed that it was better to be unhappily married than to be a poor old maid."

"Yes." Charlotte could not dispute that she had believed so in the past. Mr. Collins had certainly made her reconsider her previous philosophy, and now, she was less certain of her opinion on the matter.

Maria ignored her tea and picked up the bonnet that she had discarded earlier that morning. She began to arrange a bow of pale green ribbon. Concentrating on her task, she appeared to give little thought to her words. "I shall find security and love, I am certain of it, for I still have my beauty, but I require a chaperone to set a toe into society. Mama and Papa cannot do it, but you could. Though you continue to wear your ugly colored gowns, you are no longer in mourning and can attend balls and parties. You are an independent woman."

"My independence was hard won." Charlotte said, recalling the tediousness of her daily interactions with her husband that had resulted in her current situation. How many ponderous sermons had she been subjected to?

How many simpering compliments had she endured? And worse, how many fireplace mantels had she heard him describe in painful detail? "Note the carvings, my dear, the fluting, the ribbons. All are of the finest quality. A masterful hand created this artful mantel." And on and on he would go until Charlotte wished humanity had never discovered fire, for there would be no fireplaces on which to lavish his praise. Yes, her independence had been hard won indeed.

"But without your help, I have no hope of winning my own or of finding love." Maria looked up from her bonnet. "You must be my chaperone."

Charlotte looked at Maria's shining face and wondered if she had ever felt so hopeful. Perhaps as a very young girl she had imagined meeting the perfect gentleman and falling in love with him. Perhaps, buried deep within her the hope existed still, but she was now too practical to live for something that might never happen. Her security had not come easily, and she simply did not have the will to go into society and become swept up, and then disappointed, by the quest for love, even if it were her sister's quest and not her own.

But then there was Maria with her head full of wishes, and Charlotte knew that for some people dreams of love did come true. Her friends Jane and Elizabeth Bennet had both had the good fortune to be able to marry for love. And by pure coincidence, their beloved gentlemen had both possessed great fortunes. Charlotte had not had the luxury of marrying for love, but perhaps her sister might.

"If Mama and Papa approve, and continue to send your allowance, you may keep the small bedchamber upstairs as long as you like, and I will serve as your chaperone."

Maria squealed like a young girl, leapt off her chair, and flung herself onto the settee and into Charlotte's arms. "And may we go to the winter ball in Westerham in two weeks' time?"

Charlotte groaned aloud. She had not expected the onslaught to begin so suddenly.

"Pray, say yes, sister. A gentleman will be there whose acquaintance I do so wish to make. An *American*." Maria said the word as though it were exotic and strange. "He is said to be just about my age and is traveling with his uncle on a tour of Europe. They are relatives of Colonel Armitage and are staying at his house for the duration of their visit."

Charlotte eyed her sister. An American? What could she possibly be thinking?

The Armitages, at least, were a well-respected family of decent fortune. Colonel Armitage had been in service to England, and he had elevated his whole family's status. Mrs. Armitage was a quiet, unassuming woman, who seemed to disappear when her jovial husband was near. Their children had made very good marriages. This American gentleman came from good English stock, and if he was on a European tour, he obviously had a good income as well, but Charlotte would withhold her good opinion until she had seen proof that he was not a barbarian, which was unlikely.

"He is said to be very handsome…"

There was the real inducement, Charlotte thought.

"…and Americans are reputed to be less particular about rank and age and other things about which we English are so concerned."

Supposing it could do no harm, Charlotte smiled in encouragement. "Indeed? Well, then I suppose you must meet him."

"Then we may go to the ball?"

"Yes, I suppose we may. Quite a picture I shall make in my somber attire among all the angelic white muslin and pale-colored gowns." She plucked at the drab gray fabric of her skirts.

"It has been two years, and it is perfectly acceptable for you to begin wearing other colors." Catching Charlotte's reproving look, Maria continued, "But somber shades quite flatter your coloring. You will not make such a dour picture as you suppose. You may be the belle of the ball yet."

Maria was being kind. Absurd, but kind. Charlotte was an old widow, no matter in how loving a light her younger sister viewed her.

However, against Charlotte's will, a tiny thrill of forbidden delight coursed through her at the prospect of attending a ball, of meeting new people and conversing with old friends without the weight of Mr. Collins always about her shoulders, and of dancing again. But who would dance with her now? Her days as a debutante were over years ago, Charlotte reminded herself, quickly squashing her excitement under the weight of reality. She was just coming out of mourning for her husband and must perform her duty as chaperone to her sister.

"No one will spare a second glance at me. And certainly no gentleman."

"I would be happy if a man would only look once at me."

Charlotte sighed. "You desire a marriage so much even after seeing my own less than ideal one?"

"I do. Honestly, I do. For I have seen what is possible when one marries for love."

Charlotte understood Maria's reference perfectly, and she did not blame her one bit for desiring the same love that Jane and Elizabeth had found. "Then we shall ensure that you meet your young American, but we will do so with the utmost decorum and propriety. Otherwise, straight back to Mama and Papa you go."

Maria straightened and blinked. "What a thing to say! I shall behave myself very well."

⊱ Two ⊰

An odd mixture of scents is present in the air of any ballroom: wood smoke, perfumed flesh, cold meats, watered wine, and humanity. Charlotte had forgotten the precise combination of pleasant and unpleasant aromas. Now she inhaled deeply, attempting to ignore the stench of body odor that existed beneath the other, more pleasant, smells. The scents seemed to hold memories, and Charlotte endeavored to ignore them. Memories would do her no good. She must attend to Maria, not to her own past. Instead, she focused on more tangible elements of the chamber.

Two large fireplaces loomed at one end of the ballroom, and the sheer number of wax tapers, probably donated by Lady Catherine, who never attended a public ball but who liked to make her charity known, leant a feeling of opulence to the assembly.

Arm in arm, the two sisters wove their way through the crowd toward an empty spot near the fireplaces where they could observe the dancers. Maria sparkled in her white gown with its puffed sleeves and pale green trim around the neckline, and though she would never admit it, Charlotte felt somewhat attractive in the modestly cut lavender gown with black trim, which seemed to flatter both her face and her slim figure.

Maria jabbed Charlotte in the ribs. "That must be him." Her voice was sharp, but at least she had bothered to whisper.

Charlotte scanned the ballroom for the gentleman who had captured her sister's attention so forcefully. Maria gestured with a turn of her pretty blond head and giggled. Charlotte looked but could see no one spectacular. "Who?"

"The gentleman. The *American*." Again the word was spoken as though it denoted something unusual and not just an ordinary man. "The one standing next to Colonel Armitage."

Charlotte found Colonel Armitage easily enough, for he had a memorable physique, large and jolly, and always stood out, even in a crowded room. Beside him was a young man, who appeared to be rather tall and had dark blond hair, which had been styled to convey unconcerned wildness. She was

13

certain that such perfectly tousled wildness actually took his valet hours to achieve. He spoke to Colonel and Mrs. Armitage, gesturing broadly, and smiled just as broadly. He appeared to have engaging manner, for the Armitages attended to his every word, as did many guests, but Charlotte thought she sensed a cocky air about him.

No, she must not believe the worst of him. Not yet. Perhaps her own poor experience with gentlemen was coloring her opinion of the young man. "He looks quite…" She searched for the word. "…nice."

"He certainly does. I expected him to appear different somehow, being that he is an American. Perhaps more uncouth. But he is dressed in proper English attire."

She was quite correct. His striped waistcoat, tan trousers, and dark coat caused him to blend with the other gentlemen in attendance. "He seems to fit well indeed, but we shall see how well he gets along in society."

Maria tore her eyes from the American and turned to her sister. "You must arrange a meeting for me before another young lady steals his attentions for the evening."

How quickly Maria had forgotten her promise of good behavior. Charlotte would have to guard her carefully indeed. "I shall do my duty as your chaperone and arrange an introduction, but everything will be done in a proper manner. I certainly will not rush straight to the colonel and demand a meeting."

There were rules of behavior that must be followed without question. Appearances meant everything for a woman who hoped to gain the protection of a husband. Was she naturally witty and a good conversationalist? No? Then she must learn to be so. Was she a natural musician? No? Then she must practice until she seemed to be naturally gifted. Was she happy? No? She must pretend to be so.

A woman must be an artist, a seamstress, and a great reader, and this she must do with an air of gentleness and decorum. She must behave *comme il faut* even if she wished a thousand times a day to do otherwise. It simply had to be done in the name of keeping oneself from falling low in society and being forced to accept charity from those formerly called equals.

Maria's gaze rested again on the American. Her voice was wistful. "No, indeed. That would not do at all. I do not want to appear to be overeager."

"The best way not to appear overeager is not to be overeager in the first place."

Maria groaned. "Please do not take the pleasure out of this for me."

Charlotte took Maria by the hand, gently turning her away from the American. "I do not intend to rob you of pleasure, but neither do I intend to sit by and allow you to be injured or to injure yourself socially."

"You fret too much."

"You do not fret enough." She glanced at the gentleman out of the corner of her eye. He did not appear to be a ruffian.

Maria said, "Then together we will fret just enough."

Charlotte hoped it would be so. "We must act decorously."

The frustration Charlotte had felt from her sister seemed to vanish. Perhaps her warnings had taken hold.

"I suppose you are right, but I am so tired of being alone. I do not think a little indecorous behavior would destroy my reputation."

Perhaps her warnings had not even been heard.

Charlotte was about to offer a stern rebuke when old Mrs. Farmington and her young granddaughter sidled up to them. Mrs. Farmington maintained a powdery, aged appearance even in the generous softness of so many candles. The pattern and color of her dress, a fleshy background with a subtle chevron pattern, were also reminiscent of powder, causing Charlotte to wonder if she ordered her entire wardrobe after the substance. She groaned at her approach, for Mrs. Farmington's mind was as dusty as her appearance, and she was forever speaking out of turn.

Polite curtseys were offered and the older woman began the conversation. "Such a lovely ball, is it not, Mrs. Collins?"

Thankfully, a safe subject. "It is indeed, Mrs. Farmington."

"It has been quite some time since we have seen you out in society."

"Yes." Mrs. Farmington had put together two sentences of good sense, and Charlotte wondered if a third could possibly follow.

She gestured to Charlotte's half-mourning attire. "You do Mr. Collins credit by your devotion to him. And it was such good fortune that he was able to leave you a little something on which to live."

Apparently, two reasonable sentences were her limit.

The old lady was rude but correct. Mr. Collins had left her some money. Before their marriage, Charlotte had the foresight to maneuver him into arranging a jointure, a fitting sum of money left to her in the event of his death. Charlotte's father had encouraged her not to make any such request, believing it wisest not to be troublesome before the marriage was official. But she had ignored his advice, and at first blush, Mr. Collins, being very much against the idea, had proven her father right.

Mr. Collins had railed against the idea. A woman inheriting money was unbiblical, he said.

Then, she had reminded him of Mr. Bennet, who had made similar arrangements for his wife and children and whose house Mr. Collins himself would inherit. Of course, Mr. Collins could not allow his relation to appear to be his better. And so employing the straightforward and uncomplicated tactic of exploiting her husband's desire to keep up with his relations, Charlotte had contrived a jointure.

Straightaway after Mr. Collins's funeral, she had visited his solicitor and invested her small inheritance in the Funds, and with good luck and a high rate of interest, Charlotte had been satisfied that she would be able to exist in her widowed state.

She then sought suitable accommodations, for she was forced to vacate Hunsford parsonage so that Lady Catherine could prepare it for its next occupant. However, hoping to spare herself the embarrassing task of making inquiries of those whom she had formerly considered her social equals, Charlotte asked after another structure on Lady Catherine's estate: an unused hunting cottage inconveniently located on the fringes of Rosings Park.

Lady Catherine had agreed to rent it to her at a greatly reduced rate, a circumstance that Charlotte suspected had arisen not from charity or kindness but from a feeling of responsibility. But she did not care why Lady Catherine had given her such charity, and she certainly did not intend to jeopardize it in any way. And now that she was a lowly tenant of Lady Catherine, she was no longer invited to attend the tedious social functions at the great house.

Truly, the situation could not be more agreeable.

But it was none of Mrs. Farmington's affair. Charlotte certainly had no desire to discuss her situation with this old crone or anyone else, so she chose to deflect her line of inquiry. "Mr. Collins's death was quite a shock, but I am coping with it as best I can."

Mrs. Farmington's smile oozed pity. "Yes, yes, my dear, it is good to see you out amongst society again though I doubt there are any suitably unattached gentlemen in attendance tonight to give you a turn around the dance floor."

Charlotte did not know what reaction was proper in the face of such indiscreet comments. She could not laugh or manage to muster anger. She simply stared at old Mrs. Farmington and wondered if it were possible for her to attain the coveted blunder trio and discuss not only income and matchmaking but to comment on her out-of-fashion attire as well.

She meant well, Charlotte was certain, but rather than allowing her to direct the conversation any longer, she gestured to Maria, who stood quietly beside her. "I am acting as my sister's chaperone. And is this your granddaughter?" She nodded at the woman who stood at the old woman's side. "She looks far too grown up to be little Miss Farmington."

Mrs. Farmington beamed. "This is indeed our Constance. She is quite a good deal bigger, is she not?"

A quick glance at Miss Farmington revealed that she did not appreciate being called a good deal bigger, but she said nothing as her grandmother continued. "This is her first season out. Is she not lovely?"

Constance Farmington was a lovely young lady with chestnut hair and a sprinkling of dainty freckles across the bridge of her nose, but she rather reminded Charlotte of the red roan pony her family had owned when she was a girl. She hoped that Miss Farmington was like the pony only in appearance and not in manners, for the beast had ignored her protestations and dragged her all over the countryside in search of the most delectable grasses. That pony had taught Charlotte a great deal about the complexities of social interaction: most people—and horses—behave in ways that benefit themselves and care little for the wishes and feelings of others.

Charlotte glanced again at red roan Miss Farmington, who was clearly thrilled to be among members of the opposite sex. She leaned forward conspiratorially and spoke to Maria loudly enough for the group—and perhaps the entire assembly—to hear. "Have you had the pleasure of meeting Colonel Armitage's relatives yet?"

"No, indeed, we have not." Maria shot Charlotte a haughty look under her curving blond lashes.

"Oh, you must, for they are the most fascinating—and handsome—men as I have ever seen." Miss Farmington gestured across the room to where Colonel Armitage, the young American, and an unfamiliar gentleman were surrounded by a large group of people. "Mr. James Westfield stands there beside the colonel." She indicated the young man Charlotte and Maria had observed earlier. "He is a bit older than I, but still very handsome, do not you think?"

Maria agreed perhaps too wholeheartedly. "Yes, quite handsome. And so tall."

"His uncle stands beside him. He is quite old indeed, and his attire is certainly not up to the standard of his nephew. His name, I believe, is Mr. Benjamin Basford."

Charlotte looked at the very old Mr. Basford who was probably not more than a few years older than herself, and although his dress portrayed a certain rawness not usually seen in an English ballroom, she found him to be handsome in a rather untraditional way. His hair was stylishly tousled, although she was certain that the wind—and not a valet—had arranged it. He seemed to find the ball to be very amusing and appeared to enjoy the attention he and his nephew had generated. His expression had a rather comical bent, and he did not appear to be a serious person. Charlotte disliked his smirk immediately.

But Mr. Basford was insignificant. Mr. Westfield was the prize.

"How charming they look!" exclaimed Maria.

"Oh, they are!" Miss Farmington said. "Mr. Westfield is said to have a fortune awaiting him in America, and his uncle is apparently of no little means as well, although he certainly does not dress the part."

"Oh, how lovely. They are rich as well as handsome."

Charlotte too was pleased to hear that Mr. Westfield was of substantial means. If her sister were successful in making a match with him, she would have security, and if the dewy expression in her eyes were any indication, she might have love as well. Indeed, the situation was quite possibly ideal.

The girls continued to speak about Mr. Westfield and Mr. Basford until Mrs. Farmington became bored and, claiming a parching thirst, bustled her granddaughter away into the crowd toward the refreshment room, where lemonade, negus, and white soup awaited.

Ever the dutiful chaperone, Charlotte was soon left to stand alone to watch her sister dance with Mr. Jonas Card, an acquaintance she had made on her early visits to Hunsford. He stumbled good-naturedly through the quadrille while Maria laughed.

Though he was a well-looking gentleman, always polished and elegantly dressed, Mr. Card's fortune and property caused many of the young ladies of his acquaintance to view him as more handsome than his features warranted. Maria, however, had never looked at him twice, fortune or not, and Charlotte had always been rather sorry for that, for he was a genial sort of man who would tolerate her sister's frequent flights of fancy and was capable of financing her shopping trips.

Charlotte was contemplating Mr. Card as a potential suitor for her sister when she felt someone bump into her. Slightly off balance, she reached to steady herself against the side of the mantel and turned, annoyed, to find the offender to be a large gentleman with a shock of red hair and piercing eyes. The gentleman's gaze was intense, and he offered a slight bow. "Pray excuse me."

"It is nothing, sir." She turned politely away. They had not been properly introduced, and she did not want to invite his acquaintance by meeting his eyes again. But the man continued at her side. She could sense his gaze upon her, and she began to feel slightly uneasy.

"I do not believe we have been introduced, but I do not see how it is so wrong for an introduction to take place now that I have nearly caused you to fall. I am Lewis Edgington." He offered a proper bow. "I am an often forgotten relation of the de Bourgh family. A distant cousin actually."

Charlotte was reluctant to break with convention, but he was a relation of Lady Catherine, so she curtseyed with extreme decorum and what she hoped was a foreboding expression.

He continued undeterred by her countenance. "Lady Catherine promised to introduce us. I understand that you rent the old hunting cottage on her property. She said that you are the widow of her former rector."

Stubborn man, Charlotte thought as she stared at him. He knew very well that she had no desire to continue the acquaintance, no matter to whom he was related. Her manner exhibited that truth as clearly as if she had spoken the words aloud. She had no chance to generate a reply before he spoke again. "I am sorry to hear of the Reverend Mr. Collins's death."

"Thank you." It had been two years since he was buried. Why were so many people commenting about him tonight?

"It is good for you to venture out into society again and to mingle with others now that you are coming out of the mourning period."

Well, she was certainly glad he thought so. She often concerned herself with the inappropriate opinions of strange men. She narrowed her eyes. "I still mourn Mr. Collins, sir."

"Yes?" He considered her for a moment, and an odd expression came into in his eyes. "Well, I am very sorry to hear that."

What precisely did that mean? She did not know quite how to respond to his reply, which had been uttered with an undertone of…of…she knew not what, and could only manage to say a brief "thank you."

Relieved when he bowed and left her, she leaned against the wall. She was unused to male attention, and something about Mr. Edgington caused her discomfort. Suddenly, she wanted nothing more than to return to the safety of her home.

Thankfully, the quadrille soon ended and Mr. Card delivered Maria back to her side, bowing to her so deeply Charlotte worried that the seam of his coat would split. "Thank you for the dance, Miss Lucas. May I procure lemonade for you and Mrs. Collins?"

"How kind—" Charlotte began, but Maria spoke over her.

"—but we do not require a beverage at the moment. Thank you, Mr. Card."

At her dismissal, Mr. Card's face fell into a downtrodden expression, which he quickly covered with a bright smile. He was an obliging gentleman, and her sister really ought to have a care when dealing with him. She planned to say as much to her when he departed, but the very moment Mr. Card's coat disappeared into the crowd, Maria demanded, "Will you not go speak to Colonel Armitage now?"

Charlotte glanced through her eyelashes across the ballroom at the three gentlemen. They finally had managed to divest themselves of the crowd that had been around them all evening. "In a moment." She searched for an excuse to depart for the evening instead of seeking an introduction.

Maria was openly staring at the American. Anyone in the room might read her obvious interest. When would her sister learn the art of subtlety? Charlotte reached out to take her hand and divert her attention to a more appropriate object, but Maria spoke. "It is my good fortune, then, that Americans are a brash sort of people, for here they come now."

Colonel Armitage led his relations straight toward them, and Charlotte allowed herself only the briefest of glances, but Maria shot them an open, welcoming smile.

"Mrs. Collins, Miss Lucas, will you allow me to present my long-lost relations from America?" He indicated the older gentleman with entirely too much dark hair for his age and a witty look in his eyes. "This is my nephew Mr. Benjamin Basford, the son of my elder sister who, you will remember, disappeared to the American colonies some years ago to get married. And this is his sister's son, Mr. James Westfield."

The gentlemen bowed.

"It is a pleasure to make your acquaintance," Charlotte said with a sedate curtsey and a jaundiced eye.

She looked to Maria, who had also greeted them with a curtsey, but her eyes were wide and locked with those of Mr. Westfield. They seemed to take no notice of the others around them or to mark the pleasantries they uttered.

This was trouble indeed.

The young man spoke first. "May I have the pleasure of the next dance, Miss Lucas?"

Maria beamed. "You may."

And with that, Mr. Westfield offered his arm and led Maria, who practically floated at his side, to her place in the set.

"What a charming pair," Colonel Armitage said. "And he is just as taken with Miss Lucas as I predicted."

Mr. Basford looked at his uncle. "I heard you make no such prediction."

The colonel appeared incredulous, one hairy eyebrow raised. "I said as much just this morning at breakfast. Did you not mark me?"

"I heard you speak only of your eggs and toast, also a charming pair but hardly my nephew and Miss Lucas."

Colonel Armitage gave a frustrated snort, and Charlotte wondered that his eyebrows did not flutter in the breeze. "I mentioned Miss Lucas as a possible acquaintance for him, I am sure. Perhaps I only thought it. Ah! The joys of aging. One day you shall understand."

Charlotte murmured something polite having to do with maturation bringing wisdom, but she did not quite believe her words applied to the colonel, for tonight he seemed more confused than wise.

But Mr. Basford only laughed and said, "I hope that I never age so much that I'd begin to confuse people with breakfast items."

Colonel Armitage snorted again and turned to Charlotte. He took her hand and patted it. "All this talk of food is making me hungry, and I can take no more of my nephew's wit on an empty stomach. I must excuse myself for the buffet."

Charlotte hoped Mr. Basford might excuse himself as well, but he remained at her side, studying the room with a silent smirk while his uncle squeezed his way through the crowd. She followed Mr. Basford's gaze, which alighted on a young couple obviously being introduced by an elderly chaperone. He looked back at Charlotte, his dark eyes mischievous. "Don't you find these English introductory rules to be a little confining?"

Already shaken by her impromptu conversation with Mr. Edgington and recalling her ruminations on that very subject earlier that evening, Charlotte was taken aback at his selection of topic. She recovered herself quickly and congratulated herself for saying, "Indeed I do not, for they keep one from being thrown into the company of inappropriate, dangerous people."

He grinned at her attempt at a cutting remark. "Well, it's a good thing, then, that we met in the proper way. Since we were introduced by my uncle the colonel, you can be assured that I'm neither inappropriate nor dangerous."

Charlotte was fairly certain that he did not present any danger, but she was as yet uncertain about deeming him appropriate. She examined him for a moment. "We shall see."

"Then, while you are deciding, shall we have a dance?"

She stared at him now, mouth agape. "Can you not see that I am in mourning attire, sir?" She gestured to the black trim on her gown.

"Are you?" He looked her over once. And then once more. "My apologies. I assumed that you wore that shade because it suits you."

"I am just coming out of my mourning period, if you must know," she ground out.

"Ah, then it's fortunate that the prescribed attire suits you so well. It brings out the lovely color in your cheeks."

Was it possible that he paying her a sincere compliment? She hardly thought so, for she knew very well that she only had color in her cheeks due to embarrassment or as a result of remaining too long out of doors in the summer. He returned her gaze with an open expression, and she wondered if he was awaiting an appropriate feminine response. A swoon perhaps. Well, she certainly did not intend to concede to his expectations.

"Are all Americans as brash as you?"

"No, some are as stuffy as you. Are all English bound by pointless manners and meaningless social conventions?"

"Our manners and customs do not bind us but protect us."

"They prevent you from living freely."

Charlotte's teeth clenched momentarily. She was beginning to believe that he was, at the very least, inappropriate if not dangerous as well. She unclamped her jaw. "If living freely means bringing disrespect to Mr. Collins and being ostracized by my friends and family, then I will remain bound by convention, as you say. And while you are in England, it would be better if you followed our customs as well."

"Would it?" He spoke as if their conversation was pleasant and not laced with discomfort. "Then I fear I will not make a good impression on Westerham society while I am here."

Charlotte decided to turn to a polite subject. "And how long will you be in our town?"

"Quite some time. My sister wants James to be introduced to your English society. I am to be his chaperone."

"Then you will be forced to attend many of our tedious social functions." She certainly did not relish the prospect of meeting Mr. Basford with any frequency.

"Yes, I am afraid so, but I do find certain aspects of them rather amusing. I assume you'll be attending with Miss Lucas."

Her reply was a reluctant "yes."

He gestured to the dance floor where Maria and Mr. Westfield stood up together. Their two blond heads were easy to view among the other dancers. "My uncle was correct. They do look well together, don't they?"

Charlotte was forced to admit that they did make a handsome couple. As she watched their sunny heads bob with the movements of the dance, an imp seized her, and before she could censor herself, she said, "Like eggs and toast." Mr. Basford leaned back his head and fairly shouted with laughter, causing Charlotte to regret her allusion. She glanced around, thinking to find the entire ballroom focused on them, but no one seemed to notice his outburst or her complexion, which was certainly a ten shades of crimson.

His laughter abated and he studied her. "I find that I like you, Mrs. Collins. Perhaps at the next assembly, we can see how well we do on the dance floor."

Charlotte gawked at him before schooling her features into a mask of impassivity. Mr. Basford did not appear to comprehend the forward nature of his remark, and when she attempted to lance him with a look of disdain, he only smiled, causing her to wonder if a man such as him could possibly be cowed by anyone.

Mr. Basford bid Charlotte a polite goodbye, bowing, his eyes never leaving her face, and against her will, she noticed that he was a tolerably handsome man.

ᴥ Three ᴥ

The sisters visited their parents' home in Hertfordshire for the Yuletide. The journey of fifty miles was cold, and the public coach was cramped and unpleasant. The wet weather turned the roads to mud during the day, and the cold transformed them into a partially frozen slurry at night. The horses labored before the coach, and Charlotte fancied that she could hear their groans of protest at being forced to work in conditions that were not suitable for man or beast.

If Charlotte had not had a true fondness for her family, she would have never attempted the trip, especially accompanied by a sister who was struck dumb by love. Charlotte wished Maria had been struck mute by love instead, for she spent the duration of the voyage speaking of Mr. Westfield, Mr. Westfield, Mr. Westfield. His hair, his eyes, his wit.

They had not been enclosed within the carriage for more than half an hour before Charlotte began to fear that one of their fellow travelers might toss her sister out the window at the next mention of Mr. Westfield's name.

Briefly, very briefly, Charlotte had considered doing so herself.

When they had finally arrived at Lucas Lodge, Charlotte pulled Maria aside and said, "Do not overtax Mama and Papa with tales of romance."

But Maria had only looked at her and asked, "Why ever not? They will be pleased that I have attracted the attention of a gentleman such as Mr. Westfield."

And upon their first moments in the sitting room, which was kept uncomfortably warm to assuage their parents' fear of drafts, Maria had relayed all the details that she had been able to discern about the gentleman. Beginning with his appearance and finishing a summary of their most intimate discussions, which had apparently focused primarily on fashion.

And for the next few weeks she had elaborated.

Between Maria's discourses on Mr. Westfield, the Lucases managed to celebrate Christmas, relax together *en famille*, and eat as lavishly as their budget would allow. And Charlotte would have found her time in Hertfordshire to be restful had it not been for Maria's chatter and the obvious concern it elicited in her parents.

Aware that she would eventually be asked to account for Maria's involvement with Mr. Westfield, Charlotte had attempted to avoid the subject altogether when alone with her parents. She hardly knew how to convince them that Mr. Westfield was an upstanding gentleman when she was yet unsure.

One evening shortly before their departure, the subject could not be avoided. A fire roared in the hearth while her parents huddled under heavy blankets to keep out the non-existent drafts and Charlotte perspired.

"Now my dear," said her mother. "Do tell me about this gentleman Mr. Westham."

"West-*field*, Mama." How could she possibly get his name wrong? Maria had only spoken it with shocking regularity for the past five weeks.

"Yes, yes. Your papa and I are very concerned. He is American, is he not?"

"Indeed he is."

Lady Lucas groaned.

Sir William raised his eyebrows. "I know we have had our trouble with them in the past, but certainly they cannot be completely disreputable. If he is quite taken with our Maria, he cannot be thoroughly bad, can he?"

Lady Lucas's face was drawn into skeptical lines, her mouth pulled downward into a small frown. "But is this gentleman—this *American*—good enough for our daughter? Surely not."

Charlotte had asked herself the same question, but she did not want to worry her parents over much. So she told them the same platitudes she used to reassure herself. "Although we have not long been acquainted with Mr. Westfield, he comes from a well-respected English family and he is traveling Europe with a proper—" she was unsure if proper were the correct word to describe Mr. Basford—"chaperone. I will ensure that nothing untoward occurs."

"Yes, yes, but has he any money?"

"I understand that his family wants for very little. They are travelling our country quite at their leisure."

Lady Lucas appeared relieved and snuggled deeper under her blanket, but Sir William leaned forward. "That is reassurance indeed, but I only wish he had a title. An appointment to the knighthood. Maria is quite pretty enough to marry a person of rank."

Charlotte regarded her father. He knew very well that America did not operate under a system of rank. Perhaps his mind had dimmed more than she had realized. "I fear that titled gentlemen are rather difficult to come by in America."

"Oh, of course." Sir William looked momentarily confused and then he took Charlotte's hand. "You are a good daughter, my dear. You made a good marriage yourself, and I am certain you will ensure that Maria will also be so fortuitously settled."

Charlotte only smiled.

In the new year, Charlotte and Maria returned to the warm—but not stiflingly so—walls of the cottage in Westerham. Foul weather caused social invitations to arrive infrequently, and Maria heartily lamented her empty calendar and spent her hours planning future perambulations in sunny gardens and picnics by the river with various and sundry gentlemen. She was determined to fall in love. With Mr. Westfield if possible.

Love was also on Charlotte's mind. In her youth, she had not believed that love existed, but she had seen the proof of it. Now, she wondered at its nature. How did it feel? Maria seemed wild and willing to be wooed. But did love overwhelm or coax? Did it break in like a thief and steal one's heart? Or was it patient and kind?

Charlotte did not care for poetry, and she did not often turn her thoughts to it if it could possibly be helped. But Shakespeare's question came to her mind, "Tell me where is fancy bred, or in the heart or in the head?" Love in poetry was one matter, but what of the real world? What was love?

She was contemplating poetry! She was in desperate need of some diversion or she would certainly begin composing some lines of her own.

So when Mr. Jonas Card and his mother paid a call on them one overcast afternoon, Maria and Charlotte were both quite pleased, for Maria had gained society and Charlotte had been able to forgo her poetical musings.

Mr. Card and his mother had only just entered the sitting room, when Maria decided to enact her plotted escape, although only out to slog along the damp country roads in Mr. Card's barouche.

"Why do we not pick up Miss Farmington and drive into Westerham for a while this afternoon?" Maria asked Mr. Card in a pleading tone. "I am desperately in need of some amusement outside this house, and the weather is not so cold as to make the trip unpleasant."

"Our driver is along to chaperone, so if it is agreeable to your sister, let us be off," Mr. Card looked to Charlotte for permission. With a proper chaperone, there was no reason to thwart her sister's escape plot. Even though she did not wish to be alone with Mrs. Card for a protracted period of time, it was better than the alternative.

So she nodded her consent, and soon the young people had departed, leaving Charlotte with Mrs. Card and a pot of tea. Jonas's mother was a diminutive woman of little meaningful conversation but many words. Moreover, she was of single-minded purpose, much like a terrier. She was determined to fetch a daughter-in-law who would bend easily to her will with regard to the running of the Card household.

They had already discussed the weather and the upcoming change of seasons, and the conversation lulled, causing Charlotte to await Maria and Mr. Card's return with some eagerness. Why had she not reminded them not to tarry too long in town?

"We have not seen you and Maria about this winter. We had worried that you had disappeared into Hertfordshire for good."

"No, we still reside happily here. We merely chose to enjoy a quiet holiday with our relations. As you know, our parents must keep to the house due to their ill health. We felt it unkind to leave them during Christmas."

"A noble thing to do, but we missed you at our assemblies."

"Thank you. It is very kind of you to say. I know that Maria longed to attend those functions. She missed her companions greatly."

"I believe it is also safe to say that Miss Lucas was missed as well, especially by Jonas."

Charlotte sipped the tea, desperately hoping for a turn in the conversation, but Mrs. Card spoke again.

"It has always been my fondest wish that Miss Lucas would one day marry my Jonas."

Charlotte set her cup daintily in the saucer and then placed it on the table, giving herself time to consider a proper reply. Was there a proper reply? She was hardly in a position to negotiate a marriage contract for her sister, especially to a gentleman whom she had no wish to marry. "It is flattering to know that you consider Maria suitable match for your son. He is an upstanding gentleman."

"Indeed, they are a fine match, and I have said as much to Jonas."

This conversation was not at all to Charlotte's liking. She knew very well that her sister's affections lay with the American Mr. Westfield and not with Mr. Card, whom she viewed as little more than a toy to be discarded at her whim.

"Mrs. Card—"

"I suppose Miss Lucas is in love with that dreadful young American, like every other young lady of our acquaintance."

Charlotte sat up rigidly. Were her thoughts so obvious? Her words teetered too close to the truth. "To the best of my knowledge, Maria is not in love with anyone at the present time, and I do not believe that this is a suitable topic of conversation."

Mrs. Card's eyes hardened to something between granite and steel and then softened slightly. "Forgive me. I just worry so about my Jonas. I do want him to be happy."

Finally, some relief. "I do understand. I want Maria to be happy as well."

"I must confess that I have heard nothing negative at all about Mr. Westfield. In fact, I have heard just the opposite. It was indecorous of me to say such things, but it does feel good, now and again, to say bilious things about other gentlemen. It makes my Jonas stand out as the deserving gentleman that he is."

"Your acknowledgment does you credit." Charlotte hoped the conversation would soon land on even footing. "Mr. Card is indeed a fine gentleman and a good catch for any young lady."

"How kind of you to say. And I must say that by all accounts, Mr. Westfield is a testimony to his English lineage. He behaves in a civilized manner and is always pleasant at a party." Here Mrs. Card leaned forward in the manner of a conspirator. "It is his uncle whose behavior is questionable."

After her conversation with Mr. Basford at the winter ball, Charlotte could well believe that.

"Oh?"

"I had it from Mrs. Holloway who had it from a relative of the colonel's that Mr. Basford behaved as quite the libertine in America."

"Oh dear." Libertine was not the description she had expected. Clown or jester, perhaps, but not libertine.

"They say he was thrown out of America for indecent behavior. And to be thrown out of a country as indecent as that is really saying something."

Charlotte could believe him rude and flirtatious, but she could not believe him to be such a man as that. "Can one be thrown out of a country without some sort of trial? That seems rather unlikely, do not you think?"

"Not after the things he has done here. He is often impertinent and overtly plainspoken. He seems to laugh at us all. I would put nothing past a man such as him. Have you not marked his behavior?"

Charlotte nodded her assent and refilled her cup of tea.

"It is utterly incomprehensible to me that he would be chosen to chaperone young Mr. Westfield. He does not set a decent example at all. What could Mr. Westfield's parents have been thinking to send him across the world in such a man's care? Some people, it seems, simply do not understand the way of the world."

Charlotte leaned back, and curiosity forced her to ask, "Are you at all acquainted with a Mr. Lewis Edgington? I encountered him some months ago at the winter ball."

Her face brightened at the prospect of relating more gossip. "Now there is a man who is reputed to be thoroughly good."

"It is nice to hear a man is said to be so."

"He is a widower. He lost his wife about the same time as Mr. Collins's accident, I believe. I have heard that he keeps a very nice sort of house with a respectable number of servants, and it is said that he rarely gambles."

Charlotte was preparing to make a suitably disinterested reply when the sitting room door burst open and Maria entered followed by Mr. Westfield and Mr. Basford.

Charlotte and Mrs. Card stood abruptly, surprised at their calamitous entrance.

Maria flung herself on the settee where Charlotte had been sitting. "Lord, you will not believe what has happened to us!"

"Good heavens, Maria! This is very untoward," Charlotte said and then turned to welcome her new guests. "Please do sit down."

Mrs. Card sat down on her chair rather heavily for a person of her small size. "Where is Jonas?"

Mr. Westfield took possession of the other upholstered chair beside the fireplace, and Mr. Basford sat in the small wooden chair beside the writing desk, immediately tilting it back on its rear legs.

Charlotte stared at the airborne chair legs and imagined that she could hear the wood creak in protest, causing her to question not only the integrity of the chair's structure but also of Mr. Basford's character, for only a questionable gentleman would show such disrespect for the furniture of a lady.

No one had responded to Mrs. Card's inquiry, so she repeated herself. "I demand to know what has happened to my son."

Mr. Basford concealed a smirk, Charlotte was certain of it.

"You will never believe it, Charlotte," Maria said, "but poor Mr. Card's carriage broke down on the way out of town. Fortunately, we were soon discovered by Mr. Westfield and Mr. Basford, who summoned help and then offered us a ride home in their carriage, for it is threatening rain."

Concern crossed Mrs. Card's features. "Oh dear. Rain! Where is Jonas? He shall be quite soaked through if he does not hurry!"

Mr. Westfield replied, "The repair has been made to the carriage, and he should be not fifteen minutes behind us. He was fortunate to be so near town when the break occurred."

"I do hope he beats the rain, for I cannot bear a wet ride home." Mrs. Card arose and walked to the window, her hands clasped in front of her. The gentlemen arose as well, Mr. Basford slower than his nephew.

"Do not worry, Mrs. Card, he will be along soon," said Mr. Westfield.

"What has become of Miss Farmington?" Charlotte asked Mr. Westfield.

Mr. Basford answered. "We deposited her at her home on the way here."

Charlotte nodded and was just about to suggest another cup of tea to her new guests, and hoping her supply would stretch to accommodate so many, when Edward entered the sitting room to announce Mr. Card, who stood beside him looking somewhat embarrassed.

The gentlemen bowed, and Mrs. Card appeared to be restraining herself from going to him. "Jonas, are you well?"

"Yes, Mama, I am quite well, only a little ashamed at putting out Miss Lucas and her friend especially in such threatening weather."

"Does it threaten still?" Mrs. Card turned again to the window. "It is quite dark. Jonas, we must return home immediately."

Mr. Card smiled apologetically at Maria. "As you wish, Mama. Pray excuse us, and Miss Lucas, please accept my sincerest regrets over our ruined ride."

Maria barely tore her eyes from Mr. Westfield when she said, "The incident is already forgotten."

And Charlotte could well believe it. When Mr. Westfield was near, it appeared, her sister forgot nearly everything, good manners included.

After the Cards departed, the gentlemen were once again able to take their seats, and the party became quiet.

"Shall we have tea? Maria, ring the bell and inform Mrs. Eff that we require another pot."

Maria went obediently.

"Why do the English have such an obsession with tea?" asked Mr. Basford, still leaning precariously on the back legs of the chair. "It is nothing but a few dried leaves after all."

Charlotte studied him. "Indeed, your censure is unwarranted, for I have heard that Americans are quite mad for the stuff as well. Particularly in Boston, I believe."

Charlotte was pleased with her retort, and so was Mr. Basford, who leaned his head back, causing the chair to tilt even further, and laughed heartily.

"She has you there, Uncle."

"Yes, indeed, she does."

"Mr. Basford seems to believe that the customs of our country are quite stilted and unnecessary," Charlotte said to Mr. Westfield.

"I confess that I do," Mr. Basford replied, letting the front legs of the chair return to the ground. "Take for instance the custom of calling people by their family names. I've seen close friends referring to each other as Mr. or Mrs. Whatnot. It's ridiculous."

"In your opinion, perhaps, Mr. Basford. I have never called social acquaintances by their first names unless I have known them since childhood. It is too familiar and uncomfortable."

"That is only because you have not practiced. Call me Ben, and you'll soon see how nice familiarity is."

Charlotte looked at him with horror. "Indeed, I will not! That sort of familiarity is only permitted in private moments between married couples, and perhaps not even then!"

He spoke as if she had not. "And I'll call you Charlotte."

"Indeed you shall not!" she objected, leaning forward as though to apprehend his words.

Mr. Westfield came to her rescue. "Uncle, do stop tormenting Mrs. Collins." He turned to Charlotte. "He is still reacting to your tea comment. He does not like to be bested in a battle of wits."

Regaining her composure somewhat, Charlotte asked Mr. Westfield, "Are all people in America this informal?"

"No. In truth, the rules of propriety are somewhat relaxed in our country, but many of us are almost as formal as you. However, Uncle believes strongly in informality and fancies himself ahead of his time."

"Someone ought to tell him that it will do him no good to be ahead of his time if he is rejected by society in the present. He will have no acquaintances to speak of and even fewer friends."

"You are probably correct," Mr. Basford said conversationally. "I care nothing for mere acquaintances, but a true friend will accept my eccentricities, Mrs. Collins."

He emphasized her name, causing Charlotte to flush. "With such appalling manners, it is unlikely that you will ever develop true friends, Mr. Basford." She emphasized his last name in the same manner.

Edward entered just then with the tray, and he deposited it on a side table. He looked very pleased at having accomplished his task successfully. Charlotte smiled, while Maria began to serve the tea, beginning with Mr. Westfield. She did not concentrate on pouring, but smiled at the American, and Charlotte hoped she would not overfill his cup and spill on the rug. It was such a bother to clean rugs. The room would be in upheaval for days.

She was about to admonish her to take care, when Maria righted the teapot and spoke. "Have you heard, Charlotte? We are all invited to Colonel Armitage's house for an evening of cards."

No longer concerned that her rug would be destroyed, Charlotte considered the invitation. Maria knew that she did not enjoy cards and would not blame her for turning down the invitation. She was on the verge of doing just that when she saw the look Maria gave Mr. Westfield and the look he returned.

"We will go, of course, will we not, Charlotte?" Maria asked, still looking at Mr. Westfield.

"I do not see how I could refuse."

ꙨꙨ Four ꙨꙨ

"I should have refused," Charlotte said as the team of large-bodied gray horses pulled Mr. Card's lovely barouche—though not half so fine as any of Lady Catherine's elegant conveyances—along the well-rutted roads. "This rain has all but destroyed the lanes, and it is a dreadful evening for being out."

Maria scowled. "Do not be so sour, Charlotte."

Mr. Card looked quite discomfited and shifted in his seat. "We will soon be in a pleasant room with pleasanter company."

"That is a subject worthy of debate," Charlotte murmured to Maria. It was unlikely that the weather, or Charlotte's temper, would turn for the better before the night was out. She had passed a very taxing week. She had been obliged to call upon Mrs. Card, and after a dull quarter hour in her company, she had spent the rest of the week going over her finances, which always dampened her mood.

Maria leaned forward and asked in a hushed tone, "Why are you in such poor spirits this evening?"

In truth, Charlotte did not relish being in the company of Mr. Basford, but she did not want to confide in her sister, who could keep nothing secret. "I do not intend to be. I am certain the weather has depressed my spirits. I will be less gloomy, I am sure, when we are in company."

"Then it is quite fortunate that we arrive at Colonel Armitage's home soon, for Mr. Card and I will not have to bear your mood very much longer."

Charlotte stared out into the gathering darkness and remained silent. The sun was hanging low, and its light filtered through the cloudy, rainy sky, casting the world in a gloomy haze.

Beside her, Maria fidgeted with her dress, adjusting the dove-colored fabric across her lap so that there were no wrinkles. Charlotte observed her preening gestures, and then she looked at her own dress. She had worn mourning attire for so long that she felt odd wearing this gown of pale colored cotton with a subtle dusky blue floral motif. The decision to relinquish her mourning garb entirely had been difficult, but Maria, for once, had made good sense.

"Charlotte," she had said, "You have served your time and done your duty to Mr. Collins. No matter how much you wish to deny it, you are still alive, and as such, you need to retake your position in society."

"You speak as if I am some great lady. I am just Charlotte Collins."

"And while Charlotte Collins may not be of a noble family, she is the daughter of a gentleman who was appointed to the knighthood and is a great lady of a different, more meaningful, sort."

Tears had come to Charlotte's eyes. "How kind."

"It is not kind; it is the truth. Tear the black lace off your gowns and rejoin the world."

Charlotte toyed with the thought. "Perhaps I should."

"Indeed you should, and perchance you will find a new beau of your own."

Charlotte had laughed at the ridiculousness of that comment, for she could not hope in that direction, but she did remove the black lace and pack away her black dresses. She was going to live, and she would begin tonight, this dreary, damp, and dingy night.

At least, that had been her intention, but she could not shake off the darkness of her spirit as easily as she had dispatched with her dark clothing.

Mr. Card, who had been absorbed in watching Maria arrange her skirts, ventured a compliment. "I hope you do not mind my saying so, but you ladies look lovely tonight. You quite outshine the sun."

"I should hope we outshine the sun at such a gloomy time of day."

Mr. Card looked abashed and quickly attempted to correct himself, but Maria laughed off his words. "I comprehend your meaning, Mr. Card, and I appreciate the kind sentiment. I am afraid my sister has let the weather affect her spirits too much today."

"It is true. You should not mark a word I say this evening, Mr. Card. I hope that the fresh air will soon improve my mood."

"Good society, also, must be of some help. Pleasant conversation can certainly do no harm," added Maria.

Charlotte wondered if she would find pleasant conversation at a card party, for the most she had ever heard over a game of whist was "Aha!" or a disappointed, "How cruel you were to take that trick, Mr. Whatnot!" If her preconception held true, she was in for a dull evening indeed.

"We will pass a merry evening with our friends. I have heard such wonderful tales over a hand of cards," Mr. Card returned, and Charlotte had to smile at their very different opinions on the matter.

"Yes, Miss Farmington has promised to attend, and of course, Colonel Armitage's relations will be there."

Mr. Card leaned forward, gesturing broadly as the two continued to speak about the evening's society while the carriage finished its journey. Orange light shone out the windows of the Armitages' house, promising warmth and comfort, and Charlotte found herself eager to be inside and out of the gathering gloom.

Mr. Card alighted from the carriage, his boots making a splatting sound as they hit the damp ground.

He assisted them from the carriage. "Take care, ladies. It is moist, but we will be inside soon enough."

Charlotte picked her way to the front door, and she turned in time to witness his careful aid of her sister. She remembered the words of Mrs. Card. He did love Maria.

And this fact was certainly lost on her sister, for in her excitement to be among the others, she barely touched his arm as he escorted her to the door.

Their party had arrived slightly late owing to the poor condition of the roads, and when they were shown to the drawing room, they discovered that many games were already in progress. Maria went directly to the table where Miss Farmington and Mr. Westfield played at whist with Colonel Armitage and Mrs. Holloway, a woman with whom Charlotte did not share a particular acquaintance. She and Mr. Card overlooked their game and chatted with the players.

Charlotte received a cup of tea and took it to the window seat, where she could observe the whole room. It seemed a pleasant party even if it were an evening of cards. Wreathed in flickering yellow candlelight, the group took on an ethereal glow. Yes, the room looked quite pretty, but still, Charlotte would have rather remained at home. Leaning back into the cool darkness of the window alcove, Charlotte sipped her tea and reminded herself that she was here for Maria. She must focus on her sister's happiness. Soon enough, Charlotte could be back at her little cottage enjoying her solitude.

She heard Maria laugh loudly and glanced up at her. Her sister absolutely shone under the attention of Mr. Card and Mr. Westfield. Her blond hair was like a halo around her delicate face, and Charlotte wondered how long she would remain unmarried now that she was out in society on a regular basis. Mr. Westfield looked quite enchanted, and Mr. Card was just as enamored as ever. Would her sister ever recognize the love of a man whom she counted as merely a friend? Most likely not. Maria was a careless young woman, and Mr. Westfield distracted her completely. Poor Mr. Card was in for a hearty disappointment now that Mr. Westfield was in Westerham.

The side door to the salon opened, admitting Mr. Basford. He made quite a striking figure in his simple attire. His neck cloth was done in a simple knot compared to the more complex creations of the other men in the room, and he appeared to be dressed for a comfortable evening at home instead of entertaining a party of guests.

Not wanting to invite his attention, Charlotte looked away before he noticed her appraisal and turned again to the card game, in which Miss Farmington apparently made a decisive play and clenched the win, causing a roar of mixed happiness and disappointment to erupt from the table.

Mrs. Holloway and Colonel Armitage excused themselves, graciously allowing Mr. Card and Maria to take their places. Colonel Armitage noticed Charlotte's position at the window, paused briefly by the biscuit tray, and then, encouraged by her welcoming smile, joined her. "Mrs. Collins, how do you do this evening?"

"Very well, thank you, Colonel."

"I hope you find it a very pleasant party. I only regret that my guests were required to venture out in such wet weather."

"My sister and I are thankful for your invitation, and I can assure you that the journey was quite worth it, sir."

"Well, I am glad to hear it."

"Please have a seat." Charlotte made room for him beside her on the ample window seat.

"Thank you." He lowered himself beside her.

"It was very kind of you to give your places to Maria and Mr. Card."

"It is good for young people to gather together, do you not agree?"

Charlotte nodded.

"And we older people, having virtually no vitality left in us, must be content to bask in their youthful vigor."

On such a night when Charlotte felt the gloom so personally, she was forced to agree with the Colonel. "At a certain point in life, we all must endeavor to entertain ourselves."

Colonel Armitage sighed. "Is that not the truth? I find it a surprisingly difficult task, this business of entertaining of oneself. I fear that if left completely to my own devices I might bore myself into oblivion. That is why I host evenings such as this. By surrounding myself with youth, I fancy that I become more interesting by default."

Charlotte laughed.

"What nonsense is my uncle telling you?" Charlotte and the colonel looked up to find Mr. Basford leaning against the wall.

Appalling manners! "On the contrary, he speaks common sense."

"We were discussing the behavior of people of a certain age in society," the colonel explained.

"Just as I suspected. Utter nonsense."

Charlotte was surprised at the derogatory tone he used with his uncle, but Colonel Armitage, apparently used to such loving disrespect, laughed. "How very much like your mother you are."

"Many have said as much, Uncle."

"What is your opinion on the subject?" Colonel Armitage asked him.

"As you may well believe, it is quite different from yours. And Mrs. Collins's as well, I imagine." He looked at her for assent.

"I have no doubt that our opinions diverge, for they have not been on the same continent since we have been introduced."

"Quite so," he said. "I believe that we who have attained some maturity of years have an advantage in society. We shouldn't cut ourselves off from it.

Rather, we should use the benefit of our experience to enjoy it, for we are no longer desperately seeking our mates or worried about impressing our companions. We've already done these youthful things, and now we may simply enjoy ourselves without these distractions."

Charlotte contemplated the matter for a moment. "Perhaps this is a wise way to view life, but I am afraid this will prove to be an unpopular opinion."

The colonel snorted. "My nephew cares nothing for popularity."

Mr. Basford waved his hand dismissively. "It's not a matter of popularity. I simply do not allow the opinions of others to guide my behavior."

"Perhaps circumstances are different across the Atlantic, but here in England, we have great respect for others and show it through appropriate, acceptable behavior."

"We behave very charmingly in America. We simply do not allow etiquette to rule us."

Colonel Armitage was then summoned by Mr. Westfield, and he stood to make his excuses and take his leave. "I see I must go play host for a moment. Ben, take my place at the window and you may continue your debate."

Charlotte suddenly wanted to issue some excuses of her own and escape before Mr. Basford could accept or reject the colonel's offer. She searched her mind franticly for a plausible excuse. Did she hear Maria calling? She glanced at her sister, who sat on the far side of the room and was clearly much engrossed in her conversation with Mr. Westfield to be sufficient pretext for departure. Mr. Basford would never believe it. Did she leave the kettle on the stove at home? That would not suffice either. He would probably simply tease her about England's love of tea. Perhaps she could use an old excuse—the need for refreshment. Yes, refreshment. Not even Mr. Basford would prevent her from a beverage and a biscuit.

Too late! Mr. Basford was sitting beside her.

Even though Mr. Basford's girth was half that of his uncle, the widow seat seemed to shrink and the walls closed in, and Charlotte scooted as far to the side as possible. He only leaned toward her—the cretin—and grinned. "Hello, Charlotte."

"I have asked you not to call me that, and there is no need for another greeting, for we have been conversing for several minutes."

"The proper response would be 'Hello, Ben. How nice to see you tonight.'"

Charlotte scowled. He infuriated her by smiling back.

His voice softened. "I do not mean to make you uncomfortable, Mrs. Collins. Let's speak of a friendly subject."

"I did not think there was a subject we could discuss in a friendly manner."

"Then I'll choose the topic and prove to you that I can behave properly."

"Amaze me."

"Well, now that was very rude."

Embarrassed, she apologized, and they remained in silence a moment. At length, Mr. Basford cleared his throat. "My nephew seems to be enjoying the company of your sister."

"Yes, Maria speaks about Mr. Westfield with only the kindest terms."

"I am pleased to hear that."

"I am certain that he will miss her company when we travel abroad," Mr. Basford said.

"You go abroad?" Charlotte asked, both pleased and disappointed at the prospect.

"Yes, we depart in a fortnight. James's mother believes that a visit to the continent is essential for every young gentleman's education."

"How nice for one so young to see so much of the world."

"We tour Paris and then return to England to finish with a stay in London," Mr. Basford said.

"London is very agreeable, with many occupations for a young man such as Mr. Westfield. It is also a place of rich history." Charlotte had been into town on occasion and had always taken pleasure in the exhibits of the British Museum.

"I am afraid James may be more interested in theater and fine dining than he is interested in history." Charlotte imagined she heard a touch of regret in his voice.

"Those are also admirable pursuits."

"I am glad that you approve."

She paused. "I find that difficult to believe."

He turned his head to look at her more directly. "I thought you wanted people to concern themselves with the opinions of others. That is all I am doing now."

"I do not desire falsity, Mr. Basford. I simply desire that you present yourself honestly."

"Then, at your request, I'll do so, and in turn, you must not complain about my casual attitude."

"And you must not chide me for my polite behavior."

"Then are we friends?"

He seemed quite sincere and Charlotte smiled. He would soon be gone—first abroad, then to London, and eventually back to America. She could see nothing wrong with developing a friendship, especially since her sister seemed to enjoy Mr. Westfield's company so much. "Yes, I suppose."

His smile widened and almost drew a blush to Charlotte's face, but before she could consider the repercussions of the ruddiness of her cheeks, she found Maria before her. "Charlotte, may I speak to you a moment?"

"I pray you will excuse us, Mr. Basford."

He nodded and then moved away to give them privacy.

"I see you are enjoying Mr. Basford's company," Maria settled herself down in the spot he had vacated and arranging her skirts.

Charlotte's first instinct was to deny her enjoyment of their discussion, but then she softened and said truthfully, "Surprisingly, I do enjoy conversations with him. He is…different."

Oblivious to the profundity of her sister's revelation, Maria was focused solely on herself. "I too enjoy Mr. Westfield. May we invite them to dine with us?"

"I am afraid not—"

"But we make such a charming party." Maria's eyes pleaded with her sister. Her tone was whiny, and Charlotte was sorely tempted to roll her eyes.

"That may be true, Maria, but Mr. Basford has just told me that they are bound for France in a fortnight."

"Oh, what a disappointment! Why has not Mr. Westfield mentioned that to me?" Maria slumped over, and Charlotte was tempted to correct her posture, but she kept quiet while her sister considered her situation.

After several minutes, Maria straightened. "I had hoped…"

"I know what you had hoped, but there is no sense in wasting this evening in mourning for a future evening. Leave me and enjoy your friends."

Maria seemed to deliberate, her brows knitted together. She looked very serious. "For once your unstoppable practicality actually makes sense."

Charlotte laughed.

For the remainder of the evening, Maria did enjoy her friends, and Charlotte joined a game of whist and indulged in more than a few confections. She did not speak with Mr. Basford until the end of the evening when he accompanied their party to the door.

He escorted Maria on his left arm, Charlotte—somewhat unwillingly— rested her hand on his right arm. Mr. Card walked ahead with Miss Farmington and her grandmother, whom he handed into their carriage while the others spoke in the entryway.

"Thank your uncle for his generous invitation," Charlotte said to Mr. Basford.

"I will, and in turn we thank you for coming."

"It was a grand time, Mr. Basford," Maria paused a moment to push a curl from her face. "Perhaps when you and Mr. Westfield return from your tour of France, we shall all meet again at a ball."

Maria's addendum elicited a firm look from Charlotte.

Behind them, Mr. Westfield said, "I do hope so. Do you not agree, Uncle?"

Mr. Westfield stepped forward, took Maria's arm from his uncle, and led her to the Farmington's chaise to bid them farewell, leaving Charlotte alone with Mr. Basford, who turned to her. "I do agree. Will you be so kind as to save me a dance at the next ball, Mrs. Collins?"

Imagine having a gentleman reserve a dance at her advanced age. In fact, it had been years since anyone other than Mr. Collins had asked her to dance, and even then, dancing had not been a pleasure. Her husband had been awkward of foot, and eventually, Charlotte had begun to decline to stand up with him, pointing him instead to other suitable partners.

Charlotte was quite certain that Mr. Basford would prove to be a pleasanter partner. He at least had managed to escort her to the door without crushing her slippers.

"We shall see, Mr. Basford."

The Cards' barouche arrived before them, and Mr. Basford aided her inside. Charlotte could feel the warmth of his hand through their gloves.

"Good evening," he said with a slight bow, glancing at her earnestly.

"Good evening," Charlotte replied. His gaze really was too earnest. It caused her stomach to flutter. Odd.

Mr. Card joined them in the carriage, and it rumbled away, leaving Charlotte to watch as Mr. Westfield and Mr. Basford returned to the house. Just before the carriage rounded the first bend, Charlotte saw Mr. Basford turn and look toward the horizon. Was he looking at the carriage? She sucked back into the seat as if he had caught her spying and then chastised herself for her foolishness. He could not possibly have seen her. It was far too dark.

Mr. Card was seated across from Maria, and the two talked quietly about the evening. As the carriage wound its way closer to Charlotte's cottage, a pleasant quietness fell. The conveyance rocked gently while the rhythm of the horses' hoof beats sounded on the road.

When they arrived at the cottage, it felt warm and inviting, and Charlotte knew Mrs. Eff had awaited their return. She appeared in the entrance hall forthwith looking quite done in. Mrs. Eff had once been a soft, genteel lady, but now the palms of her hands were as rough as the course material of the apron she wore, and the hair that had once been fashioned in ringlets was now pulled into a bun at the nape of her neck. But her voice was always cheery no matter the time or circumstance. "Had you a pleasant party?"

"It was a lovely evening."

"For the most part," Maria added.

Mrs. Eff raised an inquisitive eyebrow as she helped to remove their cloaks. Although Mrs. Eff was her servant, she was a gentleman's daughter, a well-educated woman who had the misfortune to lose her husband without the benefit of jointure or relations to sustain her, and as such she had no means of support.

She was what Charlotte could have been, and she remained keenly aware of that fact.

Mrs. Eff had provided a measure of companionship and news from society while Charlotte was secluded in the early part of her mourning and she remained her friend despite the disparity in their current social positions.

"Miss Lucas's evening was full of amusements. However, I fear that she is disappointed by the forthcoming departure of an acquaintance."

"I had hoped we would be more than mere acquaintances."

Mrs. Eff patted her hand. "Ah, I understand, Miss Lucas, what it is to be thwarted in love."

"She is hardly thwarted in love."

Maria giggled. "You ought to speak to my sister about love, for she was much in the company of a particular gentleman this evening."

"Was she?" Mrs. Eff turned to Charlotte. "And may I ask who was the gentleman?"

Charlotte busied herself with removing her gloves. "Nonsense. No such gentleman exists."

"That was rather a tender farewell from Mr. Basford this evening, Charlotte. I think he is enamored of you."

"What a thing to say!" She dropped her gloves in Mrs. Eff's waiting hand. "Tender indeed. Mr. Basford was merely being polite, or as polite as a person such as him can be."

Thankfully, Mrs. Eff noticed her discomfort and changed the subject. "Do you require anything else tonight? Assistance with your gowns?"

Both Charlotte and Maria declined her offer, and Mrs. Eff retired to her chamber behind the kitchen while the sisters mounted the stairs. They stopped at their separate bed chamber doors.

"Mr. Westfield was quite attentive to you this evening."

"Yes." Maria had a strange, sweet smile on her lips.

"Mr. Card too showed great kindness to you."

"Mr. Card?"

"He sent his carriage for us."

Maria mistook her meaning. "It is ever so vexing to be always at the mercy of others for transportation. Surely we can afford a chaise at least."

Charlotte ignored Maria's desire for transportation of their own. She must make her message plain, for Maria was intent on misunderstanding her. "He is fond of you."

Maria yawned. "We have always been fond of each other, but there is certainly no attachment between us."

"Perhaps you have not noticed his attentions to you."

Maria opened her bedchamber door. "Perhaps you are the one who refuses to notice the attentions of a gentleman."

❧ Five ❧

Maria sat with Charlotte in their little sitting room with the sun pouring through the open windows. They had just finished a luncheon of cold meats, rolls, and butter and had been sharing what Charlotte had believed to be a companionable silence.

"What a crushing bore this town has become now that Mr. Westfield and Mr. Basford have gone."

Charlotte, who had been lamenting the amount of mending that had accumulated in her basket and contemplating another roll and butter, looked up from her stitching.

"Life went along quite well before they arrived. I am certain that we will survive now that they are gone."

"That is a subject that I am willing to debate."

"Well, I am certainly not willing to debate it. You will simply have to find something else to occupy yourself."

"Humph," Maria said in an unladylike manner. She had not seen Mr. Westfield since the evening of the card party, for he had been away from home when they had called on the Armitages soon after. Their visit had been brief and Maria had returned home quite put out and had been rather off ever since.

They sat a little longer listening to the tentative birdsong of early spring. Maria shifted on her chair and sighed.

"Shall we not pay a call on the Cards? It is dreadfully dull here."

Charlotte put down her mending and studied Maria. She appeared ready to fly from the cottage with the least provocation. Perhaps an afternoon out would improve her spirits.

"I can see you will give me no peace unless I agree."

Maria grinned. "You are quite right."

"Then we shall go, and since the weather is so fine, we will walk through the fields instead of the road."

"Charlotte, you know how to ruin anything that is remotely amusing."

"I find walking an amusement in itself."

"I do not know why."

"It is good exercise, it improves the spirits, and it is enjoyable to see the countryside."

"I can see the countryside just as well from the seat of a carriage or from walking the road on foot."

"Indulge me, Maria. I have not had a good walk through the countryside in quite some time. It is much pleasanter to walk with someone than to walk alone."

Maria agreed reluctantly to her sister's proposition. It was a short distance to the Cards' home, and Charlotte took great pleasure in the journey, enjoying the breezy spring weather. Maria complained incessantly. "My hair will be in such a state after walking in this wind."

"It is but a gentle breeze."

"My dress will be covered in mud."

"We have crossed no puddles."

"What if it rains?"

"It is not going to rain. The sky is blue and not a cloud in sight. Now do be quiet and leave me in peace."

The Cards' home was called Crumbleigh and was one of the finest estates in Westerham. Mr. Card had inherited Crumbleigh and a substantial fortune, making him one of the richest of their acquaintance. Maria always said it was a shame that all that money was wasted on such a man as Mr. Card, who was kind and obliging almost to a fault. She was at a point in her life when she believed that masculinity was defined by egotism, hardheadedness, and difficulty. While Charlotte appreciated both kindness and masculinity, she had rarely found them combined in the proper ratio in one man.

Mrs. Card received them cordially in a large, sunny sitting room.

"How glad I am to have visitors. And what a fine day for a long walk."

Privately, Charlotte thought that it must have been quite some time since Mrs. Card had indulged in a long walk, fine weather or no.

"That is precisely what I told my sister."

Mrs. Card smiled and then summoned the maid. "Go and tell my son that we have visitors." Then she turned to Maria. "Jonas will be very glad to see you. He has been quite dull these past few days."

"I am sorry to hear that. Has he been ill?" Charlotte asked.

"No, indeed. I believe he is in need of society. Young men these days seem to thrive more on society than sport. I believe that the two of you will do the trick."

Mr. Card arrived and was attired in a deep brown coat, tan breeches, and a creamy white cravat tied in a barrel knot. He appeared stylish yet sober and refined. He smiled as he greeted the assembled ladies and announced, "What a fine day! Shall we all not stroll through the gardens?"

"What a jolly idea," Maria said sourly.

Mr. Card's eyes widened to an almost impossible degree. "You do not wish to see the gardens? They are quite nice."

"Perhaps we could find a quiet bench and have a nice chat while Mrs. Card and Charlotte stroll. I am quite sick of strolling, and we must still walk home."

Mr. Card beamed. "There is a very pleasant bench in the rose garden, and I would enjoy sitting with you."

The four walked through the house, the women's dresses whispering as they walked, while Mr. Card's boots punctuated the quiet with gentle taps on the polished stone floors.

Charlotte had always loved Crumbleigh, although she could have wished for a less disintegrated-sounding name. She could remember visiting Mr. and Mrs. Card with Mr. Collins when they had first married. She had stood in the massive entryway and tried not to gawk even as she secretly marveled at the size of the hall and at her reflection in the sheen of the floor.

After she had been married to Mr. Collins for some time, she had lost some of her admiration for fine things. She could not recall all the times that she had listened to her husband discourse on such items as window dressings, vases, or furniture. Although they could only afford modest accoutrements themselves, Mr. Collins could not be prevented from praising the belongings of others. It had gotten to the point that Charlotte wanted nothing fine in her house for fear that he would boast about it to all he met.

Now, looking around the Cards' house, she felt not a twinge of jealousy. Maria, however, ran her hand along the cool marble trim and gazed longingly around her. Poor girl. It really was unfortunate that she had no feelings for Mr. Card, for he admired her, and she admired his home.

The group arrived in the rose garden, where Mr. Card and Maria tucked themselves on a little bench among the roses.

"Let us walk this way, Mrs. Collins." Mrs. Card directed her toward a small path. "We will leave them to speak alone for a time."

They chatted about the weather and then the subject turned to Mrs. Card's favorite topic of conversation—gossip. Mrs. Card's tongue was wicked and the breadth of her knowledge of the happenings in Westerham took Charlotte aback. Mr. Holloway had acquired a new sow, which he described to everyone as just as fat as Mrs. Holloway but better company. Apparently, Mrs. Holloway shared her husband's opinion of the quality of their time together, for she had become quite close, it was rumored, with an unnamed gentleman of their acquaintance. Mrs. Holloway had hinted at the affair but would not identify the man.

"Can you imagine? An affair amongst those of our acquaintance."

Charlotte was not very much familiar with Mrs. Holloway, but she found the idea of an affair implausible as well. "'Tis probably nothing but foul wind. Mrs. Holloway is certainly attempting to wound her husband for comparing her unfavorably to a pig."

"I must admit I quite agree with his comparison," Mrs. Card said. "She prattles on endlessly and indulges in too many confections, if you ask me. At the winter ball, I went to refill my wine glass again, and I observed her eating almost an entire tray of biscuits. Such gluttony."

Charlotte concealed a smile at Mrs. Card, who was often deep in her cups when in company. However, she could not quarrel with her assessment of Mrs. Holloway's conversation. She had to admit that she often found the company of certain barnyard animals more appealing than the prospect of an evening in the company of Mrs. Holloway—or Mr. Holloway for that matter—but incompetence in social settings did not mean that Mrs. Holloway was engaged in illicit behavior. That sort of thing happened in London, not Westerham.

Charlotte turned the conversation to safer topics, and she listened as Mrs. Card described her improvements to the gardens and Mr. Card's charity to the tenants on their land. Then Mrs. Card paused, glanced about as if expecting spies to appear from behind the shrubbery. Charlotte began to fear an uncomfortable change of subject, and that fear was not unfounded, for Mrs. Card grabbed her arm, nearly pulling her off balance. "Tell me this, and tell me truly, has Miss Lucas begun to feel tenderly toward my son?"

Charlotte was quite taken aback that she would broach this subject again and stopped midstride, causing Mrs. Card, who had not relinquished her grip, to be jerked backward. A reprimand leapt to Charlotte's lips, but she refrained and responded as politely as she could. Would this woman never cease meddling in her son's life? Not to mention Maria's. And Charlotte's for that matter. "Maria has not confided as much to me, and that is as it should be. Life is difficult to navigate without one's sister sticking her oar in. I feel that it is best to let young people work things out for themselves, do you not agree, Mrs. Card?"

Mrs. Card dragged her onward down the path. "I certainly do. It is ever so frustrating to watch people manipulating their relations, especially for monetary gain. I am only concerned with my son's happiness, but obviously he has the potential to make a desirable match among his own class."

"Maria is the daughter of a gentleman and certainly of Mr. Card's class!"

"Yes, but has she any money? Any dowry?"

Anger blossomed within her, but she responded with politeness. "Then why do you support the match?"

Charlotte knew very well why Mrs. Card was pushing Maria and Mr. Card together. She wanted a daughter-in-law who could be easily managed. And Maria, bless her, had more hair than wit.

"I have my reasons, and I may as well tell you that upon only the slightest provocation, Jonas will make an offer to your sister."

Charlotte's mouth dropped open and then snapped quickly shut.

"I can see that you are surprised, but I do not see why. Anyone may see Jonas's admiration."

"Mrs. Card—"

"Pray do not make yourself uneasy. As you said just moments ago, it is best to let young people work these things out for themselves. We shall just sit back and watch." Mrs. Card patted her hand reassuringly and then released her hold. "But I must say that I am quite disappointed in you, Mrs. Collins."

Charlotte continued walking calmly, but she imagined issuing any number of set-downs to the rag-mannered harridan.

"After our conversation on the day of that dreadful storm, I assumed you would have nudged Maria in my Jonas's direction."

There was very little to be said in response that was both truthful and polite. "I will encourage my sister to marry as she wishes, and she wishes to marry for love. She has spoken of no such feelings for any gentleman."

Mrs. Card's ears and nose turned an unflattering shade of red, and she crossed her arms in front of her. "You must see what an advantageous match this would be for her, and indeed yourself as well. I never took you for a fool."

The old cow was certainly in fine form. Charlotte took a deep, steadying breath. "I was once of your opinion, Mrs. Card. In fact, I was even more determined, for I believed in marriage primarily for the purpose of improving one's circumstances."

"And well you should have thought as much. It is a wise opinion for a woman to hold."

"I once agreed, but I have come to see the value of allowing love to color one's matrimonial decisions. If happiness in marriage is indeed a possibility, I am certain that it can only result from love."

"There is no such thing as a happy marriage."

Charlotte glanced over Mrs. Card's shoulder, willing some sort of interruption to occur. The appearance of Mr. Card and Maria. A carriage pulling into the drive. A regiment of soldiers marching through Crumbleigh on their way to battle. Any excuse to defer this conversation would suit Charlotte very well.

When none of those eventualities occurred, she unclenched her jaw. "I must disagree, for I have seen the evidence of them. I will encourage my sister to follow her heart. If her heart leads her to Mr. Card, then so be it."

Mrs. Card huffed, seeming suddenly to expand to twice her size and then deflating just as quickly. "Jonas is not the sort of man with whom women fall in love easily. He is the sort whom one comes to love over time."

Charlotte had nothing to say in response, and the two ladies walked in uneasy silence for some distance. The silence had the advantage of relieving Charlotte of both Mrs. Card's dreadful conversation and her tour of garden improvements, but it could not persist much longer. Charlotte selected a safer topic. "Have you heard that the Americans have gone to France?"

Not seeming to notice the lack of a segue, Mrs. Card's face lit. "Indeed I have."

"I understand that Mr. Westfield's mother encouraged it as part of her son's education."

Mrs. Card leaned in. "That is not at all what I heard."

"Oh?"

"I have heard that the true reason is that Mr. Basford wanted to visit," she paused and her voice dropped, "his Parisian mistress."

"Mistress?"

"Indeed."

The woman must be fabricating these stories. Two tales of such an illicit nature seemed improbable. "How could you possibly come to know that?"

"How does not matter. What matters is that I know it. We must beware of these Americans."

"If he were indeed joining his—" Charlotte could not speak the word and began again, "If indeed this were the case, why would he take Mr. Westfield with him?"

"Yes, poor Mr. Westfield. I believe it is safe to say that he will certainly return to Westerham a changed man. We may not trust him with our daughters. In fact, I would not be surprised at all to discover that Mr. Basford was Mrs. Holloway's mystery lover."

Charlotte stared at her companion. It was all so completely unbelievable. She acknowledged that evil existed in the world. She had seen it. But she did not believe Mr. Basford to be evil. She knew that stupidity existed in the world. She had seen even more of that. But she did not have the impression that Mr. Basford was particularly stupid. And Mrs. Card's accusations would mean that he was both evil and stupid.

Charlotte had no reason to mistrust Mrs. Card, however. Perhaps it was best to exercise extra caution where the American gentlemen were concerned. She had witnessed the effects of trusting untrustworthy men, and she would not allow Maria to become a victim. Society was often more harsh on the victim than on the perpetrator of the crime.

On the walk home, Charlotte was quiet, but Maria chattered on. "I am so pleased that I thought of the idea of an outing today, for it was just what my constitution required."

Charlotte trudged onward and did not bother to point out that she, not Maria, had suggested that they call on the Cards. There was not much point in correcting her, for she had already skittered on to the next topic.

"Mr. Card told me so many delicious stories, but I cannot seem to recall any of them. Have you ever had that happen? Your head is so full that nothing will come out? I suppose not, for you are far too sensible for that. Then we spoke of fashion. He said he very much hoped that the current enthusiasm over such tight fitting coats would soon pass, but I said I quite fancied a gentleman in a well-fitted coat. He seemed to value my opinion on the matter and vowed to see his tailor straightaway." Maria should have paused here, but instead she launched into yet another topic. "Mrs. Card seemed to be in spirits today. I believe I detected some color in her cheeks after her walk with you. Did you have a pleasant chat?"

"Humph," said Charlotte. It was the best response she could muster.

"Well, it was so jolly to be out, even if it was only with Mr. Card."

Charlotte regarded her sister as they walked. She wanted to clutch her arms and give her a good shake. "You speak of him too lightly, Maria. You should be careful of his feelings."

"Oh, pooh."

୧୭ Six ୬୦

Charlotte passed a restless night and arose early. She elected to enjoy a cup of chocolate, in the stead of her customary tea, as a consolation for her lack of sleep. The dark, bitter delicacy seemed to match her mood and yet also somehow brighten it. The house was quiet and cool at that hour, and the warm drink brought a measure of comfort to her restless spirits.

Knowing that Mr. Card desired to propose to Maria and that she was completely oblivious to that fact made Charlotte extremely uneasy. Maria was sweet, but she was an artless girl and ignorant of the feelings of others no matter how much her sister instructed her. She certainly would not have the presence of mind to spare the feelings of her long-time friend.

Charlotte contemplated simply telling her sister of Mr. Card's feelings. It had been a difficult temptation to resist, but resist it she did. She found it unethical for her to divulge Mr. Card's feelings even if his mother had been thoughtless enough to do so. This argument alone, however, was not strong enough to convince Charlotte to conceal the facts. It was her knowledge of her sister's nature that solidified her decision. Maria would only make a mess of the situation if she knew of Mr. Card's intentions. She could imagine Maria's obvious attempts to avoid him or to slough him off on other young women. It was a charade that Charlotte had no desire to watch.

In addition, it was quite clear that Maria did indeed harbor an interest in Mr. Westfield, and she was not going to be satisfied until she had made a fool of herself over him.

What a fix! A good man loved Maria, but she did not love him. She persisted in fancying another man, who may or may not be in the process of being corrupted by his questionable uncle. And Charlotte was caught in the middle. How had she come to be in this situation? After Mr. Collins's death, she had enjoyed a quiet life, and somehow her solitude had been replaced by vexation and confusion. Peace was nowhere to be found, and Charlotte was forced to search for solace in the cocoa plant.

After finishing her second cup of chocolate, she attempted to read, but still she felt restless. She considered a conversation with Mrs. Eff, but she was too jittery. Deciding that perhaps a walk into town and a browse around the shops would calm her, she notified Mrs. Eff of her departure and left a note for Maria, who was still asleep.

Charlotte walked briskly along the side of the road, and soon the hem of her dress was dampened with dew. Her spirits, however, were much brightened by the time she arrived in Westerham. She visited several shops but purchased nothing, and as noon approached, she walked to the Circulating Library.

She was considering a new novel when she sensed a presence beside her and glanced over to find Mr. Edgington, the red-haired gentleman who had bumped into her at the ball, perusing a volume several feet away.

"Good morning, Mr. Edgington."

"Good morning, Mrs. Collins," he said politely. "A pleasant morning for a browse around the shops, is it not?"

"Yes, quite."

"What do you read?"

"I am sorry to say that I enjoy novels."

"Why are you sorry to say that?"

"Are not novels considered to be a lower form of entertainment? Especially those whose content is comedic?"

"People who believe that must not comprehend the need for levity and release in our lives."

"You are quite right. Our lives are serious enough, and I find it odious indeed always to read books of great import."

Mr. Collins had been a dutiful student of sermons, and he had been displeased when Charlotte became bored of them.

Mr. Edgington smiled. "I concur. In fact, I am here for a book of travel narratives."

"Also an interesting subject. Far more interesting than a collection of sermons."

"Were you required to study sermons as a child as I was?" he said with a grimace. "I can vividly recall sitting in my room and reading Fordyce's tome while my friends were allowed to run free in the out of doors."

"I am also well acquainted with Dr. Fordyce's advice, but not from my childhood. Mr. Collins was a great believer in his tenets."

He looked at her earnestly. "I find many of his beliefs rather archaic. Even as a young child, I could not comprehend his idea of such severe subjugation of women. Those of your sex should be free to enjoy life just as a man might."

Charlotte was not certain that Mr. Edgington was speaking of entirely innocent subjects when he talked of release and pleasure. His tone was placid, but something in his eye seemed to suggest conspiracy. Or was she imagining it? Charlotte hoped to temper their discussion. "I find some of his advice for modest speech and action to be useful even today, but I have no scruples in admitting that I find his ideas regarding subjugation to the male of the species, no matter how worthy, to be very questionable indeed."

"Would you deem it questionable for me to invite you to dine with me this afternoon?"

Surprised, Charlotte analyzed him. Was it questionable? Was he flirting with her in an inappropriate manner, or was she imagining it? She had heard only positive reports regarding Mr. Edgington. Perhaps her feelings of unease stemmed from her suspicious mind. As long as they dined in a public establishment, what harm could there be in it? She was well beyond the blush of her youth, and it was acceptable for a widow to be in the company of a gentleman in public view. She placed the book back on the shelf. "I do not think it would be questionable, and I must confess I am famished."

He offered his arm. "Then let us dine, and if you wish to make any other confessions, about your reading habits or otherwise, you may feel free to do so."

Her face heated at his flirtation, and she hoped it was not obvious to those who observed her. Actually, Mr. Edgington was the second man who had brought a youthful blush to her cheeks in recent days.

If pressed, she would be forced to admit that she quite liked the fact that she was on a gentleman's arm. It must be a metaphor of some kind. Being escorted meant that she did not walk alone through the streets of life. Or something of that sort.

Charlotte and Mr. Edgington entered and were promptly seated in a public room where they were served some lovely bread, cheese, and tea. At first, Charlotte felt awkward, but as the conversation flowed, she found her ease and soon they were speaking like old acquaintances. When the church chimes sounded, Charlotte was surprised, for the hour was much later than she had anticipated. Charlotte stood. Mr. Edgington rose with her.

"Oh dear! I fear my sister will be worried at my long absence. I must return home. Will you forgive my hasty departure?"

"Of course, of course. Your sister will wonder where you have gotten yourself," he said solicitously. "May I escort you?"

"It is not necessary, sir, but I thank you for the meal." Charlotte picked up her reticule and exited the public room, and Mr. Edgington followed.

"It would be no trouble."

Charlotte turned, surprised to discover him so close by. She stopped. "Thank you, but it is not far, and I am not certain my sister will be up to receiving guests this afternoon."

He took her fingertips in his hand. "Then I shall allow you to go alone, but only if you allow me the privilege of calling on you in the future."

Charlotte did not know how to respond, but she had enough presence of mind to pull her hand from his grasp. They were in a public street! "Mr. Edgington, I am a widow…"

He did not appear abashed at her rebuke. "And I am a widower. Certainly we may be friends."

Charlotte began walking toward home, but he kept pace. After several more steps, she stopped again and turned. "Friends then if it will convince you that I do not need an escort." She spoke the words for his benefit, but she remained uncertain. Something seemed amiss with Mr. Edgington. She wondered why she had found being on his arm so pleasant only an hour earlier.

"May I call on you next week? We can discuss sermons."

"You may call on me provided that we do not discuss sermons."

She managed to divest herself of him only after she agreed to allow him to call, and when Charlotte finally arrived at her cottage, she was thankful that Mr. Edgington had not escorted her, for Maria was in high temper. Mrs. Eff, who had been sitting with her in the kitchen, looked relieved to see Charlotte. Even Edward, who was tending to the fire, seemed grateful for her appearance.

"Where have you been? I thought you were just doing some shopping," Maria demanded.

"I dined in town with Mr. Edgington."

"You dined with Mr. Edgington!" Maria's voice was barely under a shriek. "And just at the moment when I needed you most."

Maria stood abruptly, nearly knocking over the kitchen chair, and stormed out of the room. Charlotte glanced at Mrs. Eff, who only shook her head. She began to follow her, but Mrs. Eff stopped her. "Give her a moment to compose herself."

Seeing the value in her suggestion, Charlotte returned to her chair. "I am sorry, Mrs. Eff. You and Edward must have had a difficult day."

Mrs. Eff smiled at her across the table. "It was nothing, my dear."

"Nothing," Edward repeated, wiping his hands on his trousers and leaving behind dirty prints.

"I should have been here."

"You had to have your dinner."

"It was rather impromptu. I should have come straight home."

"You have to lead your own life." She paused. "Were you with Mr. Edgington lately of London? The relation of Lady Catherine?"

Charlotte looked down at the table, her face turning pink. "Yes, do you know of him?"

"I know he is quite handsome and has a well-turned calf."

"Mrs. Eff!"

"We are widows, Mrs. Collins. We are not dead, and we may certainly still appreciate male beauty, especially when it is housed in a gentleman of good family and substantial wealth."

Charlotte glanced at Edward, who did not appear to comprehend their conversation.

"He is handsome, but I confess that he sometimes makes me uneasy."

"Uneasy?"

Charlotte was sure that her face was as red as a poppy. "He flirts. At least, I think he flirts. But why would he flirt with me?"

"Why indeed. You have long been in need of a little flirtation."

"I am not certain that it is appropriate. Some of the things he says seem, well, risqué."

"That is flirtation! You are just unused to it."

"Perhaps you are right."

"Well, of course I am, dear."

The women lapsed into silence. Edward came and went, restocking the coal bin in preparation for their evening meal. At length, Charlotte stood and said, "I'll see to Maria now."

"I shall be here if you need me."

Charlotte found Maria pacing the sitting room. She did not appear to have benefitted from her time alone. Her hair was disheveled, and her hands grasped at the sides of her morning gown. "Maria, you must calm yourself."

Maria whirled around at her voice and threw her hands in the air, revealing the wrinkles she had put in her skirts. "I cannot possibly calm down, and you would not suggest such a thing if you knew what I have been through since you left."

Charlotte sat down on the chair by the fireplace and watched Maria take several more laps around the room. Finally, unable to track her along her dizzying path any longer, Charlotte arrested Maria's progress and demanded, "Do sit down and tell me what has happened."

Maria flopped onto a chair, ending sprawled in a very unladylike position, but Charlotte did not correct her.

"It is a disaster. It is worse than anything I could imagine."

Panic rose in Charlotte's throat.

"Has Lady Catherine been here?" Could she have heard of her dinner with Mr. Edgington so soon and disapproved so heartily? Would she require them to leave the cottage?

"No," Maria said, confusion on her face. "Why would she come here?"

Quickly, Charlotte asked, "Are mother and father ill?"

"No, indeed. What a silly question! This is about Mr. Card."

"Oh dear," Charlotte sighed and arranged herself more comfortably on the chair, preparing for a very long story indeed.

Tears quivered on Maria's blond lashes, and her blue eyes filled. "He has ruined everything. Absolutely everything."

Exasperated, Charlotte said, "For heaven's sake, tell me what has happened!"

"He arrived around eleven. I received him quite properly in the sitting room. You would have been proud. We were both exceedingly polite. Initially, I was happy to see him, for we have always been good friends. I remarked upon his attire. He looked quite fine today. He wore a particularly well-tailored green coat."

"He is always handsomely turned out."

"I have always liked that about him. In any case, we chatted, but as time progressed, Mr. Card seemed to become increasingly awkward. More awkward than usual, if you can imagine it."

"Oh dear."

"Yes, I was driven to ring for tea and biscuits just to have something to do, for he refused to leave."

"That was a kind decision."

"After our tea, Mr. Card began pacing the room, and I became very uncomfortable. I did not know what to say. And here he was just pacing back and forth. Then he began complimenting me. 'I have always admired you,' he said. And then I knew what was amiss."

"Did you?"

"He was going to propose, you see, and I did not want him to. Not at all. The only thing I could think of was finding a way to distract him. I suggested a walk in the garden. At first he seemed relieved, but he would not be dissuaded. He was quite determined."

"What happened?"

"Well, I got tired of walking. I just could not get away from him, no matter how fast I went. So I sat on the bench in the garden and steeled myself for the worst."

"Oh, Maria…"

"It was just as I suspected. He did propose. It was awful."

"I hope you were kind to him and considerate of his feelings."

"Kind to him?" Maria said in a high-pitched voice. "How could I possibly treat him kindly after he tortured me in such a manner. How could he not realize that I was trying to avoid the subject entirely?"

"Maria!"

"Oh! Do not chastise me, for I did not say anything too awful. I simply told him that I did not view him in such a way and that I never, ever would. Well, he would not accept that, so I told him that I loved another."

"Please tell me that you did not. Oh no. How did the poor boy react?"

"How should I know how he reacted? All I could think about was how to get myself out of this mess as quickly as possible."

"He must have been very upset. He has tender feelings for you."

"Do not look down your nose at me, Charlotte. You have no idea how to deal with such entanglements."

"I may not have had a number of lovers, but I do know that you should not have lied to Mr. Card."

"When did I lie to him?"

"You told him you loved another."

"Well, I do."

Charlotte was stunned.

"I am in love with Mr. Westfield."

Charlotte sat back in her chair, her spine straight as a piece of planed lumber. "But you hardly know him."

Maria looked offended. She stood in her own defense. "I know him well enough. He is everything a gentleman should be. He is clever, kind, and amusing. He is all that Mr. Card is not. And I told Mr. Card as much."

The situation was worse than Charlotte feared. Maria was not a delicate person, and she never seemed to comprehend the consequences of the things she said. Mr. Card would likely never forgive her.

"You should not have said such things to him. How must Mr. Card feel? He is a decent young man, handsome, charming, and rich. He has paid you the highest compliment by proposing, and how do you respond but by insulting him? You must apologize as soon as may be."

Maria crossed her arms. "I certainly will not. He will get over his hurt pride in short order and things will return to the way they have always been."

"Affairs of the heart are never that simple."

Maria groaned, left the room, and tromped up the stairs, leaving Charlotte to ponder the situation.

✒ Seven ✒

After her initial outburst subsided, Maria did not seem very much affected by the incident with Mr. Card. In fact, she seemed to have quite forgotten it. While ensconced in the cottage, she remained merry, spending much of her time daydreaming in the garden or reclining idly in the sitting room. Charlotte, however, knew that the storm clouds were gathering and that soon the deluge would begin.

A week later, an invitation to supper at the Farmington's arrived.

"You see, Charlotte." Maria waved the letter with an air of triumph. "This is proof that you have made far too much of my refusal of Mr. Card. We have been invited, you see, to join a supper party at Miss Farmington's house. I am certain that Mr. Card will also be there."

"For your sake, I am pleased to appear to be in the wrong." Charlotte remained unconvinced, but Maria beamed at her, unable to imagine any negative repercussions for her actions. Ah, if only imagination ruled reality. Charlotte would be beautiful and gentlemen would bring her carriages full of gold.

"I will write my reply straightaway." She crossed to the desk and selected a sheet of notepaper. She composed a lengthy reply, turning the paper and scribbling still more words, which Charlotte could only imagine conveyed untold silliness.

Meanwhile, Charlotte remained in the sitting room with her book in her lap. She attempted to read but soon abandoned the pursuit when her mind continued to wander. Despite all attempts to the contrary, Charlotte thought of gentlemen. What had become of her? She had not been this preoccupied even when she was in the prime of her youth. Perhaps it resulted from her sister's proclamation of love for Mr. Westfield. Or perhaps it stemmed from her conversation with Mr. Edgington. In any case, Charlotte continued to think of how much altered her life might have been had she experienced true love.

At first, this fictitious true love had no form or face. Then, much to her chagrin, she could not prevent herself from filling the void with the faces of men of her acquaintance.

First, she imagined her marriage with Mr. Collins. She recalled his manner and his words. She thought upon their days together and her feelings regarding him. Indeed, she would not call it love that they shared. It was rather more like strained companionship.

Next, the face of Mr. Basford entered her mind. She attempted not to think of him, knowing his poor reputation. She felt an embarrassed flush reach her cheeks merely at the thought of him. It was not proper for her to contemplate him. Any sort of amity with him would be insupportable.

Now, Mr. Edgington was a proper prospect for a woman such as her. He was a widower of excellent family and reputation, and strangely enough he seemed to have an interest in her. Charlotte had always been rather plain, and she had not had the inducement of a large dowry to entice gentlemen. Though it was difficult to acknowledge, men had little reason to show her attention.

Mr. Edgington, however, had experienced marriage. He must have come to realize that there were aspects of greater import than a fresh face, family support, and deep pockets. Although deep pockets never hurt. Perhaps Mr. Edgington was the gentleman with whom to explore the possibilities of love that had escaped her.

Charlotte scoffed at the turn of her contemplation. Such nonsense for a woman of her age and experience, but for some reason she felt strangely buoyant.

But would Lady Catherine accept her?

Likely not.

❧ ❧

The feeling of hopefulness did not last past the dinner at the Farmington's, however. The evening began well. Of course, most dinner parties have the advantage of expectation—of food and conversation and merriness. Only on rare occasions are these expectations met, and certainly, this was not one of those times.

While not as grand as the Cards' home, the Farmingtons' house was a large and welcoming residence. Miss Farmington greeted them at the door and escorted them into a well appointed drawing room. The furniture was upholstered in rich shades of jonquil yellow, and wax candles had been lit, causing the room to take on a dull yellow hue though it was past dusk.

The party conversed pleasantly until Mr. Card arrived. He entered the room, his posture erect and his hands clasped behind his back. He too was well appointed. His coat fit closely across his shoulders, giving him an aristocratic mien. His conduct and bearing were decidedly more aloof than ordinary. He surveyed the crowd, spotted Maria, and then walked purposefully in the opposite direction. No one, save Charlotte, took note.

Maria attempted to join the group with which he conversed. His bearing turned unambiguously cold, and although her sister appeared not to notice, it incited questioning glances from those who were assembled around them.

As the party moved toward the dining table, Miss Farmington arrested Maria, pulling her into an alcove in the hallway. Charlotte lingered behind them to listen to their conversation and wondered when she had lost her shame. "Maria, is something amiss between you and Mr. Card?" She need not have stood so close, for Miss Farmington's voice carried, and Charlotte hoped no one in the dining room had heard.

"I do not know to what you are referring, Miss Farmington." Although Charlotte could not see Maria, she felt fairly certain that her words were accompanied by a head flip.

"He is acting very strangely. How can this fact have escaped your notice?"

Charlotte waited as her sister contemplated a proper response. It took long moments. "If you believe him to be acting strangely perhaps it would be wise for you to question him, not me, for I am the same as I ever was."

Charlotte did not approve of that idea at all.

"Indeed I shall. It is fortunate, then, that Mr. Card is to be seated beside me."

Miss Farmington pulled Maria from the alcove and led the way to the dining room. Charlotte followed at length, found her appointed seat beside Mrs. Farmington, and was quickly engaged in conversation. Maria sat on the opposite side of the table between two of Miss Farmington's young friends, and the three of them chattered happily, completely ignorant of the others around them.

Out of the corner of her eye, Charlotte regarded Mr. Card and Miss Farmington. She could hear very little of their conversation, but she took notice of their continual glances in Maria's direction. Mr. Card's countenance was cold, and she was unaccustomed to seeing such an expression on so pleasant a gentleman.

The longer the two spoke the more shocked Miss Farmington appeared. She reached over and patted Mr. Card's arm comfortingly, and Charlotte was quite certain that she saw her call Maria an old fool.

In good conscience, Charlotte could not call her younger sister old, but unfortunately, she had to agree that she had behaved foolishly where Mr. Card was concerned. Perhaps she did deserve a measure of the censure that was certain to come her way.

For the remainder of the evening, Miss Farmington stayed at Mr. Card's side, fawning over him and making sure Maria was a witness to it all.

Indeed, Maria had seen, and she came to Charlotte in due course. "You see, the situation has not turned out as badly as you predicted. See there how

Miss Farmington is enjoying his company, and what a charming couple they make. Mr. Card will soon forget his ridiculous proposal to me."

"I do not know—"

"—Oh, pooh. You just refuse to acknowledge pleasant things."

Maria flounced away, leaving Charlotte with a reprimand lingering on her tongue. Alone again, she sat down to observe the room. It was clear that the news of Maria and Mr. Card was now known by everyone present and would soon be the talk of Westerham. Based on the cold glare in the eyes of Mr. Card and Miss Farmington—and the lack of conversation partners who had come Charlotte's way—she concluded that her sister—and herself by extension—would not appear in a positive light.

Oblivious to the entire situation, Maria spoke animatedly with the assembled company. Charlotte could hear her voice floating above the others. "I do not comprehend why everyone is so quiet this evening! Perhaps it is owing to too much of Mrs. Farmington's good wine." Her friends looked on with barely concealed disdain as she raised her glass to her lips and drank deeply.

Leave it to Maria to misread the situation so completely. It would not do to have her sister intoxicated; her conversation was questionable enough without the benefit of red wine. Charlotte resolved to stem the tide of the damage immediately. She stood and walked to the corner where Maria was in the process of questioning Mrs. Farmington about the vintage of the wine.

"Mrs. Farmington, thank you for an enjoyable evening," said Charlotte quietly, "but I beg you would excuse us."

Maria stared at her. "But it is so early."

"I do apologize, but I am feeling rather unwell and would like to be at home shortly."

"Oh dear," Mrs. Farmington said, "I will have a carriage brought round." She rang the bell and issued orders to the servant who arrived. Then she called her granddaughter to bid farewell to her guests. "Constance, do escort Mrs. Collins and Miss Lucas to the door."

"With pleasure." Miss Farmington did not attempt to conceal her rudeness. She offered her arm to Maria. "Shall we?"

Charlotte walked behind them, again listening to their conversation. Still no shame. "I am sorry to speak so in front of your sister, but how could you do such a thing to poor Mr. Card?"

They stopped abruptly at the door. Charlotte narrowly avoided a collision.

Maria took a confused step backward. "Do such a thing?"

"Your rejection of Mr. Card's proposal, of course, you ninny."

"Oh, that," Maria said lightly. "I had thought he would not mention it."

"Not only have you broken his heart, but you have done it for the stupidest reason imaginable."

"Wha—" Maria was flabbergasted.

Miss Farmington sighed in frustration. "You imagine yourself to be in love with Mr. Westfield, and I supposed you believe that he returns your feelings."

"I cannot speak for Mr.—"

Miss Farmington's eyes narrowed to mere slits on her freckled face. "Mr. Westfield is far above your station, and he certainly would never show interest in you."

Maria stared at her mutely, confusion etched in her face. Miss Farmington's visage had turned an unflattering shade of red, and her nose became so pinched that Charlotte wondered that she could continue to draw breath. "And worse, you have ruined your only hope for marriage. Can you not comprehend that? It is now certain that you will be as sad and lonely as your sister."

"That is quite enough." Charlotte spoke loudly as she stepped between the two young ladies. She touched her sister's hand. "Maria, shall we go?"

Maria managed to croak out a small "yes" and followed Charlotte weakly, her steps as careful as an elderly woman's.

Charlotte took her sister's arm and propelled her into the small, borrowed carriage as the tap of Miss Farmington's angry footsteps receded down the hall. Maria continued to look back at Miss Farmington's receding form. Her face had gone very pale and she turned to Charlotte and said, "I must speak with her."

Fearing that her sister would call out to Miss Farmington, or worse, burst in loud sobs, she said, "No. Do not say a word until we are home, Maria. Now is the time for discretion."

Maria stared uncomprehendingly. "How could Mr. Card do this to me?" Her lower lip wobbled.

"Not now. At home. The driver might overhear."

It appeared that Maria might protest her caution, but Charlotte kept her arm firmly around her sister's shoulders as they bumped along through the night. She absorbed the periodic trembling that rocked Maria's small form, and when they exited the carriage and descended into the night, Charlotte had to assist her into the cottage.

As soon as the candles were lit and the two sisters were alone in the sitting room before the peat fire that Edward had left burning for them, Maria's shock turned to anger, and she stormed to the fireplace. "How could Mr. Card do this?"

"Maria—"

"—He has ruined me. By tomorrow morning, the entire town will have turned against me. I shall have no friends. No prospects."

Charlotte remained silent.

Maria's voice rose, her face became ruddy in the candlelight. "And what will Mr. Westfield say?"

Charlotte took a place on the settee and waited for her sister to finish raging.

"Mr. Card said he loved me. Now he has done this. How could he? How could he possibly do this to someone he claimed to love, Charlotte? How?"

"He is angry and hurt, Maria. Only think of the things you said to him when he proposed."

"I said nothing terrible. I spoke the truth. There is nothing so inappropriate about the truth surely."

"You said yourself that you were cross with him. That you told him you would never love him. That you loved another. He has pined for you since your first meeting, Maria. You could have let him down more gently. How would you like to hear those things from the person you loved most in this world?"

"So I deserved all this censure?" Her voice cracked with emotion.

"No, certainly not. Mr. Card has made his share of mistakes in this matter as well. Not the least of which was confiding in that odious Constance Farmington."

Maria sighed. "What a disaster this has turned out to be."

"Yes, and now we are left to deal with it as we might."

Maria collapsed on the settee with tears streaming down her cheeks and cried silently with her sister's arms around her.

❧ ❧

The next morning, Maria did not come downstairs, so Charlotte went to her bed chamber to summon her. She lay unmoving beneath the covers, despite the sound of her sister's movements as she threw open the drapes, allowing bright morning light to flood the room.

Maria groaned.

"Get up. We are going to town."

"I certainly am not. Everyone despises me by now."

"Listen, sister." Charlotte sat on the side of the bed. "It is best to deal with matters such as this directly. You must go out and meet your fate."

"Last night you told me it was the time for discretion," Maria said, her face still covered.

"That was last night. You were in no condition to deal with this situation rationally."

"Nor am I now."

"Today, you must be. You must not hide. You must acknowledge the wrong you did to Mr. Card and make amends. It is the only way you will regain your status in society."

"Urgh," Maria said. She threw the blankets back, giving Charlotte the first good look at her face. Her skin was pale, her hair matted, and there were swollen, dark circles under her eyes.

"Did you sleep at all?" Charlotte's tone was softer.

"How could I sleep?"

Charlotte stroked her hair. Her fingers caught in the knotted strands, and she dropped her hand.

"I did behave badly to Mr. Card, did I not?"

Charlotte paused, pleased to see that the morning sun had brought with it a measure of mental enlightenment. "Yes, I am sorry to say you did."

Maria sighed and turned her head toward the window. "I was so nervous, and I simply wanted him to leave. I focused only on avoiding the issue, so when he proposed, I had no idea what to say. I had no thought in my head at all but to avoid the matter entirely. So I blurted the first thing that came into my mind."

"It is always wise to consider for a time."

"I know, and that is why I simply cannot go into town. I have no defense against my behavior."

"I really think you should face the world as soon as possible. If you hide away here, people will only have more fodder for their gossip."

Maria pulled the covers back over her head. "Charlotte, please do not make me. I am far too embarrassed."

Charlotte looked down at the lump in the bed that was her sister. Her sister, who was giddy and sweet, thoughtless and silly, but who loved society above all else.

"I will not make you do anything, Maria, but I am going to the bakery for some cream cakes."

"Let me know if you see anyone."

"I shall."

"And do bring me a cream cake."

✤ ✤

Charlotte walked to town, vaguely saddened that her sister had elected to remain at the cottage, and she felt quite dreary in spirits although the sun shone brightly.

As she walked, she felt the stares of the others she encountered. Not a one spoke to her, although she could hear snippets of their conversations, which were focused on Maria's poor behavior. Torn between anger at her sister's stupidity, pity at the situation into which she had put herself, and fear at her own tenuous position in society, Charlotte picked up her pace, her sturdy boots crunching on the ground beneath them.

Turning the corner beside the Circulating Library, she found herself face to face with Jonas Card.

"Excuse me, Mrs. Collins." His voice was polite, his manner chilly. He tipped his hat and stepped aside so she could pass.

Charlotte responded automatically. "It is nothing, Mr. Card."

They looked at each other awkwardly until Mr. Card bowed and then turned to leave, but Charlotte stepped into his path. "Mr. Card, let us not behave this way."

He faced her once again and said with not a small measure of bitterness, "How then would you suggest I behave?"

Charlotte bowed her head at the anger she heard in his voice. He was justified in his sentiments if not in his behavior. "I can make no such suggestion."

"Then what is the purpose of this conversation?"

"I confess I am not certain," Charlotte ventured. "Perhaps, I simply wanted to reunite you and my sister as friends. You have always been friends, have you not?"

"No, I have never been her friend." His eyes blazed with anger. "I have never been content to be a mere acquaintance. You yourself knew of my feelings. My mother revealed her conversations with you on this matter." His voice dropped to a whisper. "You knew that I have always loved her. Every moment I have spent as her friend has been a torment."

"Oh, Mr. Card—"

"And as for her so-called friendship for me, I do not believe it exists. No friend would reject another friend in so rude a fashion."

"Her words were thoughtless, I agree, but I do not believe that it was her intention to wound you."

"Do you not? Then why would she possibly tell me that she found me unmanly and that I repulsed her? Why would she say these things unless she meant to hurt me?"

Maria had not confessed that she had said such things to poor Mr. Card. It was wrong indeed.

"I can make no excuses for her actions, Mr. Card, but I know she regrets the words she spoke to you that day. I do wish that you would speak with her, allow her to apologize."

"Speak with her! Certainly not. I am quite finished with her."

Charlotte chose her next words carefully. "But Mr. Card, you have not been entirely fair to her either."

His eyes widened, and his lips stretched into a sneer. "Have I not?"

"By speaking—undoubtedly in righteous anger—to Miss Farmington, you have made Maria the focus of vicious gossip."

"What did I say of her that was untrue? I spoke the unmitigated truth when I said that she insulted me and that she loved that dreadful American Mr. Westfield. Do you deny that I spoke only what Maria said herself?"

"No, I cannot deny it. I wish…" She paused. "I only wish that you would find it in your heart to forgive her—"

"—I have no heart left."

She pushed on. "And I also wish that you would help alleviate the gossip against her. She is a sensitive young woman, and she will certainly be crushed by what is being said about her."

"And I wish she had accepted my proposal, but we cannot always get what we desire, Mrs. Collins. Good day."

Mr. Card turned on his boot heel and stalked down the street, leaving Charlotte standing with her mouth agape.

She did not know how long she stood in such an undignified posture when she heard a voice behind her say, "Excuse me, Mrs. Collins."

Charlotte turned to find Mr. Edgington leaning against the corner of the building. He bowed to her politely, and she returned a curtsey.

"Good morning, Mr. Edgington." She wondered if he had witnessed her ordeal with Mr. Card.

"Forgive me, but I could not help overhearing."

Oh dear. So much for discretion.

"I suppose it does not matter. The damage has already been done."

"I confess that your sister has been the main topic of conversation about town all morning."

"That has been my unfortunate experience as well."

"Shall we walk?" He offered his arm, and Charlotte took it gratefully.

They continued along the sidewalk, and Charlotte found she rather enjoyed having someone in whom to confide. "My poor sister will not be able to bear this. She has always been such a social creature, and she had just found herself back in society."

"It is sad that she is so affected by what is said about her."

"I suppose that is the trouble with living amongst people. It would be so much pleasanter to be a hermit."

He laughed and then turned contemplative. "I am also sorry to see what effect this situation is having on you, but I hope it does not cause you to turn into a hermit.

"It has not affected me half so much as it has Maria."

"Oh, but it has."

"I am afraid I do not follow your logic, sir."

"I have noticed that no one has spoken to you all morning, and I have heard what they said about you after you pass by. Does not that concern you at all?"

"Of course it does, but I must think of Maria."

They walked along and Charlotte fancied that she could feel the stares of people on her.

"Have you considered taking a holiday?"

"A holiday?"

"Yes. Perhaps a trip to London for a few weeks will allow the storm clouds to pass."

"I do not know, Mr. Edgington. I do not relish the idea of retreating and retrenching."

"Nonsense. You know the nature of society. Your current trouble will dissipate upon the occurrence of the next event worthy of salacious gossip. I simply believe that there is no reason to witness the slander of your family firsthand."

Charlotte considered for a moment. She had advised her sister only this morning to go out and face her trouble, but having witnessed the magnitude of the situation for herself, having spoken to poor Mr. Card, she could well see the advantage of waiting out the storm in London.

"Do you have relatives or friends whom you could visit?"

"Yes, I do have some cousins in London whom I have not seen in quite some time."

"Well, perhaps now is the time to renew your acquaintance," he suggested. "And London has many pleasant distractions for ladies."

They lapsed into silence, and Charlotte spent the remainder of her walk with Mr. Edgington considering her options. She took her leave of him, completely forgetting to purchase cream cakes for which she had ventured out, and returned home to discover that Maria was not downstairs. As Charlotte ascended the steps, she began to hear the sounds of sobbing.

She knocked on the door to Maria's bed chamber and found her sister sitting in the middle of the bed dressed in her favorite gown of a white fabric patterned with blue stripes and medallions. Her hair had been done, but it had slipped its hold and now strands hung around her face. Her eyes looked defeated, and Charlotte immediately felt compassion for her.

"Oh, Charlotte."

She sat on the rumpled bed beside her. The same position she had taken that morning. "What has happened?"

Maria held up a letter. "This was delivered an hour ago. From Miss Farmington. She says…she says…here, read it for yourself."

Charlotte opened the letter, which was written in a looping, exaggerated hand, a silly choice of script.

> My dear Maria—
>
> I know that you must be having a difficult time at present and are probably not anxious to venture out amongst our acquaintance. However, I know you are too polite to rescind your acceptance to our picnic next week. I will save you the pain of disappointing us by telling you are no longer required to attend.

It was signed in exaggerated swirls that Charlotte imagined was her name.

The situation was utterly ridiculous, and Miss Farmington's behavior only served to convince Charlotte that she was not like her old red roan pony at all. She more closely resembled a mule.

"Is it not awful?"

"Yes, it is." She patted her sister's arm. "What would you think of a holiday?"

Maria's face lit. "Holiday?"

"Yes, to London to visit our cousins the Emersons for a time."

Hope lit Maria's eyes, then suspicion. "But you said I must face society and not run away."

"Forget what I said this morning. Perhaps this is the best way. What do you think? Shall we go?"

"Could we?"

"I believe we should."

Maria, whose eyes had brightened despite their red rims, smiled for the first time that morning. "I must admit that a holiday would be welcome. I will prepare my trunk straightaway...after I ring for tea. I could certainly do with a fresh cream cake."

❧ Eight ❧

Westerham was twenty-five miles from London, an easy distance by most standards. Those standards had obviously been set by those who could afford to keep comfortable travelling coaches and horses of their own. Charlotte and Maria could afford only to purchase space on the stagecoach, and the accompanying horses, though large and undoubtedly powerful, looked like they deserved a respite in a grassy pasture.

They stopped briefly in Bromley to acquire fresh horses. The passengers disembarked while the new steeds, which looked only slightly more energetic than those they had left behind, were hitched to the coach.

Charlotte watched the slow, metered steps of the first team of horses as they were led to the paddock for rest, and she felt very much like them. Stiff and weary from travel. Though she had been sitting and not pulling, she had still been bruised by the jerking impacts of the coach's wheels through the rutted and hole-riddled roads. Travel, though necessary, had its own variety of unpleasantness.

Upon the coachman's call, Charlotte reluctantly took her seat, wishing she had brought a cushion, and continued the dusty journey toward London through the gathering warmth of spring.

Soon, the countryside was exchanged for the crush of the city. Buildings filled the horizon and the road became crowded with horses, wagons, and people on foot. The stage arrived at a coaching inn, which was fairly bustling with activity. Grooms dashed to care for the horses of the incoming stages, and passengers disembarked and milled about, searching for a hackney or seeing to their trunks.

Charlotte stepped into the busy yard and looked around. She wondered briefly if she and Maria would ever manage to find their cousin Harold Emerson amidst all the activity. Maria must have had similar thoughts, for she leaned to Charlotte and asked, "Will Mr. Emerson be able to find us, do you think? I am so weary and wish to be alone."

Charlotte patted her hand. She also wished to be alone. Maria had not been a pleasant traveling companion. She had complained nearly the entire duration of the journey. The coach was hot, the roads were dreadful, it was too crowded. All were valid complaints, but speaking them aloud would do no good.

Before Charlotte could reply, she spied Harold Emerson, who had appeared on the fringes of the crowd. Mr. Emerson was a pleasant gentleman of careful manners and curly auburn hair who had earned a substantial living in the practice of law, and he bowed before them. "Welcome, cousins."

The ladies curtseyed, and Charlotte spoke for them both. "Mr. Emerson, we feared we would never find you in such a throng of people. We are ever so glad that you have spotted us."

Maria nodded. "Yes, it is dreadfully crowded and hot."

He glanced between the sisters. Charlotte wondered if they appeared as dusty and bruised as they felt.

He said, "Allow me to see to your belongings, and we will be away as soon as is possible. I have already arranged for a hackney to take us to St. Paul's. Mrs. Emerson will be pleased to see you both."

Mr. Emerson disappeared briefly to look after their trunks and then he escorted Charlotte and Maria to the waiting conveyance. Charlotte was loath to sit once again, but she was eager to see her cousin Mary, and she took her place next to Maria and settled herself gingerly on the seat.

Mr. Emerson joined them forthwith and began a pleasant conversation. "How does your family do? Your parents, are they well?"

Charlotte responded to his polite inquiries while Maria sullenly studied the surrounding buildings.

Mr. Emerson then inquired after the comforts of their journey, a question to which Charlotte hoped Maria would not respond.

She did not.

And though it was not the precise truth, Charlotte said that their journey was most pleasant.

Here, Maria had uttered a sound of mild disagreement, which Charlotte attempted to conceal by asking, "And how does my cousin do?"

Mr. Emerson had been studying Maria, but he turned his attention back to Charlotte. "Mrs. Emerson has been anticipating your arrival most heartily. She is probably at the window even now, waiting for your appearance."

"My sister and I are eager to see her as well. How far are we from your home?"

"It is but a short drive."

"Oh, good!" Maria said, emitting the first genuine smile of the day. "I am quite ready to be situated in a solid structure that does not move or smell of horse."

Mr. Emerson seemed slightly taken aback by Maria's words, but his good nature would not allow him to think ill of her, and he assured her that their home neither moved nor smelled of horse.

For the remainder of their ride in the hackney, Mr. Emerson pointed out the sights, and soon, he gestured proudly toward his home. "We have arrived!"

While it was hardly the most fashionable London neighborhood, their home was clean and well-maintained, and it overlooked other similarly kept homes. Cousin Mary, a doe-eyed young woman with dark hair, greeted them at the door and ushered them immediately to the sitting room, while simultaneously managing to order some refreshments and see that their luggage was brought to their rooms.

Maria immediately made her excuses and disappeared into her chamber, but Charlotte stayed below stairs and enjoyed tea with the Emersons, who sat together on the settee. Charlotte observed the looks that passed between them with interest. It was clear that their marriage was founded on love, for Mary looked upon her husband with something akin to adoration, and Mr. Emerson, though much more reserved in his bearing, returned her affection with subtle glances of his own.

Though the couple had been married for very nearly five years, Charlotte could tell that they still enjoyed each other's company very much indeed, and she was quite certain that while not in company, they often sat much more closely.

Charlotte's observations were both encouraging and somewhat depressing, for she had never experienced such things. She had always sat as far from Mr. Collins as propriety would allow and looked on him as little as possible. Despite the jealousy that stung her as she watched her cousins, she was heartened to confirm once more that marital bliss was possible, and, quite likely, more common than she had thought.

"Thank you so much for opening your home to us. My sister was in very great need of an escape, and I confess that I too needed to leave Westerham for a time. As much as I love the country, it can become rather confining."

"We are happy to help you and poor Maria." Mary patted Mr. Emerson on the thigh, "Are we not, dear?"

"Indeed we are." Mr. Emerson sounded sincere but confused.

Charlotte shifted in her chair and appealed to Mr. Emerson. "I feel I must apologize for Maria's abrupt disappearance. She is still at sixes and sevens over the circumstances in Westerham."

"Do not trouble yourself." Mary waved her hand as if to dismiss the problem with a mere gesture. "We understand completely. As long as you are here, you must consider our home to be your home. Behave just as you would in Westerham. If Maria needs solitude, then she shall find it here."

"You are very kind."

"And you, my dear cousin, must get out and enjoy the atmosphere of London."

"Must I?"

Mr. Emerson cleared his throat and said, "Certainly. There is a great deal to be experienced, and now that you are here, you must experience it. It would not do for both of you to remain locked away in the tower, so to speak."

"Yes, allow Maria to heal in solitude. In the meantime, we will enjoy London, and when Maria is ready, she shall join us."

"I would not know which of the city's entertainments to select."

Mr. Emerson volunteered his services. "Allow me to arrange things. Shall we not begin with an evening at the theater?"

"Oh yes, dear, the theater."

"Then I shall arrange it."

·ෛ ෛ·

The very next night, the three of them left Maria to her bed and her biscuits and endured the changeable April weather to attend a performance of *The Inn-Keeper's Daughter* at the Theatre Royal at Drury Lane.

Mary's excitement over the evening's outing was infectious, and Charlotte was swept along in her tide of giddiness. The cousins spent the day preparing their outfits. Charlotte selected a short-sleeved dove gray gown, and when she saw Mary's gown of fine white muslin, for the first time, she regretted her own gown's black mourning trim.

Mary and Charlotte prepared for the theater together, and when the hour of their departure drew near, Mr. Emerson began to pace at the bottom of the stairs.

"Do not mind him, Charlotte," said Mary, as she held out two necklaces for Charlotte's opinion. "He would arrive a quarter hour early for every occasion if he could. It is up to us women to prevent the blunder of early arrival."

Though Charlotte was prepared to depart, she laughed at Mary, who was still a bit scattered. She pointed to the simple cross necklace. "I believe that will do your gown justice."

Mary hooked it around her neck and then regarded herself in the mirror. "Yes, I believe you are right. And now we may relieve Mr. Emerson's suffering."

They left the room and descended the stairs. Mr. Emerson paid them efficient compliments and then ushered them to the hackney.

Soon, the Theatre Royal at Drury Lane loomed before them. They had arrived a bit late, though Mr. Emerson said not a word of it as he escorted them quickly to their seats. Charlotte had hardly a moment to take in the edifice or the interior of the theater before she found herself seated in the balcony beside her cousin and her husband.

The production had already begun, but she easily slipped into the action of the play. Though she found herself enjoying the production, she felt rather like an interloper. The intimate ambiance of the balcony seats seemed to have relaxed Mr. Emerson, and the couple frequently glanced at each other throughout the performance and shared little comments and jokes that she could not hear. They passed Mr. Emerson's monocular opera glass between them, offering it occasionally to Charlotte, but she declined. She wanted to allow them privacy and interacted as little as possible, for they seemed to be enjoying each other so immensely. In fact, the Emersons soon seemed to forget her presence completely.

During the intermission, Charlotte took her leave of her cousins, descended the stone staircase, and strolled in solitude around the theater admiring the architecture and décor. She was well acquainted with the finer things. After all, she had been in Rosings, the great house of Lady Catherine de Bourgh, many times, but the sheer opulence of the theater filled her with awe. The sumptuous fabrics encouraged her to run her fingers across them, though she dared not, and the gilding made the room appear to glow golden. While Charlotte enjoyed a simpler style, the colors and textures of the rotunda caused her to fancy herself as a grand dame, whose closets were filled with gowns for every hour of the day, whose companions were always witty, and whose dance card was always filled.

"I thank you, but no," she would say to the wealthy baron, "I may not dance this set with you, for I am promised to the earl."

Charlotte smiled at her thoughts, knowing fully that she would never share them with anyone, for they were foolish and impractical, and they would never come to fruition. But what harm was it to imagine such *affaires de coeur*?

As she walked and dreamed, she became conscious of a familiar figure standing under an archway near one of the entrances to the rotunda. At first, she thought her mind was playing her for a fool and believed herself to be imagining the shock of red hair on his head, but as she ventured closer, she saw that it was indeed Mr. Edgington. Although not the baron or the earl of her daydreams, Charlotte was pleased to see him, especially so handsomely attired in a fine black suit coat and breeches and an intricately tied white cravat. She stopped before him and watched as his eyes lit with recognition.

"Mr. Edgington, good evening."

"Mrs. Collins!" He stepped forward and grasped her hand in his. His gaze dropped admiringly at her gown, her best. "You are looking quite well, but I confess I am surprised to see you here."

"At the theater or in London?" She slowly withdrew her hand.

"Both actually." He allowed her to remove her hand from his grasp and then glanced furtively around the room, as if he had been caught in a compromising position. Perhaps he had held her hand a bit longer than protocol dictated. Charlotte too looked about her, but she recognized no one.

When she returned her attention to Mr. Edgington, he was looking at her expectantly, and she remembered that she ought to say something in response. "Well, you suggested that I bring Maria to London and it seemed a fine idea." Her halting speech embarrassed her. She took a deep breath, hoping it would loosen her tongue and dispel the awkwardness she felt. "The theater was my cousin Mr. Emerson's method of entertaining his poor country relation."

"Are you enjoying it?"

"To my surprise, I find that I am. I never fancied myself a fan of the theater. It always seemed so improper."

"Improper! I should think not." He laughed. "How does Maria do?"

"She is healing, thank you, Mr. Edgington." Again his eyes travelled the room, and Charlotte wondered at his distraction. He appeared to be searching the crowd. But for whom? Perhaps he was at the theater with friends. Perhaps he was escorting a young lady. Yes, he was most likely searching the assembly for his companion. But what sort of person was Mr. Edgington's companion? A woman, undoubtedly. Did he flirt with her as he had with Charlotte? Was she younger and more attractive? Did she have a claim on Mr. Edgington's heart?

People began filing back into the theater, and his eyes returned to Charlotte.

"It appears that the intermission is near its end."

"I should return to my cousins."

He stopped her as she began to turn away. His hand gripped her forearm. She stared down at the hand on her arm.

"Mrs. Collins, forgive my impertinence." He released her. "Will you permit me to call upon you at your cousins' home?"

Ordinarily, Charlotte would have been inclined to deny such a request, if in fact she ever received one, but tonight—after witnessing the affection between Mr. and Mrs. Emerson and experiencing a twinge of jealousy at the thought that Mr. Edgington was at the theater with another lady—she said, "I would enjoy it very much."

She gave him directions to her cousins' home and then hurried back to her seat. She could barely focus on the performance for the remainder of the evening. Instead, she searched the audience for Mr. Edgington, hoping to glimpse his companion. His distinctive red hair should be easy to spot.

But it proved more difficult than Charlotte imagined, for the theater was quite overflowing with people.

"Mr. Emerson, may I accept your offer to use your opera glass?"

He removed the glass from his eye. "Certainly."

She issued her thanks and began to scan the crowd. Row after row, seat after seat, she searched. She began to feel very much like a foolish debutante, but envy, and natural curiosity, drove her to continue her search until she thought she espied Mr. Edgington.

She focused the lens on the gentleman. Yes, it was most certainly him.

He sat in the center of a row. On his left was a rather portly gentleman. Most likely not his companion.

But on his right sat a woman.

Charlotte squinted through her glass. She was not the lithe female she had envisioned but a slightly plump woman of questionable fashion sense. Charlotte could not discern the details of her gown, but her hair! Her hair could be seen from miles, she was certain. It was coiffed in ringlets and bound in a complicated wrap, and perched jauntily on the crown of her head was what appeared to be an entire bird's nest. Including the bird.

Perhaps a skylark or sparrow. Charlotte could not be certain from such a distance.

This woman must not be Mr. Edgington's consort, but his relation. Surely, he would have higher standards than to pursue a woman who would wear an aviary on her head. Perhaps he too was entertaining a poor country cousin. Charlotte smiled at the thought.

Mr. Edgington was available, and apparently, he was interested. Suddenly, a thrill ran through Charlotte. She felt jittery and a little sick. Did every woman feel this way when she was being courted by a gentleman? She had never imagined that love and nausea went hand in hand.

◈ Nine ◈

When Charlotte descended the stairs the following morning, she discovered Mr. Edgington breakfasting with her cousins.

She paused in the corridor at the first sound of his voice. What could he be doing here?

Charlotte's practical nature assured her that it probably signified nothing of greater import than the fact that he had come to call on the entire family, had interrupted their meal, and had been invited to dine with them.

It meant nothing. He had not come to call only on her.

Had he?

One never knew with gentlemen.

She checked her hair in the hall mirror and pinched her cheeks to lend them some color before entering the room.

"Good morning, Cousin Charlotte," said Mary over her muffin and tea. "I hope you do not mind, but Mr. Edgington arrived a few moments ago, and I invited him to share our late-morning meal with us."

Mr. Emerson and Mr. Edgington rose from their chairs and bowed to her. Mr. Emerson appeared to be studying their guest, as if to determine his worthiness to call upon his cousin, but Mr. Edgington's attention remained on her.

Surprised at Mr. Edgington's intensity, Charlotte spoke by rote. "Indeed, it was the proper thing to do."

She took a seat across the table from Mr. Edgington, and as the gentlemen returned to their chairs, she wondered if she would offend their guest if she filled her plate and then ate its entire contents, for she was really quite famished. She glanced at the dishes before her and decided she did not care much what he thought. She took a generous helping of ham, a boiled egg, and two slices of buttered toast and poured herself some tea.

Mr. Edgington was watching her, but he did not seem appalled by the amount of food on her plate. Apparently, he did not mind a woman who indulged herself occasionally.

"I had not intended on imposing upon your meal," he said, lifting his teacup from the saucer, "but I wanted to invite you on a walk this morning."

Mr. Edgington sipped. Charlotte looked to her cousins. Mr. Emerson produced a hesitant smile. And Mary shot Charlotte a conspiratorial look, which she hoped Mr. Edgington had not seen. "You have not imposed."

He replaced the cup gently on the saucer. "I am pleased to hear it, for I had no wish to disturb your morning routine." Then, he turned his charm on Charlotte. "Would you care to tour the shops with me, Mrs. Collins?"

She glanced at her cousins, almost asking permission with a look, which was foolish since she was an adult, a widow, and perfectly capable of choosing the company she would keep. Mary smiled again, and Mr. Emerson continued to eat.

She stiffened her spine. She did not require their permission. "That sounds lovely, Mr. Edgington, thank you."

Then, the conversation turned to the previous night's entertainment and later to other subjects. It was early afternoon before Charlotte and Mr. Edgington were finally preparing to depart on their ramble.

Mary accompanied Charlotte to her chamber to retrieve her bonnet and reticule. She dropped onto Charlotte's bed and whispered, "Mr. Edgington is very handsome, and he certainly seems to admire you."

Suddenly feeling like a young girl again, Charlotte sat on the bed too, grasping her bonnet in her hands. "Do you think so?"

"He called on you, did he not?"

"He called on the family."

Mary rolled her brown eyes. "Admit that he called on you."

Charlotte produced a reluctant "yes."

"And he invited you to walk with him?"

"Yes." She could not deny it.

"You see! I believe it has all the hallmarks of courtship," she said triumphantly, her eyes lighting with happiness.

Charlotte blushed.

"I see from your color that you return his interest."

"He seems to be a kind gentleman, and he has adequate resources. At this point, I have seen no reason to dislike him."

"Oh Charlotte, you must not always seek out the negative in people, and you must follow your heart for once, not your brain."

She considered her cousin's words. "You know very well that I have never been given to romance. I have always believed marriage to be a contract of mutual benefit between families. My parents encouraged that belief, and my observations seemed to prove it as well."

Mary sobered. "I know your thoughts on the matter very well, cousin. And I know that you disapproved of my marriage to Mr. Emerson—"

"—but I approve now—"

Charlotte had disapproved of her cousin's marriage to Mr. Emerson. At that time, he was but a law clerk who stood to inherit no fortune and had no family of name or rank. Any practical woman would have advised against the marriage.

Indeed, Charlotte had advised her against it. Most vehemently. For she had feared that Mary would end a bitter, lonely, old woman living at the mercy of her neighbors.

But Mr. Emerson had proved her wrong. He had earned his fortune and provided security for Mary. Charlotte was pleased to have been in the wrong.

Mary threw up her hands. "Do not trouble yourself. I know your opinion has changed." Mary patted Charlotte's arm. "I do not bring up the past to discomfit you, but to remind you that love and security are not as incompatible as you think."

Mary continued, "I dearly love Mr. Emerson, and I love you as well. I know that you were only concerned for my future and that you spoke to protect me. But it has all turned out for the best, you see. The risk you perceived was hardly risky at all."

Charlotte was still not quite prepared to wager her future on something as intangible as romantic love, but she was pleased for her cousin and she had no scruple of telling her so now. "I am happy for you, Mary, and in truth, I envy you. You are far braver a woman than I. I always seek safety. You followed your heart."

"You can follow yours as well. And there is a gentleman downstairs who seems to be ready to assist you in that."

And so Charlotte went below stairs to her gentleman.

They spent a pleasant afternoon in town touring Burlington's Arcade at Piccadilly, where Charlotte had been amused by the variety of goods for sale and by Mr. Edgington's commentary on the fashions and baubles offered for sale, and she felt vaguely disappointed when he walked her back to her cousin's home.

He too must not have wanted to depart, for he lingered at the doorstep for several minutes. When he took her fingers and bid her goodbye, she wondered if he had considered kissing her hand.

Strangely, she found herself glad that he had not, perhaps because of their location on the busy street. However, her relief at his decision did not prevent her from agreeing to join him on another walk when his business dealings permitted. He indicated that he would be busy for some days and would call on her at his first possible opportunity.

Charlotte could not help but admit to having been flattered by his attentions.

She had not had an unpleasant time, and Mr. Edgington had been very kind and amusing all day. She could only ascribe her feelings to her propensity to think on matters until her head ached. Perhaps her cousin was right when she suggested the idea of following her heart.

In her experience, Charlotte had seen few positive results when people in her acquaintance had followed their hearts. She had witnessed heartbreak and torment, and she had no wish to experience those things herself.

However, she had followed her mind and married Mr. Collins, and although she would not describe her life with him as either heart-breaking or tormented, she was not convinced that she had done right by neglecting her heart completely. Now, she was unsure how to find the median of the two. How does one use just enough heart and just enough mind?

Her friend Elizabeth Bennet, now Mrs. Fitzwilliam Darcy, had somehow managed to discover the balance. She had the good fortune to marry for love while not completely neglecting her duty to her family by securing a gentleman of good fortune.

She had chided Elizabeth about her passionate notions and had given many soliloquies on the subject of proper marriage strategies. Even after Elizabeth had married Mr. Darcy, Charlotte had only been able to see the monetary advantages of the match until later.

Once Charlotte had come to see the evidence of the true depth of emotion that existed between Elizabeth and Mr. Darcy, she had realized her mistake, though it took her many years to admit as much, even to herself.

She was embarrassed now at the memories and saddened at the rift that occurred in their friendship. Perhaps now was the proper moment to renew their acquaintance.

Sighing, Charlotte opened the door. She removed her bonnet as she walked toward the sitting room and pushed strands of her dark hair away from her face as she quickly appraised herself in the hall mirror. Her cheeks were bright from the exercise, and her eyes twinkled back at her.

Perhaps this was Mr. Edgington's effect on her. Or perhaps a result of a day in the sun. But if it were caused by the former and she appeared this youthful and attractive after just one outing with him, perhaps she should follow her heart.

But what message was her heart sending?

Charlotte could not bear to think of it any longer. She deposited her bonnet and parcel on the hall table and went into the sitting room where she found her cousins snuggled on the settee.

"Oh, pardon me." Embarrassed to have walked in on a tender moment, Charlotte prepared to withdraw.

"No, no, do come in and have tea with us," Mary said

"I do not want to intrude."

"Intrude? You are not intruding on us."

Charlotte hardly believed that.

"Perhaps we embarrass her, my dear," said her husband as he removed himself to a proper distance from his wife.

"Nonsense. Sit with us."

Charlotte poured herself a cup of tea and then took a seat across from them.

"Now tell us everything. Did you have a pleasant walk?"

"Pleasant enough. We ambled through the park and then enjoyed the shops at the Piccadilly."

"Did you purchase anything?"

"In a manner of speaking."

"Oh?"

"Mr. Edgington insisted on purchasing a pair of gloves I was admiring in the shop."

"Did he?" Mary asked with excitement in her voice.

"Yes. Is that inappropriate?"

Charlotte was certain that it was unsuitable for any young woman to accept gifts from a gentleman who was not her husband, but she had been less certain of the expectations of her position as a widow. The rules of propriety only became more clouded at the prospect of owning gloves so fine.

She and Mr. Edgington had become separated in the shop, and when he returned to her side, he had discovered her trying on a pair of delicate white gloves. She found them to be long enough, reaching just to the bend of her elbow, to be sufficiently fashionable, yet they remained practical enough to suit her tastes, for she despised garments that required continual adjustment and fuss to keep them presentable. Charlotte abhorred the current fashion of gloves so long that they necessitated the use of garters to maintain their position.

"Do you like them?" he had asked.

"Indeed. How could one not admire such fine craftsmanship?" She hurried to remove them and turned toward him, intending to leave the gloves on the display.

But Mr. Edgington picked them up. "Then you shall have them."

"I could not possibly afford them, Mr. Edgington."

"Then I shall make them a gift to you, for they suit your complexion very well indeed."

"I could not accept such a gift."

"Why ever not?"

"It simply is not seemly."

"It is not seemly for one to give a gift to his friend?" he asked incredulously.

Charlotte did not reply. He must know very well that his offer—generous though it was—skirted the boundaries of acceptable behavior. She was quite certain that his ignorance was feigned, but they were very nice gloves, and he seemed to be a very nice man.

"Please do me the honor of accepting them." His voice dropped lower, husky. "You may wear them at the next ball, and when you do so, I will know that you are thinking of me."

With that, Charlotte had allowed him to purchase them.

Now she was uncertain of her decision, but Mary looked at her with approval. "How kind! Of course, you should have accepted them, and you must allow me to stitch your initial in them for you. Embroidery is one of my secret pleasures. In limited doses, of course. Fortunately, the letter C is rather easy to stitch, and I shall have the task completed in no time at all."

Charlotte laughed at her cousin, who was an excellent seamstress. She retrieved the package from the hall table, unwrapped the gloves, and passed them to her cousin. Mary selected some pale blue embroidery threads and began to work, making small even stitches near the hem of the first glove.

"I find myself relieved that you approve of the gift."

Mary emitted a small, girlish giggle. "I think he is in love with you, Charlotte."

"Do you?" She was glad that Mary was concentrating on the gloves and did not notice the expression of confusion on her face.

"He has been very attentive to you. You must have noticed as much. Do you return his sentiments?"

Charlotte spun her teacup in the saucer, considering. "I do not know. There are instances when I am flattered by his attentions, but there are also moments when our association seems awkward and strange. I cannot explain it well."

Mr. Emerson cleared his throat. "It is not often that I intrude on women's affairs, but since I have been privy to the entire conversation, I will interject."

"Please do, dear." Mary winked at Charlotte. "It will be quite helpful to have a gentleman's opinion."

"You should relax and take time before you allow yourself to declare your feelings for any gentleman. Time is required for such an emotion to develop, for people to reveal their true selves. I knew my dear Mrs. Emerson for a full two years before I came to realize how devoted I was to her. Only then did I propose."

"But I fell in love with you immediately!" Mary protested, her eyes drawn for the first time from her work.

"You have proven the point I was preparing to make, my dear. People fall in love at their own pace, and circumstances are different in each person's life. Only think of the confusion that young Maria has experienced already. That is why I believe it is necessary to marry only when one is certain of their feelings and the true circumstances of the other party."

"There is probably a great deal of wisdom in your words," Charlotte said. "There was, however, a time when I would have disagreed with you wholeheartedly. I believed feelings were inconsequential."

Mary interjected. "Indeed, you must agree with him, for Mr. Emerson is the wisest man in all of England, and as there are few who may successfully argue against him, you may as well convert to his opinion. Besides, believing in love is ever so much more interesting than arguing against it."

Charlotte smiled at the faith Mary put into her husband. And that faith did not seem misplaced, for underneath his good nature and joviality, there seemed to be an active mind. She was certain that his courtroom adversaries often underestimated him. She certainly had.

Changing the subject in the intervening lull, she asked, "How does my sister do today? Has she been downstairs?"

A look of pity crossed Mary's face. "The poor dear. She came down in time for luncheon, and she tried to be pleasant, but it just was not in her."

"I am sorry that she has not been a good guest."

"Do not worry, dear," said Mr. Emerson. "We are her getaway. Her harbor in the storm."

Charlotte smiled sincerely.

"Would it be very wrong of us to tempt her downstairs with a cup of chocolate and some biscuits?" Mary asked.

"I do not believe so, for she has mourned long enough, and chocolate is perfect for all occasions, whether happy or sad."

Mary laughed at her cousin's words and then summoned her housekeeper. "Please bring us a plate of biscuits and a pot of chocolate and then summon Miss Maria from her room to join us."

The old housekeeper disappeared, delivered a large tray of sweets, and soon Maria appeared in the doorway. Charlotte was relieved to see a smile on her sister's face. Apparently, a week of mourning was all Maria could manage. "Come join us, Maria, for your cousins have offered us some delicious treats."

Maria descended on the tray of biscuits, popping two into her mouth in rapid succession. "You must have read my thoughts, for suddenly I am quite famished."

"You are feeling better then?"

"I am, for I realized today that I have done all I can to rectify my situation. I have apologized to Mr. Card."

"You apologized?" Charlotte was surprised that her very juvenile sister had thought to apologize to her friend. She felt rather proud.

"I did. I sent a letter almost the day we arrived here."

"Has he responded?"

"No, he has not, and I was very upset about his quietness. But I have done my best, and if he chooses not to accept my apology, then it is his affair, his wrong choice, not mine." Maria took a bite of biscuit. "Meanwhile, here I am in London, and I have not even left my bed chamber. I do not intend to waste the entire trip feeling sad or dreaming of Mr. Westfield. I want to see the city."

Mary clapped her hands together. "That is wonderful news. I had wished you would join us, for we have been so worried about you."

"My dear cousin, I appreciate your worry, and I believe London was the perfect escape for me. And I may enjoy the remainder of our stay here now that my conscience is free."

Maria plopped on the settee within easy reach of the tray of food. Apparently, she was always ready to enjoy the fruits of the household pantry as well.

"Mr. Emerson and I are pleased to hear it. It has been difficult for us to see you suffer so."

"I am happy to say that my suffering is now over. I will give no more thought to Mr. Card or Miss Farmington."

"And have you learned anything?"

"Yes, sister, I have. I will better guard my speech in the future."

Mary nodded. "That is wise."

Charlotte could not be more pleased that her sister appeared to have gained a new understanding of the ways of society. "Yes, our reputation is truly all we have, and we must guard it jealously and give no one cause to speak ill of us."

"There was a time I did not believe you, but indeed you are quite right, Charlotte. I have learned my lesson well. If I run afoul of society again, it will not be through any fault of my own."

After Maria had eaten her fill and chattered with her cousins, she went back upstairs to arrange her gowns for her coming trips into the city. Having had his fill of women's matters, Mr. Emerson disappeared into his library. With Mary occupied with her stitching, Charlotte began a letter to Elizabeth, telling her of her travels, Maria's troubles, and her meeting with Mr. Edgington at the theater.

At length, Charlotte completed her letter, sealing it carefully, and left the writing desk to join Mary on the settee.

"I am very glad that your sister's condition seems to be improving."

"I too am glad to see the improvement in her spirits. Maria is still rather young, and I want her to make a good match, but I do not relish seeing her in pain."

"Speaking of marriage, did I hear her correctly when she mentioned Mr. Westfield?"

"Yes, James Westfield is an acquaintance of ours from Westerham."

"Is he not a young relative of Colonel Armitage?"

"Yes, he is. He travels with his uncle Mr. Benjamin Basford of America. Are you acquainted with them, by chance?"

"I am. Before she went to the colonies, I was a friend of Mr. Westfield's mother. Evangeline and I were chums growing up and I was desolate when she married Mr. Westfield and went away. However, they have fared well in the New World. Mr. Westfield has become a force in the shipping industry and has a fleet based quite far south along the coast, in Savannah. Mrs. Westfield often writes of gigantic oak trees dripping with moss, mosquitoes, and unquenchable heat. It sounds dreadful to me. I knew that she was sending her son to Europe, but I never imagined that you might be acquainted with him."

"Yes, we all met at a ball in Westerham last winter."

"His mother will be pleased to hear that they are faring well in our hostile country."

"Do you correspond with her still?"

"I do, but the post is so painfully slow that our letters are infrequent."

"What do you know of the younger Mr. Westfield?"

Mary considered for a moment, as if deciding how much information to divulge. "His mother tells me that he is very charming and that he only requires the benefits of society to help him mature."

"He has certainly impressed everyone at home. The young ladies, including Maria, are quite taken with him. He is young, to be sure, but I have seen no fault with him. However, his uncle has developed a rather shocking reputation in his short time in our country."

Mary's eyes widened, and her lips parted, closed, and they parted again. "I find that very surprising,"

"Do you? I have heard from reliable sources that he is infamous in America as well. They say he uses young women for his own pursuits."

The conversation lulled, and Mary appeared to wrestle with her thoughts.

"I do hate to correct you, but I fear you have been listening to the wrong people."

"Have I?" Charlotte remained unconvinced.

"Indeed, his sister includes a paragraph or two about Mr. Basford in each letter, and I have never read a negative word about him."

"Perhaps she is censoring herself for his benefit."

"I hardly believe that. Evangeline always speaks her mind and tells the absolute truth."

"Even about her own family?"

"Especially about them."

Mary saw Charlotte's look of disbelief. "She has confessed to me in the strictest of confidence that Mr. Westfield, her own son, is something of a flirt. That is why she has sent him to Europe under his uncle's care. She hopes that seeing a bit of the world will help him to settle down at home and that Mr. Basford will influence him to find a suitable wife."

"How would Mr. Basford know how to find a suitable wife? He too is unmarried, is he not?"

"He has never married. He tells Evangeline that he has yet to find a woman who would affect his heart and induce him to contemplate marriage." Then rather as an afterthought, she added, "I think his view is rather noble."

"Yes, I suppose it is noble, but I do not see how that qualifies him to be a good chaperone."

"Do you not? Mr. Basford has exhibited a great deal of patience, and certainly, he will not allow his nephew to make any rash decisions."

Charlotte conceded that it could be a good thing, but in the back of her mind, she doubted Mary's words. How could her impressions of Mr.

Westfield and Mr. Basford be so skewed? She had always prided herself on being an excellent judge of character.

But after the episode with Maria and Mr. Card, Charlotte decided it might be best to reserve her judgment until she could observe them from a closer proximity. Whenever that might be. She had no notion of when they might return from their travels on the continent.

Mary handed her the newly monogrammed gloves. "Please do not say anything about Mr. Westfield. His mother would not wish it. She does not want him to gain the reputation of a flirt. And he may well have changed already."

Charlotte ran her fingers across the neat stitching. The pale blue letters stood in subtle relief against the material. She considered her reply.

Was it wise to withhold information from those of her acquaintance? Was Maria safe?

Although unsure of the wisdom of her words, she looked at Mary's concerned face and said, "Indeed, he may have changed. For Maria's sake, I do hope so."

✤ Ten ✤

For the remainder of their visit in London, Maria and Charlotte enjoyed the benefits of the city. Charlotte took Maria to Burlington's Arcade to admire the wares, but they could afford to purchase very little, which disappointed her greatly. She took some solace, however, in the purchase of some fine white muslin fabric, for shopping truly rivals chocolate in its ability to calm a harried mind.

The prospect of fine dresses had also tempted Charlotte beyond what she could bear. She could not force herself to remain in her out-of-fashion gowns when so many stylish women were walking the streets. Now with a dress of lovely pale striped muslin that had been sewn with the assistance of Mary, a length of Turkey red cotton, and a new straw bonnet and some fine ribbon to trim it, she was not only out of mourning for Mr. Collins, but she was in fashion. Her budget, however, would certainly suffer, and she would not have much meat on her table in the coming weeks.

Maria's spirits had been lifted by her activities in town, and Charlotte was pleased to see her joy, even if it derived from the more material benefits of the city. Her sister had begun to view life with the same youthful optimism as she had before the incident with Mr. Card.

Maria had also asked Mary to assist her in sewing a new gown, and in their unoccupied evenings, the two sat before the fire, surrounded by candles, and stitched the lightweight fabric into a gown. Unfortunately, Maria had not the temperament for such occupations, so Mary sewed alone amidst constant chatter.

Because Maria had missed their earlier foray to the theater, Mr. Emerson made arrangements for the party to attend a production of *Much Ado about Nothing* at Covent Garden. Charlotte was ashamed to admit how much time she spent readying herself for the evening, choosing her finest new gown and arranging her hair in ringlets, even though her stick-straight tresses resisted at every turn. She was even more ashamed to confess that she spent the entire first scene searching the audience for Mr. Edgington.

Of course, he was nowhere to be found, and Charlotte chided herself for her foolishness. It was a complete coincidence that she had met Mr. Edgington at the Theatre Royal. Coincidences, by definition, did not repeat themselves. And Charlotte accepted that hard reality by throwing herself into the action of *Much Ado about Nothing*, which she discovered was rather an easy task.

Suddenly, she was Beatrice, living in the exotic Italian countryside and involved in a merry war with the quick-witted Benedick. She was consoling the ill-fated Hero and demanding revenge against the evil villains who had forestalled her wedding to her beloved.

So much trouble and confusion caused by just a few blackguards, Charlotte thought. And how like her own life. Her current troubles too originated from this odd emotion called love. But would her strife end as easily? Would she be assured of gaining the heart of the handsome gentleman? Would Maria also be satisfactorily married? A play would resolve itself in five acts, but life held no such guarantees.

Leaving the theater, Charlotte, eager to discuss the play, turned to Maria. "How did you find the play?"

"It was dreadfully dull," Maria said, "but I did so enjoy being in society. Did you observe the quality of the gowns worn by the women in attendance? Oh, if only my gown could resemble those!"

"You did not enjoy the play?"

"I hardly paid it any mind. There was so much to see in the theater."

"Such as a play perhaps?"

Maria rolled her blue eyes. "Life is my play."

The sentence sounded pithy, but Charlotte knew her sister put no thought behind her words. She had been transfixed by the dresses and was probably plotting some alterations to her new gown, if only could convince Mary to help her.

And if life truly were a play, Charlotte's would be dull indeed, for she felt as though she were constantly waiting.

For Mr. Edgington.

She descended the stairs each day hoping to see him again at the breakfast table. When morning calls were paid, she hoped to hear his footsteps approaching the sitting room. But he never came.

Where was he? Charlotte wondered. Why would he have made her a gift of such lovely gloves and then disappear? She only intended to pine for a gentleman who was also pining for her. But was he pining for her?

Perhaps.

Perhaps not.

As the day of their return to Westerham drew near, Charlotte began to doubt her ever meeting Mr. Edgington again. Although she felt a twinge of loss at his continued absence, the pain tapered off quickly, and she found that she bore his disappearance very well indeed.

Maria was, however, beginning to feel the absence of Mr. Westfield rather keenly, and Charlotte began to wonder if her youthful infatuation was indeed something more.

As they strolled arm-in-arm through the park after a day of shopping, Maria admitted, "I have enjoyed my stay in London, but I am eager to be home, even if Mr. Card and Miss Farmington will not speak to me."

"I do miss our little cottage and the quiet of the country."

"Oh, I do not miss that at all. I miss the society!"

Charlotte thought of the shopping excursions and theater productions they had attended in the days since Maria had come out of her seclusion. "Did not London offer you enough in the way of society?"

Maria's eyes lit. "Do not misunderstand. I have enjoyed myself immensely. London offers a great deal of entertainment that Westerham cannot. But there is one thing London cannot give to me."

"And what is that?"

"Mr. Westfield."

Charlotte almost expected her sister to sigh and flutter her eyelashes at the mere mention of his name. Fortunately, she restrained herself to a silly smile. "Westerham cannot produce him for you either, I am afraid, for he is on a tour of the continent, and who knows when he will return."

"Still, I hope we will see much of Mr. Westfield in the future. I know you do not much care for his uncle, but I wish you would learn to get along with him. If Mr. Westfield is going to pay court to me, as I believe he will, you will be forced into his company. Unless, of course, you prefer to leave us unchaperoned."

Charlotte cast her a wry look. "No, Mr. Basford and I have put away our animosities, and we will behave as proper acquaintances and suitable chaperones." She chose not to mention Mary's positive report about him, for it also contained a tentative review of Mr. Westfield. Speaking of the matter with Maria would do no good, and she had promised she would not.

"I thought I detected a softening toward Mr. Basford." She winked. "And I am glad to hear it, for if Mr. Westfield and I marry, you will be relations, and I will demand family harmony."

Maria glanced at her sister and seeing the look of reproof in her eyes, she cut her off. "Do not scold me, Charlotte. I know it is improper to speak of marriage when Mr. Westfield has not. But if I cannot share my dreams with my sister, then with whom may I share them?"

Charlotte took Maria's hand. "I want you to share them with me, for one of us must harbor some dreams yet. And it is best that it should be you. You are younger and more able to sustain them."

"Oh Charlotte, you are not yet in your dotage."

Charlotte felt no emotion, no sting of remorse at the future before her. "Still, no one will have me now, and neither do I want anyone."

"What about Mr. Edgington?"

"I confess that I was flattered by his attentions, but he has proven his lack of interest. I have not seen him for so long. I find that I do not miss him at all."

"Certainly, we will see him again in Westerham."

"Perhaps, but truly, I no longer desire his company as I once did." She found that her words were indeed true.

Again Maria searched her face. "Perhaps you are simply injured by his inattention."

Charlotte glanced at Maria as they walked along the sidewalk toward their cousins' home and found herself the object of her sister's careful study. People passed by in groups of multicolored material and plumage, but for once Maria seemed to take no notice. She studied Charlotte as if seeing her for the first time. What was she attempting to read in her countenance? Perhaps she was searching for some sign of sorrow, some depression over Mr. Edgington's loss. But she truly did not feel any such thing.

"I see that you are not hurt. You are far worse than hurt."

Charlotte looked away. "Am I?"

At length, Maria said, "Yes. You have lost hope, and that is a much more serious condition, as you have often told me. I felt hopeless until I wrote to Mr. Card. It was miserable to have no prospects and no future."

"I am comfortably set up in my cottage. I do not need prospects to have a future." She said these words, and she truly believed them. She could be content with these circumstances.

"No, indeed you do not, for you are a strong, independent sort of woman, but would you not enjoy sharing your future with someone worthy? Would prospects not be nice?"

"I suppose they would," Charlotte agreed reluctantly.

"I confess I am surprised—and pleased—to hear you admit it," Maria said. "You have always taken too much on yourself—marrying Mr. Collins to relieve the family of the burden of supporting you, agreeing to act as my chaperone when our parents could not, and even taking this trip to remove me from trouble of my own creation. You deserve more, and if there is anything I may ever do to ensure your future, I vow that I will do it."

৶৶ ৶৶

The morning of their departure for Westerham a letter arrived from Mr. Edgington. The maid brought it to Charlotte's room as she dressed. She studied the handwriting briefly and then set the letter aside.

The long-awaited contact had been made. Unfortunately, she no longer felt an excitement over the gentleman. In addition, he had shown his attentions in an entirely inappropriate manner. A gentleman simply did not compose and send letters to a woman to whom he was not engaged.

If Charlotte needed another bell to complete the death knell of her interest in Mr. Edgington, this was certainly it. She found that she did not feel sad or distressed by the realization. Her interest had simply vanished. She finished her morning ritual at a leisurely pace before dismissing the maid. Then she opened the letter with only mild curiosity.

> My dear Mrs. Collins,
>
> I hope you will forgive me for not calling on you as promised. My long absence was necessitated by business matters that required my undivided attention. I have now fulfilled my obligations and would like to turn my attentions to a much pleasanter subject: you. I hope you will not find my words too forward, for they convey my feelings for you adequately. Please allow me to call on you at your earliest convenience. You need only send a note to my hotel in London and I will be at your side.
>
> L. E.

Charlotte folded the letter and called one of Mrs. Emerson's servants to inform Mr. Edgington of their impending departure. She dropped his letter in her trunk and donned her traveling bonnet, determined to meet her future happily with or without a gentleman at her side.

๑๑ Eleven ๑๑

When Charlotte and Maria arrived at their cottage in Westerham, no invitations awaited them, and Charlotte would not be understating matters to say that Maria was desolate. However, she soon learned that Mr. Westfield was in town, and her spirits lifted quite miraculously.

But Mr. Westfield did not come.

Charlotte began to wonder if there was a defect in the character of all males that caused them to show interest in ladies and then desert them altogether.

Soon, Maria's desolation returned, and desperate for consolation of company, she took to following Charlotte about the cottage. She followed her to the kitchen, the garden, and even to her bedchamber at night.

Charlotte was desperate for relief. She had briefly considered hauling Mr. Card and Miss Farmington to the cottage and demanding that they repair their friendship. She also considered finding Mr. Westfield and dragging him by his blond hair to pay a call on her sister. But it would not do to have him see Maria in such a state. She would certainly make a cake of herself by chattering Mr. Westfield into oblivion.

Charlotte could not have anyone else chattered into oblivion. It was too cruel a fate, as she well knew. Even now, Maria was talking, and she had not marked a word. She listened now.

"I find that yellow is the cheeriest color, do you not agree?" Maria did not even pause to allow a response. "But green is also a happy hue. Green suits me much better. You have always said so. And that is why I often wear the color. I do want to look my best, and green brings out my eyes. Well, actually my eyes are blue, but still, green compliments them very well. Blue and green match, I believe."

Charlotte stood. She did not care if blue and green matched or if Maria wanted to wear puce each day for the rest of her life.

"I am going for a walk."

"I shall join you."

93

"No!" Charlotte's voice had been harsh, and she moderated it. "I am going for a *long* walk."

"How long."

"Very, very long." She would walk to France if she could.

"Oh." Maria looked dejected, but then bounced in the direction of the kitchen. Poor Mrs. Eff. Charlotte hated to abandon her to Maria's conversation, but she had to preserve her own sanity.

Charlotte put on her sturdy boots and left the cottage before Maria could change her mind and accompany her. She shut the door quietly behind her. She could hear Maria's voice from the kitchen. She was saying something about goat cheese.

Poor, poor Mrs. Eff.

Charlotte hurried away from the cottage in the direction of the tree line. If Maria changed her mind—or if Mrs. Eff tossed her from the kitchen—she would not look for her in the dense undergrowth. She walked a few paces to the path and decided to take the direction of the pond, which bordered the Farmington's land. As she walked, her tension eased, and she became eager to explore the surrounding countryside.

At a bend in the path, she came upon a party of walkers from the direction of the Farmington's property.

Charlotte stood face to face with Miss Farmington, Mr. Card, Mr. Westfield, Mr. Basford, and a young lady Charlotte could not identify. Maria would be so disappointed not to have come, for she could have used this as an opportunity to regain her place in society.

Everyone stared mutely at each other for long moments, and then several of their party spoke at once.

Greetings were made, and introductions were given, but Charlotte was so surprised to have met them that she forgot the young lady's name as soon as it was given.

They all lapsed into silence. Charlotte did not know what to say. And given the extraneous circumstances, neither did the others.

Finally, Mr. Westfield spoke. "Mrs. Collins, we have been picnicking and are on our way to the trout pond."

"I was walking." It was quite obvious that she was walking. Charlotte felt like a fool.

Mr. Basford stepped forward. "Won't you join us?"

"Oh, yes, do join us," Miss Farmington's words did not sound sincere, but Charlotte decided to join them anyway. It was the right course of action.

Before Mr. Basford could offer Charlotte his arm, the nameless young woman reached for it and beamed. "I would not mind an escort over such treacherous terrain."

Mr. Basford allowed her to take his arm, but caught Charlotte's gaze and rolled his eyes. The treacherous terrain was a well-manicured path. Perhaps she feared that a wayward pebble might find its way into her walking boots. The horror!

Although Mr. Basford's expression conveyed Charlotte's own thoughts on the girl's behavior, it was audacious, and she sent him a look that she hoped communicated her disapproval.

He only smiled back. "Mrs. Collins, do you need assistance over the terrain as well?"

He offered his other arm.

Charlotte looked at the others who had already started down the trail. Mr. Card and Miss Farmington walked ahead with Mr. Westfield. Charlotte chose to walk alone. "I am used to navigating my way alone, thank you, Mr. Basford." She was truly content with the arrangement. She could hear the others chatting ahead of her, but she chose to enjoy the birdsong and wildflowers they encountered along the path. Before they arrived at their destination, the pond, the pace began to slow.

"I am exhausted," Miss Farmington complained.

The young woman on Mr. Basford's arm, whose name Charlotte continued to forget, agreed eagerly.

"This heat is oppressive indeed." Mr. Card said. He was sweating. But did it originate from the exercise or from Charlotte's presence? Charlotte hoped for the latter. Perhaps his discomfort would spur him to accept Maria's apologies and mend their friendship, and consequently restore her place in society.

"Shall we have a seat then?" Mr. Westfield pointed to a fallen log by the pathway. He leaned down to wipe the dirt from the bark and assisted Miss Farmington to sit.

Miss Farmington made much pretense of adjusting her dress. "What a charming spot! Mrs. Collins, will you sit as well?"

Doubting the sincerity of her invitation, Charlotte shook her head. "I take great pleasure in walking." She had developed the habit on the days when Mr. Collins remained inside the house to compose his sermons. "I think I should like to see the pond. You all relax here and I will be back as soon as my curiosity is assuaged."

"Allow me to accompany you," Mr. Basford offered.

"There is no need." Charlotte hoped to avoid being alone with him.

Miss Farmington waved a hand at her and spoke to her as if she were a simpleton. "You cannot go alone, Mrs. Collins. You could be attacked by some wild animal or a band of criminals. We will be fine resting here for a quarter of an hour."

Charlotte highly doubted that untamed animals or roving bandits occupied the Farmington's land, but she allowed Mr. Basford to guide her back to the path, and they walked for a while in silence. The woods deepened and soon the forest floor became a sea of lush green ferns accented by deep brown leaf cover. The temperature seemed to cool, and the air around them became moist and rich. Charlotte inhaled the scent and smiled. She could hear the sound of the stream as it meandered its way to the pond ahead. Charlotte was glad she decided to continue the walk, even if she was forced to be in Mr. Basford's company.

Thankfully, he remained silent and he proved to be a perfectly acceptable walking companion after all. He appeared to enjoy the atmosphere as much as she did.

Soon, the forest began to thin somewhat, and as they walked to the top of a rise, the pond came into view. Charlotte stopped and watched as some ducks took flight. The trees were reflected in the shimmering water, and someone had constructed a covered log dock.

"It's lovely."

Mr. Basford agreed. "Shall we walk to the dock?"

"Yes. I would like that very much."

They followed the path down to the wooden structure and walked to the railing. Charlotte leaned over, peering into the water to search out the fish that might be swimming below.

Beside her, Mr. Basford took a cloth from his pocket, unfolding it to display a heel of crusty bread. "I took the liberty of bringing this along. I thought I might see if the fish were biting."

Charlotte felt almost childlike joy at the prospect of something as simple as feeding fish. He broke the bread in half and gave a lump to her.

Together, they leaned over the railing and dropped crumbs while Mr. Basford occasionally told her the names of the different types of fish that appeared near the surface. Soon, they were surrounded by ducks who had regained their bravery and even some turtles had been drawn to the lure of food.

The bread was soon gone, but they lingered on the dock while the animals gradually took their leave.

Mr. Basford looked at her, and she flicked bread crumbs off her dress self-consciously. "I am sorry that you and Miss Lucas were not invited to the picnic."

"Do not trouble yourself…"

"It was wrong and I hope that you know that you will not be excluded from the ball my uncle will be hosting soon."

She felt relief for her sister. There was an additional benefit: if Maria were allowed to rejoin her friends, Charlotte would be released from her constant conversation. "You are very kind."

He waved a dismissive hand, startling a duck. They stood silently for a time and then they returned to the path, walking slowly to the rest of Mr. Basford's party.

"I believe my nephew has an interest in your sister."

"Does he?" Maria would be thrilled. The day was improving indeed.

"I believe so." He seemed to study her reaction, and she hoped that she appeared disinterested. "I think it may be wise to arrange for him to call on her sometime soon."

"I—" Charlotte prepared to resist the idea of leaving her sister alone with Mr. Westfield, but Mr. Basford held up a hand.

"With proper chaperones of course. I'll be with him, and of course, you'll be there."

Charlotte turned away, uncertain whether she should be pleased for her sister or unnerved at being with Mr. Basford again, despite their pleasant walk. "I suppose you believe that my concerns are unfounded."

"I confess that I don't relish the idea of accompanying my nephew to call on a young woman, but I know it would mean a great deal to you if I did."

"Then you are doing this for me?" She tried to suppress the panic she felt rising in her. Why would he even admit to having such a notion? It was preposterous.

"I suppose I am." He kept his eyes focused ahead as they walked. She stared directly at him.

Eventually, he turned to her and smiled, and suddenly, Charlotte was compelled to look ahead. She did not care to contemplate why.

"But I am also doing it for my nephew and his mother and because it is my duty."

She worked up the courage to look at him again. His face was serious.

"I know you still do not think much of my brash ways." He straightened his cravat and brushed imaginary dust from his coat. "But despite appearances, I am an honorable man."

Charlotte could not disagree with him and she felt properly chastised. Again, she could not bring herself to meet his gaze.

They did not speak again until they returned to the log where they had left the others. Mr. Basford rejoined his simpering nameless companion and Charlotte continued to walk alone.

৩৫ Twelve ৩৬

Time passed rather slowly as time is wont to do when one is anticipating an event. The days prior to Colonel Armitage's ball seemed to stretch out endlessly with little entertainment or distraction. Charlotte and Maria had spent their time at the cottage, receiving only a few callers, returning those calls, and occasionally writing letters to their parents, who were keeping to themselves in their small drawing room in Hertfordshire, and to Elizabeth and Mary, who demanded to be kept apprised of all occurrences of a romantic nature.

Charlotte had received a response from her missive to Elizabeth, and she was well pleased. Elizabeth had written a lengthy reply full of good natured questions and stories about her two children, Jane, who was six, and Cassandra, who was four. Their friendship, it seemed, was back on course, and Charlotte found herself divulging her interactions with both Mr. Edgington and Mr. Basford in her return letter. Although she valued the companionship and commiseration that Maria provided, there was something vitally important about having a best friend with whom to mull over such situations.

Despite Mr. Basford's words during their impromptu walk, neither he nor Mr. Westfield had called on them. Because she had not been privy to the discussion and because Charlotte had not divulged the contents of her conversation with Mr. Basford to her, Maria was not expecting him to call, and therefore, happily, she remained unaffected, but Charlotte was disappointed for her sister and angry at the entire male sex. Were all men apt to promise to call and then disappear? In her mind, she had relegated Mr. Edgington, Mr. Westfield, and Mr. Basford—and indeed most men in general—to the lowest circle of Dante's Inferno.

In her desperation for society, Maria focused on the gossip she could glean from Mrs. Eff after her trips into town. She insisted that Charlotte listen as she recounted each one.

Apparently, Mrs. Holloway was still engaged in an affair, but the gentleman had not yet been discovered. Mr. Holloway still had his pig and claimed that he would never slaughter so fine an animal, even if it meant doing without pork for a year.

Story after nonsensical story poured forth from Maria, but Charlotte could not bring herself to pay much attention, so she soon focused her efforts on embellishing bonnets and dresses with bits of ribbon or simply moped about the cottage.

When the official invitation to the ball had arrived, the serene mood was shattered by Maria's overwhelming joy.

The letter arrived on a particularly dreary morning when Charlotte had been forced to neglect her garden. She and Maria had lingered over a breakfast of toast and tea and discussed how dreadfully depressing the weather had become. Even the usually cheery kitchen with its patterned wallpaper and bright trim seemed dull.

Maria sighed dramatically. "I do not know what I shall do with myself for an entire day if this weather keeps up. I so long to be in town or to call on friends."

"This weather will not last forever." Charlotte too longed to be elsewhere.

"Indeed, it shall," Maria proclaimed, plunking down her teacup definitively. "This weather will persist just to spite me. The gods of weather know I have my heart set on Mr. Westfield, but they do not want me even to see him."

Charlotte laughed at her sister's dramatics. "I doubt very much that the weather gods, as you called them, have any interest whatsoever in your love life."

"Indeed, I suppose you are right, for I have no love life. I cannot have such a thing as long as I am trapped in this cottage."

"Have another cup of tea. It will make you feel much better."

The second helping of tea did not do as much for Maria as the invitation that was delivered soon thereafter.

Mrs. Eff entered the room and was in the process of removing soiled dishes from the table when she almost off-handedly said, "This arrived by messenger, Mrs. Collins. I did not want to disturb your eating."

She handed the letter to Charlotte, and Maria bounded out of her chair to look over her sister's shoulder. Charlotte opened and carefully unfolded the paper.

"Faster, faster!" Maria demanded. "I believe that is Mrs. Armitage's hand!"

Before Charlotte could even set an eye on the contents of the letter, Maria shrieked. "A ball!"

Mrs. Eff jumped, and the teacups clattered in her grasp.

"The ball Colonel Armitage promised to give in honor of his relations. Thank you, weather gods!"

"Maria, do be quiet and at least pretend to be civilized."

Maria scowled, plucked the paper from her hands, and returned to her seat.

"Finally, some entertainment! And I have yet to tell you the best news, Charlotte."

"Can there be something better than a ball?"

"Indeed. Mr. Westfield has already secured me for the first two dances."

"How can that be possible if you only learned of the ball two minutes ago?"

Maria blushed, her cheeks turning a deep red, her lashes downcast. "I hope you will not think it too forward, but he asked for the first two dances at the next ball—whenever it was to be held—when we last spoke all those weeks ago."

Charlotte was not entirely sure she approved of such forward behavior, but she said, "The only thing better than a ball, I suppose, is to have a gentleman with whom to dance."

"Well, of course, silly, for that is the entire purpose of a ball."

"Then I may as well stay at home, for I do not intend to dance."

"No, you may not just stay home, for I would not be allowed to attend." Her voice contained a note of panic.

"Do not trouble yourself. I know how much this means to you, and although I rarely dance, I quite enjoy balls myself. But I have other things to think of besides men."

"Well, I think you should not waste your figure. It will not last forever, you know."

Charlotte rolled her eyes and glanced down at herself. Her figure was probably her most alluring feature. Her face had always been plain, and she had accepted that, but she said, "You really ought to show more respect for your elder sister."

"And you really ought to live a little. Who knows. Perhaps Mr. Edgington will return to town for the ball and sweep you into a state of loving bliss."

"I seriously doubt that will occur at this ball or any other."

Maria tilted her blond head and said, "Only because you will not allow it."

❦

The ball was held at Colonel Armitage's home, and Charlotte, who generally preferred the smaller, private balls, found herself almost as eager to arrive as her sister. She had to prevent herself from rushing into the carriage, which the colonel sent to retrieve them. Charlotte fidgeted with her dress and adjusted her wrap. She had worn her best gown and the monogrammed gloves that Mr. Edgington had given her before she had left London. She felt odd wearing a gift from a gentleman, but the gloves were very fine, and she found she could not prevent herself from slipping them on. And they looked very well with her gown.

Maria spent the entire carriage ride chattering loudly. Her sister's enthusiasm was infectious, and by the time they arrived and alighted from the carriage, she was very nearly convinced that it was a magical night.

Charlotte dearly loved her sister's optimism, but she rarely allowed it to affect her own opinions. She preferred to avoid disappointment at all costs, and she had found that looking forward to an event and building it up in her mind was the best way to ensure that the evening would be a complete disaster. She hoped that would not be the case.

The ballroom was quite large and more than adequate to host a large ball. Located on the back side of the house, it had the advantage of an entire wall of windows with two doors at opposite ends of the ballroom that opened onto a gracious balcony overlooking the courtyard behind the building. The doors were thrown wide open, allowing sweet-smelling air to cool the dancers and freshen the room. Adjacent to the ballroom, there was a smaller room for refreshments where many older gentlemen—who were already secure in their matrimonial bonds or who no longer cared for that sort of bondage—tended to gather and consume mass quantities of food and drink.

Charlotte began the evening by standing by the opened windows. The breeze blew her skirts around her ankles as she watched the first dances. Maria fairly glowed in Mr. Westfield's arms, and although her concern for her sister's reputation continued, Charlotte could not help but rejoice in her happiness. It appeared that Miss Farmington would at least be civil, and Mr. Card had yet to make an appearance, so all might be well.

Across the room, Mr. Basford seemed pleased as well. Charlotte had yet to speak with him that evening, but the expression on his face appeared open and readable.

She was considering Mr. Basford when she felt a presence at her side. She turned to find Mr. Edgington looking at her intensely.

"Mr. Edgington, I did not expect to see you here. When did you return to Westerham?"

"Mrs. Collins," he said, bowing, "I returned only a fortnight ago."

Charlotte was surprised. The comings and goings of eligible men were not usually neglected in Westerham. She ought to have heard of his return.

"I am pleased that you had a safe journey."

He appraised her appearance. "I am more pleased to see you. I noticed that you are wearing the gloves I gave you."

Charlotte blushed. He grinned back wolfishly.

She looked down at them. "Yes, they suit my dress very nicely."

He smirked, and his red hair appeared to flame in the candlelight. He was dressed in fashionable formal attire. His deep blue coat and tan breeches fit snugly, revealing a strong, square silhouette. His boots shone, and he smelled of strong, musky cologne. He was almost overpowering.

He stepped slightly closer. "Will you do me the honor of a dance?"

She employed her standard reply. "I am afraid I did not come with the intention of dancing."

He challenged her. "You are no longer in mourning, and unless you have an objection to your potential partner, I see no reason to decline."

Charlotte shifted her weight. "I suppose it could do no harm. I only hope that you can forgive any missteps. It has been a long time since I have danced."

"Believe me, your dancing abilities are the least of my concerns." He led her to the floor.

The dance began, and Charlotte focused solely on the steps. She did not intend to ruin the dance for the other couples on the floor by her own poor skills, and even more, she did not want to make a spectacle of herself as she always had been when paired with Mr. Collins.

After the first section of the dance, Charlotte began to feel more at ease, and she was able to glance at her partner for the first time. Immediately, she wished she had not done so.

Mr. Edgington was looking at her ever so intensely. His eyes fairly burned through her. She blushed deeply and looked away. As the dance continued in silence, Charlotte could feel his stare, and the flattery initially caused by his intensity began to transform into concern and embarrassment.

She attempted several conversations, but she was unable to keep up a steady stream of distracting chatter. If only she possessed Maria's oratorical gifts! Finally, she abandoned the pretense of talking altogether.

All around them people watched and no doubt assumed that there was an attraction, at the very least, or an attachment—at most—between them. At that precise moment, Charlotte was neither attracted nor attached to Mr. Edgington, and she longed for the musicians to play the final chords of the dance, releasing her from the obligation of his stare.

She considered trying to strike up another conversation, but she disregarded the possibility quickly. Any interest she showed in Mr. Edgington would only serve to convince the people around them of an attachment that certainly did not exist.

The dance ended without another word passing between them and without Mr. Edgington looking away from Charlotte. Taking her gloved hand, he escorted her back to where Maria stood near the exit to the balcony.

He released her with a look of exaggerated remorse. "Thank you for the pleasant dance, Mrs. Collins."

Charlotte attempted to conceal her displeasure and thanked him quickly in return.

He smiled, his eyes still too intense, and said, "I hope that we will speak again before the evening ends."

Mr. Edgington then turned on his heel and disappeared into the crowd.

Charlotte turned to her sister and said through gritted teeth, "I do not know what to think of that man."

She giggled. "Well, after a dance like that, there is no doubt about what he thinks of you."

"Oh no!" Charlotte cried. "Pray, do not say such a thing!"

"Why are you so upset? What is wrong with having a gentleman interested in you?"

Charlotte was beginning to doubt that Mr. Edgington was a gentleman, but she would not say as much to her sister, and certainly not in a public place.

"After all, balls are for the express purpose of making matches. I have been working toward that end all evening."

"Lower your voice, Maria," Charlotte warned in a ragged whisper.

Maria gave Charlotte a cross look, but when she spoke again it was with a softer voice. "I have had two dances with Mr. Westfield, and he has proclaimed that were it possible to do so, he would dance every dance with me."

"I am pleased for you, but you must not be so public about your feelings."

"Maybe I am not the problem. Maybe you should be more overt about yours. Poor Mr. Edgington probably thinks you do not like him."

"Well, I…"

"You do not like him?" Maria asked, confused. "I believed you did."

"Let us not speak of this here." Charlotte glanced at those around them. Then in a louder tone, she asked, "Does not everyone look well tonight?"

"Most people do look lovely, although I find some questionable hairstyles. I believe one woman has a bird's nest in her coiffure this evening."

Charlotte was preparing to remind Maria that it was impolite to criticize other people's fashions in public, but something niggled at her mind. A bird's nest? She had seen a bird's nest used as an accessory of late. But where?

She thought for a moment and then the memory came to her. The theater. At Drury Lane in London! She had seen a woman with such an audacious affectation in her hair from the balcony of the theater. The woman whom Mr. Edgington had escorted. The plump one she had believed to be his poor country relation. Could it possibly be the same woman? Charlotte hardly thought so, but she leaned to her sister anyway. "Who is wearing the bird's nest?"

"Oh, I can never recollect her name. A plump woman. There was some gossip about her recently. Why can I not recall her name?" Maria scanned the room. "There!" She inclined her head toward a group of people beside the fireplace.

Charlotte did not instantly see the bird's nest, but when the group shifted, she saw a woman wearing elaborate wrap. Her hair dripped in bouncy ringlets. But was it the same wrap and the same ringlets that she had seen at the theater? Charlotte could not be sure until she saw the bird.

The mystery woman shifted slightly, revealing more of her hairstyle. Charlotte's heart began to flutter as the bird emerged. It was definitely the same one she had seen in the theater. It had to be. There could not be many women who would wear a bird in their hair in that very style. It must be the same woman she had seen with Mr. Edgington. She had the same build, and, now that Charlotte considered it, she thought it could be the same gown, although she was not certain.

Who was this woman? She strained, but still she could not see her face. Was she accompanying Mr. Edgington this evening? If so, why ever would he have danced with her? Had his companion observed their dance? She certainly would not have been pleased to see the rapt attention he paid Charlotte. She would be jealous indeed.

The woman turned, and Charlotte stifled a gasp. It was Mrs. Holloway!

Mrs. Holloway, who was rumored to be having an affair with an unknown gentleman. She had been with Mr. Edgington in London. She was engaged in adultery! With Mr. Edgington.

Clearly, Mr. Holloway was right to focus his attentions on a pig, for his wife was an undeserving creature.

And even more clearly, Mr. Edgington was the worst of men.

While Charlotte was deep in contemplation, Mrs. Farmington joined them with her granddaughter in tow. "Mrs. Collins, Miss Lucas, how lovely you look tonight."

Charlotte wondered how she could possibly look lovely. In all likelihood her realization about Mr. Edgington had robbed the color from her cheeks. But it would not do to behave as though something ill had occurred, and she schooled her features accordingly.

Would not Mrs. Farmington, and indeed all of Westerham, relish this news? But she certainly did not care to reveal her knowledge of this illicit affair. She wished she knew nothing of it.

Charlotte turned her attention to the older woman. She wore feathers in her colorless hair, but no bird. Her frost-colored curls bobbled as she walked and the plumage on her head waved back and forth. Miss Farmington was more attractively attired in a softly patterned blue dress with white trim. Her chestnut hair—also styled without a bird—glowed in the candlelight, and her eyes gleamed with malice as she looked a Maria. The harridan!

"And how popular you both are!" Miss Farmington looked slyly at Charlotte.

Oh! If this ninny had marked Mr. Edgington's attentions, then everyone had. Of course, no one knew that he was Mrs. Holloway's lover and was, therefore, a disreputable fellow. So she seemed safe.

"Yes, we could not help but notice how much attention Mr. Edgington paid you, Mrs. Collins," old Mrs. Farmington agreed.

Charlotte clasped her hands into fists and felt the material of her gloves wrinkle in her palms. "I can assure you that I have done nothing to invite his attentions, if indeed he paid them to me."

"He had eyes only for you." Miss Farmington sneered and made Charlotte want to clap her hand over her mouth. Fortunately, her next words changed the course of the conversation in a different, thought not entirely pleasant, direction. "And it seems that Mr. Westfield has eyes only for you, dear Maria. If I did not like you half so much, I believe I would be jealous."

Maria seemed taken aback by Miss Farmington's abrupt tone. She thought a beat. "You have no reason to be jealous. Mr. Westfield is very kind, but we have no attachment."

"He selected you for the first two dances."

"Yes, but he has danced twice with you, has he not?"

"I suppose he has."

"He is a delightful dancer."

"Yes."

"You see." Mrs. Farmington leaned in closely and inclined her head toward Mr. Edgington's group. "I was right. You two are indeed popular tonight."

"You are too kind," Charlotte murmured, still barely able to latch on to a coherent thought.

Mrs. Farmington spoke. "Are you certain you do not wish to tell us of an impending engagement to Mr. Edgington?"

"No, indeed, for we have no understanding. We had only one dance, and one dance does not a betrothal make. It does not even signify a friendship." But a bird's nest in the hair did signify an affair. "It barely even signifies an acquaintance."

"Well, you may mark my words, Mrs. Collins. Mr. Edgington will make a proposal to you very soon."

Charlotte certainly hoped not.

She was spared a reply when Mr. Basford spoke. He had appeared beside them without drawing Charlotte's immediate notice. The ladies curtseyed and greeted him. "Good evening, Mrs. Farmington, Mrs. Collins, Miss Lucas, Miss Farmington. Are you enjoying this evening's entertainments?"

Charlotte certainly noticed him now. His attire, while still somewhat informal and his cravat rumpled, was striking. His dark green coat drew her attention to his eyes, which beamed openness and honesty. Her tongue clung to the roof of her mouth, and all thoughts of Mr. Edgington and Mrs. Holloway and the bird vanished. They were none of her concern anyway.

"Indeed we are, Mr. Basford," Maria replied for her.

Old Mrs. Farmington and Miss Farmington gave their agreement.

"I am only sorry that my uncle could not be a little more in spirits tonight. He enjoys society and balls."

"Oh, is Colonel Armitage ill?" Mrs. Farmington asked, with concern in her voice. The elderly did not relish hearing of sickness, for fear that the words would somehow pass the condition on to them.

"Don't trouble yourself, Mrs. Farmington. He is quite well. It is just a touch of gout. He will be himself in no time. Until then he will have to be content to sit on the side of the action and enjoy his wine."

"We must be certain to give him our regards. Now come along, dear, I am in need of some refreshment." Miss Farmington and her grandmother bid them good evening and headed toward the door to the refreshment room.

Mr. Basford turned his attention to Maria. "I know my nephew enjoyed the favor of your dances together."

"You may tell him that I enjoyed them as well."

"It was nice to see you dancing as well, Mrs. Collins."

"I was just saying as much to her myself."

He turned to Charlotte and smiled. "Would you dance with me? We arranged it at the winter ball, if you'll remember."

Charlotte had forgotten his offer. She had not accepted it, had she? There was no obvious way of refusing him this time, so she accepted. As he led her to the floor, he subtly leaned closer to her ear. "Thank you for not embarrassing me with another rejection."

Surprised, she smiled. Standing at such close proximity, she could smell him. He smelled like the woods they had walked in several weeks ago. Without thinking, she inhaled deeply.

He continued as he led her into the dance, "I know you do not like public displays, so I'll be a proper gentleman, I assure you."

"Thank you."

"I saw you dancing with Mr. Edgington."

"Did you?" She still hoped she had imagined the attention they had attracted.

"He was very intense."

"I suppose he was."

He gave her a look of disbelief and said, "You are too kind to tell the truth."

"But I am not kind enough to think well of inappropriate behavior."

They walked forward with the other dancers, and conversation paused.

"You have reminded me of the importance of appropriate behavior several times."

Her back prickled, but there was no reprimand in his eyes.

She attempted a joke. "Perhaps you needed reminding."

He was silent for a moment, and she feared she had offended him, but then she looked into his face. His grin was somehow a mix of honesty and humor, and Charlotte smiled back. "Perhaps I ought to pass your reminder on to Mr. Edgington."

Charlotte could not repress her laughter, but she sobered at the intensely kind expression that suddenly lit Mr. Basford's eyes.

They finished the dance in companionable silence. Charlotte contemplated Mr. Basford. She had chastised his behavior almost from the moment she made his acquaintance, but it was now evident that he was a true gentleman. And more disconcertingly, it appeared that her own good judgment, which she prized, was flawed.

It did not matter now. She knew the truth. She would be kind to Mr. Basford, and she would never again hold two minutes' discourse with Mr. Edgington. It was as simple as that.

ঞ৹ Thirteen ৹৯

Mr. Basford proved to be an excellent partner, and it felt natural to move with him around the floor. Charlotte found herself forgetting about the steps and the onlookers—including Mr. Edgington and Mrs. Holloway—and simply enjoyed being on the dance floor.

When the dance ended, he led her from the floor, and she was reluctant to go. When he returned her to her place near the balcony door, he gave her hand a squeeze before releasing it. "Thank you, my friend."

She suddenly felt flushed and rather weak. A warm rush moved through her body at the sincerity in his voice.

Charlotte watched as Mr. Basford disappeared into the crowd. She realized that she was holding her hands in front of her as if to retain the feel of his hand on hers. Abruptly she relaxed her arms, letting them come to her sides and skim her skirt. She should not feel anything for him, of course, but there was warmth that still radiated through her body, and she did not know how to explain it. Thinking the fresh air might cool the heat that Mr. Basford had caused, she stepped onto the moonlit balcony.

The breeze did little to cool her cheeks, but there was no one else on the balcony and Charlotte was glad for the solitude. Mr. Basford persisted in her mind, however, and as she reviewed her interaction with him, she indulged in a bit of girlish fancy.

Mentally shaking herself, she pulled off her gloves and clutched them in her left hand. She should not be thinking of any man, not Mr. Collins, Mr. Edgington—the swine—or even Mr. Basford. She should be thinking of Maria and chaperoning her, as was her duty.

Charlotte turned to go back inside the ballroom and find her sister, but she stopped abruptly at the sight of Mr. Edgington behind her. His face was in shadow, and a shaft of light coming through the ballroom windows illuminated his fine dress clothes.

She glanced quickly around her. The far edges of the balcony were in deep shadow, but it appeared that they were alone.

"Mr. Edgington, I did not hear you arrive." Charlotte attempted to sound stern. Instead, she sounded as squeaky as a mouse cornered by a hungry cat.

"I did not mean to startle you, Mrs. Collins. My apologies."

Charlotte was on the verge of following her original intention of never again speaking to Mr. Edgington and returning to the ballroom, but he moved toward the railing, blocking her way. His face came into the light. He was smiling. He took his place near her and leaned his hands casually against the railing. "It is a pleasant evening, is it not?"

"For some, I suppose it is. But it is a very welcome relief from the rain."

"Yes, travel was quite difficult on the muddy roads."

"I imagine it was."

Charlotte leaned against the corner of the railing and looked at him sidelong. She must find a way to return to the ballroom. It would not do to be alone with this ogre.

Mr. Edgington moved slightly closer, his eyes intent on her profile. "I am pleased that I chose to return to Westerham when I did, despite the poor traveling conditions."

He was facing her squarely now, his hip leaning against the railing.

"Are you?" She kept her gaze resolutely forward and attempted to keep the malice from her voice.

"Very glad," he whispered.

Mr. Edgington appeared to be reaching for her hand, which was resting on the rail, but then he reconsidered, and he was left standing very close to her, leaving her no means of escape. She could feel his breath on her nape, causing wisps of hair to stir along the neckline of her dress. She wanted to gag at his overbearing presence, and all she could think of was fleeing him.

"I must return inside."

She expected him to move away, to allow her to pass, but instead, he said, "You are always leaving, Mrs. Collins."

"I fear I must."

Again, he did not move. "I missed you when you departed London."

"I do not think it is possible to miss someone with whom you barely associated."

"On the contrary, we saw quite a bit of each other, although not as much as I would have liked."

"It is polite of you to say, sir, but—"

"It is the truth, Mrs. Collins. I find myself thinking of you often."

Charlotte shrank back at his words. He only came forward to fill the vacated inches between them.

She looked up at him firmly. "That is very flattering, sir, but it is probably best that you do not think of me at all."

"I do not see how I can stop myself."

"I am certain that it will be an easier task than you anticipate. I am not a particularly memorable or exciting woman."

"On the contrary, Mrs. Collins, to me you are both memorable and exciting."

She glanced around. Still no one had appeared on the balcony. "Pray, do not say such things."

He leaned even closer. "I cannot help myself. I must say these things."

"One always has the capability of helping oneself when one so chooses."

He smiled and laughed at Charlotte as though she were a child who just said something very foolish. She looked sideways, searching again for an escape route, but Mr. Edgington had effectively blocked her in the corner with his large body. She began to fidget with the gloves in her hands. She wished she had not worn them. Perhaps they were unduly encouraging him. She would burn them as soon as she returned home. If she could ever get off this wretched balcony.

He glanced at the gloves, too, and reached down and took the fingertips of one glove in his and stroked them, but he did not touch her directly.

"Mrs. Collins, I would like to court you," he said with his head bowed over her hands.

"I...I..."

"I have admired you from the first, and I would like to know you better. Much better."

"Mr. Edgington..."

"Please, call me Lewis."

"No," she said sharply.

Her eyes met his, and he gave her a wry grin. "My proper Mrs. Collins."

Charlotte recoiled at the sarcastic tone of his voice. "I am not your Mrs. Collins."

His eyes turned hard, and she immediately dropped the glove that he held in his hand, releasing it to his custody. The other glove remained clutched in her fingers.

He moved back half a step, giving Charlotte a modicum of personal space. She could not see his eyes clearly now that his face had gone into the shadow. But he seemed intent on the glove that now dangled from his fingers. He transferred it to his other hand and began to follow its contours with his index finger. Charlotte watched as his fingertip reached the top of the glove that had so recently rested in the crook of her elbow. He began to trace the monogram he found there.

"I am glad you wore the gloves I gave you." His voice sounded cold.

Charlotte could not respond, but only watched him continue to examine her glove.

"They mark you as mine."

"Yours?"

"Mine."

He raised his eyes to her. "Did you not know that accepting gifts from men is often a sign of a deeper relationship?"

"That is certainly not the case here," she said in a desperate whisper.

"Is it not?" He slapped the glove gently against his opposite hand and then let it slide slowly across his palm.

Charlotte's eyes flew to his. His face was very close again, and for a moment she feared he would breech propriety and kiss her, but he did not. He simply continued to look at her with the same hard intensity.

"We have no relationship." She spoke with as much dignity as she could muster. She turned with the intention of sweeping back into the ballroom, but he shifted, effectively blocking her movement.

Acting as if he had not purposefully and rudely blocked her, he said nonchalantly, "Yes, but we could have."

Charlotte stiffened her resolve in preparation to reply in the most negative manner possible when he interrupted her.

"Before you refuse, consider, imagine, the possibilities. We have both experienced the world. We know that love is an illusion, and marriage is good for nothing other than securing a fortune or creating children."

"I certainly would not marry you," Charlotte spat.

He looked angry, but when he spoke again, his tone was even and quiet. "I will not be offended by your unkind words because I did not propose, nor do I intend to do so. My proposition, Mrs. Collins, is completely different."

He spoke her name now as though it were a slight.

"Unless your proposition is that we return to the ballroom and join the others before someone gets the wrong impression, you may be assured that I will say no."

"Dear Mrs. Collins, always so concerned about the opinions of others. My proposition is very simple. As two mature adults, we are ideally suited to take care of each other's physical needs, are we not? Widows often have arrangements with men such as myself."

Charlotte recoiled as he reached to stroke her cheek.

He smiled at her evasion. "We who are unfettered by the bonds of marriage can truly enjoy each other."

"No! Indeed we shall not, and it is indelicate and offensive of you to make such a suggestion." The pitch of Charlotte's voice was high with panic, but she tried to maintain a whisper.

He leaned closer, and Charlotte could feel the heat from his body. "What is it the poets say, 'Gather ye rosebuds while ye may'?"

"I do not trust poets, and I certainly will not let pretty words change my decision."

"All the same, you might want to reconsider." He tucked her glove into the pocket of his coat with careful deliberation. "After all, it may appear to some people that we are already so engaged. We have been alone here for quite a long while, and I have a memento of our time together. A memento that, I believe, was also a rather intimate gift."

Charlotte was stunned into utter silence.

"You may cling to your high moral principles, but you will have to content yourself with them. Your morality may be questioned by society when they see such damning evidence of your behavior."

The realization that he was threatening Charlotte, blackmailing her into an indecent relationship, registered despite her shock. Was this how he had begun with Mrs. Holloway? Was she not so much his lover but his victim?

Regardless of how he had engaged the services of Mrs. Holloway, Charlotte was ruined no matter what decision she made. She would either be a woman defiled or she would appear to be one to the rest of the world. She would devastate her family and lose her friends, or she would lose her self-respect. How could she—a woman who prided herself on common sense and propriety—have been so foolish?

"Return my glove this instant," she demanded with more confidence than she felt.

He smirked. "Indeed, I will not."

She stared, still unable to believe the baseness of his character.

"It would behoove you to reconsider my offer, Mrs. Collins."

Though her reputation was already as good as ruined, Charlotte still could not consider his proposition. "Mr. Edgington, do you find joy in blackmailing women in this manner?"

He glared. Moments crawled by. "You misunderstand, my dear Mrs. Collins. For a gentleman such as myself, it has nothing to do with the joy of mere words. I desire an entirely different sort of joy. Perhaps I ought to use the word euphoria. With this token," he said as he patted the pocket where her glove was concealed, "I have the opportunity to experience the sort of joy I desire."

Charlotte struggled to breathe. He was a monster. "Why are you so intent on torturing me? I have done nothing to merit it."

"Done nothing?" His voice became thick with barely restrained anger, "You reject me. No other man in England would have you, a cold, joyless woman, and still you reject me. I would have you."

Charlotte suddenly had the urge to throttle him, and instead of launching herself at him bodily, she struck him across the face with her other glove. Then, shocked at her physical outburst, she stared as his hand went to his cheek.

"You old fool!" he said between clenched teeth. "Do you realize what I may do to your reputation? Do you not comprehend? My connections in Westerham society, to Lady Catherine, will assure your ruin. One well-placed word from me about how you offered this glove as an inducement to an affair, and the dear old bat will see that you lose everything. Including your very home!"

Charlotte stepped backward. She knew that Lady Catherine would not hesitate to remove her from the cottage if she merely suspected her to be a part of the demimonde. Her cottage. It was her only real security. She could not lose it. But what could she do?

Her eyes darted around the balcony as if the answer would be written on the wall. But no such response appeared. After a long hesitation, Charlotte resigned herself to her fate. "Do what you will, but my conscience is clean and the truth will set me free."

He sneered. "I thought you many things, my dear Mrs. Collins, but never naïve. Truth is found in perception, and we have already been perceived," he said, gesturing to a movement on the opposite side of the balcony.

Charlotte squinted into the shadows. She could see a hint of motion, but she could not discern who had joined them.

Mr. Edgington took her hand in his rough grip and kissed her knuckles. Charlotte pulled her hand away, wiping it on her gown to remove the sensation he had imparted on her skin. Her fingers and her spirit felt bruised by his roughness. Mr. Edgington walked back into the ballroom, leaving her at the mercy of whomever had come onto the balcony.

༄ Fourteen ༄

Charlotte's mind whirled, yet her thoughts were disconnected, and she could not latch on to one before another overtook it. She felt hot and cold at the same time, and she began to fear that she might faint. She had never fainted in her life, and she refused to begin now. Not over that swine Mr. Edgington. She grasped the hard wood of the railing until her knuckles turned white, and her eyes ached with barely restrained tears.

What should she do? What could be done? She had blundered far worse than Maria ever had.

She was ruined. Irrevocably ruined.

Suddenly, she heard a voice behind her. "Charlotte?" She jumped and spun quickly to find that Mr. Basford looked concerned. "Are you well?"

She responded without thinking. She could not think. At least not rationally. "I am quite well." It was, of course, a lie. A polite lie, but a lie nonetheless.

He studied her in the dim light. "I can see, despite your words to the contrary, that something is amiss."

Charlotte bit back a sob. "No, I assure you…"

He took her hands in his, a soft, reassuring touch, but the contact of his gloved hand on her naked skin only served to remind her of her missing glove.

"What has happened?"

Aghast, she pulled her hands away and stepped back two full steps. "I cannot say."

When Mr. Edgington's slander became public, the last thing she needed was for anyone to have seen her alone in the company of Mr. Basford as well. She would be labeled as an irrevocably fallen woman and the results would do no favors for herself or her future happiness. She stared at the ground while attempting to compose herself.

"Please, I may be able to help."

She looked up at him sharply. "I am afraid no one can help. I am quite beyond it."

Mr. Basford answered her with a skeptical look and stepped back to lean his hip against the railing. His posture was much like that of Mr. Edgington, but his bearing was completely opposite. He made the position seem more amicable than antagonistic He studied her silently for several moments while she tried to gather her wits about her.

He did not move, but the concern in his eyes conveyed as much as any physical comfort he could have offered. "I saw you here with Mr. Edgington. Has he done something to upset you?"

She was shocked at how easily her façade cracked under his kindness. Tears welled again in her eyes, and she only shook her head.

He turned abruptly, searching the ballroom intensely. "I can see that he has. I'll speak to him."

"No!" She laid a bare hand on his arm to restrain him. "You must not." She desperately wanted to tell him everything, to share her burden. In fact, she could not prevent herself. "Please, I am already ruined."

At her words, he turned back to her, and her hand fell to her side. His face was drawn into a confused expression. His forehead was a furrowed as a farmer's field, and Charlotte had the strange inclination to smooth it with her bare hand. "Ruined? Impossible. You are the most upright woman I've ever met."

"It does not matter. He will tell people, and they will believe him."

"Tell people what? No one who has ever met you will believe any negative remarks about you."

"They will believe him when he shows them the evidence."

He noticed the single glove clutched in her hand, and gently, he took it from her. The cloth seemed to burn her hand as it slipped through her fingers.

She hung her head as she saw understanding begin to come over him.

"He has the other glove?"

"Yes."

"Why would he take it?" He looked at it as though it would reveal its secrets.

Charlotte shook her head, unable to speak the truth, wiping at her eyes to keep the tears from falling.

His voice came out in a harsh whisper, his eyes hard. "He is trying to intimidate you into some sort of illicit affair with him!"

Charlotte nodded but did not meet his eyes. "He will ruin me if I do not give in to his demands, and I will be ruined if I do as he wishes. Either way, my reputation in society will be completely and utterly destroyed."

Saying the words out loud caused Charlotte to comprehend the full extent of her situation. "Not only will I be ruined, but so will my family. And poor Maria will have no hope of ever marrying well. Oh Lord…. And my house. I shall lose that as well once he goes to Lady Catherine."

Charlotte covered her face, her hand shaking, but she did not even think to be embarrassed by her exhibition of feminine frailty. She cried quietly for a moment and then took a deep, fortifying breath. Now was not the time for hysterics. She must try to think of a solution.

Unfortunately, she knew very well that nothing could be done, but she reviewed possible courses of action anyway. Perhaps she could somehow retrieve the glove during the evening, but how? Impossible. In all likelihood, he had already sent for his carriage and would soon be away. Perhaps she could destroy the remaining glove and deny the matter entirely. Also impossible, for the glove bore her own initials. She could go to Lady Catherine and tell her what had happened, but why would she believe her over her own relation? Indeed, nothing could be done to save her.

"He will show them my glove, which was a gift from him many months ago. A gift that bears my initials. And that dance...." She winced. "I have been here alone with him all this time. People will believe him. They will have no choice in the face of such evidence."

She expected Mr. Basford to leave her now, to save himself from sharing in her ruin. But he did not move. He stood like a rock before her.

Seeing his implacable features, Charlotte turned to leave, to spare him if he would not spare himself. "I must find Maria and procure a carriage. I must leave here immediately! Please order the carriage for us, if you please."

"No."

He was refusing his carriage! Feeling trapped, she began to panic. How would she and Maria get home? Would they have to walk home in shame through the dark streets of Westerham?

"You must not leave, and you must not cry. What you do now will have a large impact on your future." Mr. Basford's voice sounded authoritative and calm.

Even amid her distress, the truth of his words penetrated. She must minimize the damage. She turned back to him and watched in horror as he removed his own gloves and placed one in his jacket pocket. "What are you doing?"

"You must have gloves for the rest of the evening. I understand that going without them is simply not done. People will take notice and ask you about them, and you're certainly in no frame of mind to deal with the situation directly, at least not yet." He handed one glove to her. "Put on your glove and carry this other with you. People may notice that you're only wearing one, but they will see that you carry its mate. If anyone asks, tell them that the fabric has irritated your skin and that you regret that you must carry it."

She stared at him, unsure of what to do or think. Her mind was muddled, her thinking unclear. Would it benefit her to allow Mr. Basford to come to her aid? Could she trust him? Did she have any choice?

She did as he suggested and slid her glove back on her hand. She took his glove, which she folded to disguise its masculine cut, and held it in her hand.

"But you will be without gloves."

He rolled his eyes subtly. "I'm an uncouth American. It will be expected that I would break with custom in this way."

"But—"

"Do not concern yourself with my reputation, Mrs. Collins." He offered his arm, but Charlotte only stared at it, uncomprehending, as though he were the first gentleman ever to offer her such a courtesy. All proficiency of etiquette seemed to have deserted her. "You must go inside, speak to people, and behave as if nothing has happened."

"I do not think I can." Her hands shook, and her stomach was tight. The world seemed to tilt around her, and she leaned against the wall for support.

He stood squarely in front of her. His body was very broad and strong, but his carriage was not at all intimidating. He waited until her eyes met his. His voice was firm when he spoke. "You can and you shall. You must begin to fight his lies even now. You have done nothing wrong."

She nodded mutely, taking another bracing breath as a faint glimmer of courage shone inside her heart. She knew what she must do and turned to Mr. Basford, took a deep breath. "You must dance with me."

Charlotte almost expected him to make a jest about her forward behavior, but, thankfully, he appeared to give the idea serious consideration. "Yes, I think it wise for you to dance with me, and also with any other gentleman who asks. Talk with your friends. You and Maria will depart in our carriage at the end of the evening as planned."

He offered his arm again. Slowly, she reached for it. He took her ungloved hand, tucking it in the crook of his arm, and led her toward the door.

As they walked toward the ballroom door, Charlotte tried to think through her situation. Was she behaving wisely or would she exacerbate the problem? Every emotion told her to flee, to leave the ball and continue to run, but her mind said that flight was the easy course of action. And Charlotte had often found that the easiest solution did not yield the most desirable results. The difficult road was usually the one that ought to be travelled.

They reached the doors, and Charlotte took a shuddering breath. Mr. Basford gave her a stern look. The furrows were back in his brow. "Just don't cry."

She looked at him crossly. She may be a little rattled, but did he think her so weak that she might burst into tears in public? Perhaps she had cried on the balcony, but she would never do so in the ballroom! She was stronger than that. She detested debutantes who allowed their emotions to rule their behavior, or worse, who used their tears to manipulate others. She would see herself through the evening, and she would behave with her usual grace and good sense.

She hoped.

Charlotte kept her focus ahead of her as they entered. The room was alive with movement and sound. Couples danced in dizzying patterns, and voices seemed to swirl around her. What had seemed so pleasant only ten minutes prior now overwhelmed her, and she wondered suddenly if she was capable of maintaining her poise.

Her hand tightened on Mr. Basford's arm.

He whispered, "You've spent your whole life performing for others. You can certainly continue to perform for the rest of the evening."

Again, anger cut through her embarrassment, and she glared up at Mr. Basford. Did he think her merely a performer?

He only smiled back. Pleasantly. Charlotte wanted to remove that smirk from his face, but she forced her attention to the people around her. She had a fleeting recognition of her longtime friends as they moved around the ballroom. Would any of these people ever speak to her again after Mr. Edgington's news came out? Mrs. Card and Mrs. Farmington were seated in a corner, leaning toward each other to share gossip. Maria stood nearby watching as Mr. Westfield finished a dance with Miss Farmington. Would any of these people ever deign to speak with her again?

When the next dance began, Charlotte found herself being led to the floor by Mr. Basford. The steps came automatically, and she scanned the room for Mr. Edgington. She found him leaning insolently against the far wall. Mrs. Holloway stood nearby, conversing with two women. She looked frequently at Mr. Edgington and was obviously attempting to draw him into their conversation. Charlotte wondered where Mr. Holloway was. Perhaps he was taking some refreshment or had stayed at home with his pig. It was most certainly better company than his wife.

Mrs. Holloway's ridiculous bird adornment bobbled as she spoke, still glancing at Mr. Edgington, but he paid her little heed. He was watching Charlotte. Heat rose along the skin of her neck, and angry tears jumped to her eyes.

Mr. Basford spoke to her softly. "It is a nice ball, is it not, Mrs. Collins?"

She tore her gaze away from her enemy and looked at her partner, and his gaze was intense, calling her to focus and forget Mr. Edgington. "It is indeed, Mr. Basford."

"Of course, since it was given by my uncle, it would be rude of you not to agree."

Charlotte laughed, but even to her own ears, it sounded odd, forced and unnatural.

"I find that I enjoy your English country dances more than I expected." Mr. Basford was attempting to be companionable. "We have many similar dances in Savannah."

Charlotte made her best effort to focus on the topic of conversation. "It is nice to hear you say something positive about our land."

He smiled down at her sincerely. The furrows were gone, and smooth skin took their place. He looked so attractive, even to her overwhelmed mind. His steps were confident, and each time his bare hands met her bare one she could feel his strength enter her body.

As their hands met again, he gave her fingertips a gentle, warm squeeze. "There are many things I like about England, although I may not have shared as much as I should have."

"And I find that Americans may not be as ill mannered as I originally believed."

He grinned widely, and somehow Charlotte knew that her secret was quite safe in his possession.

They made polite small talk for the remainder of the dance, and Charlotte almost managed to forget her situation under Mr. Basford's compliments and distracting comments. When the dance was completed, he offered to escort her to acquire some lemonade, which she accepted, drinking gratefully, not realizing how thirsty she had been. After lingering a few moments over the cold meats and cheeses, Mr. Basford led her to an empty place alongside the dance floor. She expected him to excuse himself, but he did not. Instead, he took his place beside her, seeming almost proprietary in his stance. Acquaintances came to chat, and still Mr. Basford remained at her side. She wondered if she ought to speak to him, tell him he could go, but she found she liked having him there.

And so conversation flowed freely, and soon, the crowd began to dwindle. Alone with Charlotte again, Mr. Basford leaned down near her ear and said, "Relief is on the way. I see that Maria is making her way across the room. It is undoubtedly time for you to return home."

She spotted Maria and Mr. Westfield as they slowly made their way around the small group of dancers who kept to the floor, talking and laughing along the way. It was good to see Maria among her friends again even if all her wounds had not yet healed. She wondered if any of her companions would remain when Mr. Edgington's slander became public.

"You have done well." Thank heaven for Mr. Basford and his ability to distract her from her thoughts. However, Charlotte knew she did not deserve such a compliment. During the last few hours, she had been relying on his strength a great deal, but when Mr. Edgington used his weapon, she would be completely alone and unaided.

She began to say as much to Mr. Basford, but he interrupted her. "Do not contemplate the future just yet. We will deal with that as it comes."

"We? This is not your dilemma. It is mine alone."

Mr. Basford looked away quickly, but she saw irritated lines cross his brow. She was surprised to realize that she might have angered him, and eager to soothe him, she turned her full gaze on him. "I appreciate all that you have done for me tonight, but you are not required to suffer for my folly."

"What folly? You have done nothing to deserve this." His voice sounded harsh, and Charlotte wondered at his tone. She studied his profile. His teeth were clenched and his lips were stretched into a tight line. He was not angry, she realized, but injured.

Her tone was gentle, as if to calm him. "Have I not? I trusted an undeserving man."

Maria and Mr. Westfield were very close now, so Mr. Basford leaned down slightly to say, "I hope that will not cause you to distrust all men. Some of us are worthy."

Before she could think of a response, her sister arrived at her side with Mr. Westfield as her escort. "Has it not been a lovely evening, Charlotte? I am sorry that it has to end already. Everyone behaved charmingly, even Miss Farmington and Mr. Card," she added in a discreet whisper. "No one suffered from the want of a partner. Such wonderful music, delicious food, and..." Maria glanced at Mr. Westfield. "...such agreeable companions."

Although she could not concur with the hearty compliments her sister lavished on the ball, she said, "I am glad you had such a pleasant time."

"Indeed, it has been a most enjoyable evening. It is a shame to see it end." Mr. Westfield's eyes were intent on Maria, and Charlotte felt hope for her sister. Perhaps he was in love with her, and she only prayed that his love was strong so that Mr. Edgington's slander would not dissolve it.

Mr. Basford, who had been watching his nephew, turned to Charlotte. "Perhaps we'll call on Mrs. Collins and Miss Lucas this week."

"Oh, yes, that would be pleasing indeed, Uncle."

Charlotte nodded her assent, grateful for the excuse to speak with Mr. Basford again soon, but she did not meet his eyes.

Mr. Basford stepped away to order the carriage while Mr. Westfield bid Maria a fond farewell, causing her to giggle, as he escorted her out the door. Charlotte remained behind.

When Mr. Basford returned, Charlotte saw that they were quite alone in the vestibule and offered his glove to him. "Thank you for this evening."

He only shook his head, and she dropped her hand. "I hope you do not object to us calling on you later this week."

Knowing that she should act demurely, she could not. She looked at Mr. Basford squarely. "No, indeed. I quite look forward to it."

He inclined his dark head toward hers. His voice was soft but firm when he said, "Until then, do not worry. We will simply tell the truth. All will be well."

ঙ৹ Fifteen ঙৡ৹

The Armitage's carriage rumbled up the cottage drive. Candlelight flickered in the sitting room window, and Charlotte knew that Mrs. Eff and Edward had awaited their return. For the first time, she wished they had not. Mrs. Eff would not be as easily fooled by her veneer of nonchalance as Maria.

The coachman assisted Charlotte and Maria from the carriage and then the conveyance disappeared with a loud growl of wheels on stones. Mrs. Eff opened the cottage door as they approached. "Welcome home. May I take your things?"

Maria removed her wrap and gloves and piled them in Mrs. Eff's arms while recounting each minute of the ball. Charlotte removed her pelisse and handed it to Edward, but she retained her gloves. She hoped no one had noticed.

Mrs. Eff handed the heap of Maria's garments to Edward. "See that these are properly stored." He disappeared down the hall, and Mrs. Eff looked at the sisters. "A fire is still burning in the sitting room. I thought you might enjoy some tea before bed."

Charlotte clutched the mismatched gloves behind her skirt, wringing the fabric back and forth. She did not want tea. She wanted privacy. Why would not everyone just go to sleep?

Maria yawned. "I do not think I could stay awake long enough for the water to boil."

Thank heavens. Now Charlotte could engineer a few moments of peace to dispose of the evidence of the night's crimes.

"Mrs. Collins?"

"Thank you for your kindness, Mrs. Eff. I think I will sit in solitude by the fire for a few moments, but I do not require any tea."

"Are you certain?"

"Yes, you and Edward have had a long day. You ought to retire."

Mrs. Eff eyed her and then nodded. "Sleep well, Mrs. Collins. I do look forward to hearing about the ball tomorrow morning."

Charlotte tried to smile and wondered if she had managed to do so. Mrs. Eff said nothing, looked at her oddly, and then disappeared to her chamber.

The door to the sitting room was ajar, and Charlotte pushed it open. She walked into the chamber as though she were moving in water. Her steps were slow, and as her arms swung at her sides, the fabric of the gloves brushed against her skirt in long, slow strokes. Whoosh, whoosh, whoosh. It was the only sound she could hear. When had the house become so quiet? Could Mrs. Eff hear the hum of fabric on fabric? Would she hear the crackles of the glove as it burned?

Charlotte stood before the mantel, and the peat fire smoldered before her. If only destroying the glove would destroy Mr. Edgington's slander. But as long as its mate existed, Charlotte was ruined.

Still, she would do what was within her power. And that was to destroy the offending article. She flung her glove on top of the smoldering peat and watched as flames began to grow and consume the fabric.

Holding Mr. Basford's glove in both hands, she stood in front of the fire and watched as it died slowly, the embers glowing and banking. In and out. In and out.

The embers should have been peaceful, and she had expected to feel relief when the glove had turned to ash, but she felt neither peace nor relief. Realizing that her back and legs ached, Charlotte turned to go to her bed chamber and discovered Edward watching her through the open door. She quickly hid Mr. Basford's glove behind her back.

"Are you well, Mrs. Collins?"

She cleared her throat. Why was she suddenly nervous? Edward was her sweet but muddle-minded servant and probably comprehended little of the intricacies of society. "Yes, why do you ask?"

"I called your name over and over."

"Oh." How could she not have heard him? She wondered how long he had been observing her. Had he seen her burn that glove? Had he seen Mr. Basford's glove?

"I am fine. Go to bed, Edward."

He studied her with steady eyes, and she thought he might speak again, but he only nodded and left the chamber.

Charlotte also went to her bed chamber, where she tucked away Mr. Basford's glove in the small wooden box that housed her hair ornaments and jewelry—some inexpensive earrings, a string of pearls from her father, and a cross pendant—and placed it in the cupboard. She would return it to him at an opportune moment.

Satisfied that Mr. Basford's glove would remain safely hidden, she removed her gown and draped it over a chair. She had barely prevented herself from throwing it onto the floor in disgust. It was a good gown, and she would not allow the memories of Mr. Edgington ruin it for her.

When she had finally laid down to rest, sleep had eluded her, and when it did claim her, she found herself dreaming of gloves and fires and dances and

Mr. Basford. Sounds began to drift in and out of Charlotte's dreams, and they became even more confused. She heard Mrs. Eff and Edward about their morning chores: the sounds of fresh coals hitting the kitchen grate and the clatter of breakfast dishes. Could it be morning already? Usually, Charlotte went down to greet them and discuss the news from town with Mrs. Eff, but instead, she turned onto her left side and pulled the covers over her head to block out the sounds from below.

Hours later—or perhaps only minutes, Charlotte could not be certain—she heard Maria moving about below stairs and snippets of her voice as she told Mrs. Eff about the ball. Charlotte knew they would be expecting her, but still, she could not manage to arise and face the day. At any moment the news of her scandal would become public, and the happy sounds of her household would disappear. She would be ostracized from her friends and family, leaving her with little choice but to take in a dozen stray cats for company.

More bewildering than the taunting sounds of normalcy that could not last was the fact that Charlotte's mind continued to stray to Mr. Basford. Each time she closed her eyes, she was on the balcony again. Mr. Edgington was gone, and Charlotte would turn and watch as Mr. Basford emerged tall and strong from the darkness. She saw the concern in his eyes and her heart began to flutter just as it had the night before.

Charlotte threw her arm over her head, trying to block out her thoughts but seeing only Mr. Basford in the crook of her elbow. He had promised to help her, but he could not possibly be able to do so. What could be done after all? Mr. Edgington had her glove, and he would not hesitate to use it against her now that she had rejected his vile offer. There was nothing to be done but wait for the inevitable to occur.

Charlotte closed her eyes and managed to doze for several more hours, experiencing dark nightmares of Mr. Edgington. His red hair had turned to flames, and he advanced on her, but Charlotte could not run. Just as he reached for her gloved hands, she would awake with a start.

Once awake, she contemplated Mr. Basford. A much pleasanter topic, but inappropriate nonetheless.

She knew that she could not stay in bed forever, and even if she were to attempt such a feat, her blankets would not shield her from the coldness of society once the scandal became known. She pushed away the linens and threw her legs over the side of the bed. The planks of the wooden floor felt cool beneath her bare feet as she washed at the washstand, did her morning ablutions, and put on her plainest morning gown. She then gathered her courage and went downstairs.

Mrs. Eff was dusting the small table in the hallway, and she looked up from her work and concern crossed her once delicate face. "I was beginning to worry about you, my dear, are you well?" She dropped the dust cloth onto the table and assisted Charlotte down the remaining steps.

Charlotte attempted a reassuring smile but failed miserably.

Mrs. Eff patted her hand. "Do I need to consult the apothecary?"

Charlotte walked with ginger steps toward the sitting room. "I do feel rather weak, but I think a cup of tea will be all I require."

"Rosehip tea then, my dear, made from your own garden. It is just the thing for an aching head. Why do you not go to the sitting room and rest a bit more?" With a kind smile, she led her to the settee. "Back in my dancing days, before our family lost its holdings, such as they were, I never felt worse than the day after a spectacular ball."

Charlotte sat down and tucked her legs under her in a comfortable yet thoroughly undignified fashion. She might as well be comfortable if she could not be proper.

Mrs. Eff arranged cushions around her. "I suppose you do not feel like talking just yet. Let me bring you some tea and toast."

Charlotte nodded at Mrs. Eff, grateful that she had suggested food. She had not realized how hungry she had become, and it was much later in the day than she had anticipated. From her seat, she craned her head to look out the open window. The sun was high in the sky, beaming on Edward who toiled in the garden. His face was content but smeared with dirt. Charlotte envied him. He truly had a simple life and took pleasure in small things. He did not have to worry over the words and deeds of unscrupulous people. He only had to tend to the rosemary.

She turned away from the pastoral scene, and her mind began to bounce from one thought to another like a young debutante in a room full of potential beaux. The news must soon become public. She must formulate a rebuttal. She must see to Maria. She must protect her assets. If only she had the energy.

A sound in the hallway caused her to jump in the anticipation that it would be a neighbor coming to confirm Mr. Edgington's story. She sat bolt upright when a knock sounded at the sitting room door. Her nerves hummed as she rearranged her skirt. "Come in."

It was Mrs. Eff. God bless Mrs. Eff, for she carried a pot of tea and a plate of toast and jam, and not the ill news she expected. The smells of food surrounded her, making her stomach clench in anticipation. Mrs. Eff offered her a cup of rosehip tea, and Charlotte sipped it, letting the warmth and sweetness of the liquid give her strength.

"Miss Maria asked me to tell you that she has gone for a turn about the garden. She was all a-twitter this morning. I suppose balls take more out of us as we age."

Charlotte wished that age were the cause of her morning depression. She said nothing, took up her plate, and selected a piece of toast. Mrs. Eff chatted about some matters of the cottage and their upcoming meals and then launched into the news from town. With the introduction of each new tidbit of information, Charlotte became anxious and then felt relief wash over her when it became apparent that she was not the focus of the gossip. Why had she ever found gossip to be an agreeable pastime?

Fortunately, there was no mention of Mr. Edgington, only of the general pleasure everyone experienced at the ball. General pleasure. Ha! Charlotte thought. It had caused her acute pain. And strangely, Mr. Basford had provided acute joy. How, she wondered, could joy and pain coexist in the same evening?

But why did not Mrs. Eff speak of Mr. Edgington and the glove? Perhaps she had heard but was too timid to speak of it. No. That could not be the case, for Mrs. Eff was always very forthcoming. Perhaps the news had not yet gotten out. Perhaps Mr. Edgington had been killed in a tragic hunting accident early this morning before he could ruin her reputation. Perhaps a wild boar had mauled him. Were boars even in season? She doubted a pheasant could do sufficient damage. A sudden mauling was too good—and too horrid—a circumstance to contemplate.

Still, Charlotte was beginning to feel a bit of relief and had almost finished eating an entire piece of toast when Mrs. Eff produced a letter from her apron pocket. Her relief was instantly shattered into splinters of fear. "This arrived this morning while you were still in your chamber. Now that you've had some nourishment, I expect you are ready for a word from the outside world."

She held out the paper to her, and Charlotte stared at it, still chewing on her last bite of toast. Was this ill news? Had the knowledge of the glove become known? She stared at the direction, but she did not recognize the handwriting. Slowly, she put down her plate and took the letter from Mrs. Eff's hands. "Thank you."

"Is there anything else I can do for you?"

"No, thank you, Mrs. Eff. You have been a great help already."

"I shall leave you to your letter then."

Charlotte watched as Mrs. Eff exited the sitting room, her skirt trailing behind her. She looked down at the letter again, and drawing in a deep breath, she opened the seal. Quickly, she checked the signature first.

Mr. Basford.

Relief raced through her and a silly smile reached her lips. She was too pleased that it was not a threat from Mr. Edgington that she did not contemplate the breach of etiquette he had committed in writing her. But the smile fell from her lips. Perhaps he had come to his senses and was writing to withdraw his support. She took a deep breath and began to read.

My dear Mrs. Collins,

I hope you will not think this letter is inappropriate, for I'm writing it with the best of intentions. Before you begin to panic, let me to assuage your fear. Don't trouble yourself. Nothing has occurred to ruin you. I'm merely writing on behalf of Mr. Westfield and myself to solidify our appointment with you and Miss Lucas. My nephew is eager to speak to your sister. I hope it will be acceptable for us to call on you both tomorrow afternoon. In the meantime, Mrs. Collins, do not trouble yourself. All will be well.

B. B.

Charlotte carefully refolded the letter and set it in her lap. She stared down at it, occasionally repositioning it on the fabric of her dress. Her heart was torn with hope and doubt. Why was he so kind? How could he possibly benefit from helping her?

Certainly he had already proven himself to be an upstanding man and very much unlike what she had expected upon their first meeting. His letter had soothed her in a manner that nothing—neither the rosehip tea and toast nor Mrs. Eff's conversation—had managed.

✒ ✒

Maria returned inside and sank ungracefully onto the settee beside Charlotte. She looked fresh and excited, her blue eyes shining. Charlotte felt like a storm cloud—a woman of dark and changeable moods—and probably resembled one as well.

"Did you enjoy your walk?"

"I would have much rather talked to you, but you refused to get out of bed at a reasonable hour. I suppose you felt ill?"

"I had a dreadful headache this morning, but I am feeling better now."

"I am glad to hear it." Maria took Charlotte's hand. "I do not say it often enough, but I do not know what I would do without you. You have given me a home and a chance to enjoy society. If it had not been for you, I would never have met Mr. Westfield."

Guilt raced through Charlotte. Maria's happiness was indeed attached to hers. And how tenuous was Charlotte's happiness! Unsure of whether she should break the bad news to her sister, she hugged Maria tight, looking down at her blond head where it rested against her shoulder. The poor girl had already been the target of the sharp arrows of gossip, but still she managed to retain her innocence and optimism. Her good nature had seen her through the loss of her friendship with Miss Farmington and Mr. Card. Perhaps Charlotte ought to rank optimism a little higher in her list of virtues.

Charlotte sighed. She feared that her brush with the slings of society would not leave her as innocent. The horrid tale would become public eventually, and it would be better to tell Maria beforehand. But Charlotte could not bear to ruin her sister's elevated mood, and there was Mr. Westfield's impending visit to consider.

Perhaps tomorrow he would propose, and engaged to the man she loved, Maria would be safe from partaking in Charlotte's ruin.

❧ ❧

Mr. Basford and Mr. Westfield arrived at the cottage the next day in the early afternoon. In the sitting room, Maria sat in a chair appearing completely composed while Charlotte fidgeted on the settee.

"Mr. Basford and Mr. Westfield." Mrs. Eff announced them at the door. Charlotte imagined that her voice held a note of finality.

The sisters stood and turned to greet them.

"Good day," Charlotte said. She tried not to seek reassurance from Mr. Basford that the news had not yet spread, but she could not help herself. Her eyes sought his.

He smiled, his lips drawing into a subtle U-shape, and she knew her secret remained safe.

She released the breath she had been holding. His smile deepened, revealing a row of nicely formed teeth. Charlotte dragged her gaze away from him and focused on Maria, who was blushing prettily as Mr. Westfield greeted her.

Charlotte forced herself to remember her role as hostess. "Please, do sit down."

"That is very kind of you, Mrs. Collins," Mr. Westfield said, "but I was hoping to have the pleasure of taking a turn about the garden with Miss Lucas. Would you grant us your permission?"

If it were possible to shout inwardly, Charlotte did so. Outwardly, she remained composed. There could be no doubt but that Mr. Westfield was going to propose! Charlotte would convey her parent's blessing forthwith, and perhaps the marriage would occur before Mr. Edgington's news could do damage. At the very least, her sister would be securely engaged when the dreadful news became available to the public.

"Certainly, Mr. Westfield. It is a fine day for walking." Charlotte had to restrain herself from pushing them out the door. Instead, she kept her seat as Mr. Westfield escorted Maria from the room, but she did wink at her sister when she turned back in the doorway and smiled hugely.

Once the door had been shut behind them, Mr. Basford said, "That was a very cheeky gesture for so refined a woman."

Charlotte elected to reply in a similarly cheeky manner. She actually felt a bit cheeky just now. "You forget, Mr. Basford, that I am—or very soon will be—a woman with a reputation. It is expected that I would behave in such a shocking fashion."

He sobered. "You don't believe that, do you?" he asked, leaning forward in his seat.

"What? That soon society in general will believe me to be only slightly better than a harlot and that they will expect me to behave accordingly? I cannot help but believe it."

"Surely no one will believe you capable of what Mr. Edgington will assert."

"I wish that were true." She looked down at her skirt. "But in my experience, people are eager to believe the worst in others."

A pause.

"What about you, Charlotte, are you inclined to believe the worst in others?"

Charlotte considered. She had believed the worst of Mr. Basford, and in reality, he was the best of men, but she had believed the best of Mr. Edgington, and he had turned out to be a pig. A serpent. A demon! She stopped her litany of insults. "It appears that I always believe the opposite of what is true. I find that I cannot read the character of others at all."

"First impressions can be deceiving."

"Indeed."

Although the conversation dwindled, the two sat comfortably together for a time. Then, Mr. Basford shifted in his chair. "My nephew is proposing to Maria."

Charlotte's head snapped up. More inward rejoicing. "I am so pleased, and I know my sister will be pleased as well. She has developed deep feelings for your nephew."

"James is quite fond of her too. He needed only a little encouragement from me to make his proposal."

"Encouragement was required?"

"Oh, no, do not misunderstand. The boy wanted to propose. He told me so himself. He simply needed a little nudge to overcome his initial hesitancy."

She was somewhat relieved. "I see. And you merely nudged him."

"I thought the timing was right."

He meant, of course, that the timing would prevent his young charge from caving in to societal pressure once Charlotte's disparaging story was known. She dropped her eyes, ashamed that she had the potential to affect her sister's life negatively. But if it resulted in an engagement, the circumstance could not be entirely bad.

"I did not tell him your situation."

"I greatly appreciate that."

He stood, crossed the room, and joined Charlotte on the settee. He sat at a respectable distance, but Charlotte slid further toward the armrest. She made a great pretense of rearranging her skirt. And then, realizing that she was preening like Maria in a room of eligible gentlemen, she took a fortifying breath and looked at Mr. Basford.

He was lounging against the back of the settee, looking calm and relaxed indeed. How could he manage to be so calm when she felt so nervous? His legs were stretched in front of him in a very inelegant position that somehow managed to suit him quite well.

Her eyes moved up past his deep blue frock coat, his loosely tied white cravat, and his neck to his face. Slowly, she met his eyes, and the events that had concerned her only moments ago seemed to disappear into insignificance. What cared she about Maria and Mr. Westfield when she felt such a pull toward Mr. Basford?

Charlotte did not know exactly what to do next, but she could not force herself to remove her gaze from his. She clasped and unclasped her hands in her lap several times before she realized she was fidgeting. How inexperienced she must appear. She dropped her hands beside her, allowing them to rest on the settee. Finally, she sat, unmoving.

Mr. Basford, however, was not so immobile. Gradually, gently, his hand moved from where it had laid across his chest. It slid ever so slowly across the brocade fabric of the settee. Charlotte saw the movement in the periphery of her vision, but she continued to meet his eyes. Her heart beat faster as his hand approached hers. Slowly, slowly, his hand continued to move toward her, and time seemed to stop as she waited for their fingers to meet.

His hand was so near to hers that she could feel the heat from his skin. A shiver of anticipation rushed through her. Her whole being was focused on Mr. Basford, and she was shocked to discover how desperately she wanted his touch and wished to experience his ever-present warmth.

The door burst open in the moment before Mr. Basford's hand met hers. His hand retracted politely to his lap as Maria and Mr. Westfield dashed in, smiling and laughing. The moment dissipated like dew on morning grass, leaving Charlotte's face as warm as if she had been standing in the sunshine.

Charlotte was thankful that her sister was unobservant, for she did not notice the blush on her cheeks, and she did not feel the tension between her and Mr. Basford. She simply hurried into the room and said, "Charlotte, Mr. Westfield would like to speak with you."

Composing herself, Charlotte adjusted her position on the settee, sitting straighter and turning her gaze to Mr. Westfield. She attempted an authoritarian demeanor, but she feared her red cheeks would hinder the facade. "Should we step into the next room?"

Mr. Westfield came forward, clearing his throat. Maria stood behind him, her face flushed with excitement. "No, Mrs. Collins, I believe everyone here will share in our joy."

He paused, glanced down at the floor, and cleared his throat again. Charlotte wondered if he had lost his nerve. Finally, he said, "I have asked Maria to become my wife—"

"I said yes!"

"Yes. Indeed, she gave her consent, but now I must ask the permission of her family—"

"And is it not true, Charlotte, that Mama and Papa have given you the power to agree to a match?"

Charlotte glanced between them. Mr. Westfield was still staring at the floor and periodically clearing his throat, and Maria was looking at her with wide, hopeful eyes.

"Yes. Mama and Papa have given me the option of granting their permission in their absence."

Maria stepped forward and grasped Mr. Westfield's elbow. "And will you grant it?"

"That depends." She glanced again at Mr. Westfield. "Sir, do you promise to make my sister happy? To provide for her? And, most importantly, to love her knowing that she has no dowry to speak of?"

Mr. Westfield met Charlotte's direct gaze. "I will do my best, Mrs. Collins, with or without a dowry."

"Then, I do grant permission."

Maria squealed with glee. She abandoned her betrothed and ran to throw her arms around Charlotte while Mr. Basford rose to clap his nephew on the shoulder.

Maria bounced up and down in Charlotte's embrace. "We must begin planning the wedding immediately!"

"Maria wants to be married as soon as possible," Mr. Westfield explained. He paused. Another cough. "As do I, naturally."

"We will see to the license while the ladies plan the ceremony," Mr. Basford assured him with a glance at Charlotte. She felt heat rise in her cheeks, and she focused instead on her sister.

"First, we must see to a dress…."

The good news of Maria's engagement to Mr. Westfield spread around Westerham, and soon there were many callers wishing to congratulate them. Mr. Basford and Mr. Westfield had procured the license and the ceremony was set to take place in three weeks' time. The gentlemen were frequent callers at the cottage, and the sisters always looked forward to their arrival.

In her happiness, Charlotte had almost forgotten about Mr. Edgington's intended blackmail, but the threat had not yet passed.

✂ Sixteen ✂

It is said that bad news spreads quickly, but whoever first uttered those words probably did not realize that there was something that spread faster: pernicious gossip.

No one was quite certain how the story began, but everyone knew without a doubt that it was true. *Someone* had seen the glove. No one was quite sure who.

The only thing that was certain was that Charlotte Collins was a fallen woman.

The news came to Charlotte in this way: she was in the kitchen stitching new ribbons onto the dress Maria intended to wear on her wedding day when Mrs. Eff, who had been with Edward in town procuring foodstuffs for the household, arrived at the cottage looking very grim. She entered and immediately sent Edward to their chambers, which were adjacent to the kitchen, instead of requiring his help with the provisions. He disappeared through the open door, and Charlotte heard him moving about.

She looked at Mrs. Eff, whose face appeared pale. Immediately, she was concerned. "Mrs. Eff, are you ill?" For once she hoped for illness because the alternative was her own downfall.

"No, Mrs. Collins. Not ill. Just sick at heart."

Oh dear.

Charlotte pushed the ribbons and cloth aside and gestured for Mrs. Eff to sit at the table. "Do tell me what is the matter." She did not really want to hear what she knew must be forthcoming.

"Edward and I have heard the most dreadful news in town."

"Has someone died?" Now Charlotte hoped for a death. Please, a death.

Mrs. Eff sucked in a deep breath. "No one has died, but a reputation has perished."

Charlotte's fingers curled around the edge of the table. The story had begun to spread. She knew it with perfect certainty, but she asked anyway, "What do you mean?"

"Word has got out that," Mrs. Eff hesitated, looking down at the floor and then back at Charlotte, "well, that you committed an indiscretion with that awful Mr. Edgington. Someone said you gave him a glove as a memento."

Charlotte's hand tightened again on the table, and her knuckles turned white. Her eyes dropped to her lap, and she knew that her face flamed with anger and embarrassment.

"It is not true, is it, Mrs. Collins?" she paused for a quick breath, and then continued, "Well, it could not be true. I told Mrs. Sinclair that myself when she told me. I told her there was no possibility that an upstanding lady like you would do such a thing."

Charlotte shook her head, but could not speak, and to her horror, tears began sliding down her cheeks. What a weak and pitiful woman she was! She could not even bear up under the scrutiny of Mrs. Eff. Imagine how she might humiliate herself in public. She would have to become a recluse. There was no doubt.

Mrs. Eff leaned forward with a look of pity on her face. "Oh, my dear. Tell me what has happened."

Charlotte took a few moments to compose herself. The kitchen was silent, and Edward had stopped knocking about in his chamber. Everyone, it seemed, was awaiting an explanation that would vindicate her. She took a bracing breath, but still her voice shook. "I was completely deceived by Mr. Edgington. Completely and utterly deceived! I believed him to be a man of good character. But he is not."

Mrs. Eff's frown deepened as Charlotte relayed the entire story, including the stolen glove and Mr. Basford's role in the debacle. When she finished speaking, Mrs. Eff leaned back in her chair, and Charlotte let her head fall into her hands.

"Well, this is quite a fix indeed."

Charlotte massaged her temples, trying to relieve the pressure that bore down on her. "There is nothing to be done, I am afraid. Nothing. Now that the slander has become public, I am ruined."

"That is not true, Mrs. Collins. Everyone in Westerham knows your good character."

"Yes, but they will have no choice but to believe Mr. Edgington. In fact, they already believe it. You have said so yourself."

Mrs. Eff let out a frustrated breath. "I cannot believe that the rumor will persist when people begin to think logically about your character. None who knows you will believe such a thing for long."

"Will they not? You know as well as I that people do not think logically about gossip. What is heard is believed. It is as simple as that." Tears continued to fall down her cheeks and she swiped them away. "Everywhere I go, his lies will haunt me. Even if I leave Westerham, I will always look behind me."

"Surely you do not think he would follow you?"

"I do not believe so, but he is well traveled. Will he happen upon me in Hertfordshire and expose me there? If I go to Bath, will the story follow there as well? Can I go anywhere to be completely safe?"

Mrs. Eff considered for a moment, and then said, almost to herself, "As long as he has that glove, he might be able to convince others, but without that proof, his power is gone."

"If only I had not accepted those gloves in the first place..."

"You cannot go into the past and undo it now, but perhaps if we could get that glove back.... Do you have its mate?"

Charlotte hung her head. "No, I destroyed it the night of the ball."

"There must be some means by which to retrieve that glove," Mrs. Eff said. "Can you not think of a way?"

Charlotte had thought and thought of how to get that glove. Each of her schemes had ranged from the far-fetched—sneaking into his home and stealing the glove—to the utterly immoral—setting his home ablaze, and the glove with it.

"There is no way."

Mrs. Eff looked a bit deflated and pondered the situation for some minutes before asking, "Did anyone see you alone with Mr. Edgington at the ball?"

"I cannot be certain, but I believe only Mr. Basford observed us. Though anyone could have looked out onto the balcony without my notice."

"I do believe that Mr. Basford is a gentleman who can be trusted."

Charlotte looked up, her chin in her hands. "I hope so. I do not know anymore. The people I think I should trust seem to turn out to be unsavory, and those I mistrust at first meeting seem to be the true gentlemen."

"Is not that always the way?"

ᔫ ᔫ

Later that day, Maria returned from paying a call at the Armitage house and dropped her bonnet on the kitchen table where Charlotte was distracting herself by arranging a vase of flowers cut from her garden. Maria fluttered around the room, searching for a biscuit to assuage her appetite, and recounted the events of her afternoon. Her conversation barely registered in Charlotte's ears. It was quite plain to her that Maria had not heard the vicious gossip. Charlotte was relieved that word had not yet reached her, but she knew she would have to confide the whole sordid, embarrassing story to her.

Charlotte interrupted her sister's soliloquy regarding her impending nuptials. "Maria, sit down. I must tell you some news."

Oblivious to her sister's grim tone, Maria perched on one of the kitchen chairs and began idly touching the flowers before her. "I do hope it is delicious news, for I have had a delightful day. Is it news of a tender nature? Has a new couple formed an attachment?"

"No, indeed. It is not news of an attachment. In fact, it is the opposite."

"Oh, then do not tell me, for I am in no mood for ill news." Maria dropped a flower back into the vase.

"I am afraid you must hear this." Charlotte pushed the vase out of the way. "For it affects you."

"How can that be? I have done nothing to warrant the gossip of others. At least not recently."

Charlotte quieted Maria with a serious gaze. "I am afraid that I am the subject."

Charlotte recounted the story, attempting to conceal the seriousness of the issue from her younger sister, but Maria comprehended the situation fully. She listened in shock, her blue eyes large and watery on her sister's behalf, and then she lapsed into anger. Her porcelain-colored skin flushed red. She leapt from her chair and rushed to her sister's side and wrapped her arms around her.

"He is a monster! What kind of man would do such a thing?"

Charlotte's eyes filled with tears as she listened to her sister's outrage and felt her comforting arms around her. She was so quick to jump to her defense and had not even considered the repercussions to her own life.

Maria rocked Charlotte back and forth in her arms, repeating, "Poor, poor, Charlotte. You do not deserve this."

Charlotte pulled away gently, wiping the tears from her eyes. "Listen to me, Maria." She held her at arm's length so she could see her face. "This situation could affect you as well."

"What? How?" A look of genuine confusion crossed her face.

"Gossip is already spreading through town. Mrs. Eff and Edward heard this morning. It is but a matter of time before our friends and neighbors are acquainted with the terrible story. I am rather surprised that you did not hear of it while you were with the Armitages today."

"Oh dear, I had not thought...."

"And you know how things like this are wont to go. The gossip never affects just one person. It affects the entire family, I am sorry to say."

"What are you saying? How can this affect me?"

Charlotte, searching for delicate words, hesitated and then said, "People might believe that you engage in the same type of behaviors of which I am accused. Or at the very least, they will look down upon you because you are related to me. You may lose more friends over this."

"Lose friends? Over nothing? How could anyone believe this of you? Even if he does have that glove!"

"I do not want this to spoil your wedding. You deserve a perfect day."

A wistful expression crossed Maria's features. "I am safely engaged to Mr. Westfield and nothing will ruin my wedding. We are so blissfully happy. Until then, I will just ignore any gossip I hear."

Charlotte mustered a smile at her sister's bravery, or her foolishness, whichever it was.

❧ ❧

The next week proceeded in the way Charlotte had expected. The story circulated through Westerham, and soon there was no one who had not heard of her supposed downfall. Visitors called on her, demanding to hear the truth of the matter. Some supported her, but a majority seemed to reject her. Still others shunned her, choosing to believe Mr. Edgington's story without first seeking her version of the event.

Soon the visits began to dwindle, and Charlotte could not decide whether to be relieved by the fact that she was no longer forced to defend herself to inconsiderate neighbors or to be upset because many of her acquaintances had chosen to believe Mr. Edgington's slander.

As the cottage became quiet, Charlotte became depressed. But when the next visitor arrived, she realized how utterly unprepared and completely naïve she herself had been.

Maria was on a drive with Mr. Westfield when a closed carriage, complete with gilded family crest and team of four perfectly matched steeds, rumbled ceremoniously into the drive. The sound attracted Charlotte to the window, and she drew away immediately at the sight, as though a view alone could injure her. And injure her it had, for she recognized the carriage as one belonging to Lady Catherine de Bourgh.

Charlotte withdrew further from the window and debated which room to choose to meet her inevitable doom. Perhaps she ought to go out and meet the carriage. Face her destruction head on. She took two steps toward the door and stopped.

No, she would not go like a lamb to the slaughter. Lady Catherine would come to her. It was the only power she retained: the power to inconvenience.

Charlotte arranged herself in the sitting room. She selected the high-backed chair by the fireplace, for it seemed the most regal, and she waited. She had hardly allowed herself to consider how Mr. Collins's former patroness and the proprietor of her rented cottage would react to the slander. Certainly, the encounter would not end well.

Mrs. Eff announced Lady Catherine, and the great lady swept into the room, skirts swirling in her wake. Charlotte contemplated keeping her seat, but then she stood. Her heart fluttered in her chest and her palms began to sweat, and suddenly, the world seemed to shrink as her vision closed in on her guest.

She closed her eyes, to regain her composure, and spoke. "Lady Catherine." The name held power, and Charlotte felt certain that merely speaking it aloud would unleash the plagues of the Day of Judgment.

When she dared to open her eyes, she saw no swarm of locusts or apocalyptic horsemen. The world was as it had been moments before, quiet and calm, only now a woman in severely fashionable attire stood before her.

"Mrs. Collins." Her voice was as severe as her attire.

"Will you sit?"

"No, I shall not! I do not hold pleasant discourse with women such as you."

Charlotte sat. She might as well be comfortable when the ill news was delivered.

"A report of an alarming nature has reached me."

"Has it?" Charlotte attempted indifference. "I find it surprising that you would come to me with gossip."

Lady Catherine's eyes narrowed, and her face hardened into planes and steep ridges. "It has come to my attention that the state of your morality has declined drastically."

"I am afraid that your information is incorrect, for my morality is as it has always been."

"The unmitigated gall!" Lady Catherine strode across the room and stopped only just before her skirts brushed Charlotte's knees. "I have researched the matter fully. My relation has shared with me the evidence—a glove bearing your very initials."

Here Charlotte attempted a protest, but words failed and Lady Catherine continued.

"This debauched behavior is completely unacceptable in anyone associated with the family of de Bourgh. You have left me with no choice but to sever all ties with you and your relations and to request your removal from this cottage." She looked around her as if Charlotte's supposed ill deeds had sullied the very walls around them. "Vacate my property before a month has passed."

Lady Catherine turned with the intention of sweeping from the room, but Charlotte stood. "You do not offer me the benefit of a reply?"

The older lady spun on her heel. "Certainly not. Mr. Edgington is of the house of de Bourgh and has no reason to speak falsely. I trust him." Again, she attempted a dramatic exit.

"Folly indeed."

Lady Catherine stopped. Charlotte stopped. The world stopped.

"Mrs. Collins, I am sorry that the situation has come to this." She sounded anything but apologetic. "I hope you will find your way back to the straight and narrow path of which your husband, the Reverend Collins, often preached."

To this message Charlotte had no reply.

It was the apocalypse of Lady Catherine, and unlike God, she had no mercy.

৯৬ Seventeen ৬৯

As Maria prepared for her wedding, Charlotte quietly prepared to depart from the cottage and return to Lucas Lodge a fallen and humiliated old widow. Her reputation was completely and utterly ruined in Westerham, and finding comfortable and affordable lodgings in town was unlikely, especially with the poor reference of Lady Catherine. Indeed, she had no desire to remain in a place that was hostile toward her, despite her need to vindicate herself.

She informed Mrs. Eff and Edward that she would have to do without their services and began to pack her few and precious books into a trunk. She did not want to remain at her parents' home forever. She had become accustomed to her independence and she could not bring herself to abandon it, even if it meant that she would live in a small abode, with no servants, and little meat. Doing without was preferable to being a burden and a source of shame to her family.

Maria came upon Charlotte as she was putting the last of her books in the trunk. "Whatever are you doing, Charlotte?"

She looked up from her task, startled. Maria was watching her with confused, concerned eyes.

"Packing my books."

"Well, that is quite obvious, but why?"

Charlotte closed the lid of the trunk, inhaling as the scent of paper and printer's ink wafted into the air. She found it impossible to explain the full truth of her financial situation to her sister, and moreover, she was unwilling to burden her with her troubles right before her wedding. So she simply said, "I hope you will not think me a weak person when I tell you this, but I have decided to return to Hertfordshire. I cannot live with the specter of Mr. Edgington's slander."

"Oh, Charlotte…" Pity was evident in her voice, and Charlotte interrupted her.

"Do not feel sorry for me. I am content with this decision. I will be near Mama and Papa, and I will be in the company of longtime friends. And with a good measure of luck, Mr. Edgington will never visit."

Maria's eyes were wide with concern, and she thought for a long moment before speaking again. "Although I am sad that you have made this decision, I must say that I approve. I would worry about you here alone. Lord knows what Mr. Edgington is capable of doing."

"Do not worry about me, Maria, wherever I am. I am a resilient person, and I will recover and rise above each new problem." Charlotte hoped her words would convince both her sister and herself.

"If anyone can survive, I know it is you. You are the strongest woman I know."

Charlotte gave her sister an encouraging smile, although she did not believe her, for at that precise moment, she felt herself to be the weakest of the weak and the poorest of the poor. She felt incapable of carrying her trunks down the stairs much less being able to carry the burdens her new life must impart.

But Charlotte forced a smile. "I am only sorry that I will not have the pleasure of receiving you and your new husband when you call on me here."

"We will call on you wherever you are. No matter where Mr. Westfield and I live, even if it is the farthest reaches of America, I will always write. Every day."

"As will I."

A bit teary, Maria took her leave, and Charlotte continued to pack her things alone. She moved through the tasks without much conscious thought, for such serious contemplation only led to sorrow.

๑๑෧ ฿๑๑

Days passed and Charlotte hardly seemed to notice. She received no visitors and was loathe to go into Westerham, so she was pleased when Mr. Basford called on her.

In fact, she almost burst into tears when she saw him riding toward her cottage with Mr. Westfield. He looked so strong and gentlemanly astride his tall bay horse. He was dressed in the same rather unfashionable attire as usual, and beside the dapper Mr. Westfield, he looked rather rough, but Charlotte saw him with new eyes.

She and Maria received them in the sitting room, which was now somewhat more bare thanks to Charlotte's packing efforts. The gentlemen did not mark the lack of accessories. Charlotte counted herself fortunate that gentlemen rarely take note of such things. A lady would have recognized the lack and commented immediately.

The conversation, mostly on the subject of the fine weather and the upcoming wedding, was strained as the four pretended that nothing was amiss.

Mr. Basford chatted amiably, keeping the conversation on the lighter side. The four laughed, but behind it was a sort of anxious restraint. Neither Mr. Westfield nor Mr. Basford ever mentioned the ugly gossip, and Charlotte was thankful. She could not bear to speak of it to one more person, and she certainly could not discuss it in front of her sister's betrothed.

When the gentlemen prepared to mount their horses and take their leave, Mr. Basford took Charlotte's hand in his, giving it a gentle squeeze. When she met his eyes, his gaze was warm and sincere, and she felt that warmth and sincerity to her core. She felt his unspoken support and was very thankful indeed.

Maria and Charlotte stood at the window and watched Mr. Basford and Mr. Westfield ride away. The sisters stood so close that their elbows touched, their silence companionable and relaxed. Despite the tension that had existed during their time together, Charlotte was sorry to see them go. She regretted not being able to have a private moment with Mr. Basford, but his visit had managed to give her a measure of strength. Still, she wondered at Mr. Westfield's relative quiet during the conversation. Usually an avid conversationalist, he had been polite, but not as talkative as usual.

"That was rather awkward at first, was it not?"

"Do not trouble yourself. All is well," Maria watched the gentlemen's progress down the path.

"Mr. Westfield, in particular, remained rather quiet, do not you think?"

"Perhaps he spoke a bit less than usual, but I see no cause for concern."

"I cannot help but worry. My situation has caused so much strife already, and I would hate to think that it would ruin—"

"Do not even say it!" Maria faced Charlotte, "Mr. Westfield is simply tired from the wedding preparations. That is all."

"But I still worry."

"If Mr. Westfield truly loves me, then nothing—not a thousand Mr. Edgingtons—would prevent our marriage. So you see, nothing you have done—or not done—can hinder our marriage."

Charlotte hoped Mr. Westfield's love was as strong as he had led Maria to believe, but only a week before their nuptials, the reasons for his awkwardness became known.

Charlotte was working the garden, gleaning the late summer flowers and preparing the garden for the autumn. It was foolish, Charlotte knew, to tend her plants when she would be vacating the property in only two weeks' time. But still, she could not stop herself. Chopping flowers off their stalks and hacking in the dirt provided a somewhat ladylike method for relieving her tension and venting her frustrations. She had just beheaded a rather pretty rose when she heard footsteps approaching at a rapid pace. Charlotte turned, the rose still in hand, and saw Mrs. Eff hurrying down the path with Edward following behind. Her bonnet had fallen from its place on her head and hung on only by its ribbon, and between her swirling skirts and the dust kicked up by her boots, Edward was almost obscured.

Charlotte stood, her knees protesting at her sudden movement, and she dropped the rose in the direction of her basket. It fell instead onto the ground, but she took no notice. "Mrs. Eff!" she called out in surprise. "What is the matter?"

Mrs. Eff stopped before her, unable to speak for want of breath. She held up her hand to halt Charlotte's questioning momentarily. Charlotte looked to Edward, who was breathing less heavily. The lines on his young face conveyed his concern.

"Maria..." he said. "So sad."

Charlotte's eyes flew to Mrs. Eff, who quickly shushed Edward. "Where is Miss Maria?" she asked in a strained voice.

Charlotte looked around her. "Still in the kitchen, I suppose. I left her working on her wedding attire. What has happened?"

Mrs. Eff raised a shaking hand to her forehead. "Oh Lord.... I hate to be the bearer of ill news."

"What is it?" she whispered, as though Maria might be able to hear her through the walls. Somehow, though, Charlotte already knew. There could be little doubt that Mr. Edgington's slander had caused more damage. And to Maria this time. But what was the nature of this damage? Please, God, do not let it be the wedding.

"Mr. Westfield and Miss Farmington disappeared sometime last night," Mrs. Eff said.

"What?" Charlotte asked, momentarily confused.

"They have eloped. At least that is the appearance."

Charlotte knew that the potential for disaster had existed in their circumstances, but this was an eventuality she had not expected. Mr. Westfield had eloped. With Miss Farmington. It was inconceivable.

But as Charlotte considered their state of affairs, everything became clear. Events crystallized in her mind. This explained Mr. Westfield's odd behavior when he and Mr. Basford had last called. Even then, he had no intention of following through with his engagement to Maria. The cur! And he could not very well call off their engagement, for such a thing was not done. Instead he chose to flee, leaving Maria again in shame and embarrassment.

And it was all Charlotte's fault. Mr. Edgington's scheme was ruining her life and now her sister's as well.

"Oh dear." Charlotte could think of nothing else to say. "Oh dear, oh dear, oh dear."

Edward repeated, "Oh dear, oh dear."

"Mr. Basford left at first light to attempt to recover them."

Charlotte could not even offer one more lame "oh dear," for her voice was now gone.

"It all seems so sudden, but it must have been brewing for quite a while," Mrs. Eff said. "Mr. Westfield had us all fooled, even his uncle, it seems."

Mrs. Eff was waiting for a reply, and all Charlotte could think to say was "Poor, poor Maria."

"I am so sorry. She will be inconsolable."

They stood in silence for a long moment. Charlotte attempted to gather her thoughts. What was she to do? How was she to break such news to her sister? Maria loved Mr. Westfield. It would break her poor heart.

Perhaps it was all a mistake. "How did you come to find this out?" Charlotte asked.

"You are well aware of the manner in which news travels in Westerham, through servants especially. I had to hurry so that Maria would hear it from you instead of from someone on the street. The vultures are gathering." She took a deep breath. "Miss Eames at the Farmington's said she saw the young lady enter Mr. Westfield's carriage very late last night. She saw it with her own eyes."

It was doubtful, then, that it was a mistake. Servants may exaggerate the goings-on in their households, but if Mrs. Eff believed this Miss Eames, then it must be true.

"Thank you for coming here to warn us." Charlotte paused. "Do you know why...why he left Maria?"

"You mean, does it have anything to do with Mr. Edgington's falsehoods?"

Charlotte nodded, fear clutching her heart at the knowledge that she had ruined her sister's chance at love. Mrs. Eff's face conveyed the truth though she did not speak a word. Charlotte groaned. Everyone found the ground fascinating for several moments.

Charlotte tried to be sensible. "Even the best of men might be persuaded to leave a good woman in the face of such a scandal in the family."

Mrs. Eff's face became a mixture of sorrow and pity, and struggling with her emotions, Charlotte only nodded. The fault was indeed hers.

No! The fault lay with the depraved Mr. Edgington, and as guilty as Charlotte felt, she must force herself to remember that fact. She had done nothing worse than trusting the wrong gentleman. Many a woman had made such a mistake, yet they did not suffer such public humiliation.

Mrs. Eff finally found her voice. "I cannot say for certain the cause of Mr. Westfield's actions. Some people say that he simply got his head turned by Miss Farmington, and some say that Mr. Edgington's story caused him to begin to doubt Miss Maria's morality."

"I do not like Mr. Edgington," Edward said. "He is unkind. And Miss Maria is sweet."

Edward was correct. Maria did not deserve such ill treatment. Charlotte winced at the pain she would suffer. Mrs. Eff hastened to say, "But that is all just conjecture. Who is to know what a man such as him could be thinking? The truth is that only Mr. Westfield knows for certain. It is impossible to know his reasons for such treachery without consulting the villain himself, and at the moment, he is nowhere to be found."

"Perhaps Mr. Basford will find him," Charlotte speculated, "but the damage is already done. She will be heartbroken."

Maria rounded the corner of the house and entered the garden. "Who will be heartbroken?"

Charlotte, Mrs. Eff, and Edward stared at her dumbly for a moment.

Mrs. Eff took Edward's hand. "Perhaps we should go."

Maria stopped them. "Oh no. Do not leave on my account. Now that you are no longer in our service, you must stay and chat with Charlotte and me. We are lonely here without you!"

Mrs. Eff looked to Charlotte, who nodded slightly, granting permission to stay, needing her support.

"Now tell me the gossip from town." Maria picked up the rose Charlotte had dropped and twirled it between her fingertips. "It will be a relief to hear something other than these heinous lies about Charlotte."

Mrs. Eff grimaced. "My dear, I am finding that gossip does no good for anyone. It is getting so that no news brings me pleasure anymore."

"What do you mean?"

Charlotte took Maria's hand, halting the twirling of the flower. "The news that Mrs. Eff has just related to me concerns Mr. Westfield."

"Oh?" A hint of worry colored her voice.

Charlotte was unsure of exactly how to divulge such sensitive information. "It seems that he has left Westerham."

"Perhaps he has gone on his uncle's business in London." Maria tried to be sensible. It saddened Charlotte all the more.

"I am afraid not," Charlotte paused and took a deep breath. "It seems that he has disappeared and taken Miss Farmington with him."

"What?" Maria shook her blond head.

Thankfully, Mrs. Eff spoke. "It is believed that they have eloped." Her voice was soft and gentle, and Charlotte was glad that she had been the one to bring the truth to light. She could not seem to find the words that would break her sister's heart.

Maria's fingers tightened around the stem of the rose and the blossom trembled slightly in her grasp. "No, I do not believe that. Mr. Westfield and Miss Farmington? The very idea is preposterous. Mr. Westfield loves me. He is engaged to me." Maria looked from Mrs. Eff to Charlotte. "He loves me. He does."

Charlotte grasped her hand in both of hers. "We know nothing for certain. That is only what Mrs. Eff heard in Westerham." Her words were meant to soothe, but Charlotte doubted their veracity. "She thought you should hear it from us first and not from someone else."

"It is no matter. It is not true." The stem of the rose bent in her grasp. "I will not believe it until I have proof of it from Mr. Westfield himself. Until then, we must assume that the wedding will proceed on schedule."

Maria lifted her chin resolutely and began to walk toward the front of the house, but then turned around. "I will believe nothing ill of Mr. Westfield. He loves me."

Charlotte wondered just whom she attempted to convince.

Mrs. Eff, Edward, and Charlotte stood in silence, listening to the swish of Maria's footsteps along the path.

"I hope she's correct in her faith in him," Mrs. Eff said.

Charlotte nodded. "As do I."

But neither of them held out any true hope.

♦♦♦

For the next few days, the cottage was rather quiet, and Maria's behavior could only be described as stoic. Charlotte was as impressed by Maria's fortitude as she was concerned about her refusal to acknowledge her true circumstances. Maria appeared to move through her days as usual, without tears, and always speaking well of Mr. Westfield. She was unusually helpful around the cottage. She assisted Charlotte's packing efforts and took long walks in the garden and surrounding woodlands, but she did not go into town.

Then, a letter arrived from Mr. Westfield.

Charlotte watched as Maria took it to her room, her face impassive. She did not return for several hours, and Charlotte thought it best to give her time to digest whatever news the missive contained.

She could very well guess its contents.

It was full dark when Maria entered the sitting room and took the chair opposite her sister. Her face showed the effects of tears, but she was no longer crying.

They sat in silence for many moments, and Charlotte was loath to speak, fearing what she would hear once the conversation began.

Finally, Maria spoke. Her voice was very soft, but it did not crack with emotion as Charlotte had expected. "I am no longer engaged to Mr. Westfield." Charlotte blinked at the detachment of Maria's voice. The sad words were simply stated as though she had just said, "Dinner is at seven," or "The weather is quite fine today."

Charlotte approached Maria's chair, not sure what to do or say. Kneeling before her, she took her hand. "I am so sorry, Maria."

Maria began to stroke the back of Charlotte's hand as she spoke. "So am I. But there is nothing to be done. He and Miss Farmington have eloped."

"Oh my dear…" Charlotte dropped her head into Maria's lap. Everything was ruined. They were both doomed to return in disgrace to their parents' home in Hertfordshire. Worse, neither of them would find love or security now that Mr. Edgington's damage had been done.

"His letter was very kind."

"Oh, well, at least he was kind."

Charlotte felt Maria stiffen and then relax. She said, "Do not be cruel, Charlotte. I do not believe Mr. Westfield meant any harm. He just went about things the wrong way."

How could she forgive him? she asked herself. Then Charlotte realized the reason. Any anger must be shared between her suitor and her sister, for she had been the cause of the problem. "The fault is mine." She raised her head to look into her sister's eyes. They were calm and almost peaceful, but she read the truth of the matter there.

"Do not blame yourself, Charlotte—"

Charlotte could not fathom the idea that the two events were unconnected. There were just too many mitigating circumstances for her to continue to believe the best of Mr. Westfield. It was far too coincidental that Mr. Edgington's lies would become public and shortly thereafter Mr. Westfield would break their engagement.

"I cannot help but blame myself. All the facts support my supposition. Had Mr. Edgington never come into my life, you would not be in this situation."

Maria pushed stray hairs from her sister's forehead. "I will tell you the truth. In his letter, he did say that he preferred not to join himself to such a scandal."

Tears fell down Charlotte's cheeks. Her sister's future happiness was ruined along with her own. Together, they would be ostracized from society. "I am so terribly sorry. So sorry."

Maria lifted Charlotte's chin. "Listen to me, Charlotte. Do you know what I think? I think Mr. Westfield is just using Mr. Edgington's slander as an excuse."

Charlotte studied her with confused, teary eyes. "What could you possibly mean?"

"I do not believe he ever loved me."

Charlotte stared, perplexed. Why would he have proposed if he had not loved her? She did not have a large dowry or a lofty title. "Of course, he loved you."

"As depressing a thought as it is, I believe it is true." Her voice was breezy. "I do not think he ever loved me. When I first read the letter, I was outraged. I cried and wanted to kill him and Miss Farmington, but then I began to recall all our past interactions. Suddenly, I felt calm. I could see what had been before me all along. It was such a strange sensation. I do not believe that I have ever thought so clearly." She seemed to ponder that for a moment. "I realized that he was always very attentive to Miss Farmington and that he only called upon me when Mr. Basford called upon you as well."

"What nonsense. Mr. Westfield wanted to call on you. Mr. Basford was merely a chaperone."

"Oh, I think Mr. Westfield had some interest in me at first, but he soon gravitated toward Miss Farmington. And why wouldn't he? She has a far bigger dowry, and she is a determined flirt."

Yes, Charlotte could well believe that. She had witnessed Miss Farmington's flirtatious behavior, although she wondered why any man would have an interest in a woman with such horse-like features. Even with the inducement of a dowry. "Then why did he propose to you?"

Maria paused, considering. "I do not know, but I am glad that we are no longer engaged. I certainly do not want to marry someone who does not love me."

Charlotte tried to recall what she had observed in Mr. Westfield, but her mind did not seem to be functioning. There was too much information to process. One thing only nagged at her. "You do not blame me then?"

"How could I possibly blame you? You have done nothing wrong."

"I trusted an untrustworthy man, and as a result you may have lost Mr. Westfield and I have lost my home."

Maria started. "What? Lost your home? What do you mean? You told me that you had elected to leave Westerham. Voluntarily."

Charlotte had not meant to break the news in so clumsy a fashion, but the words had simply slipped out. She hesitated, trying to think of a way to cover her error.

"Tell me," Maria demanded. "The truth. I am so weary of lies."

"Lady Catherine heard Mr. Edgington's gossip, and she revoked the lease on this cottage."

"That old bat!" Her voice was indignant and high-pitched.

Charlotte considered reprimanding her for not showing respect for those higher in society, but she refrained. Lady Catherine was an old bat.

"It is very unfair of her to punish you for something you would never do."

Charlotte attempted a practical reply. "It was within her rights to withdraw from our agreement. I cannot blame her."

"Bah! I shall blame her on your behalf."

"And I shall blame Mr. Westfield on your behalf."

Maria laughed softly, and Charlotte was pleased to hear the sound. "I think that is an even exchange."

They sat silently for a while. Charlotte's heart ached for her sister and for her own predicament. She and Maria had no recourse now but to slink home in disgrace.

As if reading her mind, Maria asked, "Is Lady Catherine's regrettable decision the true reason that you are returning home to Hertfordshire?"

"While I did not relish staying here to fight the gossip that surrounds me, Westerham has become my home. I have lived here for years, and I had no wish to leave it. Unfortunately, Lady Catherine has left me no choice. I can no longer live here and it will be some time before I am able to discover such agreeable accommodations on my small income."

Maria's brow furrowed. "But you will never be satisfied living at Lucas Lodge."

"No..."

"Neither would I." Maria paused. "What are we going to do? Surely, you do not intend to seek out another Mr. Collins."

"No indeed." The thought of an expeditious marriage had briefly—oh so briefly—crossed her mind. Ever since the news of Mr. Westfield's elopement had reached her, Charlotte knew that she must do more than simply disappear into Hertfordshire. She must help provide for them both since their parents' income had become so limited. "Must we discuss this now?"

"Yes, we absolutely must! Now, tell me what you are planning. I can tell there is more, and I can tell it is dreadful."

"I may have no choice but to seek employment." Charlotte observed the shock in her sister's wide eyes. "Perhaps an elderly lady in Hertfordshire requires a companion."

Charlotte knew that her parents had not the inclination to house two grown daughters, and she had no desire to become a burden to them, or to allow Maria to become so, especially since the dissolution of her engagement had been solely Charlotte's fault. She must support herself and her sister. It was her duty.

But it was impossible on her income. Lady Catherine's discounted lease fee had allowed her to live in such relative luxury. In any other circumstances, she would have been living in a tiny home with no servants at all.

Though she hated to acknowledge the fact, it was becoming painfully clear that employment was the solution. The idea was not as unbearable as the idea of a loveless marriage, for Charlotte was not afraid of toil. But what type of employment ought she seek? There were so few professions available to a woman like her. Governess, companion, or tutor: those were her choices. And they were not entirely objectionable. Now if only she could find someone willing to hire her, she could be somewhat content.

But Maria did not share her resignation to employment. A stern look crossed Maria's soft features. "You cannot be serious."

"It is a perfectly acceptable form of employment for someone of my position."

"Indeed it is, but Charlotte, you deserve so much more."

"Do I?"

"Of course you do! You deserve to have a proper husband, whom you love. A proper house and a companion of your own, if you like."

"You are only saying these things because we are related. I am no more special than anyone else."

"To me, you are special. Perhaps my reason lies in the fact that you are my sister, but I say this also because you are a worthy woman."

Charlotte smiled at her sister's vehement defense of her. "Thank you. You are very kind. But there is nothing to be done about it now."

Maria's look became quite determined.

"Indeed there is something to be done about it, and if you refuse to acknowledge that fact, then I suppose it will be up to someone else."

৵৶ Eighteen ৵৶

"Good afternoon, Mr. Basford." Charlotte stood and brushed the dirt from her hands. It was the Tuesday after Maria's wedding was to have taken place and less than a week before they had to vacate the cottage at Lady Catherine's request.

He bowed. "Mrs. Collins." Was she imagining it, or did his posture show contrition?

Charlotte had not expected him, nor had she expected the anticipation that rose in her as she had looked over her shoulder and seen him coming down the path toward her. From a distance, he had looked quite well put together in a deep brown coat and tan breeches, but as he drew nearer, she saw that he looked somewhat disheveled. More disheveled than usual. His face seemed drawn, and tired lines surrounded his eyes.

For a moment, he stood facing her. Then he turned abruptly and paced a few steps away. She watched and wondered what his odd behavior could possibly signify. She was already aware of the situation with Mr. Westfield and Miss Farmington—Mrs. Westfield, she corrected herself. "If you are here to inform me of a relationship between your nephew and Miss Farmington, I have already heard. Do not trouble yourself. All is well."

"Mmm…" Mr. Basford turned on his heel and looked at Charlotte. "I know this does not conform to proper English etiquette, but I would like very much to sit down." He laughed. "And I could really do with a cup of tea."

"I believe, as the fallen woman I am reputed to be, I am well past the need for meaningless etiquette at the moment, Mr. Basford. Do come inside."

He followed her into the cottage. They walked past the trunks and bandboxes in the hallway, and Charlotte hoped that he was too distracted to notice. She did not desire to explain the cheerless turn her life had taken. After they walked by the sad evidence in the hall, she gestured to the sitting room, offering him a seat and telling him that she would go fetch the tea.

When she returned with the tea tray balanced in her hands, Mr. Basford was standing with his back to the room. His attention was focused out the window, and he did not realize that Charlotte had entered until she set the tray down on the table with a gentle thud. He turned around and looked at her, his gaze softening.

"Tea?"

Charlotte poured his tea, handed it to him, and watched as he took a sip.

A look of satisfaction crossed his handsome features, and she was tempted to joke that England had affected him more than he cared to admit. Instead, she gestured to a chair, and he sat. "When did you develop such an affinity for tea?"

He smiled, put his teacup back on the saucer, and tipped the chair on its back legs. "As you once reminded me, Americans enjoy tea as well."

"Ah, but you claimed that you did not."

"Perhaps since being in England I have begun to appreciate it more." He echoed her previous thoughts.

They sipped in silence and a sort of uncomfortable feeling descended upon the room. Mr. Basford, too, looked rather unsettled.

Finally, Charlotte set down her cup and decided to plunge into the conversation they had been avoiding. She cleared her throat. "How does Mr. Westfield do? I understand that he is now happily married."

Chair legs hit the ground with a thunk, and Mr. Basford placed his cup on the table. He looked abashed.

She sought to reassure him. "Pray, do not concern yourself about what has happened between my sister and your nephew."

"How can I not concern myself?" His countenance was sad.

"You have done your part to rectify the matter. Did you not search for him after he and Miss Farmington disappeared?"

"Indeed, I did. It was the only thing I could do."

He stood and began pacing the room again. The furniture fairly shook under his heavy strides. Charlotte wished she could command him to sit, if only to save the floorboards. But they were Lady Catherine's floorboards, she thought with a dash of spite, so she allowed him to pace and hoped he would wear a path in the wood.

"And did you discover them?"

"Yes. I am sorry to say that they had eloped to Gretna Green. A dreadful process and so far below what was expected of him." He looked at her briefly. His brown eyes, altered by the discontent they held, seemed darker. "His mother is going to be so disappointed."

Charlotte sat back on the settee. She had secretly hoped that it had all been an unattractive rumor. But it was not, and the last vestiges of pointless hope, which she had held out for Maria's sake, drained away. "Oh."

He returned to his seat, tipped it back. "They returned to Westerham with me last night."

Charlotte did not know quite what to say. She was pleased that they had returned safely for his family's sake, but she felt pain for her sister. She managed to say only "Mmmm."

"They intend to travel to Savannah in the coming weeks."

"Will they make their home there?" She hoped for Maria's sake that they would.

"No, my nephew is quite enamored with England, and Miss Farmington." He paused, realizing that he had not used her proper name, but he didn't correct himself. "She says she cannot bear to part from her family. They will make their home here."

"I see." She hoped she sounded noncommittal and wondered what would become of Mr. Basford. His duties as chaperone had been completed. Would he too return to America? Would he ever venture back to English soil?

Before she could inquire, he stood abruptly and began pacing again. "I am so sorry, Mrs. Collins. I am sorry for what I have done to you and your sister."

His words surprised her. "What have you to be sorry for?"

He ran his hands through his hair. "I am responsible for the entire situation."

Confused, Charlotte began to twist the fabric of her skirt in her hands and tried to work out what to say next. "You cannot be responsible for Mr. Westfield's decisions."

"No, but I believe I had undue influence over his choice to propose to Maria."

She endeavored to read his face, but he had turned aside, giving her only a view of his tight profile. "What do you mean?"

Mr. Basford walked a few more paces and then faced her. The light from the window streamed around his body. "I mean that after that..." His voice tapered off as he no doubt searched for the proper epithet to use in company. "...fool Edgington began spreading those lies about you, I felt...." He paused again and ran his hand through his hair, leaving it even messier. "Well, I felt the need to take action. I knew you'd be very upset about the gossip, and after seeing people's reaction when Maria turned down Mr. Card, I had an idea of how the town would respond. I also knew that you were more concerned for your sister than for yourself. I wanted to help. I thought it would be helpful."

"I am afraid I do not understand."

"I encouraged James to propose to Maria."

"You mentioned that when we last spoke."

"No. I *encouraged* him." He said the word as if it were poison.

"What?"

"I sensed his reluctance." He paused in his speech but continued pacing. He faced the settee again. "But I genuinely thought he was in love with her."

Charlotte stood. What was he trying to say? "Did you force Mr. Westfield to propose to Maria?"

"No, I did not force him, but I did encourage him."

Sorrow and confusion rose in her, and Charlotte warred against them. There was no sense in allowing her feelings to overcome her. Emotional behavior would do her no good, and it certainly would not improve her reputation. But she thought of Maria and the valiant way she was accepting her situation. Perhaps she would not have been so upset if Maria had been upstairs crying, but the serene way she accepted the circumstances absolutely broke her heart. Maria had lost hope, and that was the worst of all possible outcomes.

Charlotte knew not how best to respond.

"I was thinking of you." His gaze was direct and unwavering, causing Charlotte's breath to catch. "I knew how concerned you were about how the gossip would affect your sister."

"I was naturally anxious given the circumstances in which I found myself," Charlotte managed to say, "but I certainly did not want anyone forced to marry Maria."

"I did not intend to force him to propose. I did not think myself to be doing so. I believed him to be in love with her. Confess. You believed it to be so as well. Did you not?"

Charlotte could not lie. "I hoped he loved her."

"I believed it was a match of mutual love. Otherwise I would not have acted as I did."

Charlotte believed him. The pain in his expression was genuine. She had just cause to be angry and hurt, but she found that she could be neither. Her common sense would not allow it. "Mr. Basford, you have always shown yourself to be an honorable gentleman of the highest morals, and I believe that the actions you took in this situation were the result of your good intentions. I am sorry that my sister was injured, but, pray, do not hold yourself accountable. Mr. Westfield is solely to blame."

They stood a moment in silence, and Mr. Basford seemed to relax. The tension left his shoulders, and his hands unclenched and fell loosely at his sides. He returned to his seat and picked up his teacup like a civilized gentleman and not the barbarian who had stalked the room moments ago, and Charlotte followed his lead, picking up her teacup and sipping daintily. The tea was cool.

"Miss Lucas's heart will mend, although it may not seem likely now."

Charlotte was not sure if he sought to reassure her or himself.

"It is not her heart that concerns me but her hope. She has lost hope, I think."

Mr. Basford's expression changed to one of pity. "I am sorry for that."

"As am I."

They sat a moment, drinking tepid tea, while Charlotte considered her next words carefully. "I do not know how to say this without giving the appearance of rudeness, so I will be frank. I believe it would be best if you were not here when Maria returns." He began to protest, but she interrupted him. "She may not appreciate a reminder of Mr. Westfield so soon."

He nodded. "I do understand. Perhaps I may call on you again, while Maria is absent of course."

Charlotte thought for a moment. She knew what she must do. She must raise herself above suspicion, and to do that she would be forced to sever their friendship, though in merely contemplating the decision, she felt as though she were severing a vital part of herself. Refusing to meet his eyes, she spoke. "Despite my great appreciation for the kindness you have shown me and for the friendship that has grown between us, my reputation is fragile. I hope you will understand when I say that it might be for the best if we do not meet privately again."

He set down his cup. Upon hearing it hit the table, she looked up. His face displayed his disappointment. For a moment, they sat, frozen. Neither moving or speaking. Charlotte wondered if he too wanted to make their final moments, though uncomfortable, last longer. Then, he stood slowly, his body tight again and his hands clenched. "I am sorry to hear that."

Charlotte desperately wanted to snatch her words back, to invite him to call as soon as was convenient. But she could not. She was leaving Westerham, and even if she could remain, it would be inappropriate for them to meet again. She remained silent, and he took his leave of her with a nod and perfunctory words of parting.

Apparently, he did not understand.

Charlotte listened as his crisp footsteps retreated, paused, and then returned.

She rose as he reentered the room. "Mr. Basford?"

He ignored her questioning tone completely and asked a question of his own. "What are all these trunks?"

"They are not your concern." She looked away momentarily, but he pushed onward, walking toward her. His facial expression was hard and then softened.

When he spoke again, his voice was quiet, and it brought color to Charlotte's cheeks. "Tell me. You're not leaving Westerham, are you?"

"I must."

"And that is why you brought the tea and not Mrs. Eff. She is already gone, isn't she?"

"I had no other option, but to dismiss Mrs. Eff and Edward."

"Of course, you do. I know Edgington's lies have done some damage, but leaving now and dismissing your servants will only confirm people's suspicions."

"Truly, I have no other choice."

"You always have a choice."

Charlotte clenched her hands and stared at him, uncertain of how much to confess. She chose to confess all. What could it hurt? She had nothing left. "Mr. Edgington's slander has reached my proprietress, Lady Catherine de Bourgh. After Mr. Collins died, she graciously provided this cottage for me at a reduced rate, but she prefers not to house a fallen woman."

Mr. Basford rocked back on his heels.

"I can no longer afford to employ Mrs. Eff and Edward. They have not been here in weeks. I miss them," she added wistfully, then sobered. "I must vacate this lovely cottage soon."

Mr. Basford's eyes were focused on the floor. "Where will you go?"

The kindness of his voice made Charlotte resent her pitiful situation. "I must go to my parents' home to Hertfordshire and take Maria with me. She certainly cannot stay in Westerham alone." Charlotte again debated how much she should divulge, but his kind eyes drew her onward. "I will seek employment. Eventually, perhaps I will be able to lease my own home, but I will always mourn my cottage here."

"I am sorry. I did not realize…." Mr. Basford's voice trailed off into quiet.

Charlotte continued, now eager to share her feelings once she had begun: "I was so pleased when Mr. Westfield proposed, for it meant that Maria would be spared my indignity. Now, she must return home with me."

"Surely the situation is not so dire."

Charlotte sighed. "Not dire. But Maria will live far below what she deserves."

"And so will you."

He appeared genuinely sad.

"Pray do not concern yourself with me. I shall be fine." She attempted to steel herself against the need she felt for his kindness and compassion. She would soon depart, and in all probability, she would not see him again. She must learn to do without his friendship.

"And this is why I am not invited to call on you? Because you're leaving?" His eyes were wide, searching hers for the truth.

Charlotte lowered hers.

She wished that her departure was the only reason she should reject his visits, but it was not. She would not lie to him, but she did not desire to injure him. She said nothing, and eventually she gathered the courage to look at him.

Their eyes met and held for what seemed like many minutes, and then, with a nod, he turned and walked out of the room.

She did not want to feel remorse at his departure, but she went to the window and watched Mr. Basford—his back straight, his stride long and ground-covering—walking away from her cottage. She would not see him again, and the thought did not appeal to her.

She had liked him.

She had liked him very much indeed.

ᴥᴥ Nineteen ᴥᴥ

Charlotte and Maria walked in the garden together. Both ladies had needed the time out of doors and a bit of physical activity to refresh their depressed spirits. Maria had been very quiet during the duration of their stroll and seemed not to be affected at all by the sunlight or surroundings, and Charlotte spent the time attempting to memorize the cottage and its garden. She committed each flower to memory, each leaf and color. Charlotte had installed most of the plants and cultivated them with her own hands. She learned by heart each stone of the cottage walls. She felt sure that the smooth brown stones would go with her in her memory no matter where her life led her.

Charlotte cast a sidelong glance at Maria. Her blond hair blew around her face and her dress wrapped itself around her ankles, making her gait seem labored. Her expression remained tense, with tiny frown lines around her mouth. Concerned that the fresh air had done nothing for her sister's spirits, Charlotte felt certain that Maria would benefit from a cup of tea and some biscuits to lighten her mood. She was about to suggest that they return inside when she heard the sound of a carriage approaching.

They turned to see it enter the drive, a dust cloud trailing behind.

A team of gray horses trotted in front of a familiar barouche, their large, well-muscled bodies easily pulling it along. The sound of their hooves was rhythmic and somehow soothing, and some of Charlotte's anxiety was carried away by the cadence.

Charlotte looked at Maria, who stared at the carriage as it drew ever closer. Her body seemed to go lax. She whispered, "It is Mr. Card's carriage."

"I think you must be right." But what did it signify?

Mr. Card alighted from the carriage almost before it drew to a halt and certainly before the coachman could assist him. Suddenly, he stopped and looked at the ground, his hand still clinging to the side of the carriage as if his courage and bravado had disappeared the moment his feet touched the earth.

Maria, however, approached him rather boldly, and Charlotte followed close behind.

Maria's voice was somehow a mixture of courage and hesitancy. "Good day, Mr. Card."

Mr. Card looked at her and removed his hand from the carriage. "Good day, Mrs. Collins, Miss Lucas."

"Good day," Charlotte repeated. She was preparing to invite him inside when he spoke again.

"I know relations between our families have been strained of late, but you must excuse my plain speech." His face was a study in consternation. He rushed on. "I have heard of your trouble. Quite frankly, I do not believe a word of it."

Embarrassed, Charlotte found herself to be the one who was looking at the ground. "Thank you for your kindness, Mr. Card. I certainly am not guilty of that which I have been accused."

"I knew it!" He raised a fist in victory and then lowered it. "I knew it simply could not be true. But Mama tells me that you are leaving Westerham."

Charlotte nodded quickly but wondered how Mrs. Card had heard about her departure. She had hoped to leave Westerham quietly, to disappear and be forgotten. She had not believed her plans to be common knowledge, but apparently, her arrangements had been discovered. She would not concern herself with the details now.

Mr. Card's voice grew uncharacteristically strong. "There is no cause for such a drastic move."

"I am afraid it cannot be helped," Charlotte said. "We leave at the week's end."

"So soon?"

"I am sorry to say it is so."

Mr. Card glanced at Maria and then back to Charlotte. "Would you grant me the privilege of speaking with Miss Lucas?"

"Certainly," she said, though she was sure that her voice conveyed her uncertainty. "It would be very wrong for me to deny you a moment to say your goodbyes."

Mr. Card said a quiet thank you. Then, he offered his arm to Maria, and she shyly accepted.

Wondering at the portents of their conversation, Charlotte watched Mr. Card escort her sister to the back garden, and then she turned to go inside the cottage. Perhaps they would repair their friendship. At least something good would come of the sad situation.

She busied herself with the novel she had been reading and managed to get through one or two paragraphs at a time without her mind wandering to what might be occurring in the garden. At length, she heard the hoof beats recede as the carriage pulled away from the cottage.

When Maria entered the sitting room, Charlotte was prepared for a torrent of tears. It was not easy to say goodbye to friends, and despite what had occurred between them in the recent past, they were friends.

Maria, however, seemed strangely serene, her spirits much improved. She entered the chamber and remained quiet, pacing slowly across the room. Charlotte watched as her sister walked to the window.

"Tea?" Charlotte offered although no teapot was present.

"No, thank you."

Maria did not turn away from her place at the window. Her blue dress was washed in sunlight, and her blonde hair glowed. "Charlotte, there is something I must tell you."

Charlotte stiffened. This did not bode well. "I do not believe I can take more bad news."

Maria turned away from the window. "It is not bad news. It is the best news."

Charlotte paused, waiting. Her body was on edge, as if poised to flee at a moment's notice.

"Mr. Card has proposed again, and—"

"Oh no!" This was certainly far worse than she had expected. Their friendship would not be repaired and Maria would leave Westerham with only unpleasant memories to console her.

"—and I have accepted."

Charlotte leapt to her feet, and her book landed on the floor with a thunk.

"What? Proposed? Accepted?" Charlotte repeated stupidly. What could Maria be thinking?

"Mr. Card has proposed again, and I have accepted," Maria spoke as though to a young child as she crossed the room to where Charlotte stood frozen in shock by the settee.

"He has struck during a moment of weakness."

"No. He has waited until I understood the truth of marriage."

"But you do not love him!"

Maria took Charlotte's hand in hers. Her grasp felt strangely steady but not at all reassuring. "I do not consult my emotions in this case." Charlotte shook her head, but Maria continued. "We are to be married."

Charlotte stepped back. She comprehended the situation perfectly. Mr. Card's proposition had come at the moment of their greatest need, and Maria fancied herself to be her savior. "Please do not make the same mistake that I made with Mr. Collins. I know our situation seems bleak now, but things will work out for our good."

Maria ignored Charlotte's protest altogether, "We will not have to leave Westerham after all. We will both be living in Mr. Card's grand house, you see."

Fear crept into Charlotte's heart, and she clutched Maria's hands even tighter. "No. Maria, do not trade your chance at love for security. No amount of money is worth a loveless marriage."

"It may not be as loveless as you predict. Perhaps I shall grow to love him."

"How can you possibly say that?"

"Have not many other happy couples begun their marriages in this way?"

"How ridiculous. You cannot be so naïve after witnessing my own failed marriage." Maria knew how absurd it was to believe that love would come after marriage, especially a marriage of convenience. "You do not love him. You love Mr. Westfield."

"No. I was mistaken in my belief. I thought love to be something shocking, like a lightning bolt or a runaway carriage, and that it would knock me over. But now I realize that love might be something else entirely. Perhaps love for Mr. Card will sneak into my heart."

"Maria—"

"Charlotte, do not argue with me." She dropped her sister's hand abruptly. Her voice was strong, almost harsh. "It has been decided. I am marrying Mr. Card, and you are living with us."

The sisters faced each other in defiance. "I know you are doing this because you are afraid for your future."

"I am afraid for our future—yours and mine—but I do feel a fondness for Mr. Card. Is that not a foundation on which to base a marriage? Yours was formed on a great deal less."

Charlotte stared in disbelief. She could make a thousand different, accurate retorts. She could remind her of the pain of her marriage to Mr. Collins. She could tell her that her notion of love was a sham, that it would never come after marriage. She could tell her that all love was a sham, for that was how she felt at that precise moment. Instead, she asked, "What about our parents' permission? I do not believe I can act in their stead and give my permission to a marriage of convenience that could bring you sorrow."

"We do not require your permission, Charlotte, though I hope in time you will come to understand my decision."

"Has he sought Papa's permission?"

"He did so when he first proposed all those months ago. So it is all settled."

"I see." There was nothing Charlotte could do. The bargain had been struck without her. She stared down at her hands. "Do not do this. I beg you would not."

"Do not look for Mr. Collins in Mr. Card. He is not there."

Maria was correct. Mr. Card was not like Mr. Collins at all, but she was no more in love with Mr. Card than Charlotte had been with Mr. Collins. "How could I ignore the similarities of our circumstances? You are not in love with Mr. Card."

"I like him, and that is a kinder feeling than you ever experienced with Mr. Collins." Maria's face was set, as though sculpted in granite. "And Mr. Card can help us."

Yes, he could help them, but the cost was quite dear. Her sister bought and sold to repair the damage Charlotte had caused by trusting Mr. Edgington. "I do not like it."

"I am sorry for that, but it does not change a thing. Mr. Card has gone to secure a special license. We will be married before the week is out, and we will all move to Crumbleigh."

Charlotte was poised to argue, but Maria looked at her earnestly. "You have taken care of me. Even before I moved here, I know you sent money to our parents. You introduced me to Westerham society. You took me to balls, hoping that I would have the love that you never had. Now I am benefiting from all the assistance you have given me. I will have a husband and a large house. It is my time to return all the favors you have given me in the past. Charlotte, let me take care of you."

"But the rumors…"

"I will not allow you to run away."

"I am not running away!" She was not running. Was she?

Maria's sardonic look momentarily cowed Charlotte.

"I know it will not be easy, but Mr. Card believes that your reputation will be restored in time, and I agree. People have short memories, and another person's scandal will make the town forget ours. Have not you told me as much in the past? And until then, Mr. Card's good name will carry us. You will see. We shall be happy and secure."

Maria paused and forced her sister to look into her eyes. The look Charlotte read there was sincere and almost pleading. "It is my turn to take care of you."

Her voice tapered off in a whisper, and Charlotte melted into her seat. She saw that Maria's mind was quite made up.

After Maria left the room, Charlotte indulged herself in an embarrassing display of emotion. Tears rolled unchecked down her cheeks, and her eyelids swelled under the strain of her sorrow.

As much as she hated to admit it, she had wanted to run away. Her situation practically demanded it. She had little money, and no one in Westerham would hire her. No one in Westerham would even hold two words' conversation with her! She simply had to leave.

Now Maria believed that her marriage would cure all the ills that had befallen them, but Charlotte knew it would not be so. It was true that society sometimes had a short memory, but Mr. Edgington still had her glove, and as long as it was in his possession, her reputation would always be in danger. Worse, once it became public knowledge that she had benefited from Lady Catherine's charity but was now shunned by her, she would be doubly shamed.

She began to consider tactics for talking her sister out of her impending marriage, but she discounted such persuasion almost immediately. Charlotte's interference would only serve to make matters worse. There was simply nothing to be done.

She would have a home, and for that she was thankful. She would have protection in Mr. Card and Maria. Mrs. Card, however, would heartily disapprove. She was known to have little compassion for people who have fallen prey to society's pressures or who have been accused of having done so.

Charlotte sighed, picked up her abused book, and placed it back in the trunk. In truth, she had little choice in the matter. Maria was an adult, and she had made her choice.

Maria would marry Mr. Card. It was as simple as that.

·ᵒᵉ ᵍᵉᵒ·

Planning a wedding is never a simple affair. Planning a wedding in less than a week is utterly inadvisable. Charlotte and Maria had the advantage of already having prepared her clothing for her aborted wedding to Mr. Westfield. So new invitations had to be written and dispatched, and a messenger was sent post haste to Hertfordshire to inform Sir William and Lady Lucas of the date.

Thankfully, Mr. Card secured the license, the church, and the minister to perform the ceremony. Because the couple had not planned a wedding trip, etiquette dictated that Mrs. Card should hold a celebratory breakfast at her home, and Charlotte was certain that she went about her duties with as much joy as a cat in a tub of water.

The day of the wedding dawned bright and clear, but Charlotte still felt rather depressed, and when the Cards' servants arrived to transport their belongings to their new home, Charlotte felt even more disheartened.

She watched as two finely attired servants removed and placed her belongings—all contained in a surprisingly small number of trunks—on a wagon. When her personal possessions had been removed, they covered the furniture, which was to remain in the cottage, with dust cloths.

Charlotte was losing her home. She was losing her independence and would now be essentially in the care of her younger sister and her husband. Any pride that she might have harbored over her independent situation was now completely gone.

Maria entered the sitting room and found Charlotte perched on the edge of the cloth-covered settee.

"Are you well, Charlotte?"

"I am attempting to be well."

"The carriage will be here soon. What are you doing sitting in here?"

"I was simply saying goodbye to my dear old cottage."

"I know you will miss it, but Crumbleigh will soon become home. And it is ever so much bigger."

"Are you ready to be married?"

Maria gestured at her dress and said, "Yes, as long as you approve of my appearance."

Charlotte studied her for the first time since she entered the room. The dress they had chosen to serve as her wedding gown accentuated her slim form, and her hair curled elaborately around her face. She looked very beautiful indeed, and Charlotte told her as much.

Then, although she knew it was far too late to take corrective action, she made one last foray. "Maria, I am not trying to insult you. You are my sister, and I care a great deal about your happiness. Are you certain about this course of action?"

Rather than becoming angry, Maria softened. "I know you care about me, but you must stop worrying. I am at peace with my marriage, and so should you be."

Charlotte did not speak for long moments, considering. She would be no better than Mr. Westfield if she suggested that Maria abandon her betrothed on their wedding day. She must wed Mr. Card. "I shall be at peace. I shall."

"Good. Now, let us stop talking, for I hear Mr. Card's carriage approaching."

With that, Maria practically ran out of the room, leaving Charlotte alone again. She would have to get used to thinking of Crumbleigh as her home, but there had been something special about these stone walls. They had represented her safety and independence, and they had given her a life that she was sad to leave.

But leave she must.

Taking a deep breath, she followed Maria to the carriage and into her uncertain future.

ᴏᴏᴏ Twenty ᴏᴏᴏ

Maria and Mr. Card's wedding was a small, quiet assembly. The speed with which the wedding was organized prevented many people, including Maria and Charlotte's parents, from attending. Numerous members of the Card family were in attendance, however, as well as several of Maria's other friends. Mrs. Eff and Edward attended at Charlotte's insistence and sat unobtrusively behind the rest of the guests. Miss Farmington—the new Mrs. Westfield, actually—Mr. Westfield, and Mr. Basford, of course, had not been invited, and their absence was not mentioned, but it was felt by all. Only the first few rows of pews were occupied, but Maria and Mr. Card did not seem troubled that their wedding was not the society event of the season.

Charlotte sat in the front pew and watched as the couple exchanged their vows. Mr. Card cut a dashing figure in his dark morning coat, and Maria clutched a nosegay of flowers while light filtered through the church windows and turned her blond hair into spun gold. Charlotte was surprised to see tenderness in her sister's bright blue eyes. Perhaps it was true. Perhaps it was thankfulness. Or perhaps she would one day fall in love with Mr. Card. If that were the case, it would be good fortune indeed.

After the ceremony, the party was bound to return to the Card home for the wedding breakfast. On her way out of the church, Charlotte was arrested by Mrs. Eff.

"It was a lovely ceremony."

"Yes, Maria seemed happy, did she not? I do so want her to be happy."

"Of course you do, my dear," Mrs. Eff gave her hand a pat. "I do believe that she is very happy."

"She says that one day she will grow to love him, but will she?"

"One never knows about love."

"One never knows," Charlotte repeated.

They had reached the church door and were standing half in sun and half in the shade of the building. "I have news, and I thought it best you heard it from a friend." Here she paused and looked around. Finding no one within hearing distance, she continued, "I had it from a servant of Colonel Armitage that Mr. Westfield and Miss Farmington were already married when Mr. Basford discovered them. There was quite a stir, naturally, when he threw over your sister, but all is well now that Maria is married."

Charlotte nodded. This she had already known, thanks to Mr. Basford himself.

Mrs. Eff continued to speak. "They returned home briefly, but, they have left town again. Apparently, Mr. Basford has now arranged matters for them."

"I know of the occurrence at Gretna Green, but what other matters did Mr. Basford arrange?" Charlotte hoped she had kept her desperate curiosity from her voice.

"He booked them all passage to America, I understand."

"Oh? All of them?" He had said nothing about departing with the newlyweds.

"Yes, I believe so."

Mr. Basford was leaving. Although she had been quite certain that he was lost to her, it was a different matter entirely to have the truth so finally laid out. Mr. Basford was returning to Savannah. So far away. Across the ocean. And between them was only the lingering tension of the broken engagement between his nephew and her sister. She wished it were not so. She wished they could have parted in friendship. Or not have parted at all.

"I believe that neither Mr. Westfield nor the new Mrs. Westfield truly desired to undertake such a trip, but Mr. Basford insisted. And Colonel Armitage agreed, so it was settled."

"And have they set sail yet?" Charlotte's question was meant to be neutral, but she could hear the emotion in her voice. She concentrated on the scene before her. The carriages were filling and pulling away from the church one at a time. Dirt kicked up by the horses' hooves rose in the air, and Charlotte wondered vaguely if Maria was minding her dress in all that dust.

"I cannot say. But I do know that they are to visit Mr. Westfield's mother for quite some time before returning home to Westerham. If you ask me, we may not see them again. Savannah is said to be quite a beautiful place, and the trip, I understand, is rather a difficult one. Mrs. Westfield may not wish to undertake it again, despite the draw of family and country."

Only one carriage remained, waiting for Charlotte to embark. "I do wish them the best," she said, trying to feel as genuine as her tone of voice sounded.

Mrs. Eff gestured to Edward, who had been waiting in the vestibule. "We must be off, my dear. I do hope you enjoy the breakfast. I promised Edward a little something from the bakery."

Charlotte hardly heard her, but nodded just the same and watched them depart, walking together down the stone steps and rounding the corner of the church. Charlotte went to the waiting carriage, allowed herself to be handed in, and sat down as a wave of sorrow washed over her. It was odd how the prospect of losing something—or someone—could cause it to become so important to her.

✿✿✿

When Charlotte joined the wedding breakfast, the group, which had sounded animated when she was in the hall, seemed to become rather subdued, and she was quite conscious that it had mostly to do with her newfound reputation as a fallen woman. She attempted to remain on the fringes of the party, but Mr. Card and Maria continued to insist that she sit near them or converse with their group. It was rather kind of them to consider her feelings in that way, but it was also awkward and tiring.

Soon exhausted, Charlotte slipped away to a quiet part of the house. She opened the door to the library and peered inside. Vacant. Charlotte smiled. A few moments of peace at last. She chose a chair beside the window and did not even bother with the pretense of selecting a book. She knew she would not be able to concentrate on dramatic fiction, for her very life was a drama, and it was not fiction.

She was weary of being looked upon with suspicion. What must people say about her in the privacy of their drawing rooms? She longed for the presence of someone who looked upon her with kindness. Who did not contemplate her alleged lewd behavior with his peers. Who believed her when she said she was innocent. She longed for Mr. Basford.

Charlotte shifted in her chair and held back tears at the thought of him. This ought to be the happiest of occasions. Her sister had wed a kind gentleman who could support both her and Charlotte. She should not be contemplating a gentleman whom she was unlikely to lay eyes on again. They would never again share a chamber or sit together on a settee. But perhaps, late at night, she would see him often in her eye's mind. She would recall their conversations, their walk in the wood, and their dances. She would remember his dress, his scent. She would remember him.

She closed her eyes and indulged herself in her memories.

She had been alone in the library for quite a little while when the door opened and Mr. Card's mother invaded the room like a cold draft.

"Mrs. Card." Charlotte straightened on the upholstered chair. She felt like a child who had been caught in mischief. She did not know precisely what to say, so she blurted, "I am glad you are here. Will you sit with me? I wanted to thank you for allowing me to move into your home."

Mrs. Card puffed up her chest haughtily and did not take a seat. Her wiry gray hair moved stiffly as she shook her head, and her nose wrinkled. "I do not sit with women such as you."

Charlotte opened her mouth and then shut it. There was nothing to be said.

Mrs. Card walked to a bookcase, and with her back to the room, she said, "Mrs. Collins, you know in the past I regarded you in high esteem."

Charlotte steeled herself. She had known that Mrs. Card would not be a bastion of support in her time of need, but she had hoped the lady would have been civil at the very least. "I appreciate that."

Mrs. Card turned, her skirts brushing the books on the bottom shelf, threatening to upend them. "But recent events have caused me to question my original estimation."

"I assure you those events have been grossly exaggerated."

Mrs. Card's chin rose slightly and her eyes narrowed. "As I understand it, Mrs. Collins, there is tangible proof."

It was useless to argue the merits of her case. Her character had already been decided. "It is not as it seems to be, Mrs. Card."

The older woman sighed. "I do want to believe you, but until further proof is laid at my door, I must protect myself and my family. I cautioned Jonas against this marriage, but he loves Maria. And Maria loves you. Therefore, you will live here."

"Again, I thank you."

Her eyes turned to flint. "Do not thank me. It is none of my doing, I assure you. Jonas had defended you quite convincingly, and I almost believe him. I just worry so about my son's reputation."

"I understand. Reputations are quite fragile things." Charlotte ought to know.

Mrs. Card sniffed, as though scenting the air for truth or the origin of an ill odor. "I find it best to retire to my house in London. I leave tomorrow."

She was leaving. It should have been a relief to have such a caustic presence out of her life, but grief rocked Charlotte. Not only had the slander caused her to lose her own home, but now it drove Mrs. Card out of hers.

She stood in protest. "Mrs. Card, I—"

"Do not speak. I am simply too old to bother with this type of nonsense." She sniffed again. Perhaps she had a cold. "Jonas reminds me that this is his and Maria's home now. She is the lady of the house. They must choose their houseguests themselves. It is no longer my place, no matter how heartily I disapprove."

The last words hung heavily in the air, and again Charlotte could think of no suitable reply.

Obviously expecting no response, Mrs. Card left the room, leaving Charlotte alone again. It seemed that being alone was to become her lot in life.

❧ ❧

Charlotte's accommodations at Crumbleigh were more than adequate. Her cottage had boasted of a small bed chamber with moderately comfortable furnishings, but the Cards' home was luxury itself. Her bed was large and covered in soft, inviting linens, and she found that her clothing, which had been unpacked by the servants, did not even fill one of the wardrobes that decorated her bed chamber. Her toiletries had been arranged on her dressing table, but her books remained in their trunk. Charlotte decided to put them in the remaining wardrobe space, even though it was not the proper use for the furniture. She wanted to have them in her chamber, and moreover, she was glad to have a task to occupy her first morning there.

When at last she descended below stairs, she felt rather lost, disoriented in her new surroundings. A servant informed her that Maria and Mr. Card had not yet risen. Charlotte had expected as much, so she entered the breakfast room alone to find an elaborate buffet awaiting her. Perhaps living under the protection of her sister and her husband would not be so very dreadful, she thought as she filled her plate.

After finishing a large meal of sausages, eggs, and muffins and jam, Charlotte pushed away from the table and wondered what to do with herself. There was no menu to plan or shopping lists to make. She had no garden in which to toil, and she did not want to leave the property without wishing the newlyweds every happiness. Besides, she had no calls to pay.

So she decided to take a tour of the house. She had seen most of the public rooms in her visits in years past, but now that this was her home, she viewed things with new eyes.

Crumbleigh was certainly sumptuous, and the rooms were large and lushly furnished, but Charlotte was drawn to the smaller morning room. It was quite a bit larger than her sitting room in the cottage, but it had the same simple air about it that the other rooms home seemed to lack. The fabrics at the windows and on the furniture were light and cheerful, and the walls were a pleasing shade of pale yellow. A small fire in the hearth chased away the morning chill. She wondered who had chosen the décor, for Mrs. Card certainly did not seem the type to choose such joyful accessories. Perhaps there was some goodness in her yet.

Charlotte remained in the morning room and settled herself at the escritoire, a much more elaborate version of the writing desk that had been in the cottage to write a letter to her parents and to her cousins the Emersons. She spent a great deal of time describing Maria's wedding and then found herself without much else to relate, so she closed the letters, sealed them with a wafer, and called a servant to see to their delivery.

Charlotte took several turns about the room and then selected a book of very poor poetry from a shelf and attempted to entertain herself with snide thoughts about the verse.

Maria and Mr. Card did not arrive downstairs until quite late that afternoon, and when they appeared, Charlotte found herself inordinately pleased to see them. She dropped the book, stood, and greeted them warmly.

The newlyweds sat together on the settee, and Charlotte found that she could not quite decipher Maria' mood. She wondered if her sister regretted her decision after only one night as a married woman. Mr. Card, however, was quite talkative, although Charlotte did not find the subject altogether pleasing. "I suppose you are aware by now that Mama left this morning for her house in town."

"Yes," Charlotte hung her head slightly. "I spoke with her yesterday at your wedding breakfast. I am afraid it is my fault that she has left her home."

"No indeed," Maria said. "She is just a closed-minded shrew who would not know the truth if it stepped on her foot!"

"Maria!"

Mr. Card arrested her with a quick hand gesture. "My wife," he blushed at the word and continued, "is quite correct, although I would not have used that precise wording. My mother has fallen victim to the unfortunate gossip that has been spread about you, but once we clear your good name, she will return home and all will be well."

"Mr. Card, you are very kind, but I do not believe there is anything to be done to rectify the situation." Charlotte glanced from Mr. Card to Maria. "I do appreciate your faith in me, but how can you possibly support me in the face of the evidence?"

"Time will make the truth evident."

Charlotte snorted.

"No, no. Listen to your new brother-in-law," he insisted. "If you will recall, Maria rejected my first proposal."

Maria's eyebrows knit together, but her voice was well-moderated when she said, "Oh, do not bring that up!"

"Patience, my dear." He turned back to Charlotte, his face set. "I have always loved Maria, and I knew that deep down, she loved me too. I just had to wait for the circumstances to make the truth evident to her. The same thing will happen to you."

Charlotte was not sure she believed him, but she smiled at his obvious fancy for Maria. If sister did not love him, at the very least, he loved her. And that was something. Perhaps that would be sufficient for a pleasant marriage. She said, "Until then, I intend to stay out of society."

"You will go mad in this house all the time, Charlotte."

"I knew you would prefer to stay out of society, which is precisely why I have taken it upon myself to make your time here more pleasurable."

"Oh, Mr. Card, what have you done?" Maria asked, concerned.

"I have made an addition to our staff. Mrs. Effingham and her son begin work in our household. Mrs. Eff will be your personal companion, Mrs. Collins. I think that you will soon be quite happy indeed."

Joy spread through Charlotte and she clasped her hands together. A smile stretched across her face. Maria appeared genuinely pleased for the first time that morning, and she spoke before Charlotte could muster a reply, "Oh, how thoughtful of you!"

"Mrs. Eff will work here?" Charlotte asked, testing the words and feeling the attendant pleasure they brought.

"Indeed she shall. I knew how attached you were to her, and I wanted to make you comfortable in your new home."

"I confess I am pleased indeed," Charlotte said, emotions rising in her throat. "You are very good to us, Mr. Card."

Hiring Mrs. Eff and Edward had been very kind of him. Not only would she have a companion, but she would have news—not gossip, news—from town and a little laughter.

Mr. Card rose and extending his hand to Maria. "Shall we take to stroll about the gardens? It appears to be a very fine day."

Maria seemed reluctant, but she took his hand and stood. "Yes, it is a very fine day."

Charlotte was quite sure Maria had not so much as glanced outside at the weather. Charlotte kept her place in the morning room and watched as they exited arm in arm.

She found that she was quite pleased at the turn of events. She had never expected Mr. Card to employ her former servants. And as uncomfortable as she was admitting that she required a champion, she was pleased to have Mr. Card to act on her behalf.

He had never struck her as the sort of man who would be a champion. Certainly, he had always been a very nice boy, but now he was acting as a proper man should. He was strong without being commanding, kind without being weak, and caring without being overly sensitive. Perhaps being married suited him, or perhaps finally being out of his mother's sphere of influence had allowed him to be the man he had always been prevented from being.

❧ Twenty-one ❧

Later that week, when the servant entered the morning room to announce the name of the caller who stood in the hallway, Charlotte could not have been more surprised, even if the butler had announced the name of the king himself. She jumped from the escritoire, where she had been composing a letter to Elizabeth, and tipped her chair backward. She caught the teetering piece of furniture just as the visitor entered the room.

The woman was plump and wore a dress of striped muslin, which defined the topography of her body, each bulging contour delineated in painful clarity. Her hair was done in tight ringlets that Charlotte knew had taken a maid ages to arrange.

But there was no bird in her coiffure at present.

Charlotte was shocked into immobility. She did not even think to curtsey. "Mrs. Holloway."

"Mrs. Collins."

The two women stared at each other. Tension radiated from Mrs. Holloway's face in tight lines that began at her mouth and stretched her puffy features until her eyes appeared thin and hard. Charlotte had the vague impression that Mrs. Holloway had arrived to demand a duel, and she sincerely hoped that Mr. Card kept no swords in the house.

"I had not expected.... Will you sit?" Charlotte gestured broadly at the room, and Mrs. Holloway chose a high-backed chair across from the escritoire. Charlotte continued to stand.

"I will come straight to the heart of the matter."

Charlotte nodded. Time seemed to slow, and she knew that something serious was amiss. She and Mrs. Holloway had never been companions. They had only one thing in common.

"This is about Edgington."

That was, unfortunately, the one thing.

Charlotte's fingers wrapped around the back of the desk chair that stood behind her. "Mr. Edgington?"

"Yes, Edgington." Charlotte began to fidget, and Mrs. Holloway stared at her again, undoubtedly noticing her discomfiture and lack of coherent response. "Are you daft?"

Why was Charlotte allowing herself to become so disconcerted? She had no reason to be intimidated by this woman. In fact, Mrs. Holloway may not be Mr. Edgington's lover, but an unwilling victim, blackmailed into an affair, just as he had attempted with Charlotte.

She felt her defenses fortify. "No, I am not daft." She turned the desk chair so that it faced her guest and sat down. "Tell me the purpose of this visit immediately."

"Edgington is mine."

Clearly, she was not an unwilling participant.

"I certainly have no connection to him."

"Do you not?" She produced something from her reticule. A piece of white fabric. She held it out and allowed it to unfold, the material sliding to dangle in midair. It took a moment for the object's identity to register in Charlotte's mind, but then she realized what it was. Her glove! "Does not this belong to you?"

"I...I..." Charlotte had never thought to see that glove again and certainly not in the hands of Mrs. Holloway. She inhaled deeply and tried to think clearly, but only questions came. Should she own it? What would that mean for her reputation? Was Mrs. Holloway also here to blackmail her?

"It has your initials embroidered here." She ran her fingers over the pale blue threads, much as Mr. Edgington had done the night he had stolen it from her.

If only Charlotte had not allowed Mary to stitch the cursed things! If only she had never accepted them from Mr. Edgington. Had never even met him.

"You may as well admit it, Mrs. Collins, for I have heard the gossip as well. You gave this to my Edgington as a token of your feelings for him."

Anger prompted Charlotte to stand. "I did no such thing. I have no feelings for him, except utter disdain."

Mrs. Holloway snorted like a nervous horse. "I also observed you with him at the theater in London." Charlotte stepped back. She had been observed with the man in London. Would her downfall never end?

"Do not appear so shocked. I concealed myself well. Even Edgington did not see me. Of course, I believed your meeting to be a product of chance, but then I saw the two of you dancing at the Armitage's ball. I knew then how you felt about him."

Charlotte remembered that dance, how he had leered. How she had blushed. "You misinterpreted."

"I think not, for in the coming weeks, I discovered this in his armoire, and I knew the rumors were true. You have been pursuing him!" She waved the glove at her. "He would have nothing to do with a woman like you. You are old and spindly. He prefers a woman with buxom qualities."

Charlotte gritted her teeth and strode across the room, rapidly closing the distance between them. When her skirts brushed those of Mrs. Holloway, she stopped and looked down at the surprised woman. Charlotte's eyes narrowed. So did Mrs. Holloway's. For a moment neither woman moved.

Charlotte leaned down and snatched the glove from Mrs. Holloway's hand. The fabric glided out of her chubby grasp with a soft whooshing sound. Without considering the consequences of her actions, she crossed the room and hurled it into the fireplace. She watched as it caught fire and listened to the crackle as it burned. Her anger smoldered.

When the glove had become nothing more than a charred mass, she turned back to Mrs. Holloway. She had not moved from her seat. Her back was rigid and her hands were balled in her lap. "I am pleased that you destroyed it," she said. "Now the evidence of your feelings for him is gone, and he will soon forget you."

Yes, the evidence was gone! He no longer had power over her. "I hope he never thinks on me again."

Mrs. Holloway looked at her for long moments, and then her face fell. When she spoke, her voice was softer, and she sounded like a young child. "I love him."

"Mrs. Holloway." Charlotte stumbled over the name. How could a married woman throw herself on the unmerciful Mr. Edgington? "I assure you that nothing is between your...companion...and me."

She nodded at the fireplace. "What about the glove?"

Charlotte hesitated. She did not want to give Mrs. Holloway power over her by telling her of the blackmail. She did not believe her to be an evil woman, but under Mr. Edgington's influence, how could she be certain? Still, she did not want her to believe it an amorous gift. Charlotte could only think to say, "It was nothing."

"You are not pursuing an affair with him?"

She could honestly answer in the negative. "I will have nothing to do with Mr. Edgington, I assure you."

Mrs. Holloway's face hardened again. The little girl voice was gone. "You may have gained his attentions in the past, but see that you do not come near Edgington again."

Charlotte looked at the ridiculous woman. Her leverage was gone, and still she spoke as though she had control of the situation. But the power now belonged to Charlotte. "See that you never mention that glove to a soul." Here Charlotte hesitated, considered, and then forged on. "For I will be forced to confirm the rumors that have been circulating about you, and I will name your accomplice. I will tell all that I know about your affair with Mr. Edgington. And I know a great deal more than you suppose."

Mrs. Holloway's eyes widened. In her anger, it was obvious she had forgotten her need to conceal the affair. Her mouth worked reflexively but only the following emerged: "I...I...."

"All of Westerham will know of your evenings spent with Mr. Edgington in London. About your forays to the theater." Mrs. Holloway's eyes widened to an alarming degree, but Charlotte pressed onward. "How do you suppose your husband will react when he discovers the truth?"

Charlotte could not fathom how Mr. Holloway might react. The sum of her knowledge of him was that his wife was unfaithful and that he had an uncommon love of porcine creatures. How was she to determine the mind of a gentleman of such tastes?

Again, the women stared at each other. One innocent, one sullied. The fire crackled in the background.

Mrs. Holloway stood. Her tense face cracked into a strained smile. "I believe we have come to an amicable agreement, Mrs. Collins, and I will trouble you no longer."

Charlotte wondered if this were some ruse, some trick to lull her into complacency. Would she now call for that duel?

But nothing untoward occurred. Both women curtseyed and bid each other good day. To any observer, the conclusion of their visit looked like any other benign call. Charlotte returned to her seat at the desk and watched as Mrs. Holloway's striped gown disappeared out the door.

Charlotte's bravado also disappeared.

What had just occurred?

She tried to think, but her mind seemed sluggish.

She had destroyed the glove. That, at the very least, was a benefit. However, she could not feel good about the methods she had used with Mrs. Holloway. Were they not the same methods Mr. Edgington had employed on her?

She sat many minutes, but soon she fancied that she could smell the charred glove amid the other fire scents. It choked her, and she took to her bed chamber where she remained until the next morning.

⚬ ⚬ ⚬

"Wake up!" a voice said all too cheerily. Charlotte heard a tray, presumably containing breakfast, deposited on the bedside table with a ceremonious thunk. She thought she could smell muffins, and she opened her eyes to confirm. Yes. Muffins.

She struggled to make her tired body sit upright and pulled the covers over her protectively. She reached for one and realized that the servant had not left.

"Mrs. Eff!" Charlotte jumped out of bed, the covers still tangled around her, and embraced her.

"Oh, go on with you now," Mrs. Eff protested. "It is not as if we have not seen each other in years."

Charlotte released her, ever so glad to have her there. "It seems like years to me. So much has occurred."

"Indeed it has. Look at you in your fine new home. And Miss Maria married. I suppose I should call her Mrs. Card now, should I not?"

"You may call her whatever you like, for I am just so pleased to see you. And how does Edward? Is he here as well?"

"He is working under the butler, a very kind man if my impression is correct. He will make a decent manservant out of my boy."

"Oh, I am so pleased, but I did not expect you so soon."

"Sometimes the unexpected can be good, and not evil."

"That has not been my experience."

Mrs. Eff observed her for some time. "Has something else occurred?"

Charlotte sat on the edge of the bed and revealed her encounter with Mrs. Holloway. "And I have descended to Mr. Edgington's level by extorting Mrs. Holloway."

Mrs. Eff had remained quiet during the recitation, her eyes serious. "I see no reason for you to experience such guilt."

"Do you not?" Hopelessness was in her voice.

"No, I do not, for you were innocent, but Mrs. Holloway is not. Moreover, she was threatening you. You had no choice but to act."

"There is always a choice."

"Oh, stop being so dramatic. Think of the good you have done. You have saved yourself. You destroyed the only tangible evidence Mr. Edgington possessed, and you have assured the secrecy of his consort. You are free."

Was she correct?

Was Charlotte free?

Mrs. Eff did not allow Charlotte the luxury of contemplation. She pulled her from her seated position on the bed. "Enough of this. Now, get up! It is time for you to get back out into the world."

Charlotte offered meek resistance while Mrs. Eff pushed her through her morning toilette and out the door, threatening to accompany her should she resist. So Charlotte did not resist. Mrs. Eff was unresistable.

The prospect of going to town had disconcerted Charlotte, but soon she became excited. Perhaps she had freed herself.

But as she walked through the shops, she was aware that people whispered about her. Of course, she should have foreseen that response. It was the treatment she had received since Mr. Edgington had slandered her. She should not be surprised, for it was the natural response of people who still believed her to be a fallen woman.

She was tempted to permit her spirits fall low again, but she had destroyed the glove! Mr. Edgington's power was effectually gone. She simply had to find a way to make her innocence known now that Mr. Edgington could no longer refute her.

Several hours had passed, and she was running out of shops to patronize and items to consider. She was beginning to lose hope of clearing her name.

Not a soul had spoken to her, and she could not initiate the conversation herself, for that would only give the appearance of desperation.

Then, in the milliner's shop, she encountered old Mrs. Farmington. They quite literally bumped into each other while searching through a table of bonnets. She had not taken note of her, for older lady nearly blended in with the powdery white walls.

They each apologized, and when Mrs. Farmington was preparing to excuse herself, Charlotte stopped her, saying, "How have you been, Mrs. Farmington? And your family, are they all well?"

"Very well, thank you, Mrs. Collins. And you?" Her voice was dry and uncertain.

"Very well indeed." Charlotte steeled herself for a difficult conversation. "You have heard that my sister has married Mr. Card?"

"Indeed I have." Her words were awkward, hesitant, as if trying to determine the course of the conversation before it occurred. "May I wish them every happiness."

"And please convey our well wishes to your granddaughter and Mr. Westfield."

A flush spread across Mrs. Farmington's weathered, pale cheeks. Charlotte was pleased to see that embarrassment, for it meant that the older woman was not going to gloat over her granddaughter's capture of Mr. Westfield.

"The marriage did not occur the way we would have done it years ago. Children today, it seems, have a different way of viewing things." She turned her head to issue a brittle cough. "I am sorry for any pain it may have caused your sister, but I cannot help but be pleased by my granddaughter's fortuitous match. I only regret the manner in which it occurred."

"Pray, do not make yourself uneasy, Mrs. Farmington. The situation served a greater purpose. It taught Maria that she had always had a fondness for Mr. Card. Now, it seems that everyone is happy."

"I know my Constance experienced terrible pain over the affair." Mrs. Farmington winced at her own choice of words. "She had always valued your sister as a friend, and it was difficult for her to be in love with Miss Lucas's beau."

Charlotte fought the urge to roll her eyes. She doubted that Miss Farmington had experienced any such difficulty. "Maria harbors no ill feelings toward Mr. or Mrs. Westfield."

"That is very kind of her, for she is entitled to be quite angry, really."

"I can assure you that Maria is far from angry, and I know she would want to convey her best wishes to the Westfields."

Mrs. Farmington sighed in relief and the two women continued to carry on a very polite conversation until Mrs. Farmington finally said, "I am surprised to see you out and about, what with the things I have heard about you of late."

For once, Charlotte was pleased at Mrs. Farmington's bent for choosing inappropriate topics of conversation. She put down the bonnet she had been considering and gave Mrs. Farmington a steady look. This was her moment of vindication, and she would not spoil it. "None of those things are true, Mrs. Farmington. Why do you choose to accept his lies about my character?"

Her features seemed to harden slightly, and she huffed. "As much as I hate to say it, Mrs. Collins, I have heard there was proof."

"Have you seen this proof?" Charlotte knew that Lady Catherine had seen it, but had anyone else? Charlotte did not know if Mr. Edgington had simply hinted at the glove's existence or if he had displayed it for the townspeople to see. Had Mrs. Holloway shown anyone? Certainly not, for she had her own secrets to conceal.

"No, I have not."

"Has anyone of your acquaintance seen proof?"

Here Mrs. Farmington paused. Anxiety filled Charlotte. "No, I suppose not."

Charlotte sighed inwardly. No one ever would see that glove. She was safe.

Mrs. Farmington continued, "But it seems unlikely that Mr. Edgington would claim to have proof that he did not possess."

Charlotte was fortified by her newfound knowledge. "I am sorry to be harsh on any person, but Mr. Edgington is an unscrupulous individual and he meant to do far worse than merely damaging my reputation."

"So you claim that there is no proof?"

"Indeed, there is none. You may apply to Mr. Edgington himself, but I guarantee that he will not be able to supply it."

"Really?" Disbelief hunched in the creases of her skin.

"Truly. Ask him. Good manners prevent me from saying anything negative about that gentleman beyond the fact that he has done me a great disservice in this community. I will hide no longer. I am not guilty of that which he has accused me."

"You sound quite convincing." Mrs. Farmington eyed her. "I do so wish to believe you, if only because of your kind forgiveness of my dear Constance."

"You ought to believe me, for I speak only the truth, Mrs. Farmington. I do not deserve the censure of this town."

"Well, my dear, all I can say is that the truth will set you free. And I hope it does."

◈◈◈

As Charlotte had hoped, word of her encounter with old Mrs. Farmington spread quickly around Westerham. Although Charlotte had grown to despise gossip, she was thankful it moved so swiftly. According to

Mrs. Eff, who had friends in many major households, it was generally agreed that Charlotte's insistence upon applying to Mr. Edgington for proof had removed any need to do so. The fact that she was willing to offer such a course of action proved that no such evidence existed and that her poor reputation had been undeserved.

Soon, invitations, which had been scarcer than a daisy in December, began to arrive. Friends began to pay calls, and Charlotte cautiously began to enjoy Westerham society again.

However, the Charlotte who returned to society was ever so much more guarded. If being married to Mr. Collins had made her wary of her reputation in society, the situation with Mr. Edgington caused her to become extremely vigilant. Her reputation was all she had. She no longer had her independence or her cottage. She was very thankful for her small income and for her sister's generosity, and she would not dishonor Maria again by her actions in society.

While Maria and Mr. Card attended almost every event to which they were invited, Charlotte restricted herself to attending only small parties or gatherings held at Crumbleigh. She declined invitations to large assemblies and balls and was careful never to be alone with a gentleman even for the briefest of moments.

Maria had told her repeatedly that she was being ridiculous, but Charlotte would not budge, claiming that she preferred to remain in the morning room at Crumbleigh rather than risk humiliation again.

In truth, Charlotte found something lacking in the society to which she had returned. The parties were not as exciting, and the concept of a ball somehow lacked the intrigue that such an assembly had formerly possessed. The card parties were duller, and the dinners, while delicious, did not inspire her the way they once had. There was no sparkling conversation that sparkled enough or clever repartee witty enough to entertain her. She considered the reasons for this lack, but she was loath to admit the truth—that Mr. Basford was the missing element.

To her great frustration, over the intervening months, she found herself thinking of him more often than she wished. Sometimes he would slip into her thoughts as she sat reading letters in the morning room with her slippered feet tucked beneath her. He appeared in her mind when she was dressing herself for bed, which disconcerted her greatly. Why would he be so stuck in her mind? He was not a suitor; he was barely even to be considered a friend. It should not be such an ordeal to forget him.

She had practically succeeded in her quest to stop thinking of Mr. Basford, except for an occasional lapse—perhaps fifteen to twenty times per day—when the letter arrived from her cousin Mary Emerson in London and brought him back to the forefront of her mind.

She read the words quickly, eagerly consuming the news of her family and friends in town, but when she saw Mr. Basford's name appear in Mrs. Emerson's neat script, she read it very carefully. Twice.

I have the most interesting news of Mr. Benjamin Basford. As you no doubt recall, I was acquainted with his sister before she moved to America. You may imagine my surprise even to hear his name mentioned in London, for I was quite sure you had told me that he returned to Savannah some months ago. However, I had the pleasure of meeting him at a dinner party given by mutual friends just last evening. After speaking at great length about his family in Savannah—all are doing well, by the way—I told him of my relationship with you, dear Charlotte.

He inquired after you with more than a passing interest and was very desirous to know about your current situation. I related the happy news of your sister's marriage and explained that you are now living at the Cards' home. I had not expected the look of consternation that crossed his features. I confess I still do not comprehend the reason for it. Perhaps you will understand.

Searching for a topic of conversation less disagreeable to him, I then told him that you believed him to be in America. He proceeded to give me the explanation for which you are undoubtedly waiting. He was, apparently, instrumental in securing passage for the new Mr. and Mrs. Westfield, and he had originally intended to accompany them when they departed, believing, he said, that there was nothing left for him in England. However, he altered his plans at the last moment, electing instead to return to London where he has taken a small house. We had a pleasant conversation about the goings on in Westerham at the end of which he asked me if I thought he would be welcome to return despite his nephew's misconduct. I hope I did not answer incorrectly by telling him he would certainly be welcome. He seemed quite eager to be off, and I would not be surprised to hear that he beat this letter to you, my dear Charlotte.

For the remainder of the letter, Mary described renovations that she and Mr. Emerson had planned for their home, but after reading the news of Mr. Basford, Charlotte could not possibly concentrate on the merits of French interior design as opposed to the current rococo fashion.

Mr. Basford was to return.

He might be in Westerham already.

Charlotte untucked her legs and sat up straighter, looking around the morning room as though he might walk in at any moment. That was absurd, of course.

She reread the letter several more times, attempting in vain to interpret the precise meaning of Mr. Basford's conversation with her cousin. He had inquired after Charlotte "with more than a passing interest." What precisely did that signify? He could be concerned merely about her living situation, but her heart wondered. Could he possibly be concerned about her beyond the boundaries of casual acquaintance?

Charlotte had felt something more from him. He had been very attentive on their walk when they encountered each other near the cottage that day. They had danced together, and the experience was not unpleasant. They were, in truth, very pleasant dances indeed. Then, there was the time when they had been on the settee in her cottage and he had almost touched her hand.

She could not easily forget the sensation that shimmered through her body as she watched his hand draw closer. She had wanted to feel his fingers against hers. And she could distinctly remember the disappointment that cut into her when Maria had entered the room.

Certainly, Charlotte would never forget the way Mr. Basford had aided her that fateful evening at the ball when Mr. Edgington had begun his campaign against her. He had distracted her and fortified her. He had danced with her, and his every touch seemed to give her strength.

Although his attempt to marry his nephew to Maria was misguided, it was meant to protect her.

He had failed miserably, and Charlotte had been rightfully troubled, but with the benefit of a little perspective, she felt kinder toward him. A great deal kinder.

She only hoped that they would have an occasion to meet when he returned to Westerham. Despite the fact that she truly wanted to have the opportunity to speak with him, she would not break her rules. They would meet appropriately. They would be in a public place and among friends. She would ask his forgiveness for her earlier outbursts, and then they would continue as good friends.

She would not allow herself to hope for anything more.

Charlotte was an old widow, and Mr. Basford had displayed gentlemanly consideration of her. Perhaps he had felt kindly toward her, but it would be foolish to dare to hope.

However, Charlotte could not help herself.

And she called herself every kind of a fool.

ᴥᴥ Twenty-two ᴥᴥ

"Pray, excuse me. Did you say something about Mr. Basford?" Charlotte asked. She was sitting at the breakfast table with her sister and Mr. Card and was enjoying some very fine sausages. She had been only partially listening to the couple's conversation, for their discussions could be quite tedious, when she thought she heard Mr. Basford's name mentioned.

"Indeed I did, Charlotte. Have you not been listening?" Maria scolded as she buttered a piece of toast.

"I do apologize. I cannot seem to keep my mind focused this morning." Or whenever the conversation centered on ribbons or methods for tying a stylish cravat.

Mr. Card put down his teacup and took up the conversation. "Maria and I saw Mr. Basford in Westerham yesterday when we stopped for lunch."

"We were quite surprised to see him," Maria interjected. "I thought he had escorted Mr. and Mrs. Westfield back to America. In fact, Colonel Armitage relayed that information to me personally. He was quite contrite over the whole debacle between Mr. Westfield and I, you see, and he wanted me to know that I would not have to come upon them unexpectedly in town and have to endure a difficult scene."

"It was a very kind sentiment, though I do not believe it was necessary," Mr. Card said.

"The colonel did not realize that nothing could possibly impede my happiness." Maria waved her butter knife in the air as though to emphasize her thoughts. "I am so content with my life that there is no room in my heart for sadness or awkwardness, even if I were to meet with Mr. and Mrs. Westfield every day of the week."

The couple smiled at each other, and Charlotte felt jealousy stir in her. Even if she was not in love, her sister seemed happy. Would Charlotte ever be so?

She steered the conversation back to Mr. Basford, asking if he seemed well.

"Indeed, he did," said Mr. Card.

"We spoke to him for a little while before our meal arrived," Maria explained. "He congratulated us on our marriage and was very kind indeed."

"Did he say how long he has been in town?" Charlotte kept her attention focused on her forked sausage.

"I believe he said he arrived last Monday and is staying again with his uncle," Mr. Card replied.

He had not called on Charlotte, and he had been in town since last Monday. More than a full week had passed. Perhaps he did not want to see her after all.

Charlotte tried not to allow herself to be disappointed.

"Mr. Card and I invited him to our dinner party on Saturday."

"And did he accept the invitation?"

"He seemed rather unsure, saying that Colonel Armitage had been keeping his schedule rather full of late and asked permission to check with him first. We assured him that he would be welcome, as would the colonel."

"I wonder what the colonel has him doing," Charlotte mused.

"Hunting, I expect. You know what a great hunter he is, and this cool weather often coaxes the deer from the woods."

"I do not see why he would choose to hunt all day and miss our party. It is possible, is it not, to attend both?" Maria whined.

"My dear, hunting is a taxing activity. Guns are much heavier than they appear. He may be quite exhausted after a day in the wilderness."

"Well, even if he may not attend the party, I invited him to call at our house any time that was convenient for him. I hold nothing against him."

Charlotte smiled at her sister's attitude toward her past circumstances, but the brightness of her smile could only be attributed to the news of Mr. Basford.

He had been invited to call.

Maria and Mr. Card continued their conversation, but Charlotte paid them little attention. Her anticipation rose even higher, causing her hands to shake slightly and her appetite to dissipate. She returned the fork and sausage to her plate and began to fidget with the napkin in her lap.

When would he come?

Would he come at all?

ঞ৹ ৹ঞ

By Thursday, several days later, Mr. Basford had still not paid a call at Mr. Card's home, and Charlotte fought her disappointment. She remained very distracted. With every knock at the door, she hoped it was Mr. Basford. Every footstep in the hallway toward the morning room was Mr. Basford's. Every voice sounded like his.

But still he did not come.

And Charlotte could not prevent herself from being disappointed. She could, however, prevent Mr. Card and Maria from seeing it, and she spent the majority of her time trying to distract herself with small jobs around the house with Mrs. Eff. That very afternoon she and Mrs. Eff were going to rearrange her wardrobe, putting away her summer dresses and taking her winter gowns and cloak out of storage. It was a rather dull task that she could have left to Mrs. Eff, but she needed to keep herself busy so Mr. Basford would not sneak into her thoughts.

Charlotte had just completed a rather fine afternoon repast with Maria and Mr. Card, but she barely tasted the sweet biscuits and Chinese tea and she hardly heard a word that was spoken.

"Charlotte?" she heard Maria say.

Guiltily, Charlotte met her eyes.

"Have you not heard a word we have said?"

"I do apologize. My mind has been at sixes and sevens today."

"That is not like you at all. Perhaps you are ill. Are you feeling quite well?"

Charlotte assured her that she was very well indeed, just distracted.

"Mr. Card and I are going for a walk after breakfast, would you like to join us since you are not ill?" She seemed to desire her company, probably to serve as a buffer from her husband.

"I think not. My mind is too preoccupied to allow me to be a proper companion. Besides Mrs. Eff and I have a project upstairs."

Maria rolled her pretty blue eyes. "Whatever you wish, but I do not see why you would turn down a walk on a lovely day for tedious indoor work."

"Do enjoy your walk. Do not worry about me. I am fine. Besides, tedium is sometimes good for the soul." Had not marriage to Mr. Collins been proof of that?

Soon, the couple departed, leaving Charlotte to her task with Mrs. Eff.

She climbed the stairs to her bedchamber, which was in a lovely part of the house that faced the front park. From her window, she had a delightful view of the small fishpond and the drive up to the house. The front lawn was elegantly manicured, and Charlotte not only enjoyed seeing it from the window, but she also enjoyed walking across the grass in the morning when it was still wet with dew.

Now it was later in the morning, and Charlotte stood in the window, waiting for Mrs. Eff to arrive and watching as sun descended through the trees that stood along the edge of the property. Their leaves had begun to change from lush green to radiant yellows, oranges, and reds.

Mrs. Eff had cracked the window slightly, allowing the cool autumn air to freshen the room. Although the air caused goose bumps to rise on her skin, she did not close the window.

Charlotte loved the fall—the scent of fallen leaves and the crisp feeling in the air.

Perhaps she should have gone on that walk with Maria and Mr. Card after all. Instead, she stood at the window and looked down the drive. She began to imagine. A single rider on a bay horse. Mr. Basford's horse. He would come. He would be shabbily dressed, but his words would not be so shabby. He would propose and Charlotte would accept. They would be married and go together into the future. A secure and happy future.

Charlotte blinked away her thoughts. She focused her mind and gaze again on the driveway. There was no movement on the horizon, but as she looked out the window, she began to become conscious of movement in her soul.

She must see Mr. Basford. She must! And if he would not come to her, she would go to him.

She could put on her sturdy boots and walk to Colonel Armitage's house straightaway. It was not so long a distance, and it was a flat path. She would be home by supper, and no one need know the nature of her trip. Indeed, she would pay a traditional morning call. There was nothing untoward about that. And if she happened to meet with Mr. Basford and perhaps attempt to make her feelings known, then so be it.

No! What was she thinking. She must not do such a thing. Her recently tattered reputation was not fully mended. She must be careful.

Charlotte's hands gripped the windowsill.

Taking a deep breath, she turned and crossed the room to the wardrobe. Inside, she found the small wooden jewelry box where she had hidden the glove Mr. Basford had loaned her the night of Mr. Edgington's deceit. Underneath her accoutrements, she saw the fine fabric of his glove. She had not allowed herself to think of that glove since the day she had put it away. She had tried not to remember the kindness it represented, and she certainly did not touch its soft fabric as she was now.

She should destroy the glove. It should meet the same fate as the gloves given to her by Mr. Edgington. She glanced at the hearth, knowing what she ought to do. She would not be free of Mr. Basford until the glove, the only remnant of their friendship, was gone.

But she simply could not do it.

Running the tip of her index finger along the contours of the glove one last time, she closed the box. Mr. Basford was gone, but she was not ready to release him completely.

୧୭୧ ୨୭୧

With each step of her boots, Charlotte vacillated between retreat and determination. Left boot, retreat. Right boot, determination. Left, right, left, right. Retreat, determination, retreat, determination. Her steps carried her onward, closer to Colonel Armitage's house.

She had planned to be careful, to be above reproach, and yet here she was, paying a call on a gentleman. What could she possibly be thinking?

She was not thinking. That fact was very plain. She was employing her heart, not her head, and she refused to allow herself to contemplate the wisdom of doing so. She simply continued walking.

In due course, she stood before the colonel's house. Of only moderate size, it seemed to tower above her now, looking ominous and foreboding. But Charlotte did not even consider the option of returning home. She had gone too far to allow her fears to dissuade her. Her heart was at stake.

Slowly, Charlotte walked up the front steps—left, right, left, right—and brushed the dust off her skirt. She checked her bonnet and tucked in stray wisps of hair. She was determined to look the best she could after such a long walk, even though she realized the low value Mr. Basford placed on fashion.

She raised her hand to knock, but stopped short, remembering to fetch her card from her reticule. Mrs. Charlotte Collins, it said in plain black script. So proper and detached. And she wondered if this prim Mrs. Charlotte Collins would recognize the slightly disheveled woman on Colonel Armitage's doorstep.

This time when she lifted her hand to the door knocker, metal struck metal, and the sharp sound seemed to echo around her. She heard the muffled footsteps of the butler approaching the door. It opened with a whoosh of air, and a large gentlemen greeted her. "Good morning, madam."

"Good morning," she handed him her card. "Is Mrs. Armitage at home?"

He took the card and glanced at her name before dropping it in the receiving bowl on the hall table, and Charlotte got the distinct impression that he did not believe the prim name on the card matched the woman standing before him. She brushed at her gown again.

"I am sorry, madam, but she is not at home this morning."

"Oh dear." What was she to do? She had depended upon Mrs. Armitage's being at home to receive callers this morning. Charlotte glanced behind the butler, hoping that Mr. Basford would appear as if by magic. But the hallway was empty.

Charlotte joined her hands in front of her gown and dropped her eyes. Was she to have gone all this way for naught? She could not allow that. She had already risked her reputation; why not see her task to completion? She raised her chin and found the butler still looking at her. "Is the family at home?"

"No, I am afraid they are all out this morning."

Out? Charlotte wanted to shout. All of them? The colonel? Mr. Basford? Everyone? How could they be out? She must see Mr. Basford. She simply must.

"Mr. Basford. Is he in?" Her words sounded tight.

"He too is out, madam." The butler was clearly losing patience. "No one is at home. They are all *out*." The last word was annunciated as though Charlotte were an imbecile.

"Oh." Charlotte's mind raced. What should she do?

"My apologies," he said, slowly closing the door. "Good day."

The heavy oak door drew closer and closer to Charlotte's face, and she was frozen, wondering what course of action, if any, to take. If the door closed, she would have no choice but to return home a failure. Suddenly, one word escaped her tight lips: "Wait!"

Startled, the butler halted the door's progress and stared at her. Charlotte had startled herself and for a moment said nothing. What would she do? What could she do? She must say something. She could not stand here staring at the butler all day.

"May I be of service, madam?"

She gathered her courage. "Yes, you may. I would like to leave a note, if I might, for Mr. Basford. I require a quill, ink, and sheet of writing paper, if you please."

He did not appear pleased by her request, but he did not argue. "Yes madam." He opened the door fully. "If you will follow me."

The butler led her into the sitting room and to a small, well-appointed escritoire. She seated herself in the chair and immediately took up quill and paper. What would she say? She had never written a letter of this nature to a gentleman. The butler's voice broke into her thoughts. "I will return for the letter in a few moments."

Charlotte had already forgotten the butler and nodded in annoyance. She understood his message. She would not be left unattended long to write her inappropriate note. Her fingers tightened on the quill, and she began the letter:

Mr. Basford—

But the words would not come. She did not know how to convey all that was in her heart in a letter with a butler waiting to sweep her out of the house like yesterday's refuse. She huffed out a sigh. Perhaps this was a poorly conceived idea after all. She dropped the quill on the paper, causing ink to pool in the corner. She stared at the stain.

The paper was ruined. She was ruined. It was all ruined!

Charlotte grasped the paper in her hands and prepared to crumple it, but a dull sound entered her mind. The butler's heavy footsteps approached from a distance. She had no more time. He would escort her to the door and not readmit her. She could not allow herself to be indecisive.

Charlotte quickly replaced the paper on the desk and picked up the quill, and after dipping it in fresh ink, she began to scribble furiously. Her handwriting barely resembled that of a genteel lady. It looked more like an animal had danced across the page with muddy feet. But Charlotte paid no heed to her penmanship and wrote:

I had hoped to find you at home this morning, but since you are away, I must compose this note. I do so to hope to

see you Saturday at the Cards' dinner party, for I greatly wish
to speak with you.

The door opened and the butler appeared at her side. "Madam?"

"A moment, please," she begged, holding her left hand in stopping gesture.

Searching her mind frantically for a suitable closing, she could find none. The butler cleared his throat, and she glanced at his hard-eyed expression. She had no more time.

Before folding the paper in a hasty configuration and handing it to the butler for delivery, she wrote one word.

Charlotte.

༺ Twenty-three ༻

Charlotte did not at first regret composing the letter to Mr. Basford. She imagined each day that he would arrive, unable to wait until the dinner party to see her. And each evening, when he did not arrive, the tiniest bit of regret crept in.

She had walked miles to pay a call on Mr. Basford. No gently reared woman would do such a thing. She had left a desperate note. No lady of sense would dare write to a gentleman, and certainly not out of desperation. And worse, she had signed her Christian name. Charlotte. No lady would do such a thing in a letter to a gentleman who was not her husband. And no gentleman would misunderstand the implication.

Perhaps Mr. Basford believed she still harbored resentment for his role in the incident between Maria and Mr. Westfield. But that could not be. Her letter was proof enough that she felt kindly toward him. Perhaps he was kindly rejecting her. A horrid thought.

By the day of Maria and Mr. Card's dinner party, Charlotte had neither seen nor heard from Mr. Basford or any of the Armitage family.

She did her best not to appear depressed when in company, but she felt her disappointment keenly. Her final hope was that Mr. Basford would appear at the party, but she knew the possibility was quite remote. He had told Mr. Card and Maria when they had issued the invitation that it was unlikely that he would be able to attend.

Still, on the evening of the party, each time the door opened to admit another guest to the sitting room where they had gathered to converse before dinner, Charlotte turned eagerly to discover who had entered. The appointed time to dine drew nearer and nearer, and still he did not come.

Charlotte talked with the guests, taking an eager interest in them. At least, she hoped she appeared interested. In truth, she had very little idea what had been said to her thus far that evening. She hardly knew to whom she talked. Perhaps she had spoken with the rector. She could not be certain.

Finally, dinner was announced, and Mr. Card escorted Charlotte into the dining room on one arm and his wife on the other. He mouthed the necessary compliments about his good fortune at having two beautiful women to escort, but Charlotte scarcely heard him. Mr. Basford had not come. Her mind cried out in sorrow, but she smiled to those around her.

The dinner consisted of numerous long courses, and each one was more highly lauded for its palatability than the last. Charlotte wished they had served only bread and cheese. It would have been faster.

She was seated next to Maria, who seemed very proud of her position opposite her husband at the head of the table. Speaking only when absolutely necessary, she listened as Maria and her guests talked and concentrated on attempting to push Mr. Basford's rejection from her mind.

The simple fact was that Charlotte would have to accept her life as it was. All in all, it certainly was not a bad life. She had financial security, a lovely shelter in the Cards' home, and the opportunity to buy a new gown now and then. She had a small circle of friends—most of whom were represented at the table—and she had Maria and Mr. Card, and she dearly loved them.

One day, she would be able to view Mr. Basford as a mere acquaintance. Until then, she would try not to think of him at all. Resolved, Charlotte turned her attention to the plates that appeared before her and ate without tasting a bite.

After dinner, the group returned to the sitting room to take tea and coffee and to engage in cards on the tables that Mr. Card and Maria had set up for the occasion.

Several guests left after the meal, citing the chilly night as the reason for their early departures, and the remaining guests chose to play at cards. Charlotte knew she would make a terrible participant in such an endeavor and took a seat on the bench near the fire. She purposefully kept her back to the door so she would not be tempted to look at every servant who entered the room in the vain, foolish hope that Mr. Basford had come.

Charlotte sat on the edge of a light blue brocade armless bench, which the servants had placed conveniently at the back of a settee to provide additional seating for the dinner party guests, with a book resting in her lap. The heavy oak door had been rather busy, admitting servants to clean up the tea things and to keep the fire stoked.

Charlotte had just congratulated herself for not turning around once to see who had come into the room when she felt someone sit on the settee behind her. She assumed that one of the card players from the table behind her had tired of the game and cried off to take a seat by the fire.

"Charlotte," a voice whispered.

Mr. Basford's voice. It washed over her like warm water.

Mr. Basford was on the settee behind her, with his back to her.

He had come!

Suddenly weak, Charlotte's arm, which had been resting decorously on the book in her lap, fell limply at her side, her fingers brushing the brocade fabric on the edge of the bench. Her face reddened, and she glanced around, hoping no one had observed her discomfiture. Everyone was otherwise occupied with their games, and no one even seemed to notice that Mr. Basford had arrived.

"Ben." The whispered word fell from her lips unbidden. She had never used his given name before, and it felt brazen.

She could sense him at her back and smell his woodsy scent mixed with the odor of sun and horses, and she realized he must have come directly from a long ride. She wanted to turn and face him, but propriety prohibited her. Propriety and fear.

"I had to see you. In public, just as you wanted," Mr. Basford whispered.

They were silent a moment, voices murmured around them and the fire crackled softly beside them. His hand casually draped itself over the low arm of the settee, and his fingers brushed against Charlotte's. She jumped at his touch, and then a fire spread through her. His fingers sought hers, first tracing the backs of her knuckles, inviting her to open to him.

She lowered her head and glanced at the card players from beneath her lashes, but there was no one to witness their inappropriate behavior. Everyone was distracted by their games.

"Ben, this is…" she began as his fingers continued to brush hers. But she did not have the will to pull her hand away as she should.

"Inappropriate. I know."

His thumb now traced the contours at the base of Charlotte's hand, which had opened into a loose fist.

His voice was even quieter now, and she had to lean slightly back to hear him. "I am sorry for missing the meal. My uncle and I were at a hunting cabin. It was quite remote, and I did not return home and find your note until this evening."

Relief and understanding flowed over Charlotte. He had rushed to see her. Never had the scent of horses been so welcome.

"And about Miss Lucas and James. It was entirely my fault. I never should have interfered. But it was never about them."

Charlotte could not reply. Her voice would not function, apparently, when he touched her. She swallowed and attempted again to form reassuring words. But they would not come.

"For me, it was never about them." His voice was quiet but insistent.

"But…" she tapered off, trying to think of something practical to say. To explain that she had quite forgotten about Maria and Mr. Westfield and his role in the debacle. That she was not angry. That she had missed him.

"It was about you, Charlotte. I am in love with you." His voice paused, but his fingers continued to stroke the palm of her hand, encouraging her fingers to accept his. "You must believe me when I tell you that I cannot forget you."

"I have not forgotten either," Charlotte said, her voice barely a whisper. Then after a moment, she confessed, "I still have your glove."

She could feel the rasp of his fingertips across her soft palm.

"Marry me." His whisper was rough with restraint.

Charlotte could not speak words of either sense or nonsense at that very moment. Instead, she opened her hand and wove her fingers between his, shuddering slightly at the intimate contact. There they remained, holding hands with the fire as their only witness.

✎⊙◎ Epilogue ◎⊙✎

"I do not think that gentleman likes me one bit," Mr. Basford said as he joined his wife on the settee. He sat closer than propriety dictated, but Charlotte no longer cared. She only snuggled into his dark brown coat and inhaled deeply of his woodsy scent.

"Who? Mr. Darcy?"

"Of course. The Darcys are our only houseguests, aren't they? Mr. Darcy is the only male, I believe. Or is there something you wish to tell me? Have we other visitors hiding in one of the bed chambers?"

Charlotte ignored his jest and answered with as much seriousness as a woman in love can muster. "Mr. Darcy is a gentleman of contradiction. He believes in strict respectability and decorum, but Lizzie tells me he is a loving husband with a humor not visible to most acquaintances. And I know that he would go to the greatest lengths for her."

She smiled as she recalled Mr. Darcy's facial expression when, not more than a half hour ago, he had observed Mr. Basford's curious sitting habits. She giggled. "But I thought he would not be able to contain his disgust when you tilted back on the rear legs of that desk chair."

"I recall seeing that very same look cross your face when I first came to call."

Charlotte leaned back so she could look at him more fully. He had a handsome face, even when he chided her. She lifted her hand and stroked his cheek. "I did not know you as well as I do now. You too are a gentleman of contradictions. You appear to be an uncouth lout, but in reality, your character has many things to recommend itself."

Mr. Basford took hold of Charlotte's hand and brought it to his lips. "And these recommendations are what convinced you to marry me?"

"Indeed. And the fact that I was desperately in love."

"Yes, it was all part of my plan." He grinned. "I gave you no option but to marry me."

Charlotte tucked her feet beneath her, snuggled close again, and thought back on their wedding, which had taken place on an autumn morning in Mr. Collins's former parish church. She found it appropriate that she would marry the man she truly loved in the church where Mr. Collins had delivered countless mind-numbing sermons.

The majority of the sanctuary had stood empty—much as it had for Mr. Collins's Sunday services—but Charlotte hardly noticed. She had begun to be influenced by Mr. Basford's beliefs regarding the need to gain society's good opinion, and although she had not yet done away with her concern completely, she certainly placed a great deal less emphasis on it. Her family and close friends had come to share in her happiness, but she was so besotted by him that she would have been almost as pleased to marry Mr. Basford with only a clergyman and a witness present.

As a wedding gift for his new bride, Mr. Basford had attempted to purchase Charlotte's treasured cottage, but he had met with the resistance of Lady Catherine, and even his charms—and a very large sum of money—could not persuade her to part with the property. Disappointed, he had confessed his attempt to Charlotte. She had been saddened at the news initially, but upon further consideration, she decided that Lady Catherine's unforgiving nature had resulted in a blessing, for the specter of her former patroness would no longer hover over her life.

Although Mr. Basford could afford to purchase a large country manor, the couple had decided to lease a moderately sized house in Westerham, which they christened Basford Cottage. Following the wedding, they took possession, electing to enjoy the peace of the house before departing on their voyage to the New World the following year.

Maria and Mr. Card were frequent visitors to Basford Cottage, and the two couples often went into society together. Mrs. Eff and Edward returned to positions in Charlotte's household. Mrs. Eff served as her lady's maid and confidante, and Edward became Mr. Basford's valet, which he declared to be the perfect position for the young man. Mr. Basford said, "The boy knows very little about fashion, and I find that essential in my valet. Another manservant might attempt to persuade me to adopt some *English attire…*" He spoke the last two words as though they were an epithet. "…and that is unacceptable."

And so their situation at Basford Cottage was ideal.

The Darcys had arrived several months after the wedding, and in the morning room of which Charlotte had become so fond, she and Elizabeth had been able to enjoy their friendship as they had in their youth.

Charlotte, suddenly serious, glanced at her husband. "I am glad Lizzie is here, even if you do cause Mr. Darcy discomfort."

"I believe our fishing excursions are helping him warm somewhat to my informality and casual bearing. Why just yesterday he loosened his cravat before making his first cast. Perhaps before he departs, he may tip his chair onto its back legs."

"I doubt that very much. But I am pleased that Lizzie sees that I have shed my preoccupations with money and propriety and followed my heart." Charlotte smiled. "Of course, she was equally delighted to discover that you could provide well for me, both in feeling and in the security with which every woman must concern herself."

Here Charlotte allowed Mr. Basford the liberty of a long and satisfying kiss. Or perhaps she was the one who had taken the liberty. Nevertheless, their lips met, and he hauled her across his lap, settling her so that more liberties could be taken.

At length, the kiss dwindled, but Charlotte remained draped across Mr. Basford's lap. She sighed into the lapels of his coat, for she knew that she would never have to fear for her security again. For the first time in her life, Charlotte truly believed that she had gained both happiness and security, which did not rest in a large income or in the good opinion of society, but in the relationships she had with her family and friends and in the love she shared with her husband.

❧ Author's Note ❧

I am most indebted to Jane Austen for her creation of the wonderful world and characters of *Pride and Prejudice*. I would also like to thank my family and friends, who ceaselessly supported my dreams. For their contributions to this book and to my life in general, I would like to express my deep gratitude to Bert Becton, Marilyn and Robert Whiteley, Octavia and Ed Becton, Laura Daley, Blaine Rankin, Brenda Godbee, Jill Huggins, and Beverle Graves Myers. Though any errors within this text belong solely to me, I will do my best to foist them upon someone else.

❧ ❧

Maria Lucas

A Short Story

❧ Maria Lucas ☙

"Oh, Charlotte, I have made the most dreadful mistake."

These words came forth from the lips of Maria Card, née Lucas, the moment her sister Charlotte opened the front door and discovered her on the stoop. Behind her, stood her husband Mr. Jonas Card's fine barouche, and its driver was unloading a fine number of trunks and hat boxes from it.

Observing the scene and her sister's countenance and no doubt supposing the reasons for both, Charlotte, in her very practical way, first addressed the parcel-laden driver. "They will fit there, I suppose," she said as she gestured to an empty spot in the foyer. And then to Maria, she said with true feeling, "Oh dear, you must come in and tell me what has happened."

Upon entering, Maria's cold-numbed fingers worked at the ties to her cloak and bonnet, both of the finest quality fabrics of the winter season, and looked at her sister. "What has happened? Why, you may guess the reason yourself, for you predicted it from the beginning."

Finally free of her outerwear, Maria was quite tempted to pitch the lot on the floor in vexation and grief, and but for the actions of her sensible sister, she would have done just that.

"The servants are abed at this hour, and there is no sense in leaving your coat to wrinkle. I will hang it myself." She took the garments from her hands and hung them on pegs while Maria watched, immobilized by the unreality of the drastic actions she had just taken.

Standing there in the hallway of her sister's new home, her hands hanging dejected at her sides and all her worldly goods carried in by the driver, she said, "I do not love my husband." Here, her voice broke, but she shed no tears, for she found she had none left.

Charlotte said not a word, but only took her by the hand and led her to the sitting room where a warm fire burned in the grate and where they were also conveniently away from the ears of her husband's servant. Sensible Charlotte. Always trying to save her from herself. But this time, she doubted there was any sense in trying.

Maria lowered herself onto the settee and looked around the chamber, suddenly feeling loath to elaborate on her sad situation, so she chose to expound on her sister's. "It is a great deal too cheery in this room to suit my disposition. And the hour is quite late for such a fire. It will hardly be banked by morning."

"Yes," Charlotte said, "It is probably a great extravagance in fuel, but I find a nice blaze staves off depression. As you know, my dear sister, my own husband has been in town this past fortnight on business, and I find myself quite unable to sleep without his presence. I have spent a great many hours there in my husband's chair before this fire with a book in my hand."

Maria winced. "You cannot find rest without your husband, and I cannot find rest *with* mine! You were correct in cautioning me against marriage, but I was determined to save us both from destitution. I should have known that I am not the salvific sort."

Charlotte stirred the fire a bit, doubtless taking a moment to collect her thoughts on the matter, and then joined Maria on the settee.

"But it has been months since your marriage, and you have seemed quite at peace until this moment."

Maria could not suppress a long sigh, for she had been holding it in lo these many months. "I suppose for a time I was at peace. I had saved us from returning to our parents' home in shame or, worse, into employment as governesses, and my husband was such a true friend that marrying him seemed but a small sacrifice."

"Has he mistreated you, my dear?"

Maria very nearly giggled. "Mistreated me? No, indeed." She could barely even imagine Mr. Card with enough strength to injure her either physically or emotionally.

A little crease—either born of irritation or confusion, Maria knew not which—formed between Charlotte's eyes. "Then, do tell me what has happened, and do not make me guess, for I am destined to be wrong every time."

Maria tried to keep the resignation from her voice, "After you departed from Crumbleigh, so, it seems, did Mr. Card."

"What do you mean? He has been living elsewhere."

"In all other ways but physically, yes, it seems he has."

"Maria, state plainly what has happened. I am more confused now than when you first arrived."

"Those first days of our marriage hinted at happiness. On the night of our marriage ceremony, we stayed awake until dawn and talked of everything. He told me that he loved me and that he knew one day soon I would fall in love with him as well."

"I view nothing unusual in that."

Maria held up a hand, and she feared that her cheeks had turned pink. "Is it also not unusual for a husband to defer the intimacies of marriage?"

Charlotte reddened. Then, she coughed a bit, and Maria could tell by the mixture of pain—undoubtedly from her memories of her married life with Mr. Collins—and embarrassed pleasure—obviously arising from her current matrimonial situation—that such deferment had not been her experience in either case.

"I thought as much," Maria began and then checked herself.

Charlotte seemed to take a bracing breath. "You have an unusually platonic relationship. In some cases…" Maria knew by the grimace her sister's face pulled that she was referring to Mr. Collins. "…that might be considered a benefit."

"And so I believed at first. Mr. Card was adamant that we would become physically united as husband and wife only when our hearts were first united in love. But upon failing to win my affections over the first month at Crumbleigh, Mr. Card began to disappear more frequently from the house."

"You suspect him of keeping a…."

Apparently, Charlotte was unable to say the word, so Maria supplied it for her, "Mistress?" Here, she paused and thought a bit. "I had not even given a moment's thought to such an idea, and I meant nothing of the sort. But I suppose, however unlikely it seems, that it could be true. But I do not wish to discuss such intimate matters, for they are much too uncomfortable to speak of, even with you my dear sister."

"Oh, thank heavens." Charlotte's entire demeanor relaxed visibly, and as the tension in her face drained away, Maria had the most terrible compulsion to giggle. Though twice married—and thoroughly, Maria imagined, pleased by her current husband—her sister's prudish leanings could not be completely stifled.

Maria, however, was not so becalmed, and she had to issue the prologue to the worst news of all. "Mr. Card's pursuits have seemed much more wholesome, if not precisely prestigious. He has thrown himself into the lands at Crumbleigh. You know how his mother forbade him from acquainting himself with such duties. She always believed him to be above the management of his own lands and so his land agent has always acted on his behalf."

"Yes, your mother-in-law has always been quite opinionated. On all matters it seems, even those that are not her concern." Maria winced at the bitterness in her sister's voice. The pain of Mrs. Card's ill treatment of her lingered, it seemed, and Maria wished that she could remove the sting for her. Unfortunately, Mrs. Card's stingers were responsible for her pain as well.

She continued, "Now, Mr. Card has taken to his role as landowner almost as if it were a vocation. He behaves like any lowly tenant might. Rather than taking infrequent forays into his land on horseback, he has been joining the laborers right there in the fields."

Charlotte seemed to consider for a moment. "That sounds very unlike Mr. Card."

"Does it not?" Maria imagined her husband in the fields wearing his fine frock coats and wielding a hoe with his soft-skinned hands. "It is quite ridiculous indeed, for he is not a physical sort of man."

"However, we must consider his mother's role in determining his interests. Until he defied her wishes in making a second proposal to you, he had probably never made a serious decision in his life. Perhaps, he is enjoying his newfound freedom from his mother's bluster."

Maria shook her head, realized that it ached, and pulled the pins from her blond hair to ease the strain. "If only such a notion were true! But alas, I fear he is behaving unwisely, for he has made a shocking eviction from Crumbleigh."

Always willing to trust in Mr. Card's goodness, Charlotte said, "Well, he must have had a very good reason."

"In this case, I do not believe so, for it was me who was asked to leave."

As much as Charlotte's ordinarily impassive face was capable, it registered her abject shock. "Mr. Card asked you to leave?"

"Yes," Maria said. Ordinarily, she would have been reduced to tears, but she had grown since her sad dealings earlier this year, and now she was prepared to face her problems—if not headlong—then at least with the righteous anger that was due her as the wronged party. "He sent me to London."

"But you came here."

"Yes, I could not bear to do his bidding, even if he does have a fine home in town. You know his mother has vacated the property and married some wealthy tradesman. Can you imagine? What gentleman—even a gentleman in trade—would have such a yapping mutt?" Maria's anger burned through her despondence. "If Mr. Card desires to foist me off and then expects me to trot obediently to London with no explanation for his withdrawal and coldness, then he is bound to be disappointed. He does not treat me as a wife ought to be treated, and therefore, I will not act as one."

"But what do you intend to do, for you cannot stay here everlastingly?"

"I intend to discover his reason for sending me away, and...." Maria took a steadying breath. "...if I find that he simply desires to be rid of me—that he no longer loves me and wants to woo me—then I will do him one better. I will disappear into London and from his life forever."

Once tucked upstairs in her sister's best guest room, Maria began to feel the true weight of her situation.

Her husband, who claimed to love her and who vowed to win her heart, had sent her away.

She had disobeyed him, and such defiance felt surprisingly pleasing. She would not go quietly from his life, for it was the place she had chosen, for right reason or wrong, and Crumbleigh was her home.

And truth be told, Maria had borne Mr. Card's clumsy attempts to win her heart quite well. Perhaps she had enjoyed the attention he gave her more than the method, but it was disappointing to think that she no longer had his admiration and affection.

And despite the persisting feelings of friendship that would not yet give way to love, she had hoped her feelings would change. If sheer force of will could create romantic love, then she would have loved Mr. Card long ago.

But something was missing.

Some spark. Some feeling of excitement and yet also some feeling that Mr. Card was a confident gentleman and not just the boy who was awkwardly trying to woo her. His attempts to win her heart had been awkward, for he was behaving quite apart from his natural character. He had attempted poetry, rhyming "lady" with "baby," she recalled with a grimace. He had sung songs of love out of tune. He had surprised her with a romantic picnic on the hottest day of the summer, and though both had returned home thoroughly overheated, it had nothing to do with their passion for each other.

Oh! Was she doomed to unhappiness? Would she never feel her blood race with passion? Would she ever experience true love? Would Mr. Card give up on winning her?

No, she could not bear to think that she had finally alienated him.

Dear, sweet Mr. Card, who had stood by her and her sister during the darkest of hours, who had always been her friend, and who claimed to love her. He could not suddenly send her away without good reason.

And Maria vowed to discover just what that reason was.

She would go to the lands at Crumbleigh and observe Mr. Card all day until she found out the truth of the matter. Then, and only then, would she know how to proceed: whether to implant herself in Crumbleigh and refuse to be moved or to disappear into London forever.

She would attack at dawn.

ঞ৩ এ৯৪

Dawn came and went.

Maria's attack began somewhere in the vicinity of noon, for she deemed it too cool to go mucking about the countryside in the morning hours. Besides, what could she learn at dawn that she could not also discover at noon?

Although Charlotte offered her carriage—and the advice to speak frankly with Mr. Card instead of sneaking about the property and spying on him—Maria took neither. She set out on booted feet and in her warmest cloak for Crumbleigh. When the house was in view, she took a hard turn and skirted the property, heading for the fields where the tenants ought to be plowing for the spring wheat harvest.

And it was there that she first saw Mr. Card, although she did not at first recognize him.

Maria kept herself concealed in the wooded boundary of the field and watched as the ploughboys worked the earth in long straight lines and other men dragged harrowers through the dirt clumps, making a field suitable for growing.

Believing Mr. Card to be in the barn overseeing the threshing of corn or inspecting the sheep, Maria was preparing to leave her hiding spot in the field when she saw a coat that looked suspiciously like Mr. Card's, only worn by a man whose work-hardened body belied his fine outerwear. Clearly, Mr. Card had lent his coat to a laborer.

This man appeared to be her husband's age, but his body seemed to have been hewn from rock. There was no softness around his middle, no extraneous movement, as he worked the earth.

Truly, this man was a specimen to be admired.

And admire him Maria did.

She tucked herself further into the shadows of the trees and watched as his strong arms worked the harrower and as his calves flexed and contracted with each step. He drew closer to the edge of the woods, working the soil with his back to Maria, and she took advantage of the view, enjoying the way his muscles strained against the seams of Mr. Card's coat.

And then he turned.

Maria stifled a gasp.

This was no tenant farmer or ploughboy.

This was Mr. Card himself.

But he was so entirely altered.

His body was hardened from the months of work, and even his face had changed. Gone was the boyish expression, the shyness vanished from his eyes. He was all man, in control and sure of himself.

Maria rocked back on her heels and watched him.

How had such a transformation occurred?

And when had he learned to operate farm implements? She had not thought he had the strength for such work, but clearly he had, for she had been admiring her own husband's prowess without even realizing it.

She had not known her husband had prowess to begin with.

And how had she not noticed the great changes taking place in both his form and his demeanor? Why, she had seen him just the other day when he told her he was sending her to London.

She had certainly noticed that his demeanor had hardened against her, but beyond that she had not looked upon him at all.

What a fool she was!

Thinking back, she realized that she had probably not actually *noticed* Mr. Card since well before the harvest. But now that she reflected on him, she could see the transformation happening from the very moment she had agreed to marry him.

That day he had become more powerful, but she had scarcely realized that the trend had continued.

In her stubbornness, she had refused to see what was before her. And she had loved him as any friend might love another friend, but she had never imagined she could feel romantically about him, no matter how much he tried to woo her or how much she wished to be wooed.

How wrong she had been.

For sitting in her concealed place in the woods, she felt a sudden rush of passion for her husband. His new confidence called her out of hiding and his body begged for her touch.

But did he still want her?

And worse, had her thoughtless treatment of him caused him to seek out the company of a mistress, as Charlotte suggested?

She must find out.

⚬⚬⚬

Maria remained hidden in the woods until Mr. Card strode in the direction of the threshing barn, and she gathered her skirts and stumbled along in the branch- and rock-littered woods after him. She tripped through the shadowy underbrush, stubbing her toes countless times, but still she persisted.

Because she had to remain on the periphery of the field, Maria's journey took much longer, and by the time she arrived at the barn, Mr. Card had already departed.

To see his mistress?

Her heart clutched at the thought, and she turned on her heel to follow him when she heard a distinct voice from inside the barn. "Mr. Card is a fine gentleman. No other landlord would work beside us like he has."

"Yes, I believe he will sure make things right, even at great cost to himself."

Peeking through the joints of the wooden barn, Maria saw Mr. Grimes, Mr. Card's manservant, speaking with an unknown tenant.

"I do not mean to speak ill of my betters, but now that Mr. Ransom has been dismissed, I believe circumstances may improve, though we will be in want this winter. The harvest was the smallest in years, and we sold all we gleaned for rent. Now, we have hardly enough stores to last the month, but we must endure until spring."

"Mr. Card has already seen that the tenants will be more fairly treated by hiring you as bailiff. And indeed, he will see to it that you are all fairly compensated for the years of mismanagement. Even now, he is gone to see about selling some head of cattle."

"Shame to be selling cattle."

"It is what must be done when the corn crop is so poor. No doubt Mr. Card would sell off his very land to right this wrong."

Realization washed over Maria like a cold rain.

Mr. Card was having financial difficulties. The harvest was poor, the tenants had been mistreated and were on the verge of starvation, and it had been all Mrs. Card's doing. Now, Mr. Card was doing whatever it took to make things right.

That explained his sudden disappearance from the house, but how did it relate to his decision to send her away?

She began to shiver and decided the best course of action was to return to her sister's home and discuss matters with her.

ఞ ఞ

"I was reduced to hearing the truth of Mr. Ransom's dismissal from the serving staff. Can you imagine?"

"Servants, even the most loyal, may not always be trusted," Charlotte said. "Perhaps the tale is untrue."

"In this case, I find I must believe them, for Mr. Grimes is Mr. Card's most trusted servant, and his words explain my husband's behavior so entirely that I cannot but believe them." Maria's elbows dropped to her knees, and her head rested in her hands as she continued, "Mr. Ransom has been most unkind to Mr. Card's tenants, and his farming practices—or whatever they might be called, for I know naught of such things—have practically left everyone without sufficient grain to endure the winter."

"But your harvest seemed so bountiful this year."

"No," Maria shook her head in her hands. "It was not so, for the crops that were given as the first fruits due as payment to Mr. Card turned out to be the bulk of that which was harvested."

"How can this be? Crumbleigh has always been the most respected home and had the most bountiful fields in the county."

"I daresay Mrs. Card is to blame. You know what an old goat she is. She and Mr. Ransom must have been careless in their dealings with their tenants for some years, and the effects are revealed only now."

"I cannot believe Mrs. Card was guilty of outright duplicity, but it did seem odd that she was so evidently willing to abandon her lifelong home for the crushing throng of London and then to marry so quickly to a gentleman so beneath her station. Perhaps she knew of the forthcoming financial difficulty."

"Well, you may believe Mrs. Card guilty of both misjudging you and of defrauding the tenants she was sworn to care for, and the result is that Crumbleigh's lands may be on the verge of being dismantled and sold piece by piece, for Mr. Card will not allow his tenants to suffer."

Upon speaking those words aloud, Maria realized the truth of them, and suddenly, the reason for her dismissal became clear.

She plunked down in the chair behind her. "Oh Lord, that is it."

Mr. Card sent her away not because he had fallen out of love with her or taken a mistress; he attempted to remove her to London so she would not discover his financial difficulties.

It made perfect sense.

She had made no pretence of the fact that she had married him for security, and if he was suddenly insolvent, he would not want her to know, for it would only serve to thwart his plans to romance her.

He loved her yet.

"What?" Charlotte looked at her with concerned eyes. "You have gone very pale. Can I bring you some tea?"

Maria held up a shaking hand. "No, no tea." She stood up. "I must get to my husband immediately."

"Truly, you are too ill to go home now. Besides it is too late in the evening. Wait until tomorrow."

"I must go now. If you will not order me your carriage, I shall walk." Upon those words, Maria left the room, intent on finding her cloak and walking once again all the way to Crumbleigh, only this time she was bound for the house and not the fields.

"Wait, I will ring for the carriage." And with that, Charlotte disappeared, and after a brief time, the conveyance appeared and so did she. "Will you return tonight?"

Maria blushed, thinking of Mr. Card as he worked the fields earlier that day. A warmth rushed through her. "No, I do not believe so."

◦◦ ◦◦

Maria found the doors to Crumbleigh yet unlocked, though she encountered no one, not even a servant, at the entry.

They did not expect her, and she had purposely stopped the coachman early so that she could furtively enter the premises.

She could not account for her sudden need for stealth other than the fact that she felt oddly unsure of herself.

Maria intended to seduce Mr. Card, but she knew not how to woo a man, especially one who had sent her away not two days before. She did not want anyone to witness her failure, should the worst occur.

And, oh, she greatly hoped that it would not.

The great house was silent as Maria sneaked—as well as can be done on booted feet—across the marble entry. There was a chill in the air, for the fires had been extinguished long before, but the cold was not what caused her hands to shake.

No, she shook out of the fear and excitement and uncertainty of newfound love.

At the top of the stairs, the temperature seemed to warm a bit, or was it the temperature of her blood that caused the illusion? Maria knew not.

She tiptoed down the hall and did not allow herself to hesitate at the door to her bedroom. She would not stop now.

On she went to the door of her husband's bedroom. She had, of course, entered the chamber before, but on those occasions, she had viewed him as nothing more than a friend. Now, the prospect of entering held new meaning.

The large mahogany door stood between them, and that was all.

Should she knock?

Or should she simply turn the knob and go forth to meet her future?

With as much boldness as remained in her, Maria turned the knob, and the door opened a crack, just enough for her to peek inside and find no light to see by. He must be asleep.

Tempted to back away, she forced her lips to move. "Jonas," she whispered into the darkness.

Though very little sound emerged, she heard him stir immediately.

He cleared his throat. "Maria?"

Maria felt herself blush and was very glad he could not see her. "Yes."

"What in the name of God are you doing here?"

He sounded angry, but Maria now detected the underlying fear of discovery in his voice, and that gave her the courage to open the door further and step inside.

"I came for two purposes, and I would ask you not to speak until I have said my piece."

"In this, I will obey you, though you have not given me a good example of obedience to follow."

"I find it impossible to be obedient to a husband whose wishes are based on untruths and misapprehensions, and I have committed no less than espionage in order to come here and set matters to rights."

She heard the bed linens rustle as he moved, and though she could not see him, she imagined him now sitting upright on the edge of the bed.

She closed the door behind her lest any servants be about to hear her words. "I know why you sent me away. I know about Mr. Ransom, the poor harvest, and even your mother's role. I know that our tenants have been greatly wronged and that you are doing your duty to them." She heard his sharp intake of breath and took a few steps closer.

"You know what a foolish creature I have always been, Jonas. You are aware of my reasons for marrying you. You know of my weakness and greed, and so I cannot fault you for sending me away. You could not help but believe that I would be irrevocably lost to you if I knew of your financial troubles."

From across the room, she heard him clear his throat again, but he said nothing.

"But Jonas, it is not to be so."

She walked a few steps closer, but still a wide chasm separated her and her husband.

Now, she must confess her feelings.

"When first I saw you in the fields working the harrower, I believed it was you who had changed. I saw the newly bronzed skin and…" She paused, remembering how he had looked in his coat and breeches. "…lean form…and I was taken with you in a manner I never was before.

"But when I heard your servants and tenants speaking of your sacrifice and kindness to them, I realized that you had not changed at all. For all at once, today, the scales on my eyes fell away, and I saw the real gentleman you have always been, but whom I was too foolish to see.

"I had seen you only as a friend and a rescuer, and I was grateful to you, but now I see that I have loved you all along."

The words were out. The confession made.

And her husband did not speak.

Maria wished she had not forced him to keep silent, for now she knew not how to proceed.

So she pushed forward, ignoring the potential embarrassment.

Her boots made soft noises across the polished wood floor, and soon, her skirt was brushing against his knees.

She could see him now, his face in shadow, as he sat immobile on the bed, and she reached down with both hands and held his face in them.

"Will you have me, Jonas?" she asked, as she lowered her face to his and brushed her lips against his cheek.

Still, he did not speak, and Maria decided to be yet bolder. Her hands pushed into his hair, and she let her body drop into his lap. She felt his warmth and hardness around her.

"Jonas?" she whispered as she pressed against him.

Her husband let out a groan that he had obviously been fighting to restrain, and she was catapulted forthwith onto the bed and crushed under him.

"Good God, Maria…"

And that was all he was able to say before the flames of passion engulfed them both.

·� 𝓞�·

Because of the poor harvest that year at Crumbleigh, Mr. Card had been forced to forego the traditional harvest home feast for his tenants and laborers. But upon the Yuletide, invitations were sent to them all.

On the night of the feast, Crumbleigh was festooned with greenery and fires burned bright in every hearth to fend off winter's chill. All of the Cards' friends and family were in attendance as well as every tenant and laborer who had been victimized by Mrs. Card and Mr. Ransom.

And after a large meal of every good thing, Mr. Card stood to address his guests.

"At the close of this year and on the eve of the new, and on this joyous holiday no less, I am pleased to welcome you to Crumbleigh. While our harvest this season may have been small, I have kept my vow to make up for past wrongs. And on that score, please accept a repayment of all that is owed to you on behalf of me, my wife, and the estate of Crumbleigh. This money will see you through the winter, and together, we will make Crumbleigh the great house and estate it once was."

A cheer went up among the gathered laborers, and they all sought Mr. Burgess, who had begun to dispense the money to each tenant and worker.

When Charlotte was able to hear over the din of the crowd, she asked, "But how was it done?"

"It was quite simple," Maria said as she took her husband's now-muscled arm and smiled. "We sold the house in London. It was not to my taste anyway, and the money was much better spent here."

"Indeed, it was, my dear," Mr. Card said.

Charlotte looked at her sister in astonishment and whispered to her, "You have fallen in love with your husband, have you not?"

"Indeed I have, and as you can see," she said, turning to him, "he did not fall out of love with me, even when I was silly and selfish."

"I almost lost her. When I absented myself to deal with land, I left our potential romance to lie fallow." Mr. Card gave her a long look that conveyed much, and said, "And love cannot grow where there is no one to attend it."

❧ ❧

Caroline Bingley

Caroline Bingley

A Continuation of Jane Austen's *Pride and Prejudice*

JENNIFER BECTON

A WHITELEY PRESS BOOK

For

Every reader of *Charlotte Collins*.

Without you, this book would not exist.

Thank you.

Well! Evil to some is always good to others.

ꙮ Jane Austen ꙮ

༄ One ༄

Banished.

The word echoed through Caroline Bingley's mind with each beat of the horses' hooves, and she felt the stab of her own mortification with each bone-jarring jolt of the hired carriage in which she was imprisoned. Her brother Charles's own hand had locked her away in this dreadful post chaise, which was presently being drawn by a second-rate pair of horses, and the entire conveyance was bound for the worst place she could imagine: her mother's home in the north of England.

Caroline glanced at the woman seated beside her. This, ostensibly, was her traveling companion, for it was quite improper for a woman of Caroline's status to voyage alone. In truth, their current mode of transport—two women traveling alone by post—was verging on impropriety as it was.

She thought her companion's name was Rosemary, but she had not taken the initiative of remembering. After all, Charles had been the one to employ the impertinent widow to accompany her while in transit and to act as her companion once in the tedious, unvarying society of Kendal, Cumbria.

While she could not blame Charles for hiring a servant to attend to her while navigating the public roads and dealing with the unsavory individuals one often encountered at posting inns, it was beyond the needs of propriety to have retained her for the duration of her stay in the north. Caroline did not need a chaperone; nor had she reached that unfortunate stage in life wherein she required the services of a paid companion. She was no doddering fool, but a wealthy young woman of sound mind and good judgment.

Caroline lifted her chin against the humiliation and anger rising within her breast. The presence of a companion was an insult to be sure!

To think that she had become a prisoner in her own life—with the right to make her own choices stripped from her—was intolerable. No, she had chosen neither the voyage nor her companion, and she certainly would not have elected to embark on such a long journey so late in the year when the weather was apt to turn foul.

Ha! It was all a good joke. This was no journey. This was a prison sentence, and Rosemary was her jailor.

Rosemary.

Caroline winced at such a gauche name. She certainly hoped that her memory had failed and that the woman's name was not Rosemary, for she did not like the pert flavor of that particular herb in servants any more than in a roast of beef. Besides, her parents must have been quite inelegant to name their daughter after such an ugly, sprawling plant, and Caroline had no patience for inelegance.

Unfortunately, the name seemed to suit both the woman's piquant personality and her gauche posture, for Rosemary was currently slumped in her seat, asleep with her head lolling in rhythm to the motion of the carriage as strands of strawberry blond hair swayed across her forehead. A woman of her age—why, she must be nearly thirty!—should not sit so indecorously.

Caroline leaned forward to scold her, to remind her how a lady ought to recline, but then she sat back and sighed. What was the point of correcting her now? They were going to the country, where posture was unimportant. For who of worth would be present to observe and reward such correctness of bearing?

She considered the woman and her vexing ability to rest despite the ruts and bumps of the byways they traveled. How could Rosemary possibly sleep at such a time? It was just the sort of incommodious thing the woman would do. For her own part, Caroline found that she could not possibly relax. She sat perfectly erect, hands crushed together in her lap, looking with great regret in the direction from whence they had come, back toward the remnants of her dreams and desires. Now her life was in shambles, and the winter-worn roads that led her inexorably into a dismal future did nothing to lull her into the forgetfulness of sleep.

Here was the sad state of her situation: Caroline not only failed to win the regard of Mr. Fitzwilliam Darcy, the only gentleman she had ever admired, but she had lost him to Miss Elizabeth Bennet, a headstrong young woman of neither breeding nor fortune. As a result, Caroline's thoughts of becoming one of the wealthiest women in England and mistress of the great estate of Pemberley had been ruined. Indeed, she had forfeited the most excellent society of Mr. Darcy and endangered the shy companionship of his sister Georgiana.

To make matters worse, she had also been unsuccessful in thwarting her brother Charles's unwise marriage to Miss Jane Bennet, and now, it seemed, no one would forgive her for having been opposed, and justly so, to both matches.

Though Caroline had never believed such a possibility to exist, her beloved brother had ostracized her, sending her away for the sake of family harmony or some such nonsense.

Her crimes?

Attempting to elevate her family's position by seeking an advantageous marriage? Hoping to prevent her brother from marrying a young lady so beneath the status to which he should ascribe?

Indeed.

But what had she done that any woman of sense would not have done? Would not the sainted Miss Elizabeth Bennet herself have shifted the heavens in order to prevent her sister Lydia's disastrous match to that scoundrel Mr. George Wickham? Caroline believed so, and as she had done nothing out of the common way in attempting to separate her brother from Miss Jane Bennet, she did not believe she deserved the censure she had received. Why, Mr. Darcy, who had been chief in instigating the entire scheme, had already been forgiven by all involved.

It was utterly unfair.

Tears of frustration welled in her eyes.

'Twas a centuries' old struggle in which she had been engaged, a struggle whose outcome had not been in her favor.

Society dictated that the Bennet girls must aspire to such gentlemen as Charles and Mr. Darcy. For was it not the duty of all children, be they male or female, to marry as well as possible for the benefit of their families?

In the same way, family loyalty had ordained that Caroline must wage a campaign against them. For was it not the duty of every family of wealth and consequence to guard against the infiltration of low-class fortune hunters?

Caroline had been forced to act after Charles had shown his admiration for Miss Bennet at their first meeting at that silly little public assembly in Meryton. Upon developing a deeper acquaintance with the lady in question and her rather wild, country family, Caroline had become concerned that her brother might have fallen in with a lady, kind though she may seem, who only sought his fortune.

She had shared her concerns with Mr. Darcy, and he had agreed wholeheartedly with her assessment. In fact, he had been the one to declare that Miss Bennet seemed to emit no real feeling for Charles, and they both shared reservations about her low-born relations.

After much strategizing, it was decided that it would be best to remove Charles from Hertfordshire before he could become the victim of a one-sided marriage to a fortune hunter wearing a dowdy country frock.

Being naturally humble, Charles had been easily convinced of Miss Bennet's indifference, and he had allowed himself to be taken to London. After learning of Miss Bennet's true feelings, he could not forgive himself for having doubted his own. His anger at Caroline's interference had been complete, and try as she might, she could not convince him that she had been acting in his best interests. She had wanted to protect him.

Caroline's cheeks moistened with tears, and she swiped them away as she considered the other charge leveled against her: her abhorrence of Mr. Darcy's decision to marry Miss Elizabeth Bennet.

As to that, she could not claim such innocence. She had considered Mr. Darcy to be her ideal match. He was everything a gentleman ought to be if he possibly can. He was handsome, well-spoken, dutiful, and rich, and he had accumulated his fortune in the most acceptable manner—through inheritance.

Caroline's own fortune, though substantially smaller than Mr. Darcy's, would assure her lifelong comfort, but her wealth was tainted: her father had earned the bulk of her inheritance through trade, a fact that Caroline always sought to conceal.

A union with Mr. Darcy would have ended the necessity of concealment and raised Caroline in the esteem of society.

And so she had sought the good opinion of a gentleman through those arts—flattery and a bit of flirtation—that all women use, and through conversation and comparison she had sought to make him aware of the obvious inferiority of any woman other than herself for matrimony.

In this, she had failed, and now she was truly a prisoner of society's whims, for though she was wealthy, she was not free.

Again, Caroline turned to look along the muddy road toward the past, as if merely looking in the direction of Pemberley might somehow transport her back in time, might change her circumstances, might win her the gentleman she had admired.

But it was not to be.

The carriage only swept her further from the comforts of her brother's household and from her dreams of permanency of station and home. Caroline braced herself against the seat, wishing she had thought to demand extra cushions when they had stopped to change conveyances at the last posting inn, for there was nothing more irksome than to arrive at one's destination with a sore posterior. She glanced about the coach for a cushion, and seeing no other suitable option, she folded her lap robe and positioned it beneath her. Fortunately, it was warmer today and dry, so the covering was not necessary to ward off the cold, though her feet were a bit chilled. The robe did little to absorb the shock of the carriage, but at least she had taken some action.

Hoping to forget the jarring of the rented carriage and her circumstances in general, Caroline forced her attention out the window. Only now, she looked ahead toward her destination, her future. Yes, even in winter's gray gloom, the countryside was quite lovely—rolling hills and all that—and had she been in the right company she might have said something poetic about the picturesque landscape of the Lake District. But the dozing Rosemary was hardly proper company, so Caroline remained silent, finally finding consolation two hours later when the coach crossed the arched stone bridge into Kendal and then bumped its way into the drive of the final posting inn.

Feeling quite bruised all over, Caroline pulled the robe from beneath her, attempted to smooth the wrinkles, and folded it into a neat square. She touched her hair, knowing it must look a fright, and adjusted her bonnet to hide the greater part of the damage.

As they drew closer to the inn, Caroline felt her heart leap a bit in her chest at the prospect of seeing her dear mother again.

Her mother, Elthea Knowles Bingley—now Elthea Knowles Bingley Newton—was the very best of women, always kind, generous, and self-effacing. If the meek were to inherit the earth, as the Scriptures said, her mother would certainly be a beneficiary. She was ever thinking of others above herself, a trait of which Caroline could not quite approve.

The post chaise pulled in front of the inn at Kendal, and Caroline spied her mother and Mr. Augustus Newton, her husband, awaiting them at the window. Her mother waved and then disappeared from view, likely rushing heedlessly to greet her in the stable yard instead of remaining inside and out of the cold and mud.

The postilion halted the team, and the horses sighed at the pleasure of resting. Caroline decided that was as good a sign as any that it was time to awaken Rosemary from her slumber. She issued her a gentle nudge to the shin. Her companion's eyes fluttered open, and she scowled as she reached down to rub her leg. "Can I be of assistance, Miss Bingley?"

"We have reached our destination."

"And that required a kick to the shin?" Rosemary asked with narrowed eyes. "Mr. Bingley is not paying me enough to be kicked."

Impertinent woman!

"Do not be dramatic. I am wearing slippers, not boots, and it was only a nudge to rouse you from slumber."

Rosemary mumbled something under her breath and then glanced outside. Then, she said, "Oh, it is lovely. In the face of such a lovely place, I have found it in my heart to forgive you."

Caroline was on the verge of telling her that she was looking at nothing but another dreadful posting inn, and more, she had not begged her forgiveness, but the postboy opened the coach door and assisted her out of the conveyance and into her mother's arms.

"Oh, Caro!" Mrs. Newton whispered as she wrapped her pudgy arms around her daughter and held her close. "How pleased I am to have you here."

Caroline was briefly inundated by feelings of so tender and unfamiliar a nature that she could not name them. She inhaled deeply of her mother's scent, and tears welled once more in her eyes. She closed them tightly and willed herself to keep her rampant emotions in check.

She was not generally prone to so many displays of feeling in such a short time. Nor was she often compelled to share every tribulation and fear she experienced, but she was tempted to do so now as she rested in the comforts of her mother's embrace.

Caroline steeled herself against these emotions, for she simply could not tell her mother the humiliating truth of what had occurred.

❧ Two ❧

On that dreadful October evening, Caroline had endured long in the company of her sister Louisa and her husband Mr. Hurst at the inn in Scarborough, where the three of them had come to tour. After some weeks of incessant shoreline walks, Caroline had become bored, and thoughts of her brother and Mr. Darcy had begun to assail her.

The course of her musings often returned to her last glimpse of Mr. Darcy on the morning she, Louisa, and Mr. Hurst had entered the carriage bound for the shore, while her brother and Mr. Darcy, who claimed some mysterious business in town, had stood on the stone staircase at Pemberley to see them off.

As Caroline turned to offer them a departing wave, a most overwhelming feeling of inevitable change had crashed over her. Her brother and Mr. Darcy stood at the foot of the immovable Pemberley, but it was as if the whole building had somehow shifted or perhaps the earth itself had changed position in the heavens. Yes, something indefinable—and yet somehow also tangible—had altered since Miss Elizabeth Bennet and her companions had visited Pemberley, and Caroline had known then, as the carriage carried her away, that her circumstances would never again be the same.

But what precisely was occurring? She must know.

So distracted was Caroline with thoughts of her former companions that she had taken up Mr. Hurst's custom and began ignoring Louisa, who was opining again on the virtues of the seaside for improving one's complexion, when there came a knock at the door of their private sitting room.

"Oh, why must they bother us in our private chamber after such a pleasant meal?" Mr. Hurst moaned from his chair in the corner where he had been feigning interest in a newspaper.

"It is quite damaging to the digestion and such an inconvenience for someone to knock at this hour," Louisa agreed. "It is rather a jarring sound indeed."

Caroline's only reply had been to bid the servant to enter, for he might possess a letter bearing news of what had occurred since she left Pemberley.

To her greatest delight, the servant said, "A letter, ma'am." He presented the missive on a silver tray, bowed, and exited the room as swiftly as he had entered.

"Oh bother!" Louisa said as she touched a hand to her forehead. "Is it from Charles?"

Caroline checked the handwriting on the direction and nodded as anticipation welled within her.

Louisa leaned back into the sofa cushions and sighed. "Charles never has anything of consequence to say, but now we are obligated to take the trouble of writing back."

"Do not trouble yourself," Caroline said as she broke the seal and unfolded the letter. "I shall make the necessary replies, for he likely has no interest in hearing of the seaside's improvements on your skin coloring."

Louisa regarded her with an icy expression. "You are in a fine temper tonight, Caroline. Perhaps you might take some fresh air...."

Louisa continued speaking, but Caroline did not hear a word of it, for as she began to decipher her brother's messy handwriting, the room around her fell away.

Several strategic words fairly leapt from the page: "pleased to announce my engagement to Miss Jane Bennet...other happy news of Mr. Darcy's proposal to Miss Elizabeth Bennet...double wedding in Hertfordshire."

No, it could not be, Caroline thought, as she reread the letter more slowly this time.

Each word stabbed at her heart and pricked at her soul. It was true. Mr. Darcy was to be married.

There, in that blasted inn at Scarborough as her sister's voice droned in the background, Caroline's heart had rent in two. All her dreams of Pemberley had been spoiled and all her hopes for her brother destroyed in one practically illegible epistle.

She quickly thrust the letter into her sister's hands and excused herself from the Hursts' company.

Behind her, she heard her sister say, "Ah, you take my advice after all and are seeking some night air. It will be a benefit surely...."

Caroline did not respond to her sister, but rushed to her chamber, determined to hide her feelings somewhere deep within her and do her duty. She would write to her brother immediately and assure him of her felicitations, for that was what a sister ought to do, even if she believed he had chosen to wed a fortune hunter.

And that is precisely what Caroline did, though she gripped the pen with such ferocity that it nearly shattered. She looked upon the paper with tears in her eyes, and the words came in fits and spurts as she struggled with her sentiments. She knew what she must say, but she certainly did not want to say it.

She must say how pleased she was to hear of both engagements, how eager she was to attend the double wedding, how everyone would surely be blissfully happy from now on. But she simply could not issue a statement of outright approval.

How could she?

It had been the brightest wish of her family, especially of her father, that Charles might marry a woman of standing, and to see him shackle himself to a lady of significantly lower rank was painful. Caroline could neither approve nor rejoice in his decision.

But truly, Charles did seem pleased with his choice. Of course, Charles was easily pleased by everything and everybody he met. This was precisely why Caroline had been forced to conspire with Mr. Darcy to remove him from Miss Bennet's sphere early in their acquaintance.

Their party had stolen away to London, but Miss Jane Bennet could not be so easily thwarted. Under the encouragement of her sister Elizabeth no doubt, Jane had also gone to London to stay with her relations in Cheapside, causing Caroline and Mr. Darcy the trouble of concealing her presence from Charles for the duration of their stay. Caroline had not enjoyed her deceit, but she had believed herself to be acting only in the best interests of her family.

She had hoped that such a separation from Miss Bennet would remind Charles of his duty to his family and allow him to meet another young lady, albeit one who boasted a large dowry or who hailed from a titled family, with whom he might be equally pleased.

Unfortunately, his attachment to Miss Bennet was complete, and his feelings for her were much more deeply felt than Caroline and Mr. Darcy had imagined.

Yes, she had misjudged her brother and the force of his sentiments and had taken actions that injured him, but she had done so with the best of intentions. Indeed, both she and Mr. Darcy had nothing but the very best of intentions.

But now Mr. Darcy was to be married as well.

And to Miss Elizabeth Bennet!

One of the wealthiest, worthiest gentlemen in all of England was to wed a mere country miss of no fortune or standing.

Each time this thought entered her mind, Caroline was forced to lay aside her pen and paper for fear that her tears might cause the ink to run, leaving evidence of her brittle emotions for her brother to observe.

Caroline did not care for such displays of her own fragility. She did not care for the appearance of weakness in anyone, especially herself.

She must remain aloof and practical.

She must find a method of coexisting peacefully with the Bennet sisters, and the most expedient method for that was to scribe a letter to Jane, for she had a softer heart and more forgiving temperament than her sister Elizabeth. Besides, Caroline had no wish to throw herself upon the mercy of Miss Elizabeth Bennet, the woman who had been the source of her greatest sorrow: the loss of Mr. Fitzwilliam Darcy's favor.

And so when she had finished her letter to Charles, she added a page to Jane:

> My dearest Jane,
>
> It is with true joy that I write to you this day, for I have just received my brother's letter, which informed me that I will soon be able to call you my sister. A happy thought indeed!
>
> I hope you will not misinterpret my behavior to you in London, for I was acting based upon a misunderstanding of the true nature of my brother's fondness for you. Had I but comprehended the violence of his affection for you, my dearest friend, I would have never taken such pains to protect you from what I believed to be certain disappointment. My hesitancy to call upon you and your relations in Cheapside or to invite you to dine in Grosvenor Street issued from nothing more than my earnest desire to protect you from sorrow.
>
> However, once I became aware of my brother's true feelings, which he had experienced from your first meeting at the Meryton assembly, I have been free to treat you in the manner in which I have always viewed you—as a most honored friend and, now, sister.
>
> Please accept the most humble declarations of warmest emotion from
>
> Your most devoted sister,
Caroline Bingley

Caroline remained determinedly practical until the moment she sealed the letter and rang for the servant, who came in short order with the promise that the missive would be posted on the morrow.

Then, upon the servant's departure, Caroline pushed away from the small escritoire, walked calmly to her bedchamber, and collapsed atop the bed linens as grief for the loss of her fondest dreams overwhelmed her. Pemberley, Georgiana, Mr. Darcy, a life of confidence and ease…they were all lost to her now.

Would Caroline never be able to exist without the fear that someone might discover her secret history? Would she always be forced to hide her lowly origins in trade? Would she be locked forever in an attempt to scrabble her way out of the middling classes toward the stability of polite society?

No matter how great her inheritance, society would always view her as a pariah, an unworthy outsider, unless she married well or managed to insinuate herself into the very best company. Now she had no hope of either.

It was utterly unfair that Miss Elizabeth Bennet had been chosen to rise in society while Caroline, who had worked to gain an education, to become well versed on any topic of conversation, and to excel at every worthy accomplishment, had been bypassed.

Caroline wept bitterly the night through, but in the morning she showed no hint of her true distress. If her eyes were a bit reddened, she would only claim that it must be the salty sea air that had irritated them.

⚬๑ ๑⚬

Having been so certain of her victory in assuaging the feelings of the entire Bennet clan with one simple letter, Caroline had been quite surprised when, upon returning to Netherfield Park in November to prepare for her brother's wedding, she discovered that Charles had not been as mollified as his fiancée.

And what, pray, had been Charles's response?

He had begun thus: "Caroline, that letter was abominable."

Caroline had laid aside the book of history she had been pretending to read and looked into her brother's usually docile blue eyes. They flashed cold with anger, but she remained calm, saying, "Whatever can you mean, Charles? To what letter do you refer?"

His blue eyes flashed again. "You know very well to which letter I refer: the one you wrote Miss Bennet."

"Oh, that!" Caroline said with as much innocence as she could muster. "It was a letter of congratulations to your betrothed."

"Congratulations, indeed!" Charles clasped his hands behind his back and came off looking very regal, his head of light brown curls held high, as he continued, "Yes, you may have touched the heart of my dear, forgiving Miss Bennet, but from a brother's perspective, it will not do."

"Will not do?" Caroline repeated. "If Miss Bennet has seen fit to accept my felicitations and explanations, then I can see no reason why you may not."

"Do you not, Caroline?" He paused for a moment, clearly pondering his next words, and then he took on an air of determination. It was rare for such an expression to grace Charles's open features, but when he wore it, his desires must be respected, for he was the head of the Bingley family. "I am aware that you and Darcy conspired to separate Miss Bennet and me, and I am deeply ashamed at my own spiritless decision to believe you both when you proclaimed that she had no true feelings for me. Miss Bennet is so modest and reserved that I can well believe you both thought your interpretation of her behavior was accurate and that your actions were for my own good."

"Yes, I was only—"

He held up a hand and his expression hardened further. "But Darcy confessed his part in the matter and the intentions behind it. He has apologized, admitted his wrong, and made amends."

Caroline could hardly believe her brother's words. "Have I not done as much in my letter to Jane?"

"No, Caroline, you have excused your actions and made no amends, and though Miss Bennet may allow the goodness of her heart to sway her opinion of you, I may not be so charitable. I cannot." He paused, seemingly in contemplation. "Perhaps…no, indeed, there are others to whom an apology may be given."

Caroline stood and turned away from her brother, for she could not bear the force of his gaze. "To whom should I apologize?"

"Well, to those you offended, naturally."

Over her shoulder Caroline said, "You refer to Miss Elizabeth Bennet."

"No," he said. Caroline's surprise at his denial caused her to face him as he continued to speak. "I refer to Mrs. Fitzwilliam Darcy, as she shall be in a few days' time."

There was a long silence during which Caroline pondered her choice of response while Charles paced the room with a grim set to his face.

"Miss Elizabeth was most upset by your actions toward her sister," he said, midstride.

Here, Caroline very nearly made an unladylike snort. She knew well that Miss Elizabeth Bennet's anger had its origins in more than Caroline's actions toward her sister. She disliked Caroline for her attempt to gain Mr. Darcy as a husband and to become mistress of Pemberley.

And Caroline found she could not blame her, for she despised Miss Elizabeth Bennet for attempting to win him and succeeding.

Caroline's hands clenched the book she still held, its pages wrinkling a bit under her harsh grasp. No, the prospect of apologizing to Mr. Darcy's choice of bride was not to be borne.

"Even for you, Charles, I cannot do it," she said.

"But you must." Charles stopped pacing and turned to look full upon his sister. He appeared to be mustering his courage to continue, and Caroline knew that he was attempting to exert his own will and not allow her to influence him again. "Yes, you must. Mr. Darcy is my closest friend and is betrothed to Miss Bennet's sister. We shall all be permanently linked. A family! If you cannot find it within yourself to make amends, then our family will always be divided, and you, I fear, will always be…." He hesitated again. "You will always be the person cast aside."

Caroline sucked in a breath at the harshness of her brother's tone. He could not mean it. He simply could not cast her aside. But as she pondered his words, she realized their truth.

Jane and Elizabeth Bennet were close, and they would often keep company together.

Jane, of course, was easily swayed, and Caroline had thought to turn this to her advantage, but Jane was more influenced by her sister, and that had to be taken into consideration. If Elizabeth never accepted Caroline, then neither would Jane.

And if Jane never accepted Caroline, then Charles would not be free to make her a member of his household once again.

Mr. Darcy, of course, would not invite her to Pemberley if Elizabeth were against her.

And this was intolerable, for an invitation to Pemberley and social intercourse with her brother and the Darcy family were crucial to her status in society.

Alas, Miss Elizabeth Bennet was the key to Caroline's return to society.

Caroline studied Charles. What was to be said that might alter the course of his discussion? Could anything accomplish such a task? It was easy for Caroline—for anyone really—to believe that her agreeably inclined brother might be managed in every circumstance, but it was simply not true.

Why, she only had to recall his treatment of her when every Bennet in Hertfordshire had arrived at Netherfield to check on Miss Jane Bennet, who had remained there to nurse her little cold. Yes, his countenance had clearly told her that she had better remain polite. The expression on her brother's face then—when he required Caroline to be civil to the girls' dimwitted mother—bore a great resemblance to the one he currently wore.

Only now, his expression was even more resolute. This was the result of his romance with Miss Jane Bennet.

He had allowed his family and friends to influence him more than his own heart, and he had suffered greatly. Realizing the error he had committed in being overly agreeable, he had clearly become determined that he should never again let anyone influence him.

He was exercising that decision as he handed down judgment on Caroline.

But Caroline was in no mood to accept his decision so easily. "My letter was kindly meant, even if you believe it to have been so poorly written. I do hope you can find it within your heart to offer me your forgiveness."

At this, he turned away, leaving Caroline to look at the hands clasped resolutely behind his back and to face the following words: "I forgive you, for you are my sister, and I cannot believe that you would purposely attempt to ruin my future happiness."

Hoping he had softened toward her, Caroline stood and placed a hand on his shoulder. "No indeed, brother. I only wanted to save you from an unequal marriage."

He turned his head so that he could meet her eyes fully. His expression held a sincerity that surprised Caroline as he said, "But a marriage is not unequal where there is an equality of love."

Caroline could not conceal her disdain. "Can you name any unequal marriages that did not end in misery for one or the other?"

"Those were marriages of unequal minds."

"Unequal fortunes must have the same effect," Caroline reasoned, "for does not money provide the opportunity for the improvement of the mind? I can hardly believe that Miss Bennet is your equal if she spent her youth without the benefit of a governess. Why, she can probably barely embroider a cushion, much less play the pianoforte!"

A muscle worked in Charles's jaw, and Caroline feared an outburst of anger, but then he sighed. "And this is precisely why I must take bold action. You refuse to see the truth before you. I love Miss Bennet, no matter how much money she has, who her relations may be, or how talented she is with needle and thread. She will be my wife, and I am unwilling to begin my marriage by inviting one who harbors such unrepentant disapproval to share our home. I shall not allow myself to be persuaded against my own good judgment, Caroline. I must act."

Cold fear rushed over Caroline, and her legs seemed no longer capable of supporting her, so she returned to her seat. She looked up at Charles, whose face was resolute, and realized that her situation was worse than she had anticipated.

"I think it best if you removed for a time," Charles said. His tone held an alarming ring of finality. "You must go home to Kendal."

"Home?" Caroline could not withhold her protest. "I have no home in Kendal."

"You shall go to our mother's home, then, if you insist on grammatical precision."

"Yes," Caroline said as her hands balled into fists. "I do insist upon it, for Newton House is not my home and it never shall be."

His reference to Newton House as "home" wounded Caroline more deeply than he could have realized. There were few people who knew how greatly she despised the very notion of home. Though she was a woman of no little fortune—20,000 pounds could hardly be considered insignificant—she had been denied the benefit of such a place from her infancy. Her father— heaven bless him—had expired before he had been able to purchase the estate his family deserved, and the inheritance, the bulk of which had been left to her brother Charles, had not yet been invested in family lands.

No, instead, it had been spent on the lease of a country manor in Hertfordshire and would soon be spent further on her brother's marriage to a country maiden. Imagine. Charles had the fortitude to commit to a woman, but not to a piece of real estate.

These were great vexations indeed, for above all else, Caroline had always yearned for a home of her own. The ownership of such a place meant far more than the possession of a piece of property. It meant a husband: a landed gentleman or perhaps someone with a title. And it meant security and status that could not easily be wrested from her.

To all outward appearances, Caroline was a woman to be envied. She wore the latest fashions, attended the most lavish balls, and associated with the wealthy and titled—and she had always tried to reflect an attitude superior to the confidence she felt inside herself—but in reality, she was nothing more than the homeless daughter of a tradesman.

Yes, Caroline would own to it: she had hoped to gain a home of her own in the form of Pemberley, but instead of gaining the home and husband of her deepest desires, she had succeeded in angering her brother, losing the good opinion of his betrothed, and humiliating herself.

"No, indeed," Caroline repeated. "I shall not go to the north of England. Surely, a journey of that magnitude is not necessary. I shall stay with Louisa in London."

"Your destination is already decided. I have written to Mama of your coming."

Caroline would not allow the mention of her mother to dissuade her from objecting again. Yes, she loved her mother and yearned to see her, but not in this manner. "Mama will bear up under her disappointment, for I refuse to go such a distance for no purpose."

Charles's jaw clenched. "But it is required," he said, and then he walked from the room, leaving only hurtful words in his wake. "Caroline, you shall not be welcome in my household until you make proper amends, and I can assure you that your welcome at Pemberley has been suspended until such a time as well."

Caroline sighed. There must yet be something she might attempt to rectify her situation, for she would neither apologize nor go to the north.

❧❧ ❧❧

Louisa surely must have pity on her, Caroline reasoned, for her sister had been chief in both separating Charles from Miss Jane Bennet and advising her about how to proceed with Mr. Darcy. Having little experience with romance, Caroline had sought her sister's advice and followed it closely.

Yes, Louisa would understand and would save her from Charles's disastrous plan. She would not allow her beloved sister to suffer for committing the crimes in which she herself was an accomplice.

"But Mr. Hurst and I do not go to London, Caroline," Louisa said, "or else you should be most welcome, certainly."

Shocked at the lack of regret in her sister's tone, Caroline demanded, "Do not go to London? Whatever can you mean? Where do you go?"

"Mr. Hurst has engaged us for a large house party in Devonshire."

"In Devonshire?"

"Indeed," Louisa replied airily.

"But," Caroline protested, "Mr. Hurst may find just as much amusement in London, may he not?"

Louisa set aside the letter she had been composing and turned her attention to her younger sister. "Caroline, do not be obtuse. His schoolfellow has invited a house full, and we are to spend several months at cards and fine foods. It was the only inducement he could want."

"Cards and food are not exclusive to Devonshire," Caroline said as she slowly walked closer to her sister and slid her fingertips along the top of the escritoire. "Why must you stay with his friends?"

Louisa rolled her eyes. "Why, for the simple reason that we were invited. Can you not comprehend that?"

There must be a method of convincing her sister to alter her plans. Caroline thought for a moment and then said, "You have never before desired to be in the company of Mr. Hurst's friends. I recall you saying that they were a group of bloated fools, in fact."

Indeed, she could hardly imagine her sister willingly placing herself in such company. Mr. Hurst was a gentleman of fashion and fortune, but he was not known for good sense or impressive companions.

"I desire to socialize with them now." Louisa's expression clearly meant to convey more than her words made obvious. "And that is all that matters."

Caroline deliberately misunderstood.

"Then, though the company does not sound particularly educated or interesting, I shall be happy to attend."

Louisa looked up at her with surprise, and then her expression hardened. Her next words were spoken in the manipulative tone Caroline knew well. "Why, I believed you to be on your way to Cumbria to visit Mama. Charles has arranged it all, including a traveling companion, I believe. He said Mama's disappointment at missing his wedding could only be assuaged by his promise to deliver you to her door."

Caroline was affronted. Charles had arranged everything. He had consulted their mother and Louisa, and everyone, it seemed, was in agreement but her.

She chose to speak plainly. "So I am to be sent away."

Louisa blinked with feigned innocence. She was fully acquainted with Caroline's actions in London, and she was also privy to the workings of her heart where Mr. Darcy was concerned, so it surprised Caroline that not even the slightest expression of pity stole across her features.

She could pretend to misunderstand Louisa's intentions no longer. The simple fact was that her sister was removing herself entirely from the altercation. She, who had been of like mind when it came to Jane Bennet, was now more interested in staying out of matters than in supporting her own blood kin.

But Caroline's vexation and grief over her sister went far deeper.

She had divulged the full truth of her feelings to Louisa. To her, she had confessed her deepest longings. Louisa knew of her desire to marry Mr. Darcy and to gain her own home, to become mistress of Pemberley. Louisa had even offered her advice on how to influence a gentleman, and yet, when all her tactics had failed and Mr. Darcy had proposed to Miss Elizabeth Bennet, her sister had abandoned her.

"I am sorry for you, my dear sister," Louisa said, though she did not sound sorry at all. "But I cannot say I am surprised."

Caroline found herself overcome by shock at her sister's words. "Can you not?"

"No, for your intentions with Mr. Darcy were far too overt. It was, at times, painful to watch your interactions with him. You must learn, Caro, to employ a bit of artfulness if you should like to ensnare a gentleman such as my Mr. Hurst."

A feeling of betrayal settled upon Caroline at that moment. She was neither angry nor embarrassed, but her shock was utter and complete.

"What do you mean, Louisa?"

"Why, precisely what I said. You were ever trying to provoke Mr. Darcy by mentioning Miss Bennet and her connections. Though you believed yourself to be mocking her, you succeeded only in keeping the lady at the forefront of his mind." Here, Louisa paused in contemplation. "You may well be the most successful unintentional matchmaker in the country!"

Ire rose in Caroline at this suggestion, and her fingers gripped the edge of the writing table. "If that is true, Louisa, then you must also accept that you share that title, for it was chiefly your advice that I followed."

The sisters eyed each other for many long moments before Louisa said, "Do not you think it wise, sister, to retrench? To take some time away? Perhaps a fresh perspective will be good for everyone."

"Retrench?" Caroline could barely pronounce the word, so far from her nature was it to retreat from conflict. "I need no pause for perspective."

"Do you not perceive the benefits?"

"No, indeed. No good can come of such dissemination of our party."

"Can it not?" Louisa asked. "Our family is suddenly very different. We welcome a new sister to the fold, and naturally, we must all find our footing in the new order. In fact, I am anxious to be away so that I may return as if none of the unpleasantness in London or at Pemberley ever occurred. You ought to do the same."

Caroline was so angry she could not utter a syllable.

"I perceive your anger, my dear sister," Louisa said, her eyes now full of false pity, "but you must understand that this decision is for the best. *Our* best." She offered Caroline another look that was all condescension. "You must weigh your choices. Is it more important to flatter your vanity or to preserve peace in the family? And I should think that you would like to retain your welcome at Pemberley."

With the latter, Caroline could not argue. She closed her eyes and allowed herself to contemplate Pemberley, the estate she had one day hoped to call home. In her mind, she could see the massive stone edifice, she could smell the roses that bloomed all summer in the manicured garden, and she could even feel the soft breeze that blew across the pond in the evenings. She could imagine herself ascending the massive staircase in the evenings after she indulged in a quick trip to the kitchen for a bedtime biscuit or glass of wine. She could feel the cool stone underfoot as she padded silently up to her chamber.

"I would never forfeit my rights to visit Pemberley," Caroline whispered.

"Then off you shall go to Mama."

"I suppose it is so," Caroline said.

◦◦◦ ◦◦◦

And here she was.

In Kendal.

Standing ankle deep in mud at a wretched coaching inn and endeavoring to conceal the full truth of what had taken place from her own mother, the woman she held most dear.

❧ Three ☙

Perhaps the long journey and the uncomfortable accommodations over the past six days had taxed Caroline beyond what she had expected, and now she was suffering from an excess of sentimentality. Yes, exhaustion was to blame for the warm sting of tears in her eyes and the heavy pull in her heart.

"Oh! How I have missed my youngest daughter." Mrs. Newton stepped back, holding Caroline at arm's length so she could better observe her. "But you have matured so much that you hardly resemble the little girl I sent to London all those years ago."

Caroline briefly lowered her eyes and smiled at her mother. "Mama, it has not been so long as that, for we have seen each other numerous times since I left the seminary."

"Yes, the seminary returned quite a changed young lady. Even your accent was different. You could have hailed from an aristocratic London family. But you were yet a little girl." Mrs. Newton caressed her daughter's cheek and then took both her hands. "Now, however, after a short two years in charge of your brother's household, I find a beautiful young woman before me."

Caroline forced a smile, but at that precise moment, she appreciated neither the benefits of her education nor her experience as mistress of her brother's household. Though outwardly she might appear to be a composed woman of sense and education, she felt more like a lost little girl than a woman of twenty years. She had no direction, no friends, no husband, no home, and—for the moment—no siblings.

Mrs. Newton squeezed Caroline's hands and then turned to Rosemary, who had also escaped the confines of the coach and was standing at a polite distance. "And will you introduce me to your friend, Caro?"

Caroline turned to regard the woman, her companion, whose full name she still could not recall. Covering her embarrassment, she said, "I should have thought Charles had supplied the name of his employee when he wrote of my arrival."

As Mrs. Newton's eyebrows raised and then drew down in confusion, Rosemary stepped closer and looked at Caroline with appraising eyes. Again, Caroline willed herself to remember the woman's surname, but it did not come.

Caroline's embarrassment only deepened when the woman supplied the name herself: "My name is Rosemary Pickersgill, and I find I am already most indebted to your family for its graciousness in seeing to the employment of a widow such as me."

Caroline gawped. Pickersgill! Her surname was far worse than her first name. Caroline cleared her throat, composed her expression, and continued by saying, as if she had been cognizant of the appellation all along, "Yes, Mama, this is Mrs. Pickersgill. And this is my mother, Mrs. Newton."

Her mother had shown no reaction to the horrid name. Instead, she said, "I am very happy to make your acquaintance, Mrs. Pickersgill, but I find I must correct you at the outset. *I* am already in *your* debt, for you have seen my daughter home to us safely."

At just that moment, Mr. Newton joined them and immediately took Caroline's hand and pressed it in his. To her consternation, she found he had neglected his gloves and was gripping her kid gloves with his bare hands. Not only was he without proper attire—either to be seen publicly or to combat the winter weather—but it reflected poorly on his wife for having allowed the circumstance in the first place, and Caroline did not like anything to reflect poorly on her mother. Besides, his hands must be quite cold.

Despite the temperature of his bare hands, he spoke with warmth, saying, "Caroline, you have been too long away from us. Your mother has missed you greatly."

Caroline concealed a wince. Mr. Newton was a kind man even though he had acquired the sum total of his fortune through the building trade. He purported to be an engineer, had been a visitor at the Royal Society in London, and claimed that the design of bridges was more complicated than it appeared, but Caroline harbored doubts. Was not a sturdy piece of timber and some supports all that was required to construct an adequate? It seemed a task that required no special acumen, but he had traveled about the country assisting in their design and accumulating vast wealth.

Caroline forced a smile to her lips and said, "I hope I find you well, Mr. Newton."

He offered her a grin so wide that his graying sideburns seemed to shift their position upward. "Oh yes, I have a new bridge to design, and I cannot be unwell when my mind is so happily occupied."

"A new bridge?" Caroline asked quietly as she shot a look toward her mother. Here was Mr. Newton already discussing his trade and in public. "How quaint."

How unfortunate that his manners displayed no real improvement from his travels and his vocabulary showed no mental aptitude out of the common way. He was wealthy, to be sure, but had he allowed that circumstance to improve him?

Not that Caroline could discern.

In fact, Mr. Newton had always worn his wealth as if it were a newly starched shirt.

Uncomfortably.

Still, Caroline smiled at him, all the while thinking it was perhaps best that he and her mother remained tucked away so far north. Here, he could not cause as much of a scene, for there were few people of polite society to take offense.

He released Caroline's hand and smiled openly at Rosemary. "And who is your friend?"

Mr. Newton and Mrs. Pickersgill acknowledge each other with bow and curtsey as the presentations were made.

"Mrs. Pickersgill," he said with a broad smile, "you are very welcome to the Lake District and, indeed, to our home as well. And now, let us be off to Newton House, for you must both be exhausted."

"Yes, my dears," Mrs. Newton said with a sweep of her arm, "do allow Mr. Newton to see to your belongings and come along to our carriage."

Caroline trudged behind her mother across the inn yard to the waiting conveyance, all the while taking care to keep her skirts lifted away from the mud. She did not relish yet another ride, but this trip would be mercifully brief.

The ladies settled themselves within the carriage, and Caroline watched with annoyance as Mr. Newton helped the postboys remove the trunks and boxes from the basket at the rear of the post chaise and carried them to the corresponding basket on the Newton's coach.

Caroline shook her head as her mother's husband heaved a large trunk across the inn yard. She had not approved of her mother's marriage to Mr. Newton for just this reason. Her own excellent father, though born to no social graces, had made certain that he fit into any society. Unfortunately, he had succumbed to fever before he could feel its full benefits. Mr. Newton's philosophy, however, dictated that he would practice only those manners that made others comfortable and not those that were designed to demonstrate his true position in society as a now-wealthy landowner.

What good was such a position if one did not take hold of all the benefits the status afforded? To Caroline, it was unfathomable. And worse, it kept her mother removed from most good society as well. They would be welcomed in no homes of worth in London.

"Oh Mama," Caroline said when she could bear it no longer, "can you not encourage Mr. Newton to behave himself?"

Mrs. Newton looked quickly to her husband. "Has he done something amiss?"

"Only look at how he carries his burden like a common plow horse. Why must he insist on undertaking such labors when there are servants about?"

Mrs. Newton turned back to her daughter with a vague look of disappointment on her face. That expression discomfited Caroline greatly, for she did not like to draw her mother's displeasure.

Mrs. Newton's lips drew into a cheerless smile as she said, "You must forgive Mr. Newton, my dear. He prefers being useful, and we must make certain allowances for those we love."

This had long been a point of contention. Her mother was always willing to make excuses whereas Caroline saw the world for what it was—a harsh and fearsome place—and endeavored to protect those she loved from its criticisms. Caroline sighed and said, "Can you and Charles not understand that reputations—and indeed marriages—are built on more than just feelings?" Her words had barely broken from her lips when regret impelled her to snatch them back. She had not meant to disagree with her mother so overtly, but could she not see that the fates of entire families rested on each action in society and on each matrimonial decision? That entire reputations could be destroyed so easily?

Mrs. Newton took both Caroline's hands in hers once more. "Oh, Caro, let us not begin with such a dismal subject. I am too pleased to have you back with us to spare a thought on a little difference of opinion."

Caroline answered her with only a tight smile and a heart full of regret.

ᴥᴥ ᴥᴥ

After three quarters of an hour on a lovely stretch of undulating terrain, Caroline had heard her fill of Mr. Newton's narrative on every winter-brown pasture, rock wall, and quaint cottage in sight and was relieved when they arrived at Newton House.

When the coach stopped before the main entrance, Mr. Newton exited and assisted the ladies to the ground, and for a moment, they all looked at the edifice before them.

Caroline was forced to admit, if only to herself, the beauty of the house despite the fact that it held no connection with an ancient family and was, unfortunately, newly built. No sprawling additions or wings of different architectural styles cluttered the building's façade. Newton House was of unified theme with little adornment. Large windows lined the exterior in perfect symmetry, and the double door placed precisely at its center was now opened in invitation. And though it was not of the imposing scale of Pemberley, it was one of the largest homes of the neighborhood and was well situated on a comfortable acreage.

In all, Newton House would make as a serviceable a prison as any home in the countryside.

Still, Caroline could not help but wonder how long she would be confined within its walls. When would her banishment come to an end? How would she rectify matters with her brother and return to his society? She must conceive of a method for doing so soon, for though this home was pleasing to the eye, it was yet her jail.

Mrs. Newton was the first to speak. "Well, as you see, it is still standing, and you have at long last arrived. I am ever so pleased at the prospect of a house full of guests." She took Caroline's arm. "Now, do come in."

"Yes, indeed, you are most welcome," Mr. Newton said as he offered Rosemary his arm and escorted her up the stairs.

Caroline shook her head at Mr. Newton's undue attention to a servant and listened with displeasure as he made a great pretense of pointing out every feature of the house as they entered the foyer.

"You see, my dear Mrs. Pickersgill, I built Newton House myself."

"Did you, Mr. Newton?" Rosemary asked as she untied her cloak and bonnet and handed them to the maid who was awaiting them in the entryway. She looked about her with apparent interest, her eyes finally alighting on the towering ceiling, which had been painted to represent the sky. "It is lovely, and I must say how much I admire your high ceilings. Their ornamentation is quite pleasing."

"The painting was Mrs. Newton's idea," Mr. Newton said with a smile, obviously pleased that someone had noticed his wife's addition to the design. "I am far too practically minded to have thought of something as artistic as that. You see, high ceilings can make a room difficult to heat, but with proper hearth placement and design, it can be done quite effectively. Only come along and allow me to show you...."

They disappeared down the hallway, leaving Mr. Newton's voice in a trail behind him as he no doubt gave Rosemary an account and view of every room on the first floor, including the servant's quarters. The woman would likely be required to hear minute details of each chamber from the dining room to the music room.

"Come, Caro," Mrs. Newton said upon shedding her outerwear, "I have ordered some refreshments to be laid out in the sitting room, and your belongings will be placed in your chambers momentarily. Then you may spend the rest of the day in recovery from your journey."

Caroline felt true joy at the prospect of a proper buffet after often having to endure food of poor quality in the posting inns over the past six days, and she followed her mother eagerly in the direction Mr. Newton and Rosemary had walked.

"Mr. Newton," Mrs. Newton called toward the back of the house, "do stop explaining the nuances of engineering to our friend and allow her to join us in the sitting room for a cup of tea."

Mr. Newton's face emerged from around the corner. "I do become quite carried away, do I not, my dear? We shall join you at this moment."

He disappeared briefly and then reemerged with Rosemary in tow.

Mrs. Newton shook her head. "You must excuse my dear Mr. Newton," she said to Rosemary. "He forgets that not all people are as interested in brick and mortar as he is."

Caroline, for once, agreed with her mother's assessment, but she did not say so.

"Not at all, Mrs. Newton," Rosemary said. "His descriptions have been most instructive."

"Well, then you will certainly have your fill of instruction here," Mrs. Newton said. "Now, come along, for I have had the servants lay a tray of cold meats."

"That is very kind, Mrs. Newton," Rosemary said as she lagged a bit behind the others. "But shall I not oversee the trunks while you enjoy your time with your daughter?"

"Indeed, I shall not hear of it, Mrs. Pickersgill, though it is kind of you to offer." Mrs. Newton led the women along the hallway, turning to share her joyous smile with them. "I am in a mood to celebrate my daughter's arrival, and you must take part. Were it up to me, we would have killed the fatted calf and celebrated all night now that Caro is home, but I did try to be sensible. Though there is a bit of ham on the tray."

Mrs. Newton pushed open the sitting room door to discover a blond-haired gentleman standing over the selection of meats and bread. "I see that we are not the first to discover the refreshments," she said with a laugh.

The gentleman turned and smiled broadly. His blue eyes rested on Caroline before they returned to her mother. "Guilty. This elegant display was too tempting to resist."

Intrigued, Caroline studied the man. He was average in height or a little taller, but he had a breadth of shoulder and a depth of musculature that gave him the appearance of being larger. He seemed familiar, but she could not quite place him.

"Ah, Rushton," Mr. Newton said from the doorway. "Once you have filled your plate, join me in the study so that the ladies may not be bothered by business. I have some design ideas for the Fairmont Bridge."

Rushton.

Caroline narrowed her eyes as the gentleman acknowledged Mr. Newton's request with a nod and a wave of his plate. Yes, she remembered him now.

Patrick Rushton. He was the son of the unfortunate Mr. James Rushton of Keswick. While the Bingleys had been ascending in wealth and status, the Rushton family was in decline. Through several generations, they owned a large tract of land that included a graphite quarry, but the mine was yielding less graphite, and with each passing year the Rushton clan had fallen a little lower.

When Caroline was a young girl, she could remember her parents discussing the elder Mr. Rushton's decision to support his family by selling as much land as was permitted in the entail. By the time Mr. Rushton had died, he had already divested himself of much of his property in order to pay his debts, and still they were not satisfied. By now, their circumstances must be dire indeed, and their family home had likely fallen into hopeless disrepair.

How very pitiable to lose one's wealth and standing in such a way.

Based on her memories of Mr. Patrick Rushton, Caroline thought it was unlikely that he would be the one to rescue the family from their plight. She remembered him as an insolent sort of youth, and based on the fact that he was currently engaged in stealing food from her mother's sitting room, he was, in her estimation, unchanged in adulthood.

"Caroline, my dear," Mrs. Newton said, "you remember Mr. Rushton, do you not? Our families have been acquainted for generations, you know, though I do not believe you ever played together as children, for he was a bit older than you. He was at university, I think, when you went to the seminary in town."

"Yes, Mama, I do remember Mr. Rushton." Caroline strode forward and curtseyed with extreme decorum. "Mr. Rushton, how very..."—she chose the word carefully—"surprising it is to see you in my mother's home."

Mr. Rushton studied her for a moment before setting his plate aside and bowing in return. "Miss Bingley," said he in an ironical tone, his eyes mischievous, "the years have not altered you, I find."

Caroline blinked at his tone but was not distracted enough to neglect her duty. "You and your family are well, I hope," she said.

"Yes, my family is in good health, Miss Bingley. Thank you for inquiring. I shall not make the same inquiry of you, for I can see that your nearest relations are all well, and your mother has assured me that your siblings do well too." He looked at Rosemary. "And will you do me the honor of introducing your friend?"

Caroline gaped at him as he crossed to stand before Rosemary. Why did everyone persist in describing this horrid servant as her friend? Could they not tell that Rosemary Pickersgill was an old widow who was not of her social class and thus not suitable for an association—much less a friendship—with Caroline?

Mrs. Newton spoke for her, saying, "Mr. Rushton, allow me to present Mrs. Pickersgill, Caroline's companion from London. We are ever so pleased to have her in our home this winter."

He gave her a polite bow, they exchanged a few civil words, and then he turned to Mr. Newton, who had been lingering with some impatience at the chamber door. "Well, Newton, shall we see to those bridges?"

With a nod at the assembled ladies, Mr. Rushton picked up his plate and departed.

৵৹ Four ৹৵

Once the door was closed and the men's voices receded, Caroline turned to the buffet, wondering idly if Mr. Rushton had left any victuals for their intended recipients. Finding that there was a sufficient supply, she began to fill a plate.

"Mrs. Pickersgill, do join Caro in taking some nourishment, if Mr. Rushton has left anything. That young man certainly has an appetite."

Caroline restrained a laugh at Mr. Rushton's being called young, for he was quite a few years older than she was. "What does Mr. Rushton do here at Newton House, Mama?"

"Why, he is Mr. Newton's business partner."

"Business partner?" Caroline forgot the piece of ham she had been transporting to her plate, holding it aloft, and frowned at the question. "Why should Mr. Newton require a partner in throwing a few logs across a river?"

"Indeed, Caroline, I believe the construction of bridges is more complicated than that," Mrs. Newton said as she crossed to the buffet. "Poor Mr. Rushton is always welcome in our home, and you must not taunt him, for he has had quite a difficult time of late."

"Has he?" Caroline asked, not truly caring whether or not he had suffered. She suddenly had no taste for ham and dropped it back to the tray, taking a large piece of bread instead.

"Oh yes! If you apply to anyone in town, you will find that he has developed the unjust reputation of a confirmed fortune hunter." Mrs. Newton turned to Rosemary to explain. "His poor father lost a great deal of money, my dear, and their estate is only now recovering. He was to be married to a wealthy young heiress, but there was a dreadful split just before the union was to take place."

"Oh dear," Rosemary said, her eyes wide. "That must have been quite a scandal. A broken engagement always brings disgrace to one party or other."

"And so it did to Mr. Rushton. No one knows the full story—for Mr. Rushton has never volunteered his perspective—but everyone says that the lady jilted him when she discovered his true circumstances."

"I could well believe him a fortune hunter, Mama, and I do not like to see him in your household," Caroline said, truly concerned.

Mrs. Newton only laughed and said, "Oh, do not believe a word of it, my dear. I have always been an excellent judge of a person's true character, and so you must believe me when I say that he is no fortune hunter."

"How can you be certain?" Caroline asked, for though she had only become acquainted with the story a few moments ago, she was now greatly afraid that her mother had been duped by a cad. "You have just confessed that Mr. Rushton has not denied his part in the dissolution of his engagement."

"What reason can he have to deny anything? No one would believe him now. Besides, it is simply not in Mr. Rushton's nature to worry over such matters or to take the easy course. Why, after university, he came home, showed an interest in engineering, and that was all that was required for Mr. Newton to take him under his wing. He learned quickly, and the two have been partners for some years now."

How unfortunate, Caroline thought, though she could not decide whom she pitied more: Mr. Newton for having to put up with Mr. Rushton's wit or Mr. Rushton for having to contend with Mr. Newton's ramblings on inane subjects.

"Now, let us forget this business with dear Mr. Rushton. Settle yourselves by the fire, and I shall bring the tea," her mother said as she arranged the cups on their saucers and lifted the silver teapot. As she turned to deliver the full cups to her guests, she said, "Caro, you will also be pleased to find another old friend in the neighborhood."

"Shall I?" If this neighbor were anything like Mr. Rushton, she was certain she would take no pleasure in the hearing.

"The Honorable Miss Lavinia Charlton—Mrs. Ralph Winton now that she has married—has been at Oak Park for several months." Mrs. Newton turned to Rosemary and explained, "Lavinia and Caroline have been friends since their days at the seminary."

"Oh?" Caroline asked, ignoring Rosemary's part in the conversation as she scooted to the edge of her seat and leaned forward a bit. This was news of great consequence, for Lavinia was the only daughter of Lord Charlton, who held a large barony and retained great wealth and status in the county. "Lavinia is in Kendal?"

"Indeed, and the whole county is well pleased to see her again. She has not returned since she was sent to London all those years ago." Mrs. Newton again turned to Rosemary. "After Lord Charlton's wife died, Lavinia was packed away to London to be educated, for her father was in no position to educate a female when he had two sons—Harold and William—for whom to account."

Rosemary, whom to Caroline's eye was trying to impress her new mistress's mother by behaving so politely, set aside her teacup and saucer. "Yes, Mrs. Newton, that often seems to occur among those of rank. Young ladies become rather disposable objects."

Caroline recalled how upset Lavinia had been over her removal from Oak Park, having been educated her whole life at home. "Come," Caroline said, "you must admit that if she had to be removed, it was at least to pleasing circumstances. She went to 'ladies' Eton' in Queen's Square, one of the most prestigious female seminaries in Town. I found it to be a first-rate seminary, and Lavinia soon came to share my opinion."

To Rosemary, Mrs. Newton said, "Caroline's father always intended to send his daughters to London for an education, so he elected to send them to Queen's Square also, and that is how their friendship grew."

Yes, Caroline's time in Queen's Square had been a great benefit to her, for she had finally been able to associate with Lavinia on the comparatively level footing the school provided.

They had indeed become fast friends, but distance had separated them when, upon leaving the seminary, Caroline had begun traveling with Charles and Mr. Darcy, and Lavinia had eventually married Mr. Ralph Winton, an excessively wealthy London gentleman.

They had exchanged a few polite letters over the intervening three years, and Caroline had been satisfied that their friendship was safe. She had not realized until just this moment how superficial the correspondence must have been, for she had not known her friend had returned to Kendal. Obviously, Lavinia had withheld some facts from her.

Almost to herself, she said, "Lavinia said nothing of a return to Kendal in her letters."

"Oh no?" Mrs. Newton asked as she joined the women by the fire with her cup and saucer balanced in her dimpled hand. "Mrs. Halstead—you recall her, do you not?—tells me that the Charlton household has been in quite an uproar. I imagine Lavinia has not had time to write of her current circumstances."

Caroline's eyes widened. "What are her current circumstances?"

"Oh my! You must not have heard." Mrs. Newton set her cup and saucer on the side table and reached for Caroline's arm and gave it a soft pat. "Her brother Harold has died."

At first, Caroline could only look at her mother to seek further confirmation, and then her mind began to process the information. "This is shocking news indeed," she said. A death in the family must certainly warrant a word or two from her friend on the subject. "Lavinia said nothing of this tragedy either."

"I am grieved to hear of the loss," Rosemary offered politely with a glance at Caroline, seemingly to gauge her reaction. "Was he a close acquaintance of your family?"

"How kind of you to offer condolences, my dear," Mrs. Newton said, "but our families were only a little acquainted, mostly due to Caroline's friendship with Lavinia. Mr. Harold Charlton was the eldest son and heir to the barony, so we associated little with him, but occasionally we were invited to Oak Park. Customs of rank are not so strictly adhered to in the country, you know."

"How did he die?" Caroline asked.

"Consumption," Mrs. Newton said with a shake of her head. "It happened last summer."

Caroline could not stifle her curiosity and asked, "Was he married? Did he leave an heir?"

"No, unfortunately, Mr. Charlton never married, and that leaves William to inherit the title."

"Oh, that is an interesting development." Caroline's eyebrows raised at the thought of William Charlton, the younger son, holding the barony. She recalled him as a pleasant but indulged young man. Beyond that, as a younger son, he was often forgotten, even by his own relations. "I admit I cannot imagine William Charlton sitting in Parliament. How has he taken to being trained for the title and its resulting duties?"

"Not well, I fear. I expect he planned to retain his carefree ways." Mrs. Newton leaned forward and whispered, "Mrs. Halstead told me in the strictest confidence of a conversation she had lately with Lord Charlton on this very subject. Young Mr. Charlton, it seems, has shown the greatest reluctance to rise to the peerage and run the estate."

"I cannot imagine any rational gentleman being so disinclined to ascend in society." Caroline shook her head. "I confess that I do not comprehend it."

Rosemary surprised Caroline by responding, "I have found, Miss Bingley, that not all people are so inclined to grasp for rank, though some will do anything to attain it."

"How very…"—Caroline considered her words again—"obvious a statement to make."

Mrs. Newton took a sip of tea and then resumed her conspiratorial posture. "You know, my dear, that I do not care to indulge in idle gossip, and I pride myself on only sharing news of a factual, verified nature. But," she said with a swirl of her teaspoon, "I must tell you that Mr. Charlton has developed an infamous reputation since you have been away, and unlike the gossip surrounding Mr. Rushton, I find I must believe it, for he has been linked quite reliably with a servant in his household."

Caroline leaned back to consider her mother's news. "I do recall," she said, "that as a child Mr. Charlton was fond of creating mischief, but to dally with a maid so openly? That is something one often sees in London, but in the country, it seems likely to be nothing more than tittle-tattle."

"You must take into account his circumstances. He is a member of the titled class and a younger son after all. If his reputation is based on truth, it should not surprise you," Mrs. Newton said with a glance at Rosemary. "Is that not so, Mrs. Pickersgill? Are not many of the titled classes, wherever their domicile, engaged in such behavior?"

"It is quite often so, I have found, Mrs. Newton."

Caroline shook her head at Rosemary's response. What did the opinion of a servant matter? "Come, Mrs. Pickersgill is hardly qualified to offer any wisdom on this subject."

"Caro! One must only glance at Mrs. Pickersgill to see that she is a woman of breeding and good sense."

Caroline glanced at Rosemary but saw neither breeding nor sense.

Rosemary set aside her teacup and crossed her hands in her lap. "It is true, Mrs. Newton. I am nothing more than your daughter's companion and ought not offer my opinions so openly." She met Caroline's eyes and added, "Accurate though they may be."

"But—" Mrs. Newton said, apparently on the verge of pursuing this line of conversation. Caroline was uninterested.

"But is there truth to these rumors?" Caroline demanded of her mother instead.

Both women looked abruptly at her.

"About Mr. Charlton. Has he been proven unworthy?"

"That I cannot say for certain," Mrs. Newton said slowly and then smiled. "I am pleased, however, to find that your time in London has not persuaded you to accept such behavior."

Caroline winced a bit. She wished to blend thoroughly with London society and accept the behavior they found suitable, but she could not deny her innate abhorrence for the practice of keeping mistresses or conducting affairs, accepted though they may be. She, who prided herself on being erudite and sophisticated, had never been able to shed her country upbringing so wholly as to approve of such affairs between gentlemen and women who were not their wives. But if that is what polite society demanded of her, then she would strive to alter her judgment.

Rather than opining on her own conflicting views of fornication, she chose to focus on the opinions of another. "Lord Charlton must be displeased, for the barony has always maintained the highest of reputations."

Mrs. Newton nodded. "Indeed, Lord Charlton must be quite concerned, for he has arranged for Lavinia to see to her brother's well-being. Lord Charlton has already departed for Town, I believe, though Parliament will not open until March. Lavinia runs the household now."

"I wonder that Lavinia's husband could spare her," Caroline said, setting aside her plate and focusing only on the conversation at hand.

"From what I hear, it is fortunate for the entire Charlton household that he could." Her mother paused a moment to sip her tea and continued, "Her six months of mourning for her brother have just ended, and certainly, she will call on you as soon as she hears you have come."

"I do not doubt that she will call, for Lavinia and I were fast friends at the seminary," Caroline said with more confidence than she felt.

Then she stood for no other reason than to expel some of the nervous energy that now coursed through her. She crossed to the buffet but did not look at its contents. Her mind was already at Oak Park, for within its walls lay her opportunity.

An association with Lavinia Winton could very much ease the damage of having been excluded from Charles and Mr. Darcy's company. To be connected with the family of a baron, though less wealthy than Mr. Darcy, would be a coup indeed!

Yes, Lavinia must come!

Caroline attempted to modulate her tone, which she knew must hold more than a hint of excitement. "Have you already shared the news of my return with Kendal society, Mama?"

Mrs. Newton nodded. "Why, yes, indeed I did, for I could hardly conceal my anticipation from my acquaintances, could I?"

Caroline smiled, pleased that her mother's easy manners for once had benefitted her. Word of her arrival would soon spread, and surely Lavinia would do her duty and call on her old friend.

She stood for a time at the buffet and imagined Charles's surprise at the turn in her circumstances. He would expect to find her contrite after her banishment, but she would greet him from a higher vantage point.

Her heart seized a bit with regret at the course of her thoughts. She did not relish the idea of Charles as her enemy and had no wish to consider their relationship as a struggle for power. She simply longed to be with him, to have his companionship once again. She wished he had never sent her away, but he had.

He had forced this disjointedness to enter their relationship, and she must deal with it as she saw fit, and she did not see fit to apologize to Miss Elizabeth Bennet.

No, she would simply have to show Charles how desirable her company was to prominent people. She would become the center of Kendal society, and when her brother returned for her, he would see his error. He would know that she was worthy to be in his society once again.

Caroline's thoughts of her brother so distracted her that she hardly heard as Mrs. Newton went on to the next topic and then the next. When finally there was a break in the conversation, she managed to say, "Mama, I beg your pardon, but fatigue suddenly overwhelms me."

Mrs. Newton's hands flew to her mouth. "Oh! Of course, of course, you are fatigued from your long journey, and here I sit nattering away." She leapt from the sofa, drawing Caroline and Rosemary with her. "Allow me to escort you both to your chambers."

They ascended the stairs in a tangle of skirts and apologies, and Mrs. Newton directed Rosemary to one of the house's finest bedchambers. "Mrs. Pickersgill," she said as she opened the door with a flourish, "I hope you will be quite comfortable here."

Rosemary sucked in a breath. The room was all plush linens and comfortable furnishings, and the large window looked upon a vast green meadow beyond. "I assure you I shall! It is a lovely room."

Caroline curbed her temptation to ask her mother why she should put a servant in such a fine room, for she truly was too exhausted to mention it.

"And it is adjacent to Caroline's room, so you two may stay up until all hours of the night chattering away as girls do," Mrs. Newton said.

Caroline grimaced. There would be little chattering with Rosemary, she felt certain.

With Rosemary shut securely in her room, Caroline walked alongside Mrs. Newton to her customary chamber, a lovely large corner room with both a view of the meadow and a delightful prospect of the pond.

"It is just as you recalled, is it not?" Mrs. Newton asked as they entered the chamber.

Caroline ventured to the window, her fingertips brushing across the bed linens as she passed. "Oh yes, Mama, the room is as lovely as it ever was," Caroline agreed.

Mrs. Newton took a seat on the bed and patted the space beside her. "Come sit with me."

Caroline was about to protest, reminding her mother of her fatigue, but one look at Mrs. Newton's hopeful face convinced her to obey.

"I am so pleased that you have come home to me, my girl, but you must tell me the truth. Has something happened between you and Charles?"

Caroline blinked at her, surprised at her mother's accuracy. Her mother may want to offer people the benefits of her trust and good opinion, but she always seemed to see straight to the heart of the matter when required. Still, Caroline could not confess the truth to her. Charles would not wish it, and neither did she. "No, why ever would you think such a thing?"

Mrs. Newton cocked her head skeptically. "Come, I know you have no wish to be here in Kendal. You aspire to a life in London and nothing less will do."

"I do love London." That was the half-truth, but she must yet conceal the unhappy portion from her mother.

As if her mother had read her thoughts, she said, "But you do not seem happy, Caro."

Caroline laughed to cover the correctness of her mother's assessment. It came out sounding bitter and sad. "Of course, I am happy. I am with you."

Mrs. Newton leaned forward, her eyes soft. "And I am happy too, my dear, but I cannot help but wonder why you left your brother and sister so suddenly."

"I missed you."

Her mother softened. "And I missed you, Caro, but I also know how well you enjoyed the benefits of Charles's household."

Caroline cleared her throat. "I found myself longing to see you again, and I knew you would be anxious to hear about Charles's marriage ceremony since you were unable to attend. It seemed the perfect opportunity to come away. Louisa and Mr. Hurst have gone to Devonshire, and of course, Charles has a wife capable of overseeing the running of Netherfield Park in my absence."

"And that is all?"

"Indeed, Mama, that is all."

Mrs. Newton did not appear truly satisfied, but she allowed the conversation to end.

·ର Five ଜଡ଼

The onslaught of calls began promptly the next morning, and the complete rite—call and requisite return of call—endured full a week. Every member of polite society in Cumbria, it seemed, had been alerted to Caroline's arrival, and the ladies seemed all to desire to call at once.

All except the one lady whom Caroline most wanted to see.

Lavinia Charlton Winton.

She, most decidedly, did not come.

Still, from ten in the morning until after two in the afternoon, a parade of neighbors passed through the drawing room of Newton House, where Caroline sat with her mother and Mrs. Pickersgill to receive them. She responded to so many inquiries as to her health and that of her siblings that she began to wish she had been ill so that she might have avoided the morning call ritual altogether.

Were Caroline not as easily given to politeness, she fancied she might greet each caller at the door herself and say, "Good morning to you, Miss Nonesuch. How lovely to rekindle our acquaintance. Allow me to save time by telling you that my family is in good health, I am pleased to be in Cumbria—though the weather is indeed horrid—and I am pained at leaving my siblings but delighted to be with my mother. Leave your card, for I am required to return your call and hold this precise discussion with you once again within the next few days."

Alas, such a thing could not be done, and so Caroline remained in her chair and made the required chitchat with all who came. Rosemary behaved admirably, and though Caroline could not be proud of the woman, she was at least not embarrassed by her, for she sat correctly and behaved to all appearances as a well-bred lady.

In fact, she was quite sure that Rosemary had charmed more than one old widow with her stories of Town and its residents. Mrs. Halstead had quite fallen in love, Caroline thought.

Mrs. Newton was always perfectly civil and reserved with her country guests, and often, she followed the conversation as she took up a bit of sewing. On the second morning, Caroline had sneaked into the drawing room early to remove all items of underlinen from the work basket. She simply refused to allow her mother to darn stockings if there were a chance that her schoolfellow Lavinia Winton might pay a call at any moment.

That moment, however, did not come until a week later. When Lavinia finally called upon the ladies of Newton House, they were absent on another visit.

Caroline, Mrs. Newton, and Rosemary had returned home through a dull drizzle of cold rain after returning a call to Mrs. Halstead, which had lasted quite a bit longer than Caroline had anticipated, and now the whole day was wasted and her spirits much depressed. She had quite given up the idea that Lavinia might call and was sure she had been snubbed, and she had no wish to do anything besides sit before the fire with a tin of biscuits and a pot of tea.

She shed her cloak and bonnet, eyeing the silver salver full of calling cards without the least feeling of hope.

Mrs. Newton pounced on the cards, however, and with shining eyes, she turned to Caroline. "Look, my dear, and you will find that your mother is always right. I told you Lavinia would call, and here is the proof."

Caroline felt her eyes widen in disbelief, and suddenly her pulse began to pound. Was it true? Had Lavinia called?

She looked down at the card her mother had extended to her.

The elegant black script read simply, "Mrs. Ralph Winton."

Caroline had the most girlish impulse to squeal and bounce up and down with glee, but she only looked at her mother and said, "I am pleased."

In truth, Caroline's relief was nearly complete, but the emotion was tainted by fear that Lavinia might have purposefully called at an early hour to avoid an actual visit and instead simply leave her card.

At least, Caroline reminded herself, Lavinia had called. She had not been slighted.

Now, it was upon her to wait on Lavinia, which she would do with the utmost courtesy and speed.

"We shall call upon her tomorrow first thing," she declared with a quick glance at Rosemary, who was watching her with a quizzical eye. "You will want to wear your nicest morning dress, Mrs. Pickersgill, for we wait upon the sister of a baron tomorrow."

Mrs. Pickersgill smiled faintly. "Indeed, a baron! I shall do my utmost to comport myself correctly."

"Yes, tomorrow is an important call." Thinking to avert any disasters that might arise from being forced to travel with her companion, she said, "It would be best if you remained as quiet as possible while we are at Oak Park."

Again, a faint smile. "Thank you, Miss Bingley. I shall take your recommendations on the value of silence into consideration. Now, if you will excuse me, I think you have long been desiring my absence."

Mrs. Pickersgill disappeared upstairs, leaving Mrs. Newton and Caroline alone in the entry hall.

"Caro, do you think it necessary to caution Mrs. Pickersgill? I have heard little of her history, but she has behaved as a well-mannered lady the entire week through, do not you think?"

Caroline was unsurprised by her mother's gentle defense of Mrs. Pickersgill, for it was just the sort of thing she would do. However, Caroline was acquainted with the wider world, and she knew the power of the titled to inflict social wounds upon the unsuspecting and the unmannered, and she would do everything she could in order to prevent anyone from bringing shame upon her family. If that meant risking slight rudeness at cautioning Mrs. Pickersgill, then so be it.

"She has been adequate, certainly," Caroline admitted, "but one cannot be too careful when one associates with the titled class. One slip and shame could rain upon us."

"My dear, you are far too dramatic for your own good," said her mother, as if Caroline's words held no greater import than newspaper gossip. "Now, do come into the music room, for I have not heard you play a note since you arrived, and you know what great pleasure I take in music."

She allowed her mother to lead the way to the music room, even though she was not in the mood to perform at the moment. She had much rather think on tomorrow's call, her wardrobe, and topics of conversation that would display her in the best light. Instead, she asked, "Have you retained the old square pianoforte then, Mama?"

"No, I believe you will be surprised to find that we have a new instrument for you to enjoy."

Mrs. Newton opened the door to a large chamber off the main hallway. The room was surrounded by casement windows, which were wonderful for allowing in light but less conducive for the highest sound quality. Today, they only admitted a dull gray and amplified the sound of the rain as it struck the large glass panes.

Several intimate seating areas were spread about the perimeter, and the furniture was comfortably upholstered in rich fabrics, but Mrs. Newton had clearly arranged the room around the pianoforte that stood at its center.

It was a beautiful instrument.

Caroline circled it, not allowing even the fabric of her skirts to touch it, as if the slightest human contact might somehow sully its perfection. Made of polished rosewood and standing upon elegantly turned legs, the piano was beyond what Caroline had anticipated.

"A Broadwood," she breathed. "I did not expect you to have acquired one so fine as this."

"I know! It was indeed a lavish expense for a household with no musical occupants, but we often have musical guests, and of course, I had hoped one day you would return and play for us."

It was a great extravagance, but Caroline could not disapprove of it. It was a sign of her mother's wealth and status, and it was indeed a thing of beauty to behold.

And she longed to play it and hear if its intonations matched its exterior beauty.

Caroline pulled the stool away, seated herself with her customary ceremony, and placed her fingertips on the cool ivory keys. She nearly sighed aloud at that simple pleasure. Seemingly without conscious decision, she began to play, her fingers automatically beginning the piece she often chose in company. It sounded even more beautiful on the Broadwood. Yes, the pianoforte had a sound as deep and lush as the darkest of chocolates. The music glided about the room and wrapped its hearers in a spell of sound.

At the seminary in London, Caroline had practiced long hours, for her father paid a great deal for her to have lessons with the music master. She could hear him now, saying, "Caroline, you must learn to play the pianoforte very well indeed, for the ability to produce a great performance on the instrument is one hallmark of an accomplished young woman, and one day, it will win you a gentleman of great worth. Mark my words."

Indeed, she had taken to her lessons with great vigor, but she could not give her father the credit for having inspired her. She had loved to play, and soon she quite outshone the other girls at the seminary.

Now, Caroline played with singular focus on her task. She knew each piece from memory, and though she had played them many times at countless parties and dinners, she fancied they still served their purpose.

And her mother's applause confirmed it.

"Oh!" she said. "Now, Mr. Newton may never chide me again for having insisted on the pianoforte, may he, Mr. Rushton? Caroline has certainly made the purchase worthwhile."

Caroline looked away from the pianoforte to discover Mr. Rushton languishing on the periphery of the chamber.

He was giving her the oddest look, and she found she could not quite meet his eyes. She looked away, and inexplicably she found herself fighting not to blush.

Then the gentleman spoke. "It was a well-rehearsed performance and very pleasing to most listeners, I am certain."

At this, Caroline did meet his gaze, for she could not take his meaning, so she chose the most direct approach and simply asked him. "What does that signify, 'well-rehearsed'? It sounds as if it were a compliment, but your tone of voice implies some sort of hidden meaning."

He smiled. "I meant just what I said. Your performance was practiced. In fact, you are so well acquainted with every note and nuance of that piece that you hardly even need to hear the actual music anymore."

"Do you mean to insinuate, then, that practice is somehow to be discouraged? I have always found, Mr. Rushton, that no great accomplishment can be made without taking the opportunity of practicing. A lack of rehearsal results in mistakes, and those can never be to one's benefit, can they?"

"I would not argue with you, Miss Bingley. I may only say this: there is also something pleasing in the unbridled joy of making errors."

"Unlike you, sir, I take no pleasure in my blunders but seek to minimize their existence."

"How unfortunate, for I have found that my greatest mistakes can sometimes yield the greatest pleasures."

Caroline laughed at this outright. "I am certain you believe yourself to be clever by speaking in paradoxes, but it shows me only how very impractical and foolish you are."

"I would expect you to think nothing different." He spoke these words with an undeniable tone of irony.

But before Caroline could question him further, her mother spoke. "Oh, you must stop teasing my daughter so, Mr. Rushton. You know very well that she plays beautifully."

"Indeed, she does everything beautifully," he said as he bowed to Mrs. Newton. Then, he turned toward the pianoforte and bowed to the musician as well, and as he raised himself back to his full height, Caroline was surprised to see a smirk on his face.

It was as if he had just negated his compliment with his sarcastic expression. Caroline scowled back. "Sir, your countenance belies your accolades, and I feel sure you must be insulting me."

"I would never presume to insult you, Miss Bingley."

"I should think not," Caroline said with venom, "for I have heard of your actions since I have been away."

"Have you indeed?" he asked with a grin. "And what, pray tell, have you heard?"

Caroline studied him in silence for a long moment, deciding whether or not to mention his broken engagement. One look at her mother told her it would be wise to hold her tongue, but upon glancing back at Mr. Rushton, she found that his expression nearly begged her to continue.

He seemed to be having fun.

And that is what kept her from saying another word. She only smirked at him as if she harbored a secret about him that even he did not know.

"That smile intrigues me, Miss Bingley."

"Does it?"

"Yes, I wonder what stories you have heard and what you have been foolish enough to believe."

"I assure you, Mr. Rushton, that nothing I have heard is likely to be as dreadful as what you have actually done."

He gave a hearty laugh. "Indeed, Miss Bingley, that is probably the truth."

"Oh come," Mrs. Newton said in his defense, "you are as upstanding a young man as ever I have seen."

He smiled genuinely at her. "I am pleased you think so, Mrs. Newton, for I hold you in the highest regard." He glanced at Caroline. "But I must depart. I was drawn to the room only to hear the performance, and Mr. Newton has now been waiting many minutes for my return to the study and our bridge plans."

"Go on, then," Mrs. Newton said.

To which Caroline added, "We will not miss you here."

Mr. Rushton only smiled once more as he exited the music room.

Caroline rose from the stool and chose a seat next to her mother. "I do not comprehend why you allow him in the house. He is a most confounding man."

৵৹ Six ৹৵

Caroline awakened early the next morning to prepare for her call upon Lavinia, and her excitement over the prospect must have overflowed to the rest of the household, for her mother had arrived with Rosemary close behind to help her dress.

So full of anticipation was Caroline that she could not even chide her mother for foisting Rosemary upon her.

She only sat at her dressing table and watched as her maid brushed her long brown hair into smooth waves.

Mrs. Newton and Rosemary sat on the bed, already completely dressed for their morning call, and observed. "Mrs. Pickersgill, you will like Oak Park."

"Will I? If you say so, Mrs. Newton, then I truly look forward to seeing it."

"It is the finest in the neighborhood, excepting my beloved Newton House of course."

"Oak Park is a lovely property," Caroline said from across the room. She was surprised at the wistfulness of her tone as she spoke. "But I do so wish you might have seen Pemberley, for it will quite spoil your view of any other home in England."

"But I have seen Pemberley," Mrs. Newton assured her daughter, "through your description. You make it sound so lovely that the reality cannot possibly match it. Besides, you know how I abhor travel. I would not enjoy myself if I were to venture so far from home. Oak Park will be the finest house I shall ever enter."

Caroline met her mother's eyes in the mirror. "I have always marveled at how different you and Papa were in your opinions on the subject of travel."

Mrs. Newton laughed. "Oh yes, we were certainly disparate in many of our opinions. He loved to wander. It was no sacrifice to him to go all the way to the Indies to earn his fortune, and though he always said he wanted to purchase an estate, I do not think he would have ever settled down enough to undertake it."

Caroline smiled at the memories of her father that were evoked within her. "I think he would have, eventually, for he knew that land is crucial to rising in society. And he desired for all of us to rise."

"Yes, he did, and you have all done so. You have such fashionable friends and have been about such interesting entertainments. And you have brought one such friend to visit us." She patted Rosemary's hand. "But I have always thought, my dear, that even the largest of houses and the finest of properties could not ensure the happiness your father and I desired for you, Charles, and Louisa. I am pleased that my children have all found their own sort of happiness and even remained as friends. It warms a mother's heart."

Caroline could not continue to meet her mother's eyes, even in the mirror, and she made a great pretense of studying her comb instead. Not only had Caroline failed to accede to her father's wishes of raising the status of the Bingley family, but she had made herself and everyone else unhappy in the process.

But this morning she had the opportunity to remedy her mistake. Today she would solidify her place in Kendal society, and from there, well, from there she could not say.

But she would rise, and it would all begin with her call on Lavinia.

∽◦❀ ❀◦∾

As Mr. Newton's coach turned onto the long approach road to Oak Park, Caroline had the oddest inclination to leap from the conveyance, for it was traveling slower than normal, surely, and dash to the door. Instead, she clasped her hands in her lap and watched as the house began to rise upon the horizon. She experienced a moment of pure envy.

Oak Park was an elaborately constructed stone edifice that took up what appeared to be the equivalent of an entire city block. Unlike Newton House, Oak Park had grown over time, with one wing decidedly neo-classical and another of Gothic influence. Somehow, the dissimilar architectural styles melded together in the domed entryway that once had served as the entire main house.

It was nothing to Pemberley, of course; few properties could rival it. Still, Oak Park represented a particular stability of rank and standing within the community that could not easily be ignored or forgotten.

It was not possible for anyone to look down upon Lavinia or Mr. Charlton, no matter what missteps they might make, for they had been fortunate enough to be born to the life to which all people aspired. They had received the best education, had access to the finest society, and lived quite at their leisure. They could behave as they chose, and no one could oust them from their proper place. Their positions were as settled as the foundation upon which Oak Park itself rested.

It was vexing to Caroline to realize that she had no such advantage. Her family had money, certainly, and that was not something to be ignored. Money was important indeed, but she knew very well that it was only one component in the quest for happiness.

And she had indeed attended the finest London seminary, she did retain access to many people within polite society, and she did live at her leisure, but she was also acutely aware that one ill-placed word of her family's origins in trade could damage every advantage she possessed.

She had no ancestors of note and no ancient family lands to lend her credibility in the face of her potential detractors.

And worse, Caroline's inheritance of 20,000 pounds was controlled by her brother until her marriage, whereupon it would be controlled by her husband. Certainly, Charles was generous with her allowances, and she would admit to having occasionally spent more than she ought to have, but the truth of the matter was that she, like every other lady, would never have the opportunity of managing her own wealth without the interference of some man or other.

Oh, how she wished for the permanency and stability afforded by a house such as Pemberley or even Oak Park, for at the very least, a woman's place was in the management of the home. It would be her place.

"Did I not tell you, Mrs. Pickersgill?" Mrs. Newton said as they drew nearer to Oak Park. "It always has been the loveliest house in the neighborhood."

Looking upon it now, Caroline could not but agree. It was lovely, especially on such a day when the sun was bright and cast upon the structure a glow of warmth and welcome.

Rosemary, however, did not seem to agree, for she said, "It is the largest, certainly, but I cannot say it holds any beauty over Newton House."

Caroline shook her head. "You are not required to flatter my mother, Mrs. Pickersgill."

"It was not mere flattery, Miss Bingley, for I expressed my honest opinion of the matter. A large house is not necessarily more pleasing to the eye than a small one. It is simply, well, larger."

"Clearly, you have never experienced the pleasures of a large house. I am certain that once you enter one as grand as Oak Park, your opinion will change."

"Oh, Caro, not everyone has the same taste," Mrs. Newton said with a smile. "You may allow Mrs. Pickersgill to admire a small house if she wishes. Besides, it will please Mr. Newton greatly to hear that she does."

Caroline was on the verge of saying, "Oh, hang Mr. Newton," but she restrained herself, realizing that there was no point, for an opinion was difficult to change, even one's own.

Rosemary cocked her head to one side and studied her through narrowed eyes. Then, as if having come to a satisfactory conclusion, she said, "I will defer to your judgment, Miss Bingley, for I see you are in no mood for debate."

"I am always in the mood for debate, Mrs. Pickersgill, but on this subject, there can be none. A woman of sense cannot prefer a small house to a large one. It is utterly ridiculous."

"Indeed, Miss Bingley."

Rosemary's voice held a distinct note of irony, but Caroline did not comment on it. In fact, the ladies did not converse again until they had completed the ride along the approach road, were received into the grand house in question, and were announced at the sitting room door by a manservant of stern countenance.

"Mrs. Newton, Miss Bingley, and Mrs. Pickersgill, madam," he said. His voice sounded strangely ominous to Caroline's ears as his words rang into the vast room and echoed off the high ceilings and art-covered walls.

Indeed, the room was lavishly done. The furniture was of the highest quality and was arranged so that it could be shown to its best advantage and not for the comfort of the room's occupants. Matching sofas, upholstered in gold and white brocade, stood in front of each of the towering windows that flanked the carved stone fireplace, and the sheer span between the two seats would likely make conversation—and even visual contact—awkward. Two high-backed chairs completed the arrangement while floor-to-ceiling draperies of heavy gold material framed the whole scene. The drapes had been pulled aside, allowing light to stream into the cavernous chamber in bright beams. Even the sunlight, it seemed, had been arranged with purposeful formality, for it descended in a most appealing manner on various points in the room.

Even though the chamber was not conducive to intimate conversation, Lavinia had seen to every other comfort. The fire had obviously been laid with care, small enough not to cause overheating but large enough to take the chill out of the air. On the far wall stood a buffet covered with full decanters and carafes of wine, sherry, and port, and crystal glasses were lined up like soldiers at the ready, always prepared to receive libations. Books were fortuitously arranged on polished wooden side tables, and a writing table was settled along the far wall. Every detail had been seen to, every necessity provided. Lavinia was obviously adept at managing her father's household, and if true comfort was lacking, it could be forgiven in the face of sheer opulence.

And Caroline was ever in favor of opulence.

As the door closed behind them, Lavinia emerged from her place in a high-backed chair like a butterfly from a cocoon. The light behind her was so dazzling that Caroline was forced to blink often as she attempted to look at her friend.

At that precise moment, Caroline could have allowed herself to be intimidated by her friend's grand appearance, by her family's even grander estate, or even by the sheer scale of the room, but she would not permit herself to be susceptible to such a weakness of emotion.

Why, she herself had very nearly been the mistress of a great household. In any case, she had visited Lavinia's home numerous times in the past, and she had been acquainted with her long before she had made the transformation from awkward caterpillar to the beautiful winged creature that now stood before Caroline.

The perfectly styled woman converged upon their party forthwith and curtseyed in Mrs. Newton's general direction. Then she smiled at Caroline, saying, "My dear friend! How good it is to see you."

Lavinia leaned in as if to take both Caroline's hands, but she stopped short and only managed to touch one hand briefly.

Caroline straightened herself. "I am very pleased to be at Oak Park again. It holds so many pleasant memories, and I find it has not altered one bit, though the view from the drive, I find, is more stunning than ever."

"How very gracious of you to notice," Lavinia said and then turned to Mrs. Pickersgill. "Caroline, will you do me the honor of introducing your friend?"

Caroline did as she was bid, and upon the pronouncement of her companion's name, Lavinia cocked her head to the side. "Pickersgill," she said. "What an odd surname, but it is strangely familiar."

Rosemary glanced at Caroline, and her expression seemed to convey surprise and perhaps a hint of dread.

Caroline, wishing to divert the conversation away from her companion, said, "A unique surname such as Pickersgill is bound to attract undue notice, I am sure, even if it is not attached to a family of dignity."

"Yes, I suppose that is so." Lavinia gestured toward the grouping of furniture where she had previously reclined. "Now, do sit down, and I shall ring for tea."

The visiting party walked dutifully to select their seats while Lavinia strode across the large chamber and rang the bell. As she made the return trip across the space, she straightened her already perfectly arranged hair and then settled herself on the sofa across from Caroline and her mother.

Lavinia looked much as she had as a schoolgirl—a lithe figure, unblemished skin, and wavy dark hair that had been the envy of more than one young lady of their acquaintance. She gave all the appearance of a distant, untouchable aristocrat. Indeed, with the sun's rays and the distance between the furniture, this was far from the intimate reunion for which Caroline had hoped.

In short course, a maid arrived with a tray, poured the visitors' tea, and then crossed the room to deliver the beverage to her mistress. The maid was of diminutive stature, and her small steps made the trip from sofa to sofa seem as though it were a journey of a thousand miles.

"Will there be anything else, madam?" the maid asked.

Clearly annoyed, Lavinia looked to her servant, saying, "No, you may go."

The maid offered a slight curtsey and made the trip from the sitting area to the door with admirable endurance.

Caroline picked up her teacup and saucer. The china was so fine that it was nearly translucent, and the aroma of the tea was so heartening that she almost sighed.

"This tea is lovely, Lavinia."

"I am so glad it pleases you," Lavinia said. "And now tell me; is your family in good health?"

And though Caroline despised repeating these bothersome social conventions she reminded herself that this was the most important call they had paid since her arrival in Kendal, and went to the trouble of responding to each inquiry and of asking the proper questions in return. When the requisite dialogue was complete, she searched for a subtle way to steer the discussion in a direction that would result ultimately in an invitation to continue their acquaintance now that they were living within so easy a distance of each other.

Perhaps, Caroline thought, it would be best to remind Lavinia of their former association, their many hours of girlish chitchat while at the seminary, or of their—admittedly sparse—written correspondence over the past years. Such memories might incite feelings of nostalgia, which naturally would lead to a renewal of their friendship.

And this was essential, for Caroline would not allow herself to languish in her exiled state.

Yes, nostalgia was the proper tool.

Caroline lifted her chin and had just resolved to speak of their shared history when the door to the chamber jerked open and in strode William Charlton.

The ladies all rose with alacrity, and Lavinia, with a hand to her breast, said, "Oh! William, you startled me!"

The Honorable Mr. William Charlton, the second son of Lord Charlton and now his heir, appeared equally surprised to have discovered the room to be occupied, and he bowed awkwardly to the gathered ladies. "I do apologize, Lavinia, but I did not realize morning calls were still taking place."

Lavinia's brow furrowed. "It is yet morning, as you see by the position of the sun through the window."

As the rest of the party turned to observe the sun's placement in the sky, Caroline studied Mr. Charlton. She had not seen him in the past few years, but time had been beneficial to him. He had filled out in both height and breadth, but he was still rather thin, and Caroline could not complain about his choice of clothing or coiffure. Yes, he had gone from having all appearances of youth and irresponsibility to improving in manliness, though perhaps not in responsibility.

Or so she had heard.

Mr. Charlton turned away from the window and adjusted the sleeves of his coat, his dark head angled down in concentration. "Yes, yes, apologies again. I have been at the accounts for so long I assumed it must be nearly sunset! But that is neither here nor there, for no matter the hour, I must not neglect our guests." He lifted his eyes and surveyed the women, his gaze stopping briefly at each one. "Mrs. Newton, a pleasure to see you. And will you not introduce me to your companions?"

"This, sir," Mrs. Newton began as she gestured to Caroline, "is my youngest daughter Caroline. Surely, you must remember her from your youth."

"Ah!" he said with a bow. Caroline curtseyed deeply and then raised her eyes with practiced allure to find that his expression had brightened considerably. "I do remember you. Did you not attend the seminary with Lavinia?"

"Indeed, I was most fortunate to spend a great deal of time with your excellent sister while we were both in London as girls."

Mr. Charlton smiled at her, and his polished air and appearance struck Caroline. He certainly had changed.

"And this," continued Mrs. Newton, "is Caroline's companion, Mrs. Pickersgill."

Bow and curtsey were exchanged, and then the ladies returned to their seats. Mr. Charlton took one of the high-backed chairs for himself and smiled broadly at Caroline, saying, "I am very pleased to see you back in the Lake District, Miss Bingley. I do hope you and Mrs. Pickersgill intend a long visit, though I myself would much rather be in Town for the season."

"I could not be in better agreement, Mr. Charlton. I have the greatest fondness for Town and will be very pleased to return there as soon as my visit here is through."

"I do not know, my dear," Mrs. Newton said. A small frown tugged at the corners of her mouth. "I have always had a certain fondness for the countryside. I hope you will not rush back to your brother and his friends in London before regaining some appreciation for the county in which you were born."

"Indeed, Mama, I do not mean any insult to Kendal. I only wanted to convey my preference for a different sort of life, one that contains more variety than may be found in a less populated region. Do not you agree, Lavinia?"

Lavinia seemed momentarily at odds with herself, and Caroline found that rather surprising. But perhaps she had imagined the confusion, for her friend's next words were rather definite. "I prefer Town. The company here is unvaried and tedious, but I will remain as long as I am required, for it is my duty to our family."

Mr. Charlton smiled, tight-lipped and rueful. "I do so wish that such duty had fallen upon neither of us. When Harold departed this mortal coil, he left us quite ensnared. He was so much better suited to the barony, its seat in Parliament, and the overseeing of this estate than I shall ever hope to be. I regret every facet of the situation."

Caroline could not believe that he was foolish enough to value his title so cheaply. "While I certainly feel deep sorrow at your brother's untimely death, I cannot imagine viewing the inheritance of a barony as a thing to be regretted."

"Can you not, Miss Bingley?" asked Mr. Charlton.

"My brother has always been perfectly at ease with his station as second son," Lavinia added.

"I do not deny it! I have no wish to."

Caroline nearly followed her impulse to snort at Mr. Charlton's naïveté and then corrected herself. Less than a month in the country and she was already losing the polish of Town. When she spoke, she made certain that she did so with the highly cultured tone she had affected over the years. "Your beloved brother was a gentleman of the highest order, respected by all who knew him. But it is human nature to improve one's mind and position, is it not?"

Brother and sister remained silent, and sensing a dark turn in their countenances, Caroline struggled to speak, but Rosemary's cultured voice next filled the room. "My friends tell me, Mr. Charlton, that you will be adequate to the title once it becomes yours."

He smiled. "It is clear that Mrs. Newton and Miss Bingley are much too generous in their opinion of me, for I intend to make at best a mediocre member of Parliament. It is only through my sister's good graces that Oak Park remains running at all, for given to my control, it would surely have disintegrated by now."

Caroline nodded. "Mrs. Winton is well suited to running a large household."

Mrs. Newton's large brown eyes studied Lavinia, but she smiled as she said, "It was kind of Mr. Winton to spare you, but it must be difficult for you to endure the separation. I do not like being parted from Mr. Newton when he is required to travel."

"I bear the distance as best I can, Mrs. Newton." Lavinia looked pointedly at her brother before continuing. "And indeed, Mr. Winton has been very generous in sparing me."

Conversation paused as brother and sister exchanged another look, and then Mr. Charlton said brightly, "Shall we all not walk about? I would greatly love an excuse not to return to my papers."

He stood and offered Lavinia his arm, which she ignored. "I believe I shall stay here if Miss Bingley will remain with me," she said, glancing now at Caroline. "I would cherish time to hear what she has been doing these past years."

"I would be honored," Mr. Charlton said as he transferred the offer of his arm to Caroline's mother, "if you would join me, Mrs. Newton. Do give me an excuse not to be about my labors."

Mrs. Newton looked between Lavinia and Caroline before nodding her assent and taking his arm. "I would not wish to hamper your business, Mr. Charlton, but I do hope my daughter will be able to rekindle her friendship with Mrs. Winton, and so I cannot deny you."

"I do so appreciate a woman who cannot deny me," he said with an innocent smile. "And you, Mrs. Pickersgill, can you deny me?"

Mrs. Pickersgill stood. "I am certain I could deny you under the correct circumstances, sir, but I find this is not one of them. I will walk with you and Mrs. Newton."

With that, they disappeared from the room, leaving Lavinia and Caroline to stare at each other across the vast physical distance that separated them.

Caroline had the oddest impression that the divide was composed of more than mere space, but she could not say why she thought that. It must be a fleeting feeling brought on by the sudden silence in the room.

"Do take the seat beside me, my dear, so we can speak more freely." Lavinia gestured toward the space beside her.

Gratefully, Caroline covered the distance, keeping in mind to move without haste, and lowered herself onto the stiff cushions. She gestured about the chamber. "I can see very well that you are suited to keeping your father's household, though I am certain you dislike being away from Mr. Winton so long."

"Yes, Mr. Winton...." Lavinia tapered off and then studied the room as though she were looking for the minutest imperfection in her decor. "I quite fancy myself the queen of the castle here. I take great pride in the daily running of the household, planning meals and such for my brother, but I had much rather not have had reason to come. I dearly miss Harold."

"I have no doubt that you still grieve his loss."

A shadow crossed Lavinia's face, and then the weather seemed to clear. "Harold is very much missed by us all. It was such a disappointment to lose him just when he had come into his own. William, especially, feels the loss, for he must face the prospect of the barony without adequate preparation. Harold would have been a credit to the title."

Caroline recognized what was unspoken. William, of course, was not a credit. He was more like a debt that would never be paid.

"It is a shame, then," she said, "that your eldest brother did not leave an heir."

Lavinia's eyebrows knit together briefly. "Indeed, that was a great loss, but at the very least, the barony is in no danger of being displaced by entail."

"Oh, that is good news indeed. But who is to inherit it? I believed your younger brother to be unwed." A bit of errant disappointment crept into Caroline at the thought of an eligible gentleman of title being taken from the marriage mart.

Why, she had never thought of the younger Mr. Charlton as anyone of significance, but now that he was to be a baron, he was ever so much more attractive.

"Good heavens, no, William is not married," Lavinia said on a laugh, and then she sobered. "Do not misunderstand. I have no intention of speaking ill of my dear brother, but he has a bit of a rakish tendency. He has shown no inclination to marry."

Caroline wondered how true Lavinia's words were. Was there any inducement that might cause Mr. Charlton to marry?

"It is of little consequence, for the title is safe," Lavinia continued. "My own son Samuel is already being groomed for the position. He is set to inherit the title and land, so, you see, it has all fallen to me. I must preserve the house and land and see to providing an heir. The only thing I may not do is sit in Parliament."

She laughed, but it sounded hollow to Caroline's ears.

"Women are, more often than not, left to pick up where their masculine counterparts have fallen short," Caroline said. "Of course, we do not receive credit for our actions. But by all accounts, you have succeeded, Lavinia. I am certain your son will do the title credit."

Then, only because it was the polite conversation topic, she inquired after Samuel. It was Caroline's experience that mothers found no greater pleasure than discussing their children, and opening the subject resulted in long discussions of such things as spittle, babble, and random excreta that, relating to an adult, would have been highly improper.

Apparently, Lavinia was not like other mothers, for she quickly looked around as though Caroline's mention of her young son would cause him to appear. "He is well and with his nurse, I should hope."

"Is he very much grown?"

"Oh, indeed he is. It seemed that he crawled for no longer than a week before he began to walk, and from there, he started running all about Oak Park. I do so love the boy." Lavinia sighed. "But I confess that I much preferred him when I could hold him in my arms like a little doll. But now he is up and dashing about the house. I quite fear for my upholstery."

Caroline felt that perhaps Lavinia wished to discuss another subject, and she did not mind a change in conversation. Children in general were lovely, and they ensured the survival of the family name and property, but one could not speak of them everlastingly.

Caroline caressed the arm of the sofa. "It is lovely fabric."

"Do you like it? I ordered it from the continent, and William did not approve of the expenditure. He ranted for days that the pattern was hideous enough to be hanging in the windows of a squalid coaching inn, but I believe it has quite grown on him now. Why just yesterday, he commented...."

Lavinia spoke on about the fabric for some minutes before a pause came into the conversation. Caroline was preparing to inquire again after Mr. Winton, Lavinia's absent husband, but instead, her friend turned to the topic Caroline had wished to avoid: "I must tell you that when you wrote of your..."—here, Lavinia paused as if searching for the correct noun— "...circumstances, I was incensed on your behalf."

"I thank you." Caroline lowered her eyes and began to wonder if her hastily dashed missive to her old friend had been a wise idea. She had been desperate to find someone who might share her outrage over her expulsion from Netherfield, but perhaps she had shared too much.

No, that could not be the case, for it was right and proper to have divulged her anger and distress to a friend as dear as Lavinia. And it was not as if she had shared her full humiliation regarding Mr. Darcy. No, she had perhaps hinted that she had once had hopes in his direction, but she was certain that her friend was unaware of her true feelings on that subject.

"Abominable the way your siblings have treated you," Lavinia continued. Her voice seemed inordinately loud, and Caroline looked about her. She had no desire to discuss her situation so openly with her mother in the house.

Had she happened to hear? Had anyone in the household not heard?

"Quite so," Caroline agreed more quietly.

"Now, I must know all the details of the situation that brought you to us, for your last letter was too vague for my tastes. What occurred to cause your family to behave so abusively?"

Caroline attempted to meet Lavinia's gaze steadily, but she could not manage it and looked away. The story was far too embarrassing to be shared. "It is hardly even worth a sentence or two, much less an entire discussion."

"I can see very well that you have been injured over the matter."

"Injured! No, indeed. I am outraged." Caroline knew very well that Lavinia was baiting her into divulging her secrets, but she did not care. She suddenly needed to commiserate with someone. "I have done nothing except that which any well-bred woman would do to protect those she loves. And that is all there is to the matter: I rightly opposed Charles's marriage to Jane Bennet and attempted to separate them, and now they are angry with me."

Lavinia sat up straighter, giving the appearance of being incensed for her friend. "You did only what you believed to be right. I would have done nothing less had I believed an unsuitable woman cast her eye on Harold. Or even William. They really ought to forgive you."

"But there is nothing that requires their forgiveness! I was protecting my brother from a social climber."

"Of course you were, my dear. We must be careful of our brothers, must we not? Else they would all marry inappropriate women."

Caroline was about to make a suitable reply when she heard her mother's voice in the hallway. "We are grateful for the turn about your sculpture gallery, Mr. Charlton, but I fear we have intruded upon your time long enough."

As the party entered the sitting room, Lavinia asked with a rather blasé tone, "Oh dear, must you go?"

"I fear we must."

"I am sorry to hear that," Mr. Charlton said. "Lavinia, shall we not escort our guests to their conveyance?"

"Indeed." The response came with little energy, but Lavinia stood, and when Caroline did the same, she interlaced their arms together.

As they walked through the marble entry and toward the door, Caroline looked at Lavinia with some trepidation, which she hoped was well concealed. Would Lavinia issue an invitation? To dine? To drive? To do anything? Caroline would accept any of them.

Certainly, Lavinia would not snub her, for they were schoolfellows and friends and had just shared intimate conversation.

But now, as Mr. Charlton assisted her mother into the coach, it was almost too late. She was right behind and would soon be trapped within and back on her way to Newton House.

Finally, the words of salvation came from the lips of Mr. Charlton. "My sister and I would be delighted if you would join our dinner party on Thursday. Everyone in the county is to be present."

Only then did he look to his sister for approval.

From her vantage point on the stairs, Lavinia looked down upon them all. Her features were schooled into elegant perfection, and only the barest hint of a smile appeared on her face as she said, "Yes, indeed, you are most welcome."

"And do bring Mr. Newton and Mr. Rushton along. Would that suit you, ladies?" Mr. Charlton added as he took Caroline's hand and assisted her into the coach.

"We are honored, sir," Caroline said, looking upon Mr. Charlton with new eyes.

The idea that had begun to edge its way into her mind earlier struck her with full force. Yes, here, right before her, was a most tempting situation.

Here was an unwed gentleman who would one day inherit a barony, and he was ripe for the taking. Indeed, he possessed all to which any woman might aspire: land, an ancient family, and a title.

A smile spread across Caroline's face, and she studied him from underneath her eyelashes. Certainly, he was a well-looking man: clean, properly attired, and unspoiled by the stench of trade.

She must admit to having never thought upon him with such designs when he was but the second son, scampering about England and leaving his reputation in tatters. Of course, in the eyes of the elite, a bit of a sullied character was perfectly acceptable.

As if sensing the course of her contemplation, Mr. Charlton turned his dark eyes upon her. Caroline leaned her head away with as much coyness as she could muster given her current turn of thought.

Yes, this would solve all her problems. A union with Mr. Charlton would accomplish so much. She would no longer be required to humiliate herself by groveling before Miss Elizabeth Bennet in order to return to her former life. Her welcome at Pemberley would be renewed simply by virtue of the fact that she would one day be Lady Charlton, and who would not want the wife of a baron in their household? Her brother and sister would again invite her into their company, and finally, finally, she would be able to rest comfortably in the fact that all her education, improvements, and accomplishments would prove her worthy. She would be shed of the yoke of the middling classes, and her family's legacy would be secure.

✍ Seven ✍

"What an unfortunate evening for Mrs. Winton's dinner party," Caroline said more to herself than to the other occupants of Mr. Newton's coach. "The weather has ruined everything, and we shall arrive quite soaked through."

Showers had been threatening all day, and by the time the good people of Newton House pointed their carriage in the direction of Oak Park, rain was descending from the sky in cords.

Foul weather was quite a vexing prospect, for Caroline had been many hours at her dressing table and had used the service of more than one of her mother's maids in preparing her clothing and coiffure for the evening. She wanted to be certain that every nuance of her appearance was perfect, and as near as she could tell in the smallish looking glass in her bedchamber, she had accomplished her goal.

She had chosen every article of clothing to accentuate the fact that she was no longer a little girl. She could not afford to be viewed as nothing more than the youngest child of a neighboring family. She must be seen as a woman, capable and accomplished.

Yet she must also be seen as fresh and youthful, and so she had chosen to arrange her hair in ringlets, which she had always fancied as the most becoming option. Instead of the ostentatious hair adornments she had chosen in London, Caroline opted for three strings of pearls to be woven through her tresses. The effect was most pleasing. She appeared both mature enough to be considered for marriage to a baron and young enough not to be perceived as being in danger of imminent old-maidenhood.

It had been a delicate balance to achieve.

And now it was raining, and all her preparation would be for naught if her hair were to be ruined.

Across from her in the carriage, Mr. Rushton glanced at her with a sardonic eye and responded to her complaint about the weather, saying, "Yes, Miss Bingley, we shall all catch our deaths from mild discomfort."

Caroline narrowed her eyes at him. "You deliberately misunderstand me. I meant only that Mrs. Winton has chosen an ill night for a party."

"I misunderstand nothing." His blue eyes held a knowing quality that vexed her greatly. "I understand very well to what you were referring. You feared for your silken slippers in all this mud, did you not?"

"Indeed, I did not," she said truthfully, for she had feared for her hair.

His gaze had traveled to the slippers in question, and Caroline pulled her feet into a position that she hoped was out of his view, for she did not relish the idea of his looking at so intimate a detail of her person.

He did not respond, but only looked at her with a hint of a smile playing about his lips.

"I meant, Mr. Rushton," she said, adopting her most superior tone, "that weather of this sort does nothing for one's demeanor or digestion."

"I am sure that the rain may also be blamed if the evening's selection of meats should turn out to be overcooked."

"Do not be absurd, Mr. Rushton. Poorly prepared food has nothing to do with climatic issues. Surely, that may be blamed on the servants."

"Surely." He then lapsed into silence, but he continued to look at her with the hint of a smile. Caroline met his stare for as long as she thought proper and then glanced away, returning again to her previous musings.

Worse than weather and the possibility of overcooked meat was Caroline's trepidation of meeting again with Mr. Charlton and his guests in the presence of her less-than-socially-apt party. Would her tenuous association with the foremost family in the neighborhood survive the combination of Mr. Newton and Mr. Rushton? Would Mrs. Pickersgill behave as a proper companion and remain pleasantly silent for the duration of the evening?

One glance at Mrs. Pickersgill in her evening ensemble told her that she made a refined, if somewhat uncooperative, picture. She sat with her hands folded in her lap, but her smirk showed how much she had relished the exchange between Caroline and Mr. Rushton. It could be a bad omen if one's companion took so much pleasure in seeing her mistress thus challenged by a gentleman of the middling classes.

Caroline then looked to Mr. Newton, who was as he ever was: largely untouched by any social graces. He sat with a broad smile on his face as he looped an arm around Mrs. Newton and whispered something to her.

Caroline wished very much that he would behave like a gentleman, and she was tempted to say just that. But her mother appeared so happy and at ease that she could not bring herself to disturb her.

Mr. Rushton was not her responsibility, and she would do her best to dissociate from him as soon as was prudent.

When their party arrived at Oak Park, servants greeted them at the coach with umbrellas. Caroline found the entire disembarkation process to be rather untoward as she endeavored to stay out of the blowing rain, all the while dodging puddles, which would certainly ruin several pairs of ladies' silk slippers before the night was through, just as Mr. Rushton had suggested.

Caroline felt a presence at her elbow and found Mr. Rushton there. She narrowed her eyes at him.

"Allow me to help protect your slippers, Miss Bingley, for we simply cannot have them ruined."

Before she gave him leave to assist her physically, his hands grasped her elbow and helped her navigate the path to the door.

Once they had gained footing on the stone staircase of Oak Park, Mr. Rushton shifted slightly, and Caroline found her hand resting demurely on his forearm. Unaware of precisely how she had come to be in that position, Caroline began to experience growing horror at the prospect of entering the house on Mr. Rushton's arm. It would be better to enter unescorted than to be seen on the arm of a gentleman who was a known fortune hunter.

As they ascended the steps, she fought the temptation to shake herself free of him, but it would not do to behave in such a way in so close a proximity to Lavinia and Mr. Charlton or their guests.

She glanced at Mr. Rushton and was even more appalled to find that he was watching her with an expression of amusement. He knew precisely what he was about by putting her in this position, and he was relishing her reaction.

Well!

She tightened her fingers on his arm, feeling the rasp of the fabric of his coat against her kid gloves. "Your assistance is no longer required, Mr. Rushton, and I should thank you to concern yourself with Mrs. Pickersgill's slippers if you are so intent upon being the savior of ladies' footwear, for owning only one good pair, I am certain she would appreciate having them protected from the elements."

Mr. Rushton did not appear to be influenced by her command in the least and only smirked at her. He was clearly aware of her intentions to remove him from her presence, but he was not offended at all. In fact, he seemed to find the situation rather droll, and that mystified Caroline. He ought to be a great deal angrier or perhaps embarrassed at her desire not to enter Oak Park on his arm.

Caroline shook her head slightly at him and continued toward the comparatively arid environment of the entrance hall. She attempted to retain as much dignity as possible as she slipped and slid across the polished stone floors and toward the receiving line.

Mr. Rushton steadied her with a hand to her elbow and laughter in his eyes. "You see, Miss Bingley, if I had acceded to your demands, you would have ended in a puddle on the floor. Now, are you not pleased that I ignored your foolishness?"

Curse Mr. Rushton!

"Indeed, I am not thankful," she said quietly as she pulled herself away from him. Then, louder, she added, "Your services are no longer required as I am on dry ground now, Mr. Rushton."

Based on his jovial countenance as he looked upon her unsteadiness, he could not have been more unconcerned about her treatment of him. He only looked at her with bright blue eyes.

It was unnerving.

Well, she would not look upon him any longer!

Instead, she concentrated on the receiving line.

In total, four and twenty guests had arrived at Oak Park, and to her consternation, Caroline discovered that the number of ladies and gentlemen was unequal, which would make the seating arrangements at dinner a tedious affair, for no female guest had the least desire of being seated beside another lady.

Caroline put the dining dilemma from her mind, trusting that Lavinia would see that she was adequately seated. Instead, she tried her utmost to remember the names and ranks of each person to whom she was introduced, be they lady or gentleman. She had learned that it was to one's best interest to remember as much as possible, for one never knew who might become important in the future.

Of highest consequence, of course, was the Dowager Lady Kentworth, who was adorned in a bulbous gown of copper-colored silk. Caroline found her an awfully small woman to be able to carry such a dress, not to mention such a lofty title, but she seemed to have a keen eye. The older lady appeared to approve of Caroline based upon their introduction alone. After studying her entire appearance from the tips of her slippers to the ringlets in her hair, the Dowager Lady Kentworth had given her a nod accompanied with the words "Very nice, my dear."

Most of the other guests were distinguished in their own ways. They seemed either to be wealthy, from a titled family of an adjacent county, or both. At the very least, most stood to inherit or marry into fortunes or titles. It was the finest society the country could offer.

Caroline wondered again how her little party would fare among such company. It was a testament to her long-standing friendship with Lavinia that they had been invited at all, for though Mr. Newton was quite one of the wealthiest men in the county, his money was incorrectly gained.

Though Caroline herself was used to moving in the finest circles in Town, her family party certainly was not. When seen in the company of the gathered assembly, they seemed slightly out of sorts. As she surveyed those who were sequestered in the large drawing room for aperitifs and conversation before dinner, it was obvious that her family's clothing was not quite correct and their manners were altogether too relaxed. Mrs. Pickersgill and Mr. Rushton blended somewhat more convincingly, perhaps because they were both youthful and therefore more easily adaptable. That must be the case, for Mrs. Pickersgill's dress was rather plain and Mr. Rushton, well, he was a great nuisance.

Her mother and Mr. Newton, however, had drawn no small amount of attention to themselves already.

They appeared to be conversing with the Dowager Lady Kentworth, and a group of onlookers had gathered around them.

Oh dear.

That could not bode well.

Before Caroline could cross the room to smooth the situation, Mr. Charlton appeared beside her.

"Good evening, Miss Bingley," he said with a bow.

Caroline returned his greeting with a curtsey.

"I observed you here alone, and I had the greatest desire to escape my duties for a few moments." He leaned in closer and whispered, "I am required to dine with the Dowager Lady Kentworth this evening, and I can think of nothing duller than listening to the old lady drone about the past."

Caroline smiled. Mr. Charlton's face was still rather near to hers, and she was able to study him at close proximity. He was a well-looking gentleman indeed, even at such a short distance, which often revealed flaws that could remain unobserved in more distant circumstances. His skin was clear and glowed with health and vigor, and his eyes were framed by the longest eyelashes she had ever seen. Overall, he exuded a charm that was not wholly unappealing to her. "It is impolitic to say such a thing about a woman of such high rank, but," she said as she leaned closer still and inhaled his cologne, "having said that, I do not envy your position."

His grin turned conspiratorial. "Ah! I knew you would agree with me. And now, allow me to ensure for you a slightly more appetizing meal. An aperitif? A glass of sherry?"

She would not have turned down any suggestion he made, and he returned with two small glasses of sherry and his open smile. "Now we can be assured of a truly appetizing meal, for we have had the correct beginning."

"Have we?" Caroline asked as she raised the glass to her lips.

"At the very least, we shall now be slightly more immune to dull conversation, shall we not?"

Caroline sipped her sherry again. "One can only hope it is so."

He laughed and then winced as Lavinia appeared at his arm.

"Oh dear, my keeper has arrived," he said to Caroline, and then he turned to Lavinia. "Have you come to ensure that I do not slip out the rear door before the meal begins?"

Lavinia did a poor job of concealing her annoyance.

"Mrs. Winton," Caroline said as a means of distraction, "I must compliment you on this lovely assembly. It is a great testament to you and your family to have such faithful friends with whom to dine."

Lavinia smiled. "And now you are counted among their number."

Caroline dipped her head, as if embarrassed by her friend's words, but truly, she was concealing her pleasure at having reinstalled herself amongst the acquaintances of the first family of the neighborhood. "I thank you for it."

"You will perform a small favor for me, will you not, Miss Bingley?"

Caroline could not but agree as Lavinia wrapped her silk-clad arm around Caroline's and led her gently from the center of the room, where she had purposefully positioned herself to be seen to the best advantage, toward the doorway through which she had originally entered.

"Certainly, I will perform any service you require of me." Caroline was pleased to assist her friend, for it spoke of their close relationship and would make her appear indispensable.

"William has insisted that I invite several guests of the lower social orders," Lavinia said softly so that her brother could not hear, and she looked around the room as if seeking out each lower-class offender. "And I do have some concern regarding their behavior tonight."

Caroline nodded and also looked about the room. "That is an understandable fear."

"If you, my dear, would be so kind as to occupy Miss Brodrick until dinner?"

"Which is Miss Brodrick?"

Lavinia pointed out a pale, slight creature who was sitting alone at the back of the room.

"Come, I shall introduce you."

The trio crossed the room to the young lady in question, and when they had drawn close enough, Lavinia said, "Miss Brodrick, I have the greatest desire to introduce you to our dear Miss Bingley."

Lavinia made the introductions, the ladies curtseyed to one another, and as she straightened again, Caroline took her first notice of the young lady.

Miss Brodrick appeared to be of no more than seventeen years, and she was everything that was fragile and slight. Even her face seemed small and was composed of delicate features and porcelain skin. Her hair was of the finest blonde coloration and decorated with a small white feathered ornament.

"Miss Bingley, it is an honor," said Miss Brodrick in a soft voice, and Caroline had to lean closer to hear her properly.

"It is equally my honor, I assure you," Caroline lied. She could not have cared less to have made her acquaintance, but it had proved her value to Lavinia, and that was all that was necessary to make her amenable.

"Miss Brodrick is recently returned from one of our old haunts, Miss Bingley," Mrs. Winton said.

"Oh?" Caroline asked, though she was quite uninterested.

"She was also a student at ladies' Eton."

"Ah, yes? Such a beneficial education for a young lady to receive," Caroline said with a glance at Mr. Charlton. "And you have certainly been admitted to society that will only serve to improve upon it."

"Yes," Miss Brodrick said in her whispered voice, "Mr. Charlton and Mrs. Winton have been very gracious in inviting me to attend."

"I do hope you will continue to think me gracious after I steal my brother away for a few moments," Lavinia said as she transferred her arm from Caroline's to her brother's. "A host's duties are never complete, it seems."

"Oh dear," Mr. Charlton said, "I must be away."

"Yes, the Dowager Lady Kentworth requires your presence." He rolled his eyes, and Lavinia sighed. "Do not be difficult, William."

Mr. Charlton bowed first to Miss Bingley and then to Miss Brodrick. "You will excuse me. It seems I must see to my duty, but you, Miss Brodrick, are in excellent care. Miss Bingley will ensure that you are not without amusing conversation."

"Excellent," Lavinia said as she held to her brother's arm and walked with him through the crowd toward the far end of the room, which held the entrance to the dining room.

Though she had the impression that he would like to slink away like a chastised child, Caroline watched as Mr. Charlton straightened his back and walked with dignity toward the opposite end of the room.

Caroline turned to Miss Brodrick. "Indeed, we shall enjoy becoming further acquainted, shall we not, Miss Brodrick?" Despite her disappointment in Mr. Charlton's departure, her pleasure in his kind words made her more able to bear it. "And so, tell me, who is your family?"

Miss Brodrick stepped back slightly, but responded with little hesitation. "My father owns a graphite mill."

"Graphite?" Caroline attempted to conceal her distaste. "I was unaware that the product was still being mined."

"Not mined, Miss Bingley. Milled."

"I see," she said, although she did not really know or care to know the difference.

"My father imports raw graphite from France and processes it so that it can be formed into proper English pencils."

"He sounds a very industrious man, though"—Caroline lowered her voice—"I would caution you, Miss Brodrick, not to make your family's dealings in trade so very public."

Miss Brodrick looked at her with pale blue eyes full of questions. "Why ever not?"

"Darling, have you learned nothing in Queen's Square?"

"I learned a great many things, Miss Bingley, among which was to value the livelihood that allowed me to be sent there."

"You may be grateful, but not quite so vocally, certainly."

"I shall not dissemble, Miss Bingley," said the pale creature. "I feel no shame; neither shall I pretend to."

"Then it shall be to your detriment," Caroline warned. "For you must realize how lowly the better classes regard such a history."

Miss Brodrick did not appear to give adequate weight to Caroline's words before she said with quiet confidence, "Then I suppose I shall just have to risk being seen as an oddity. It does not bother me, and neither should it trouble you."

"I assure you it does not. It was advice kindly meant."

"And it is kindly rejected, Miss Bingley, but I trust it will not damage our acquaintance."

Caroline smiled. Silly girl. They had no such acquaintance.

But she said, "Certainly not."

The conversation lulled, and Caroline turned to discover that Lavinia had begun the subtle organization of guests that preceded their entry into the dining area. The Dowager Lady Kentworth was already on Mr. Charlton's arm, and they were proceeding out of the drawing room. The rest of the assembly followed suit.

Caroline looked around as a feeling of panic descended over her. Everyone, it seemed, had found their escort—all except her and Miss Brodrick.

In a party composed of an uneven number of ladies and gentlemen, it was vital to secure a male dining companion early, but now it was almost too late. Caroline found herself in the company of a female and quite at the back of the party.

If she did not act quickly indeed, she would be doomed to dine in the company of Miss Brodrick.

Disaster!

She had hoped to wrangle the arm of an unattached gentleman and then select a seat as near to Mr. Charlton as possible. She would then ensure that she was well within his line of sight as she charmed her dinner partner, whomever he should be, with elegant conversation and wit.

Mr. Charlton would see what a desirable partner she was and seek her out for conversation after dinner.

A marriage proposal would be the next logical step, of course.

But now, her plan was spoiled, and she must reverse the damage if she possibly could. And quickly.

First, her eyes sought her mother and Mr. Newton. Perhaps they had been chatting with a gentleman on whose arm she could enter. She caught sight of their backs as they left the drawing room. She was already too late.

Next, she searched out Lavinia. Perhaps her friend had thought to hold aside a gentleman for her. Lavinia would prove a strong ally, certainly.

No, as Caroline looked about the chamber, she could not locate Lavinia. Likely, she was already in the dining room to see everyone comfortably settled.

Last, she looked, and not without a certain amount of desperation, for Rosemary and Mr. Rushton. Perhaps they had managed to enter a conversation with a gentleman with whom she might dine. Or, at the very least, perhaps she could enter on Mr. Rushton's arm.

If she must.

She spotted them sauntering along as if they had all the time in the world while the room emptied as guests were lured toward the scents of the meal that had been tempting them. Caroline hurried across the large drawing room toward the stragglers.

She had traversed half of the cavernous chamber when Lavinia emerged from the dining room and looked about the drawing room.

"Oh dear, Miss Bingley, I had thought you were already seated," she said. "What do you do all the way over there?"

"I..." Caroline paused as she studied Lavinia, who must have recalled leaving her at the back of the room to entertain Miss Brodrick not a quarter hour before. "I was detained."

"Ah, well, that is unfortunate indeed. And Miss Brodrick too has dawdled, I see." She ushered Mr. Rushton and Rosemary toward the door and then motioned for the young ladies. "Miss Bingley, do follow the example of your friends and come along, would you?"

Rosemary turned, her eyes seeking her mistress's. Caroline expected to find a haughty expression on the woman's face, but instead, she had the decency to appear embarrassed at entering before her mistress and on the arm of a gentleman when they were so very scarce that evening. Indeed, she was flushed red to the roots of her strawberry blond hair.

Good.

She may have the distinguishment of entering on Mr. Rushton's arm, but she would do so looking as red as a poppy.

Caroline attempted a look of nonchalance, but inwardly she seethed. To be forced to walk behind her companion. Her servant!

"Come, come!" Lavinia called to her again though they were practically side by side now. "Let us join the others. I fear, however, that you will not like your seat."

As soon as they crossed the threshold into the dining room, Caroline was escorted in the opposite direction whence Mr. Rushton and Rosemary had traveled to the other end of the long table, and Caroline did not mind being separated from them. Adequate distance was of the highest import, for she feared what she might say.

The evening was not going at all according to her plan. Mr. Rushton may have thought it appropriate to joke about it, but clearly, the rain had been an indication of the unfortunate course the evening would follow.

The dining table was so long that it would be well nigh impossible for conversation to flow between those seated at the head and those at its foot. Mr. Charlton was, of course, at its head, and Caroline found herself being directed to the midsection of the table, closer to the foot. She had no hope even of overhearing conversation that might prove useful later. All she could hear at the moment was the scrape of chairs' legs across the floor as servants assisted the guests to be seated.

Though she attempted to prevent it, her eyes sought Mr. Rushton and Rosemary. She watched him escort her to a pair of empty chairs near the head of the table—talking to a lady here, laughing with a gentleman there—and she felt her face flush with anger.

Still, Caroline would comport herself with dignity. She must do so, she reminded herself, in order to carry her plan to satisfactory completion. And though her first attempt at drawing nearer to Mr. Charlton had been thwarted, she would not give up.

It mattered not that the evening had begun in a manner so far at odds with her original design; it could be salvaged yet.

She must focus on the benefits she might glean from her current position.

She glanced at her dinner companion and discovered Miss Brodrick to be eyeing her.

Caroline already knew she would gain nothing from an association with her, so she looked across the low candle flames to those on the opposite side of the table.

There, she found a gentleman of middling age with a woman entirely too young to be his wife seated beside him. She could not remember having met either of them.

The room grew quiet, and Mr. Charlton stood and offered a few words of welcome before the servants began ladling soup for each guest.

While the servants went about their tasks, Caroline looked to her family party.

Neither her mother nor Mr. Newton seemed to notice her consternation over the order of entrance, but Mr. Rushton, it seemed, was not so dense. He was watching her, his roguish blue eyes shining.

Yes, oblivious though he seemed, she knew that he comprehended her dilemma perfectly and was reveling in it. He took pleasure in her awkwardness. It likely made him feel better about his own ineptitude and gracelessness. He appeared on the verge of smirking at her, but then he offered her a small half smile. It conveyed, well, a sort of camaraderie. That made little sense. Perhaps Caroline was misreading him. She was looking at him from across the vast expanse of the dining table after all.

Caroline raised her chin and looked purposefully away.

✤ Eight ✤

Caroline was concentrating on arranging her skirts under the dining table to prevent as many wrinkles as possible when she felt a small tap on her arm. She looked down at the appendage, almost expecting to find that an insect of some sort had landed on her.

It was very nearly an insect. It was Rosemary Pickersgill. She was leaning close, her fingers resting on Caroline's arm.

Caroline concealed her surprise with irritation, narrowing her eyes at the woman.

"Miss Bingley?" Rosemary voice came quietly, but it arrested Caroline's movements almost as if it had been a shout. She looked at her companion, who seemed to be considering her words with extreme care. "I know this is very untoward, but something of great urgency has occurred to me and I must speak with you privately."

Caroline gaped at Rosemary. "What? Now?"

The soup had been served, and, in near unison, the members of the party had appropriated the proper utensil and were dipping delicately at their fare.

"If you please."

Could any more social faux pas occur this evening? Caroline hardly thought it was possible. It appeared that she had little choice but to leave the table and exit the room. She followed her companion into the drawing room and turned to face her. "What is it?" she whispered with as much harshness as she could muster. "Can you not see that dinner has begun?"

Rosemary hesitated, gave her a considering look, and then studied the floor.

"Stop looking at your toes, and tell me why you have dragged me out here!" Caroline demanded.

Another hesitation. Then, Rosemary spoke. "I could not sit down to a meal with you staring at me as if I had done you a desperate wrong."

"I hardly think this is the time for a discussion on all the ways in which I have been wronged by you," Caroline said. "We ought not to have left the table, and our absence will undoubtedly cause vexation to Mr. Charlton and Mrs. Winton. If their dinner party is ruined, I shall not shelter you from their wrath."

Caroline was intent on returning, but Rosemary's hand stopped her. "As your companion, Miss Bingley, I must explain." Her eyes appeared weary, as if she were the one who had become frustrated with their conversation. "Mr. Rushton would not allow me to leave his side."

"Lovely," Caroline said. "You make a very nice pair indeed."

Yes, they were well suited—insolent both of them.

"I attempted to decline, to take your place at the table amidst the unpaired women, but it is impossible to thwart him."

Caroline could hardly argue with that, for it seemed that Mr. Rushton often contrived to gain exactly what he desired, but she would not concede the point to Rosemary.

Instead, she looked down at the woman with as much pride as possible and said, "Well now, you have told me. Let us return."

Expecting Rosemary to tromp ahead of her, Caroline hesitated, but upon finding that the woman remained unmoving, she swept back into the dining room ahead of her.

The room was now filled with the low murmur of conversation and the clinking of glassware as liveried servants poured wine. Upon her reentry, one of the servants pulled out the chair beside Mr. Rushton, the very one that Rosemary had vacated, and waited expectantly for Caroline to take it.

And so she did.

What good fortune, Caroline thought as she took her rightful place. She watched as Rosemary was seated beside Miss Brodrick, who smiled at her new dining partner. Yes, they would do nicely now that their places were reversed.

She glanced about her to see if anyone had noticed the shift. Aside from the somewhat confused nods of her new dining companions, no one acknowledged the change.

Caroline smiled. Her situation had improved undeniably, for she was seated far nearer to her object, Mr. Charlton. Though she could not converse comfortably with him, she was now settled within a distance that would allow him to admire her without obstruction, and if she were diligent, she might overhear his conversations.

She might hear them if she could manage to ignore Mr. Rushton, with whom she was partnered.

From her left, Mr. Rushton spoke without so much as looking at her. "Mrs. Pickersgill, I find, has abandoned me to your company."

"Yes, she confessed she could not bear you a moment longer and would rather sit alone all evening than be made to suffer another minute with you," Caroline said with satisfaction. "As her superior, I felt it my duty to relieve her of such pain by sacrificing myself to your conversation for the duration of the meal."

Caroline glanced at Mr. Rushton, hoping to find him affronted, but he did not appear to be considering her speech at all. Instead, he was looking at Rosemary. And inconceivably, he was smiling. Rosemary returned it.

Why?

Then Mr. Rushton's eyes turned to Caroline's, his expression knowing and somewhat superior.

And she understood.

Rosemary had pulled her from the room in order to exchange seats, to give Caroline the place of higher honor.

Caroline did not know whether to be angry, embarrassed, or thankful. Anger came the easiest, so she scowled at her companion across the vast expanse of table and candles that separated them.

She refused to be indebted to that woman. After all, Rosemary had only surrendered to Caroline her rightful place at the table. She would not allow one act to change her opinion of this enforced companionship.

But Caroline was no longer doomed to be partnered with a lady for the evening, and against her will, something inside her—a very small portion—softened toward Rosemary Pickersgill. She glanced at her out of the corner of her eye, and Rosemary offered her a small smile.

Caroline frowned again in return.

"That was rather kind of your Mrs. Pickersgill, do not you agree?" Mr. Rushton asked with a deceptively companionable tone.

"Kind?" Caroline would never admit it.

"Yes, kind. She observed you seething down there at the foot of the table beside sweet Miss Brodrick, and she had mercy on you."

"Mercy was not her motivation. I am certain she was more interested in retaining her position within my household than anything else."

"Yes, I find I quite like Mrs. Pickersgill," Mr. Rushton said as if he had not heard a word Caroline spoke. "I am surprised that you would find such a charming companion who would remain so faithful."

To suggest that some flaw existed in Caroline that would prevent her from gathering faithful friends was ridiculous. She was preparing to chastise him severely for his audacity when she found him smirking at her openly.

He was baiting her and quite enjoying himself in the process.

Well!

Caroline would not give him the satisfaction of a fight. Instead, she said simply, "I find I do not like you, Mr. Rushton."

Then she cut her eyes demurely toward the head of the table, foregoing any further attempts at conversation with Mr. Rushton in exchange for observing Mr. Charlton as discreetly as possible through the soup course.

Dinner proceeded as dinners invariably do. Servants deposited food before the diners, removed the soiled dishware, and replaced it with another course. Soon, the soup bowls were gone in favor of Lavinia's finest china plates, which had been arranged artfully with beef, quail, boiled potatoes, and assorted vegetables.

Caroline and Mr. Rushton ignored each other quite charmingly through the early courses, but soon, as other dinner partners spoke, their silence grew more noticeable.

"We must hold some discourse, Mr. Rushton," Caroline said.

"Ah," he replied. "So you have decided I am a worthy companion after all."

"I would not say you were worthy, but you are my evening's companion nonetheless. We must make the best of it."

Mr. Rushton smiled, and candlelight seemed to shimmer in his eyes. "I am surprised to find that you have such a practical bent, Miss Bingley."

"Indeed, I am quite practical when it is required. I have run my brother's household for several years, and my reputation as a hostess is impeccable, I assure you, though I always maintained the strictest of budgets. My management was unimpeachable."

"I see," he said, leaning back and pretending to look under the table, "that you are not one for frivolous purchases, such as silken slippers and pearls for your hair."

Caroline met his challenge fully. "There are moments, Mr. Rushton, when even the most austere woman splurges. I enjoy the finer things, and I always will, but I am not a squanderer of fortune."

She eyed his fine suit. "And you, sir, are finely attired this evening," she said, only mildly shocked at herself for commenting on someone's attire in public. "You are not moderate in all your purchases, I see."

"You have me there, Miss Bingley. I am not always moderate. At times, my passion quite gets away from me. We may not be so different after all."

"Perhaps not," Caroline said, though she was not convinced.

He lapsed into neutral topics, which required of her little by way of response, and thus their pleasant truce endured straight through dessert.

But no longer.

After the meal, Caroline retired dutifully into the drawing room with the other ladies, while the gentlemen remained behind to smoke, consume port, and carry on without them. She hoped to catch Lavinia alone so that she might be in her presence when the gentlemen—most especially her brother— joined them. Then, perhaps, she might find the opportunity to charm Mr. Charlton a bit since dinner had proven an impractical venue for flirtation.

However, this did not come to pass in quite the way she had hoped.

Rosemary entered the room after the other ladies had already assembled, and Caroline wondered vaguely where she had gotten herself, but she decided not to take the trouble of asking. It mattered not where she had been. She could not make any mischief if the gentlemen were busy smoking and the ladies were all in the drawing room.

Rosemary looked about the room, and upon seeing her mistress quite alone, she approached. Their conversation would have seemed benign to any eavesdroppers, but in actuality it was a cryptic treaty.

"Had you a pleasant meal, Miss Bingley?" *Can we make peace?*

"Tolerable." *I suppose it may not be necessary to be enemies.*

"May I join you?" *I am here at your brother's request, but that does not mean I must be a hindrance to you. Did I not see that you were settled more happily in the dining room?*

"I suppose there is room on the sofa, but take care not to crush my gown." *I understand your gesture of kindness earlier this evening, but do not allow yourself to believe that we are now friends. We are simply not enemies. And do take care not to crush my gown.*

"I will take care." *I understand.*

Rosemary sat carefully beside Caroline, and the two women remained for a time without speaking. The silence could have been awkward, but Caroline found the quiet companionship rather pleasant. Groups chattered around them, and the gentlemen soon returned.

Mr. Charlton entered, and after speaking briefly with Lavinia, Caroline was pleased to see him pour himself a glass of sherry and meander toward the sofa where she and Rosemary were seated.

Though she was tempted to shoo her companion, Caroline held her tongue. Instead, she smiled at Mr. Charlton and asked, "I thought you believed sherry to be the ideal aperitif, but is it also your choice for digestif as well?"

"Sherry was the first decanter available, and I do so despise waiting." He leaned forward, his dark hair falling in his eyes, and continued. "Generally, I prefer brandy, which has a much more calming effect on the stomach, especially after a questionable meal."

"You found the meal questionable?" Rosemary inquired.

"No indeed, and that is why I found it perfectly acceptable to have sherry in the place of brandy. My stomach did not require calming." As though to demonstrate proof of the quality of the meal, he finished the sherry in one long sip and then placed the glass on the side table. Then he glanced at Caroline with meaning. "My mind, however, did require a little soothing."

He was referring to his tedious conversation with the Dowager Lady Kentworth no doubt.

"I quite know how you must be feeling," Caroline said with a quick glance at Miss Brodrick and Mr. Rushton, who were engaged in conversation nearby.

He followed her gaze and then smiled. "Ah," he said. "Yes, we are not always free to associate with those of our choosing, are we?"

Mr. Charlton paused as he seemed to contemplate Miss Brodrick or perhaps his lack of freedom; Caroline could not be certain. Then, without preamble, he turned his lean body back to them and said, "And now, ladies, shall we not discuss a socially acceptable subject of great import and dreadful dullness?" He grinned, clasped his hands behind his back, and rose briefly to his toes. "What topics are of interest to you? Politics? War with France? Travel? Farming? Literature? What is your pleasure?"

"I am certain that you shall find Miss Bingley is well versed on any subject," Lavinia said, having descended unseen upon them. Apparently, they had left their flank unguarded. "But she is much in demand at the pianoforte."

Though Caroline was ordinarily appreciative when her friends offered her the opportunity of exhibiting at the pianoforte, she could not have been more displeased at Lavinia's timing. She wished for nothing more than to continue conversing uninterrupted with Mr. Charlton. "Oh, it is very kind of you to ask, Lavinia. But I beg you not to require it of me, for I am not in the humor for music tonight."

"But you must play for us, my dear. I shall appeal to your mother to persuade you if you will not agree."

And upon those words Lavinia called Mrs. Newton to join them, saying, "Caroline says she shall not play tonight. Do convince her."

Mrs. Newton appeared surprised. Her eyebrows were raised upon her plump face. "Oh, I would be so disappointed not to hear you this evening."

"You are both very kind," Caroline said as she glanced toward the pianoforte, which was settled far to one side of the room. She happened to glance at Mr. Rushton, and after recalling his vague insults regarding the rehearsed nature of her playing, she felt even less inclined to exhibit. "I had not the least intention of playing tonight."

"Nonsense," Lavinia said, as she pulled Caroline from her place beside Rosemary and led her toward the instrument. She leaned in close and whispered, "Do not be cross, my dear. Not only will this show your talents to their best advantage, but it will ease some tensions that are developing between Mr. and Mrs. Palmer."

She nodded in the general direction of the hearth, and Caroline observed a couple, the Palmers, obviously in the throes of some sort of heated debate.

"That," Lavinia continued with a sniff, "is why I am so thankful that Mr. Winton is so often away. We have no time to develop tensions."

Though she doubted that a few musical notes would do a thing to improve the course of the Palmers' marriage, Caroline relented. "If you insist, I shall play."

Lavinia did insist. In fact, she practically shoved Caroline onto the stool and then called out to the room in general, "Miss Bingley, my oldest friend, will now delight us all with a song."

All eyes in the room were now upon her, and Caroline began to feel a prickly, heated sensation radiate across her body. It felt strangely akin to nervousness, which was ridiculous, for she knew several appropriate pieces by heart.

Nervous? No. It was Mr. Rushton.

His oblique insult to her playing had shaken her confidence. That was all.

Caroline closed her eyes and took a moment to compose herself. Then, with purposeful hands, she arranged her skirts, which had wrinkled when Lavinia pushed her onto the stool, and finally made a great pretense of riffling through the music books before her.

She selected a volume of Italian airs. This particular collection was unknown to her, but as she studied the tiny black notes that danced across the page, she felt a little thrill of delight.

If Mr. Rushton believed her former performance had been too studied, then she would unleash upon him her talent for sight-reading. He would soon see that her accomplishments went far beyond simply memorizing a few show pieces.

No, she was truly a musician.

As she placed her fingers on the keys, her vision seemed to contract, and the music became her whole world. Gone were the arguing Palmers. Forgotten were Mr. Charlton and Lavinia. Even Mr. Rushton and his snide remarks receded.

Energy washed through her, and she began to play.

Perhaps her performance lacked a bit of polish and—though she was unwilling to admit it—her fingers did misplace themselves on occasion, but her listeners did not seem displeased. When she chanced a glance away from the page, she noticed several toes tapping.

She played three tunes and decided to stop, for it seemed an appropriate number. It was always best to leave one's audience desiring to hear more.

As Caroline sounded the final notes, she happened to glance at Mr. Rushton, who was looking at her with an odd expression. He was leaning against the far wall, arms crossed in front of his chest, feet crossed below him. He was studying her, but she could not discern any criticism in his expression.

Excellent.

A smile of victory spread across Caroline's lips.

Yes, her proficiency had impressed Mr. Rushton, and that gave her great pleasure indeed.

The rest of the room's occupants looked upon her with admiration, except for the Palmers, who were glaring at each other across the mantelpiece. At least they were no longer arguing.

"Shall you not delight us again, Caroline?" Lavinia asked.

Caroline knew that this was a query born more from politeness than a true desire for her to continue, so she declined. The interlude had served its purpose. The Palmers were silent, and it was time for her to relinquish the stage, which she did.

Caroline had many flaws—indeed, she admitted it—but the propensity of exhibiting too long was not among them. As she lifted herself from the stool, she looked over her shoulder at Mr. Rushton. He was yet watching her, and though she could not explain it, she felt herself blushing under his gaze.

✦ Nine ✦

Mr. Rushton should not be Caroline's concern. Her hopes lay in an altogether more superior object, and as she made her way back to the sofa, she discovered that her object, Mr. Charlton, awaited her there.

Mr. Charlton had engaged Rosemary in conversation. Much to her surprise, he seemed more than willing to condescend to her, waiving the privileges of his rank to hold what appeared to be a pleasant conversation with a paid companion.

As Caroline walked as gracefully as she could across the room, hoping to offer just the right amount of sway to her hips and allure to her gaze, Mr. Charlton stopped mid-word. He smiled overtly at her, and she knew she had accomplished her aim. Perhaps Mr. Darcy did not discern the merits of her movement, but Mr. Charlton apparently did.

Strangely, the thrill she had hoped to feel at catching the gentleman's interest did not spark within her.

But she smiled at him anyway as he stood to make room for her to sit.

"Ah! Miss Bingley, I had forgotten how well you played. The years have only served to improve your abilities, I think."

"I thank you, sir," she said as she lowered herself to the sofa, made great pretense of arranging her skirts, and met his eyes. "I do find much enjoyment in music."

"And it certainly was evident in your performance this evening. I do not believe my sister's pianoforte has ever sounded quite that lively."

Caroline lowered her gaze. "I thank you."

She smiled to herself. Mr. Charlton, thank heaven, seemed much more easily impressed than the dreadful Mr. Rushton.

"And I was just saying as much to Mrs. Pickersgill." He turned toward her. "Do you play as well?"

"I play a bit, sir, but very ill," she replied.

"Yes," Caroline interjected, "I am certain Mrs. Pickersgill would do well to avail herself of my mother's instrument while we are in Kendal."

Mrs. Pickersgill gave Caroline a bland look. "I do not believe any level of practice could improve my playing. I was not born to it, but I thank you for your kind offer."

The party was silent for a moment, and then Mr. Charlton spoke to Mrs. Pickersgill. "I do not believe you have yet had the opportunity to see much of Cumbria."

"Indeed, I have yet to see much of the area, sir." Her face had returned to a somewhat distant expression, and Caroline noted her well-moderated tone of voice and the manner in which she held herself. She sat like a lady, ankles crossed, hands in her lap, back erect. She did possess a certain amount of grace. She appeared to be any genteel young lady and not the unwanted companion that she was. "But it is a vast deal different from my home county."

"And from what exotic, mysterious land have you come?" Mr. Charlton asked. "I do not believe I had a chance to inquire when last we spoke."

"No, I do not believe so, sir." Rosemary laughed politely then, and said, "My family hails from the exotic county of Shropshire."

Mr. Charlton threw his head back, exposing a smooth, strong throat, and laughed loud and long. Then he turned his smile again to Rosemary. "I had no idea that Shropshire was so exotic and mysterious."

"One would not think that Shropshire holds many beauties," she said seriously, "but I have found that each county has unique charms of its own."

"Yes," Mr. Charlton said, giving her what appeared to Caroline to be an ironic look. His face was appraising and his eyebrows were raised, but a smile lingered. "Unique charms indeed."

Rosemary did not respond, and Mr. Charlton continued, "And how did you become acquainted with the family? Miss Bingley, I do not recall hearing that your family was connected with that part of the country."

"No indeed, we have no connections there," Caroline said. She was preparing to respond to his question regarding the nature of their first acquaintance, but she realized abruptly that she did not know how her brother had met this woman.

Mrs. Pickersgill said, "I became acquainted with Miss Bingley's brother in London."

"Ah! How very vague an explanation you offer, Mrs. Pickersgill. But of course, I must excuse you, for it is clear why Miss Bingley, who has exquisite taste, opted to make you her companion."

"And why might that be, Mr. Charlton?" Caroline asked. "Do enlighten us."

"Why, because she gives the appearance of a lady of worth, and you would choose nothing less for your companion, would you not?"

Caroline acknowledged his words with a nod, but she greatly wished the conversation might turn in another direction. "I do prefer to surround myself with the best company, and my family holds Mrs. Pickersgill in high regard."

"And well they should," said Mr. Charlton, "for she seems an amiable creature."

The amiable creature in question only offered a small smile.

❧ ❧

The dinner party at Oak Park concluded well after midnight, and the Newtons, Mr. Rushton, Rosemary, and Caroline departed for Newton House through cold and wet darkness. She undressed quickly with the help of a servant, and soon she lay down on the cold sheets and closed her eyes, but she found that sleep would not come.

Having kept these wretched country hours for so many weeks, Caroline ought to have slumbered easily, for early hours, morning calls, and polite conversation with one's neighbors was often more taxing than it sounded.

Caroline rolled to her side and looked out the rain-streaked window. The landscape was barely visible in the semi-dark, but she could see the silhouettes of the trees as they blew in the cold wind.

It was most beautiful, and yet somehow also it caused an ache within her breast.

How she missed Town. How she ached to be returned to those golden days when she had traveled with her brother and Mr. Darcy before the discovery of the Bennet sisters.

But now, she had fallen.

Hers, at least, was a quiet descent. Her family and friends had silently set her aside, but that was enough.

She had once again become Miss Caroline Bingley, the daughter of no one in particular.

By discovering the presence of Lavinia and the advent of a new gentleman to inherit the barony, Caroline's despair at her future prospects had been reversed.

This was her only opportunity.

Certainly, Mr. Charlton and Lavinia knew of her past. They knew precisely from whence her family's fortune came. They were acquainted with Mr. Newton, the bridge builder. And though she had been much frightened by Lavinia's laxity in paying a call and her apparent hesitation to invite her to dine at Oak Park, she was now certain of her acceptance there.

That family represented Caroline's salvation.

She had planned to pursue Mr. Charlton at a leisurely pace, allowing him to fall in love with her and propose just in time for her to join him as his wife for the London season, but after having been at Oak Park that evening and in his company, she was suddenly reinvigorated. She simply did not want to wait.

Her failures at the dinner party were the results of chance. Circumstances had hardly allowed her to converse with Mr. Charlton. She had been pulled away by Miss Brodrick, shackled to Mr. Rushton at dinner, and required to play the pianoforte. She had not a moment alone with her object, and that was required to win a gentleman, was it not? She must contrive to find him alone.

Caroline smiled at the thought of being alone with Mr. Charlton. Yes, she would undertake any task, bear any burden, and overcome any obstacle to entice Mr. Charlton.

She sat up in bed at that thought. She felt animated, ready to enact the next phase of her plan, but she could do nothing in the middle of the night.

She lay back down.

She fidgeted with the covers and adjusted her position, but sleep did not come.

Resigning herself to the fact that she was not going to drift easily into pleasant oblivion, Caroline sat up again and struggled to light her candle.

The small flame hardly lit the room, but she could see well enough to move about without crashing into the furniture. In her youth, she had sneaked below stairs to indulge in a bit of biscuit or chocolate and sit by a banked fire alone for a few moments. She longed to do so now.

And so that is precisely what she did.

After donning her wrap and a pair of slippers, she padded to the door, opened it, and peeked down the hall. She saw no one, heard no sound. She could certainly make the trip unnoticed. Of course, she was adequately covered should she come into contact with a male servant, Mr. Newton, or Mr. Rushton.

She did not want to encounter the latter, but she also did not want to remain trapped in her room, unable to sleep.

So Caroline crept down the corridor, feeling like a child in the midst of mischief, and managed to sneak into the kitchen without attracting notice. Caroline did not often enter the kitchen. As a very young child, before her father had made his fortune, she could remember helping her mother with food preparation. She knew that refined young ladies did not undertake such menial tasks. So now, Caroline generally kept as far from that room as possible.

When she had run Netherfield Park, she had consulted with the cook in the library, not the kitchen.

But occasionally, she needed to indulge in a small delicacy, so she would venture in when no one was about to notice, just as she was now.

Newton House's kitchen was designed in much the same manner as the rest of the house. It was arranged for maximum efficiency and comfort, but had little ostentation. Unlike in many of the finer houses, the room was adjacent to the dining room for the convenience of the servants. Mr. Newton obviously gave no thought to the lingering odors a kitchen was wont to produce and their effects on a lady's furniture. But her mother did not complain.

Caroline entered the pantry, rummaged a bit, and produced a tin of biscuits, which she carried to the large pine worktable that stood at the room's center. Placing the candle at a safe distance on the scrubbed wooden surface, she pulled out a heavy chair and turned it so that it was facing the banked fire that smoldered in the grate beside the stove.

She sat down and pulled the lid from the tin, and as she ate, the room seemed to cocoon her in its intimacy. Caroline smiled at the delicious feeling of warmth that spread through her and even stretched her legs toward the fire.

It was in that exact posture that Mr. Rushton found her when he entered the room with a brusque swing of the door.

Caroline looked down at the biscuit in her hand and panicked. She did not want to be caught in the throes of something as uncultured as reclining in a kitchen and eating biscuits. A lady ought to be seen at edifying tasks.

But it was too late now, for Mr. Rushton was already regarding her with a quizzical eye. "Good evening, Miss Bingley."

She returned his greeting, pretending to be absorbed by the play of the fire in the grate, but she allowed her displeasure to show on her face in the hopes that he might behave politely and leave her to herself.

That, of course, was too much to expect.

"What do you do about at this late hour?" he asked.

"Why, cannot you see?" She waved her biscuit at him. "I am penning a great work of fiction."

"Ah," he said. Then nothing more.

Caroline allowed herself to glance up and found him leaning a hip against the edge of the worktable. He was still wearing his dinner attire, but he had removed his coat and loosened his cravat.

And here she sat in her night attire! It was wholly inappropriate. He ought to leave.

She sat up straight and tucked her feet beneath her dressing gown.

He was watching her movements and smiling at her with an infuriatingly ironic expression in his eyes. "I should have expected to find you here after observing how little you ate at dinner."

Caroline willed herself not to blush. Of course, it did not matter if her face turned purple, she chided herself, for in this semi-dark, color was quite washed away. But indeed, she was embarrassed. It was true that she had been able to consume little at Oak Park. Her nerves had been much too strained by her circumstances. "I wish you would not observe me, Mr. Rushton. It is very rude."

His smile returned, and Caroline had the urge to remove it from his face, by force if necessary.

"May I join you?" he asked in a pleasant tone of voice.

"I wish you would not," she returned with exaggerated coldness.

"Excellent," he said as he came around the table, pulled out the chair beside hers, turned it around, and sat.

Caroline scowled at him. "A gentleman would leave. This situation is quite improper."

Mr. Rushton emitted a sort of throaty growl and said, "I would ask if you would do me the honor of sharing that tin of biscuits, but because I am certain you will respond in the negative, I find I must take them without your permission."

Before he could snatch the tin from her, Caroline handed it to him. "I would not deny you, Mr. Rushton."

She had expected him to say something mocking, but to her surprise, he said nothing, and that was infinitely worse. He merely chewed and looked at her intently.

He offered her a biscuit from the tin he now possessed.

She thought to feign disinterest, but she had come for this very purpose after all. She took one.

"And so if you will not deny me, Miss Bingley, tell me, what has really brought you all the way to the blighted north?"

Caroline stopped chewing and looked at him.

Mr. Rushton continued, "For I smell something suspicious in the air, and I must track it down. I cannot believe a woman, who so obviously desires the pleasures of town, would ever come here of her own accord."

"Can you not, Mr. Rushton?" Caroline studied him a moment and decided to deflect his line of questioning. "I should have thought a gentleman of property in the region would have reason to boast of its bounties."

"Indeed, it is a region of bounty and beauty, Miss Bingley, but have you not grown accustomed to the bustle of London?"

"I do not pretend to hide my regard for Town, but I also dearly love my mother." She lowered her eyes. "And she has brought me here."

He turned his head slightly, as if gauging the veracity of her statement and deciding he was skeptical.

"You do not believe I love my mother, Mr. Rushton?"

"No indeed, I am quite certain of your affection for Mrs. Newton," he said as he finished another biscuit, recovered the tin, and wiped his hands on his trousers. "In fact, it is one of your most redeeming characteristics."

"How very kind of you," Caroline said as she rose from her chair to look down upon him. "In you, I have found no such redeeming traits, and I wish very much that you would prevent yourself further thought on my account. I have nothing to conceal."

He had the audacity to snort in disbelief.

"You, on the contrary, seem to have a great deal to conceal," Caroline said.

He did not even possess the shame to look away under the force of her accusation. He simply stretched his legs and crossed his ankles. "You have heard the rumors then?"

"I am sure there are few who have not."

He only smiled.

"You are not contrite?" Caroline asked. How could a gentleman face the allegation of being a fortune hunter with such carelessness?

"Why should I be?" he asked with a shrug. His white shirt rose and fell with his movements, somehow exposing more of his chest. Caroline blushed again as he continued. "I have done nothing amiss. I am innocent. It is you who have chosen to believe idle gossip."

Caroline very nearly laughed. "On the contrary, I never believe idle gossip, only that which has been confirmed."

"Ah," he said with a smile. "So my guilt is confirmed then, in your mind?"

"It is."

"And what is your evidence?"

Caroline tucked her chair back under the table and pulled her wrap tighter around herself. "Every conversation I hold with you convinces me further of your unworthiness to be in my mother's household."

He laughed again and watched as she turned on her heel to depart.

"Good night, Mr. Rushton," she shot.

"Good night, Miss Bingley," he said as she swept past him toward the door.

She had almost made her escape when she heard him call out, "Miss Bingley."

She nearly ignored him, but something compelled her to look back at him. "What?"

When he spoke again, his voice was rather hushed. "I am certainly glad for whatever it is that brought you here. You amuse me, Miss Bingley. You amuse me."

"I am sorry that I cannot return those sentiments, Mr. Rushton, for you do not amuse me."

꧁ Ten ꧂

From the night of Lavinia's dinner party forward, Caroline could not step into the Charltons' society without Rosemary trailing alongside, keeping unending watch over her charge, but one day in late February, chance finally worked in her favor.

Rosemary had come down with a most horrifying cold, and her nose had turned cherry red. She was not fit to be seen in company, nor had she even exited her bedchamber in several days.

This offered Caroline the ideal opportunity to pay a call on Oak Park unaccompanied by her companion. And the occasion was even better than Caroline had ever dared hope, for she knew with certainty that Lavinia would not be at home that morning.

Indeed, Caroline must now seize every opportunity to associate privately with Mr. Charlton, for she could not properly woo a gentleman with her servant always about to remind her of his inaccurate reputation. And Caroline had no desire to call upon Lavinia. She went for the sole purpose of encountering Mr. Charlton.

Perhaps chance would smile upon her again and her plan would prove successful.

Caroline sat at her dressing table and studied her reflection in the mirror.

Today, she had chosen a cool blue dress that clung to her slim figure and complimented her skin tone. Her maid had worked for hours on a casual hairstyle with curls placed to frame her face as if they had fallen of their own will.

Caroline pinched her cheeks and hoped that her nose would not turn too red on the carriage ride to Oak Park. She had no wish to look as if she had fallen victim to Rosemary's cold.

Mustering her resolve, Caroline gave herself one last look in the mirror, stood, and walked quickly down the stairs and toward the waiting coach.

As she passed the sitting room door, she heard her mother call out her name.

Caroline stopped, removed all traces of annoyance from her expression, and moved to the open doorway.

"You are calling upon Mrs. Winton this morning?" her mother inquired from her seat before the fire.

"Yes, indeed."

Mrs. Newton laid aside her mending and said, "I do wish you might wait until Mrs. Pickersgill is well enough to come along."

"But why, Mama? Lavinia is my oldest friend. Surely, I do not require a chaperone to call upon her."

"Yes, you and Lavinia have long been acquainted. I only fear—" She broke off, studied Caroline a moment longer, and then seemed to change her mind about her next words. After a moment's hesitation, she said, "I fear that our Mrs. Pickersgill has not made many friends here in Kendal."

"Nonsense, Mama," Caroline objected. "She could not help but acquire acquaintances, for she has been with me every moment since we arrived."

Mrs. Newton's eyes seemed to issue a warning that Caroline could not quite comprehend, but she only said, "Yes, I suppose you will enjoy time alone with Lavinia. It is only...." Her voice trailed off.

"Only what?" Caroline said with unconcealed annoyance. The carriage was waiting, and she must hurry if she hoped to catch Mr. Charlton alone.

"Do you not find Lavinia altered since you last saw her?" Mrs. Newton asked.

Caroline stepped back in surprise at the boldness of the question. "No indeed, Mama. I find her exactly as I left her."

"Ah, perhaps I am mistaken about Lavinia then, but I do not believe the same can be said for Mrs. Pickersgill. There is a sadness about her that I do not quite comprehend. I believe she is lonely. I wish you would coax her to join us tonight at supper. It cannot be good for her to remain so long in her room."

"She is ill, Mama," Caroline said. "We must not endanger her health by pulling her from bed too quickly."

"No, I suppose not, but if she is feeling better, I think you must invite her. Company often diffuses melancholy."

Caroline had noticed no such sadness in the woman, and she certainly had no compulsion to make any effort on behalf of a servant, but she would do anything for her mother, and, at the moment, she would do anything to be in a carriage on the way to Oak Park.

"I shall do just that, Mama. Tonight, I promise."

Her mother smiled, and that pleased Caroline. "Now, be off with you, and send my best regards to Lavinia."

Caroline complied and set off in the carriage to Oak Park.

As the carriage turned onto the approach road and the house came into view, Caroline surveyed the property, all that might one day soon be hers. Of all this, she could be mistress. The thought of such prestige caused in her a strange feeling of nervousness.

This was an important visit indeed.

Caroline exited the carriage and waited on the doorstep as the coachman directed the vehicle toward the stable to wait. She raised her hand slowly to the door knocker, gathering herself, but when she knocked, it was a quick, heavy sound that indicated that she was a woman of purpose.

The door opened, revealing a plain-faced manservant.

"Good morning, madam," he said.

"Yes, good morning," Caroline said as she looked past the manservant and into the house beyond. "Is the mistress of the house available?"

"No, madam, Mrs. Winton is not at home. Would you like to leave a card?"

"Indeed." Caroline removed a card from her reticule and handed it to him, again taking the opportunity of peeking over his shoulder into the house.

A heavy step echoed through the entryway.

Then she heard a male voice. "Dash it, Peters, I can find nothing in this house since my sister arrived. Where the devil is my…. Oh! Miss Bingley, I did not realize you were here."

Caroline offered Mr. Charlton a look of surprise in return. "And I did not expect to discover you here. I have come to call upon your sister, only to find that she is not at home."

Mr. Charlton approached the door, dismissed the manservant, and then leaned against the doorframe casually. "Yes, she has gotten off to some neighbor or other. I cannot keep up with her."

"How disappointing." Caroline looked up at him through her lashes with an expression gentlemen had always seemed to prefer. "Will you not be able to offer me some sort of consolation?"

Mr. Charlton smiled at her broadly and brushed a curl from his eyes. "I was just about to walk into Kendal. Would you care to join me?"

Caroline despised walking, and she had no inclination to go as far as town in this cold.

"I enjoy walking a great deal, Mr. Charlton, but I have not the time for a walk to Kendal this morning. Shall we not take a turn about your garden instead?"

If his expression showed a bit of disappointment, he covered it quickly. "Yes, a turn about the garden would be a rather pleasant diversion. Thank you for the suggestion. I should have accomplished nothing valuable in town at any rate."

Caroline was pleased when he offered his arm, and she made certain to reward him with her most appealing smile as she took it.

"Come, let us go to the back garden. The plants appear to be a little less dead there than those in the rose garden at this time of year."

"I am certain that even your dead plants are appealing." Caroline heard herself utter those words and immediately wished to snatch them back. If she could not discover a method of showing her interest in Mr. Charlton in a less obvious manner, she would never succeed in winning him, and she would be subject to her brother's punishment forever.

They had taken one full turn about the garden, which was quite as dead as the rose garden to Caroline's eye, before Mr. Charlton spoke again.

"Tell me, Miss Bingley, do you not find yourself surprised at the changes taking place?"

Believing him to refer to the advent of spring and the transformation it brought, Caroline looked about the winter-wilted plants, and seeing no signs of life at all, she said, "No indeed, for spring occurs every year."

Mr. Charlton smiled. "Your interpretation is rather more literal than I intended."

"Oh?" Caroline asked, perfectly ashamed at having misunderstood him. "I do not care for figurative language, Mr. Charlton, but do enlighten me."

"Kendal. Have you not sensed the changes here?"

Caroline looked at him, but not in the coy manner she had used only moments ago. This look was full and questioning. Was he referring to his new status as heir? "A great many things have changed, Mr. Charlton. Do you object to these alterations?"

"I find that I do object. I quite enjoyed my life of leisure, but now I find myself pulled about by the whims of others."

"You speak rather too plainly, but I confess that I can well understand your position," Caroline said. Not caring to elaborate, she only added, "We must make of our circumstances what we can. It is useless to mope about and lament what cannot be altered."

"But changes are happening all around us. Only look at how families rise and fall in wealth. Those who were poor are now rising."

"You refer to the middling classes?" she asked with disgust.

"Indeed, I have read that one in seven people in London now account for the middling classes."

Caroline was indeed surprised. "That is a shocking number, but it changes nothing of true status."

"Does it not? Even here in Kendal, one must look only to Mr. Newton and perhaps even Miss Brodrick to observe the new stature afforded to such people. And Mr. Rushton, though he is a gentleman to be sure, had descended in wealth only to have risen again."

"Mr. Rushton is not wealthy," Caroline protested.

"Indeed, he is. Have you not seen his home in Keswick? His home in Town?" He studied her. "No, I suppose you have not. But I assure you that he has returned his family to the respectable situation it held in the past."

Caroline rather doubted this. Besides, true wealth constituted more than mere money. What of land, title, ancestry? "But Mr. Rushton has sold most of his family property, has he not? If he has no ancestral land, he cannot truly be counted as a gentleman."

"What does family land matter?" Mr. Charlton asked as he gestured broadly around him. "What does all this gain me? It is lovely, to be sure, but no one cares to work the land any longer."

"But do not you agree that land is a hallmark of a great family, of connections to the best of society through the ages? And these men of whom you speak, who have no land, they are but half-gentlemen; they have no breeding. And though they have money, they will always want for decent connections."

He looked down at her. "Yes, connections are important, as my sister has often reminded me."

"Mrs. Winton is very wise," Caroline said with what she hoped was a sage nod. "We must all cultivate our connections to our best advantage."

"Yes, yes, so she has said." He glanced around him, and when he spoke again, his voice held an edge of frustration. "She also speaks of duty and other such notions, but I cannot help but feel as if a life of freedom was ripped from me, and now I must behave in a completely new way. I wish most ardently to leave the business of Oak Park to someone more suited for the burden than I."

Caroline laughed aloud at his absurdity. "Why, Mr. Charlton, I find it utterly incomprehensible to hear you speak that way about your inheriting a barony! Only think of the advantages it provides. You may have your pick of friends and society, and any young lady would be honored by your acknowledgment of her."

Here, Mr. Charlton stopped, and again, Caroline looked at him through her lashes, letting them flutter a bit.

"Do you believe that? Any woman would be honored by me? What if I had no money at all, and only family name, reputation, and land to recommend me?" He gestured broadly at the house and land around him and then turned to Caroline. "Would you be honored by my acknowledgement of you then, Miss Bingley?" He studied her for a moment, shook his head once, and then looked toward the ground.

Caroline knew not how to respond.

"May I speak plainly?" he asked, his eyes wide and questioning.

"Of course, sir," Caroline said. She wondered if he might be on the verge of proposing marriage.

He cleared his throat and turned to face her fully.

"I have a dreadful fear that I shall destroy Oak Park when I run it without the oversight of my father and sister. I cannot seem to retain money. It slips through my grasp, and I do not quite know how. I do not wish to end a pauper."

Caroline studied him, trying not to show her surprise at this turn of conversation. Was he already losing his family's fortune?

She hoped not, but this could be a fortuitous error, for perhaps he would more quickly see her advantages if money were at stake. She did have a large dowry, and she would excel at managing Oak Park if he did not care to do it himself.

Yes, she would make an excellent baroness, especially if she had full control over the entire estate.

"Well, Mr. Charlton, you ought to use your attributes—your home and family name—to secure a wife of large dowry and leave the running of Oak Park entirely to her."

"And have you a large dowry, Miss Bingley?" he asked, his voice now a whisper. He leaned close as if hoping to catch her response, and Caroline backed away slightly.

"I do, Mr. Charlton," she whispered. Her whole body seemed to vibrate suddenly, and she could not tell if the sensation arose from hope or fear of his proposal.

He smiled and leaned closer. "And would you fancy running Oak Park?"

Mr. Charlton's lips were a breath from her, and Caroline could scarcely move enough to say, "Indeed, I would."

Her eyelids fluttered closed, and she was waiting to feel his lips upon hers when suddenly, a voice ripped across the garden. "William!"

Caroline's eyes flew open, and she jumped back, looking around for Lavinia. Had she seen her brother leaning in so closely? Had she been attempting to stop the scene from unfolding?

Lavinia was nowhere to be seen.

Caroline sent her questioning gaze to Mr. Charlton, who had righted himself. His eyelids lowered in disdain as he explained, "My sister is home and has already seen the ledger, I assume. She is likely crowing at me from the library."

"Oh," Caroline breathed. She knew Lavinia would not thwart a romantic scene between her closest acquaintance and her brother, and she felt rather silly for having momentarily doubted her friend.

"I must go," Mr. Charlton said. "I would invite you to come inside and socialize with my sister, but I fear you will not like her mood. Will you excuse me?"

"Indeed, Mr. Charlton, I would not stop you."

"I shall have your carriage sent around," he said as he took her gloved hand in his and brushed his thumb across her knuckles. "I shall call upon you soon."

Mr. Charlton then gave her a flirtatious smile and left her standing alone in the dried-up flower garden that one day she hoped to own.

〰 〰

Caroline counted her interaction with Mr. Charlton as an unmitigated success despite his abrupt removal. She had managed to discuss all the subjects she had hoped to address with him. They had discussed marriage, and it seemed that he had very nearly kissed her.

Though Caroline's own emotions were unsettled as a result, she had lashed them tightly into place now. Sentiment was hardly a creditable reason to decline a proposal of marriage to a baron!

She would continue to put herself in his path and show herself to best advantage. From there, the logical progression for him was to consider her as a specific partner in marriage.

Caroline spent the remainder of the afternoon in her chamber at Newton House contemplating her next interaction with Mr. Charlton. Her calling card in Lavinia's salver ensured a return of call from her friend, and it was likely that her brother might accompany her, for it was he who had last received her. They had some sort of connection, though she was rather unsure how to define it.

As twilight began to fall, Caroline knew she could no longer ignore her promise to her mother to coax Rosemary out of the sickroom and into their company.

With reluctance, Caroline left the comforts of her room and knocked once on the door to her companion's chamber, entering before she was bid to do so.

She discovered Rosemary still abed.

"Mrs. Pickersgill, how do you do?"

Rosemary eyed Caroline with more than a hint of irony in her expression. "As you can see, Miss Bingley, I have not recovered."

Caroline took a moment to study the woman. Her eyes were red rimmed, her nose swollen, and her face puffy. "Yes, you do look dreadful."

"How kind of you to say, Miss Bingley," she said as she dabbed at her nose with a handkerchief. "May I be of service to you?"

"No, but you may be of service to my mother. She would like you to join us tonight if you are not too ill."

Rosemary looked away. "I do not want to disappoint Mrs. Newton, but I cannot...." Her voice trailed off, almost as if she had begun to cry.

Caroline studied the side of Rosemary's face as if it might divulge something to her.

She had never looked upon Rosemary as anything other than a servant. She had never considered that the woman experienced emotions.

She moved around the side of the bed and looked down at her. It appeared that her mother had been accurate in her earlier assessment; the woman did have a particular sadness about her. Caroline had never marked it before this moment.

This realization elicited a strange reaction on Caroline's part, for she experienced a wave of pity that nearly overcame her when she saw a tear fall down her companion's cheek.

She was suddenly almost overcome by the urge to sit on the edge of Rosemary's bed and have a chat with her, as she had done many times in the past with Louisa when they were young girls. Caroline edged closer and nearly settled beside her, but something prevented her from doing so.

Uncomfortable, she moved toward the window and pretended to look at the surroundings. She did not like the peculiar feeling that had risen in her.

"My brother would not approve of his servant neglecting her duties," Caroline said, almost by rote.

There was a silence so lengthy that Caroline finally turned again to observe Rosemary, who was staring blankly ahead, but the tears had been wiped from her face.

"Yes, he would have cause to terminate my employment today," Rosemary said and then paused. When she spoke again, her tone was rough and breathy. "I beg you would forgive me, but I cannot join your family for dinner. I cannot."

That peculiar feeling nudged Caroline forward again, and she came nearer, almost without her own volition. "What is the matter, Mrs. Pickersgill?"

"Forgive me, Miss Bingley, but I care not to share my sentiments with one who asks only out of"—she squinted up at her—"a convoluted sense of duty."

Rosemary's words stung, and Caroline was surprised to hear herself say, "I am sorry to hear that, for in my brother's absence, I am responsible for you and cannot have you skulking about and neglecting your duties."

Her companion sighed heavily, her strawberry blond hair fluttering around her face upon her exhale. "I have had a letter late this afternoon. It contained ill news."

"Ill news? Of what nature?"

"Of a private nature, Miss Bingley. I beg you would forgive me, but I cannot speak of it to you."

"But this news, it has further sickened you?" Caroline's words sounded harsher than she had intended. Of all people, she comprehended the physical effects one might experience from an emotional blow. "Was it regarding a gentleman?"

Rosemary nodded slowly. "In a manner of speaking."

If Rosemary were suffering the same emotions that Caroline had experienced over Mr. Darcy's marriage to Miss Elizabeth Bennet, well, she would not berate her.

Instead, she approached the bedside, and though it was hardly an intimate gesture, her proximity surprised them both. "I shall make your excuses to my mother."

Rosemary looked at her, and relief crossed her features. "I thank you, Miss Bingley."

Caroline, suddenly uncomfortable with her feelings, turned away. "And then you may return to your duties."

She went to the door and had nearly shut it behind her when she heard Rosemary say, "Thank you, Miss Bingley."

ᨀᨂ Eleven ᨂᨀ

"Shall we all not ride out?" asked Mr. Charlton. "My sister and I have come dressed for it, as you see, and our horses are at the ready. This early March weather is shockingly warm and rather appealing. What say you?"

"Oh yes, William," Lavinia said as she clapped her hands together, "what a good idea. Our ride from Oak Park was invigorating, and I do so long to take a turn around that little pond out back."

Caroline looked at her friend in abject horror. Did she not recall what had happened the last time they had ridden out together?

Likely not, for that had been years ago, and as Caroline studied her friend's countenance now, she saw only an innocent pleasure and desire to be in the saddle.

Caroline sighed. She had been pleased when Lavinia and Mr. Charlton had called upon her that morning at Newton House, but she had not anticipated such an outing. Perhaps she should have, for Lavinia and Mr. Charlton had arrived on horseback looking quite pleased with themselves.

"Oh dear. Though you are charmingly attired, I fear I am not correctly dressed for equestrian activities," Caroline said, hoping desperately that this excuse would suffice.

"Oh, 'tis nothing, Miss Bingley," Lavinia said with a wave of her hand. "We shall wait for you to don your riding habit."

"But…," Caroline said as she sought a way to avoid riding horseback. Her eyes landed upon Rosemary, who had been sitting quietly in the corner. "I do not believe Mrs. Pickersgill cares to ride."

Rosemary did not look up from the mending in her lap to see the intent expression on Caroline's face. She simply said, "I would be happy to ride if it is required."

"You see!" Lavinia said. "It is the perfect day for riding, my dear. Everyone agrees."

Caroline clenched her fists in her lap. She had no wish to ride, and she could not fathom why going about on horseback was revered as a skill a young lady ought to have. Why, that was the reason carriages were created, was it not? To prevent young women from being forced to set themselves on the back of a wild beast and gallop madly about the countryside. Yes, a carriage was much more sensible.

She sighed. She must make sacrifices if she were to win Mr. Charlton, and this must be one of them. Caroline could not turn away this opportunity to converse with him.

She relented. "Then, I suppose, we shall ride."

"Do hurry and dress, Caroline." Lavinia waved a hand at her. "You too, Mrs. Pickersgill. William and I shall await you here."

Caroline and Rosemary went upstairs, and while the maid assisted her in changing into her riding habit, Caroline thought back on her illustrious history with equestrian activity.

It was not pleasing.

It had begun when she was but a young girl and still wearing her family's newly gained wealth with all the comfort of overly tightened corset stays. Her family had only recently been able to afford to keep a donkey for the children, and Caroline had not yet found her confidence with the animal. Her father had managed an invitation to a harvest celebration on the grounds of Oak Park, and Caroline would be able to interact with the children of the upper classes for the first time in her young life.

At the celebration, the adults had been about their conversations and activities, leaving the children to their own devices. Someone had proposed pony rides, a suggestion that horrified Caroline. She was supposed to try to impress her companions by showing that she had the same accomplishments they had, but she could not ride. She also knew, however, that her hesitancy to participate would only be evidence of her status.

So she had gone to the stables with the other children, and because there were not enough mounts, they took turns riding or leading each other about the grounds. It had all been surprisingly pleasant until it had come Caroline's turn to ride.

Caroline could not recall what happened, but she knew for certain that she had hit the ground after only a brief time on the pony's back.

The breath had left her body, and she had struggled to inhale. Tears formed in the corners of her eyes, but she did not allow them to fall. She continued to gasp as a shadow appeared above her. She wondered if it were death coming for her and closed her eyes, willing death away, and continued to attempt to draw breath.

"Caroline!" The voice was not that of death, but Lavinia Charlton, the girl she admired most in the world. Caroline opened her eyes to find her idol leaning over her. Her young face blocked out the view of the sky above her. "What is wrong with you? Relax. Just try to slow down a bit. You will soon be able to breathe."

She had only been able to cough and choke in response, but Caroline was quickly able to inhale and exhale normally, and she began to feel awkward.

"Are you well now?" Lavinia asked.

Cough. "Yes."

"Are you certain?" the girl demanded.

Caroline had nodded quickly.

"Good," Lavinia said loudly, "for I have not gotten a ride and I do not want to have to take you back to the house."

Lavinia grabbed her by the arm, yanked her into a standing position, and said more softly, "What could you possibly have been thinking? You know nothing of horses, do you?"

Caroline stared at her, and she stared back. Time seemed to freeze while her blood heated. "No."

Lavinia glowered. "You have never ridden before?"

Caroline narrowed her eyes. "I have ridden my family's donkey."

"Donkey?" She looked appalled. "You should go home. You do not belong here."

Caroline had only stood and watched as the children continued their game. Yes, she should return home. She looked down at her muddy dress. It was likely ruined, and her mother would not be pleased.

But Caroline's displeasure had come from another source. Lavinia's words had haunted and humiliated her, and she had vowed that one day she would belong amongst the elite, and then Lavinia herself would accept her.

And today, even as she allowed herself again to be swept along to the stables, Caroline vowed that she would not end on the ground in humiliation. She would devise a method for avoiding the ride altogether.

Along the way, she reviewed some potential dodges in her mind.

Perhaps she could muster a convincing fainting spell. She rejected this immediately, for she had no desire to be viewed as a swooning female.

A sprained ankle? No, indeed, for that would necessitate an undignified, unattractive limp for the remainder of the day at least. It would not do to be seen dragging about when she was trying to show herself to best advantage.

A sudden head cold? Apoplexy? Gout?

She dismissed them all.

No, Caroline was not a creator of excuses; she spoke plainly. It was a matter of pride.

She would simply have to register her objections to riding, and perhaps if she manipulated the situation correctly, Mr. Charlton would volunteer to rest with her while the others rode out.

She and Rosemary caught up to Mr. Charlton, who was walking briskly alongside Lavinia, and was discouraged to see the childlike joy in his expression. Everything about him radiated anticipation and glee. His eyes were bright, his movements quick, and even his dark curls blew about despite the tall black hat that sought to keep his hair under control. Lavinia too appeared eager to be at the stables.

"Mr. Charlton," Caroline said. "I am so pleased that you thought of inviting me to ride with you this morning."

"Ah! Think nothing of it, Miss Bingley." The stables came into view over a small rise in the landscape, and if possible, Mr. Charlton seemed to quicken his pace further as he said, "I confess that this warm weather has quite given me the desire to be outdoors."

"Indeed, it has had the same effect on me," Caroline lied. "I have found the loveliest little spot in the garden and have been many hours in the sun there."

Mrs. Pickersgill glanced sidelong at Caroline, who returned a look of defiance.

Yes, of course, it was a lie. She had not rested out of doors all week, for the wind was far too brisk, and she had not the faintest urge of damaging her hair.

"So the lure of spring has drawn you too, Miss Bingley," Lavinia said.

"A nice spot in the garden is good for the spirit, or at least our mother used to say as much," Mr. Charlton added.

"Indeed, your mother was a wise woman," Caroline said, hoping to have made headway with Mr. Charlton. "I wonder if you should care to see my little niche. I should gladly give up a ride to have the honor of showing you."

"Oh, I would not give up a ride for anything," Lavinia said for him. "And neither would my brother nor your companion, I think, for it is too fine a day to neglect the horses, is not that right, Mrs. Pickersgill?"

Rosemary smiled. "It is a fine day for riding."

Well! Caroline was going to have to resort to honesty and forget the idea of keeping Mr. Charlton behind. Their party had arrived in the stable yard, and the stench of manure, hay, and leather assaulted Caroline's senses. She was preparing to make her excuses as she approached the barn's ingress, where she discovered Mr. Rushton awaiting them.

Apparently, he was to be a part of the riding party. He stood beside his horse, a hulking grey beast, and watched her approach as if she were the only person arriving.

She did not give him the satisfaction of an acknowledgment. In fact, in recent days, she had attempted to avoid him as much as possible, a difficult task given that they were residing in the same house. But manage it she had, and they had spoken but little. Besides, he and Mr. Newton had been busy mucking about in the library and debating bridge schematics. That was hardly conversation that might interest Caroline.

"Good day, Miss Bingley," he said with all evidence of politeness, but his eyes held mischief.

Any idea of making her excuses and avoiding the ride disappeared. She would not give Mr. Rushton the satisfaction of seeing her wheedle out of their equestrian activities. He had an uncanny way of reading her motives, and she had no wish for him to witness her giving in to fear.

There was much shuffling about the stable as mounts were chosen and readied. Caroline kept herself out of the way of the commotion as well as she could, and far too soon, the horses were prepared and led to the stable yard for mounting.

Mr. Rushton found her at the back of the group and gave her a curious look.

"Allow me to present your mount, Miss Bingley." He left his horse by the fence and headed toward a small bay pony a few yards away. "This is Mossy, your mother's mare."

The pony mare looked at Caroline with dark, unconcerned eyes. Even this calm creature seemed much too big and powerful to consider sitting upon, but if her mother rode this pony, she ought to be able to manage one outing. Besides, Caroline had been able to survive her equitation lessons at the seminary. Certainly, her education would not fail her.

Caroline stood by the pony, and Mr. Rushton seemed to be awaiting her for some reason.

"Am I required to introduce myself to the creature?" she demanded.

His pale brows lowered as he considered her. "Most people give them a pat on the neck at least."

"If you insist," Caroline said as she reached out her gloved hand to the pony's neck. Mossy flinched at the sudden movement, and Mr. Rushton again eyed her.

The others had mounted, and Mr. Charlton called down to them, saying, "Mr. Rushton, assist Miss Bingley, if you please. I am anxious to be away."

Mr. Rushton hardly acknowledged the order, but he nonetheless assisted Caroline to mount Mossy. He stood on the ground beside her and watched as she fumbled to position the reins and riding crop in her hands.

"Are you well?" he asked, his blue eyes earnest. "We do not have to ride if you are unwell."

He was offering her the option of making her excuses, just as she had been scheming to do earlier, but his suggestion of it infuriated her.

"I am certainly able to ride!" Caroline snapped. "It is only that I am unused to this tack." She gestured broadly about her with her crop, hoping that "tack" was indeed the correct word for one of the things strapped to the horse.

She glanced at Mr. Charlton, hoping that he had not observed her awkwardness, and was delighted to discover that he and Lavinia were deep in conversation. Their horses strode slowly about the yard in a circle. They presented quite an elegant picture, and Caroline hoped that she looked as well as they did.

Then Mossy shifted her weight, causing Caroline to gasp at the unexpected movement.

Everyone looked at her, and she managed a tight smile. "There was a bee," she lied.

"Dashed insects," Mr. Charlton said. "Let us be off before they swarm and ruin the ride before it begins."

With that, Mr. Charlton, Lavinia, and Mrs. Pickersgill led the way out of the stable yard. Caroline urged Mossy to join them while Mr. Rushton mounted his own horse.

The mare's gait seemed smooth enough, but Caroline's feeble confidence seemed to erode with each stride away from the security of the stable.

Caroline tried to steel herself against her weakness.

Yes, fear was indeed her weakness.

Fear of exposure. Fear that her family's dubious background might haunt her forever. Fear that she might never have a home of her own. Fear that she might be flung from the back of this pony and humiliated in front of Mr. Charlton, Lavinia, Rosemary, and Mr. Rushton.

But, she reminded herself, people had been riding horses since time began. Certainly, they were no more capable of controlling the animals than she was. She could keep her seat and contain her fear on a leisurely stroll about the grounds.

Mr. Rushton had taken a bit longer to move off and was quite a bit behind her. Caroline and Mossy, as well, had fallen rather behind the others and were quite alone. Ahead, the horses seemed content. They were not snorting fire or prancing. Perhaps Mossy would take her cue from the rest of the herd.

That, however, was not the case, for suddenly, her mare seemed incapable of maintaining a slow pace. In fact, she sped up progressively. As Mr. Charlton and the ladies continued further down the wooded path, Caroline was forced to circle her obstinate pony continually in the hopes that she might calm down enough to walk like a civilized creature.

The animal remained, however, uncivil.

Caroline's hands clutched the reins, and her leg muscles ached from gripping the pommel of the side saddle as the group rounded the far end of the fish pond on their frustratingly controlled mounts.

When Mossy lost sight of the other horses, she became even more animated in her movements. Her head raised and her gait changed from smooth to springy. Caroline fancied that she could feel her pony's back muscles tense through the layers of skirt and saddle leather.

Yes, the animal was indeed tense.

This would result in no good, certainly.

Caroline looked about her, hoping to find some aid from the rocks and trees, but instead, she discovered that Mr. Rushton had ridden his mare beside her.

"Miss Bingley," he said, tipping his hat as if he were meeting her in Hyde Park for a morning excursion. His eyes held a look of superior amusement that irritated her. But almost frozen in fear, Caroline found that she could not issue a proper set down for his sardonic tone.

Instead, he continued, "I have never seen this pony become so agitated. What have you done to her?"

Something broke free within Caroline, and she snapped at him. "What have I done? What have *I* done? Sir, I can assure you I have done nothing but attempt to ride the beast. There is something amiss with this animal, not me!"

She saw Mr. Rushton set his jaw. "Stop her," he said, as if Caroline had the power to arrest the movement of a creature that outweighed her by quite a good deal.

"If I could stop her from this infernal bouncing, I would have done it long ago. I have pulled back on the reins and circled since we left the stable yard."

He looked her over from stirrup to reins and issued the following order: "Unclench yourself, Miss Bingley. You are making that pony nervous."

"Ha! I am making her nervous. Tell her to calm down first and I shall, as you say so vulgarly, 'unclench.'"

He studied the bouncing mare again, then reached inside his saddle bag and drew out a leather strap. He aligned his horse with her pony, leaned down, and fastened the clasp to her pony's bit.

"What are you about, Mr. Rushton? I do not see how another piece of leather is going to make this situation any more pleasant."

"Release the reins," he ordered. "I will lead you for the remainder of the ride."

Caroline refused. The reins were her only hope of gaining any semblance of control. "I do not think this a wise idea."

He did not seem to be listening as he slowly reeled in Caroline's pony until its head was near his horse's shoulder, and she found her body bumping against his leg.

"Release the reins," he repeated, "and trust me to help you out of this mess."

She looked up at him. His face held no amusement now. She found that she must trust him.

So she did as he requested and dropped the reins, but she punctuated her action by grasping at the pony's mane and saying, "I do not care for horse riding."

"You are afraid of horse riding," he replied in a conversational tone.

It was the tone that disarmed her. Had he made such a comment with smugness or conceit, her hackles would have raised still further and she would have felt the need to defend herself. Instead, she allowed him to continue.

"Do not be ashamed. Many people find moving at such heights and speeds disconcerting."

Caroline could not see what Mr. Rushton was doing to the pony, but her gait was beginning to smooth, and their pace slowed. They rode along quite calmly now and were following the same course that the others in their party had taken. She could barely see their companions ahead, and this provided her some relief, for though Caroline had desperately hoped to remain near Mr. Charlton, it was better that he did not witness her ineptitude.

She and Mr. Rushton continued in quiet for some time, and eventually, Caroline was able to relax herself further. Though she felt no more confidence in her current position—being banged about on Mr. Rushton's riding boot—she began to feel a bit of her customary passion return.

"I believe my mare has calmed herself sufficiently. You may release us, Mr. Rushton."

"Indeed, I shall not. At least not until you can prove that you may control this animal without sending her into a panic."

"I can assure you that we shall be fine now. Look. We are both calm."

"You assure me of nothing until you take up the reins and show me."

So, with hidden trepidation, Caroline gathered the reins and hoped that she would not humiliate herself again.

Mr. Rushton uncoiled his leather lead, giving Caroline a bit of slack and thus the opportunity to be in control of her own mount.

She was excessively pleased that the mare did not immediately set to bouncing like a ball.

Instead, she seemed to slow down.

That did not seem such a bad prospect, and so she did nothing to encourage the pony to move any faster.

This turned out to be an error in judgment, for eventually, her pony and—by extension, Mr. Rushton's horse, for he was still connected loosely by the lead—began to dawdle beside the pond.

The ground was damp by the water's edge, and the mare's hooves made sucking sounds as she plodded along. The other horses had already reached the tree line, and she saw that Lavinia and Mr. Charlton had turned around to check their progress. Though she wished to join them and shed herself of Mr. Rushton, Caroline's mount slowed to a stop beside the tall reeds and then threw her head down, yanking the reins from Caroline's fingers, to snatch at the burgeoning grass.

Mr. Rushton appeared amused, but he did nothing to aid her. He simply allowed his horse to amble along beside Mossy.

"What is wrong with this animal?" Caroline demanded. "First, she would not stop; now, she will not go. If you have chosen this mount as a jest, I assure you, it is not amusing!"

"This is the calmest pony in the stable, Miss Bingley. I would never over-horse a rider such as yourself."

"A rider such as myself?"

"A fearful novice."

"Humph." Her embarrassment—and the knowledge that Mr. Charlton might be observing her even now—caused her to act more bravely than perhaps she ought. She put her reins in one hand and moved the crop to the other. She hesitated and then administered a very light tap to the horse's right flank.

The mare did not move. She continued to munch grass.

"Miss Bingley! I caution against the use of the crop."

Caroline ignored him.

A harder tap.

The mare's head came up, ears back. Mossy was displeased but not motivated enough to move and dove again for the grass.

Caroline grasped the crop tighter and contorted herself to give the horse a good smack. The crop hovered in midair, preparing to fall on the mare's haunches, when several ducks suddenly flapped out of the reeds.

The mare moved then.

The onslaught of ducks had caught the pony by surprise, causing her to spin sideways and trot quickly along the pond's edge away from the ducks. Caroline closed her eyes to block out the fear, and through sheer force of will and the extreme desire not to embarrass herself, she managed to keep her seat.

And then she heard a splat as if something had landed on the boggy ground. Laughter rang out from the tree line.

She opened her eyes, wondering what had happened. Mossy had already returned to eating grass as if the startle had never occurred.

Caroline looked to the tree line where Mr. Charlton, Lavinia, and Rosemary were laughing. Even from the distance, she could see clearly that Mr. Charlton was amused. He called, "Miss Bingley, do see to Mr. Rushton. We are off on a gallop."

Only then did she look down and see Mr. Rushton lying face first in the muck beside her pony, his hands still resolutely holding the lead. His horse stood alongside him, and Caroline swore his mare had a quizzical expression on her equine face, likely wondering what her rider was doing on the ground.

Caroline was wondering the same herself.

Unsure of what she ought to do, she remained on her pony, which was still grazing on the lush grass that grew alongside the pond.

Mr. Rushton began to pull himself out of the mud. For long moments, Caroline could not see his face, but certainly, he would be angry.

Gentlemen did not care for public humiliation any more than she did.

Caroline felt the familiar temptation to exploit the situation. She could offer the snide remark that came so quickly to mind, but something prevented her from doing so. And that was odd. Here was the opportunity to prove her superiority of wit. To turn the accident to her advantage.

But was not his current humiliation her doing? She had opted to ride despite her distaste and displeasure in the activity, not to mention her complete ineptitude.

Again, these thoughts were odd. Ordinarily, Caroline would refuse to admit—even to herself—any culpability in such a situation, but at that moment, she could not deny that she bore some blame for his current state of filth. But unaccustomed to offering sympathy, Caroline simply sat without speaking a word.

Mr. Rushton stood with slow deliberation, and now he looked up at Caroline as she sat on the pony's back. He had managed to keep his face from landing in the mud, but his riding coat was caked with the substance. His lower body, however, seemed to have landed on dry ground, for his trousers were largely undamaged. He wore a neutral expression, and then it began to transform.

A burst of laughter escaped him.

Caroline's brow furrowed in confusion. "You are laughing?"

Mr. Rushton did not respond except to continue laughing.

"You are mad," Caroline said.

"No, indeed," he said as he shook some muck from his hands. "I have not been unhorsed in years, and you and this little pony have managed what unbroken colts could not."

"You *are* mad."

✧ Twelve ✧

Mr. Rushton smiled at Caroline as he offered his assistance to her in dismounting the pony. "Come along, Miss Bingley. We shall not be joining the others."

Again, Caroline had the strongest urge to offer a set down. A lady need not bow to the whims of a gentleman. She may make her own choices. But really, did she have a choice? She could no more control this pony than she could control the weather.

"To the stables then?" she asked.

"In time," he said. "First, do allow me the opportunity of repairing some of the damage done to my pride."

From the saddle, Caroline eyed his mud-encrusted hand with disdain and chose to reject his aid. She unlaced her leg from around the pommel and slid as gracefully as possible to the ground.

"Can such a thing be accomplished out of doors?"

By the look of him, he required thorough bathing and a change of clothing.

"Not properly, no," he said as he handed her the pony's lead.

She looked at the now-docile pony and decided she would not be dragged across the countryside if she held the line.

"Now, if you will permit me, I will remove this soiled garment and wash my hands as well as possible in the pond."

Mr. Rushton did not await her permission, so Caroline did not give it. She simply watched as he removed his riding coat, turned it inside out, and stored it in his saddle bag. He wore only his white linen shirt and waistcoat, which really was not proper in the company of a lady.

Caroline ought to complain, but she found that she rather admired the way the cloth stretched across his shoulders and back. She turned away, suddenly discomfited, and cleared her throat. "It seems, Mr. Rushton, that if we may not be together without becoming embroiled in some sort of altercation, we ought not to be in each other's company."

323

"Altercation?" he asked as he bent to rinse his hands in the pond. "Yes, I suppose we have had our share, but this is not an argument. I find I am not in the mood to quarrel. If I had been interested in fighting with you, Miss Bingley, I would have begun this conversation by asking just what the devil you thought to accomplish by riding out when you had no business doing so."

"And I would not explain myself, of course," Caroline replied.

He stood up and shook his hands in an attempt to dry them. Water flew in all directions, catching the sunlight as it fell. "As I expected," he said.

"And I might ask why you had selected such a difficult mount for me, Mr. Rushton, if you suspected my dislike for riding."

Caroline watched as he walked slowly toward her, his gaze keeping contact with hers. "And I would remind you that you were settled upon your mother's pony, which has never so much as had a subversive thought in her head."

They were standing within arm's length now, glaring at each other.

"Then," Caroline said, "I think it best that we do not speak about it."

"Indeed," Mr. Rushton said as he brushed past her and took up both his horse's reins and the pony's lead. "Come," he said as he walked to the base of a nearby tree. "We shall sit for a few minutes."

Caroline watched as he secured the horses and then sat on the ground without so much as a cloth between his trousers and the earth.

She supposed it did not matter to him.

She, on the other hand, attempted to perch herself on a large exposed root.

"Horses are emotional creatures, and they reflect the emotions of their riders," Mr. Rushton said without preamble.

Caroline sighed. "I thought we were not going to discuss this."

He continued, "One need only look at one's mount to understand everything about the person astride."

"Oh," Caroline said, understanding his intention. "What, pray tell, does today's adventure reveal about me?"

He studied her for a moment and then looked away. "It would be impolite of a gentleman to speak of it, Miss Bingley."

"Oh, come, I have invited your opinion. You are safe."

He laughed. "Now that you have said that, I am reassured that I am indeed not safe. When a lady assures a gentleman, it is only because she believes he will then flatter her."

"And what you say shall not flatter me?" Caroline asked.

"What I say would have been the truth."

"Then, speak it."

"The truth," he said, "is better discovered oneself."

Caroline was silent for a moment, but she was determined to discover his meaning. "Do you accuse me of a lack of skill then?"

"Lack of skill?"

"I was given proper instruction in all matters equestrian. It is an integral part of every lady's education." She would never admit that she remembered very little about the endeavor.

"Yes, that much was evident." He laughed. "You knew which end of the horse to which to apply the whip."

"You jest, but I was well taught."

"I do not refer to your lack of skill." When he spoke again, his voice was soft. "Indeed, Miss Bingley, I believe there are but few skills that you have not artfully mastered."

She looked at him but could not read his expression, for he was facing forward again. His tone sounded wry, but his words were complimentary.

She hesitated and then said, "I believe, Mr. Rushton, that is the first time I have ever heard a compliment escape your lips."

He faced her now, and his expression was as wry as his tone. "Did I compliment you? My apologies. It was quite unintentional."

She laughed at him despite herself, but sobered quickly.

"You are indeed a truly accomplished performer," Mr. Rushton said. "But one may not perform when horses are involved. They have a way of revealing one's true self."

"Then they are wiser creatures than I have given them credit for being."

"Yes, Mossy has revealed quite a great deal today. I comprehend you now. Perfectly."

"Oh?" Caroline adjusted on her perch. "Enlighten me."

"Women, I find, are the finest actors. They perform continually to entice a gentleman and then drop the charade once he is caught."

Caroline spoke without thinking. "How would you suggest we behave, then, if not by showing ourselves to the best advantage?"

"You should portray yourself as you are, of course. It is foolish to perform. And it is even more foolish to overestimate one's skills on horseback. You ought to have known that."

She pointed an accusatory finger at him. "Ah, but I have heard that you, Mr. Rushton, are also a great performer."

Mr. Rushton studied her. "You have thrice laid this accusation at my feet, Miss Bingley. Why not speak plainly? I will not object."

She decided to do just that. "I have heard that you were once engaged to be married to a young lady of large fortune."

"That is true," he said, his face still open.

"And that the lady terminated the engagement when she discovered your family's true situation."

"Also true," he confessed.

"So you admit to being a fortune hunter!"

"Indeed, I do not."

"Then I fear, Mr. Rushton, you will have to explain yourself."

"I will do so happily now that you have asked and not based your entire opinion of me on supposition and gossip."

Caroline crossed her arms over her chest, waiting for him to proceed.

"My father was a proud man, and his humiliation at having sold off so much of Rushton House was complete. He vowed that before he died he would see our fortunes restored, and so with that in mind, he arranged for me to marry the eldest daughter of a wealthy London family when we were yet children. He, of course, did not divulge the status of our estate, only that I was to inherit an ancient house and land. They believed us wealthy and stable, but we needed the money desperately."

Caroline nodded.

"The old dear truly believed that my marriage would save the family, but before we reached the appointed age, my father became ill and died, making me promise that I would fulfill my vow to the lady and save our family land. I agreed, but as our wedding day approached, guilt assailed me. I could not bring myself to withhold the truth from her, so I brought her to Rushton House, which was then in quite a state of disrepair."

Caroline could well imagine the condition of the property. It would please no woman.

"Simply put," Mr. Rushton said, "she broke the engagement, and I allowed it."

"But your vow to your father?"

"I did not break it. The lady ended the engagement, and I said nothing ill about her. In fact, I said nothing at all on the subject, which is why the fortune-hunting rumor still abounds. And I did restore the family land, every piece."

"But how?"

"Through my association with Mr. Newton. Bridge building can be quite lucrative."

Trade, Caroline thought. It always seemed to return to trade.

"So you see, Miss Bingley, it was through my blatant refusal to perform—to present myself as anything other than I was—that I restored my family to rights. And I speak from that experience when I tell you that it is best not to perform for others, whether human or equine."

They were silent a few moments, and Caroline found herself watching the horse and pony as they grazed, to all appearances, peacefully.

"Mr. Rushton, you really should not pretend to have some keen insight into my character or temperament based on my interaction with unpredictable creatures."

"Horses are only unpredictable if their handler does not know their true nature." He too studied the pair of grazing beasts. "Men often experience similar dilemmas in their interactions with your fair sex. If a man does not know a woman's true nature, he cannot adequately predict what might occur next."

"Yes? And now you believe you may predict what I shall do next?"

He smiled. "I would not dare to insult you by admitting it."

She only looked at him, trying to comprehend his meaning.

Then Mr. Rushton stood and reached for her hand. "Come, I find I am quite dried out enough to attempt the walk home."

And with that, he assisted her to her feet and gathered the horses, and together, they returned to Newton House in silence.

As they walked, Caroline looked over her shoulder in the hopes of spying the others of their party, but they were nowhere to be seen.

There was no hope left of cultivating time alone with Mr. Charlton. Depressing as it was, this disastrous outing would likely be her last opportunity of being in his company for some time.

This was a heavy discouragement indeed, but such stumbling blocks only served to embolden Caroline. She may not have triumphed as quickly as she would have liked, but the game was not over.

She would have her baron yet.

༄ Thirteen ༄

The best course of action, Caroline decided, was to apply to Lavinia for assistance in her quest to marry Mr. Charlton, and she must do so as soon as possible, for the London season was already in progress, and though her friend's brother seemed to show an interest in her at times, he had not yet proposed. And Caroline had the greatest wish to rejoin society as the wife of a future baron. Then her triumph would be complete, her humiliation finally forgotten, and the requirement to make amends with Miss Elizabeth Bennet nullified.

"Do get your bonnet, Mrs. Pickersgill," Caroline said into the quiet sitting room where the ladies had been reclining, "for we must pay a call on Oak Park this morning."

"Yes, Miss Bingley," Rosemary said as she rose to gather her outerwear.

Once in the carriage, Rosemary looked at Caroline with curiosity.

"You seem to be rather purposeful in this visit, Miss Bingley. Is something amiss?"

Caroline scowled and lied, "Of course not. It is a visit. Nothing more."

"Ah," Rosemary said, not sounding convinced at all.

They remained quiet on the remainder of the ride, and when they arrived, they were escorted again to the cavernous drawing room.

Caroline joined Mrs. Winton on the sofa, while Mrs. Pickersgill chose a seat on the opposite one and took a book from the nearby table, obviously giving Caroline her privacy.

After a bit of polite conversation, it was time for Caroline to reveal her motivations for calling.

"Lavinia, I have come to speak with you about a matter of a deeply personal nature," she whispered as she glanced across the room at Mrs. Pickersgill, who appeared to be engrossed in her book. It seemed safe to speak, albeit softly.

"Oh?" Lavinia asked as she leaned in, eyebrows raised in curiosity.

"I trust that we have been friends long enough that you must have already guessed what I might say."

Lavinia blinked at her and then laughed. "You could not be more mistaken, for though you are one of my dearest friends, I have not the slightest conception of what you might say."

That disclosure did not hearten Caroline. She had hoped that her friend might already be aware of her desire to marry her brother and that she would approve and assist her in that goal.

"Then, because you have not guessed already, I will speak plain. Our families have long been acquainted, and, I daresay, no one would argue that we have been the closest of friends for many years."

"No indeed," Lavinia said. "No one could argue that point, but I do not comprehend your hesitancy to speak such an obvious truth."

Caroline took heart at Lavinia's tone and pressed onward. "I hope you will not think me too presumptuous when I say that our families could only grow closer by the arrangement of a strategic union."

Had Lavinia not been one of her dearest schoolfellows, Caroline would have thought her expression momentarily registered shock. However, the look lingered but briefly, so she could not be certain that she had seen it at all.

"Union?"

This question was asked with perhaps more volume of voice than Caroline had hoped to hear. She looked quickly to Mrs. Pickersgill, whose head was still bent over the book. She appeared not to have heard.

Caroline took a bracing breath and then spoke aloud. "Indeed, I hope I might have your support in convincing your brother, Mr. Charlton, that a closer connection between our families might be a benefit to both."

A small crease formed between Lavinia's eyes. Caroline could not tell if her friend's countenance showed her bafflement or anger, but she could certainly feel the searching nature of her look. Lavinia's intense exploration of Caroline's face was both disconcerting and more than a bit bewildering.

Could Lavinia have not guessed her motives?

"My dearest friend, tell me. Are you suggesting an"—here, Lavinia's voice seemed to catch, but she continued—"alliance of a marital nature between yourself and my brother?"

Caroline nodded.

Lavinia straightened her back and cocked her head to the side, asking an unspoken question.

Well, Caroline would explain her motives, and then Lavinia would comprehend the necessity of such a merger.

"Our association would be advantageous to all parties." Caroline watched as Lavinia's features went entirely blank. There was no joy, sorrow, or conflict to be had within her expression or demeanor. Only a confusing vacancy. "You and I would be sisters. Your brother would be wed." She lowered her voice to a whisper. "And the rumors about his proclivities of socializing with those so decidedly beneath him would be ended. And though I do not fancy my fortune to be a large enticement, it would no doubt aid in its own little way."

Lavinia's blank expression altered, and a smile slid across her features.

Yes, money was ever an enticement, Caroline thought.

When Lavinia finally spoke, her voice had taken on a new tone that was not entirely comprehensible to Caroline. "I may make one promise to you, my oldest and dearest friend: I will do whatever is in my power to ensure that both our families get precisely what is warranted."

A snort from the opposite side of the room impeded Caroline's sense of relief. She lanced Mrs. Pickersgill with a sharp stare. "Mrs. Pickersgill, if you are ill, kindly remove yourself from this chamber so that you do not infect us all."

"Pardon me, Miss Bingley," Rosemary said with a decidedly unapologetic tone. "I am not ill, and I certainly did not intend to distract you from your tête-a-tête." She then went back to her reading without the least hint of appropriate embarrassment, and Caroline reminded herself that she ought to continue to speak in hushed tones.

To Lavinia, she whispered, "I am relieved indeed to find that you favor the match."

"Indeed, I am glad to offer you some relief," Lavinia said, her head still held high.

"I hope you will direct me in the best way to convince your brother of the rightness of such unification of our families in that manner."

Lavinia reached out and patted Caroline's hands, which had been clutched in her lap for the balance of the conversation. "Do not give my brother the least thought, for I shall design the strategy myself."

⁂

After their return from Oak Park, Caroline and Rosemary spent the afternoon in the cutting garden with Mrs. Newton, and Caroline had just gone to clean the soil from her hands and change into her dinner attire when a knock sounded at her bedchamber door.

"Pardon me, miss," said the rather fresh-faced young maid, "but Mrs. Newton bid me to inform you that Mr. Charlton is awaiting you in the sitting room."

"Mr. Charlton?" Caroline asked. Lavinia was an efficient worker if he had come this very day to make his proposal.

"Yes, miss," the maid affirmed.

Caroline quickly surveyed herself in the mirror. Her light blue dress had a white chevron pattern and was suitable for a country meal, but it would not do now. Not with Mr. Charlton about to make his proposal.

"Go and find my green silk gown and help me redress quickly," Caroline commanded the maid, who dashed to the wardrobe and began to search through the gowns stored there.

She did as Caroline asked, returning to her side with her finest London gown that seemed to accentuate her features nicely.

She managed to don the gown in a timely fashion, but then she realized her hairstyle would not do for such an occasion, and she demanded that the maid help rearrange that as well.

In the end, her decision to redress quickly took her almost an hour to accomplish, but when she entered the sitting room, she was pleased to have made the choice she had, for Mr. Charlton's eyes seemed to lighten upon his first sight of her.

He leapt off the high-backed chair where he had been sitting and speaking with Rosemary. "Oh! Miss Bingley, there you are."

Rosemary also stood and took in her mistress's appearance, and her eyes narrowed with suspicion. "Good evening, Miss Bingley. You look lovely."

A crease formed between Caroline's eyes as she tried to eke some hidden purpose from Rosemary's words, but who could fathom what that woman was thinking? She would do better not to try to interpret her at all. Instead, she turned her pleasure upon Mr. Charlton when he said, "Yes, indeed. You make quite a picture, just as Mrs. Pickersgill said."

Caroline stood for a moment longer so that Mr. Charlton could admire her further if he wished, and then she took a seat on the chair opposite his.

Mr. Charlton watched as she sat, and Caroline believed she might have seen a twinge of regret in his expression, but she only smiled at him and said, "We are so pleased to have you in our home this evening."

"I have been here too long already," he said as he removed his watch from the fob pocket of his breeches and glanced at it, "but I found myself quite compelled to stop here on my ride back from town."

Caroline blushed. "I am honored," she said.

"I simply could not leave Kendal without taking leave of you," he said.

Caroline's blush suddenly drained, and she felt her face pale. "Leave Kendal?"

"Yes, unfortunately, Lavinia had a letter from our father just this morning, and we have been called immediately to London."

"London?" Caroline repeated lamely. She knew she was staring at him with confusion and questions in her eyes, and that it was a most unsophisticated expression, but she could not prevent herself from looking at him thus.

On the periphery, she saw Rosemary look from her to Mr. Charlton.

"It seems a rather abrupt decision," Rosemary said into the awkward silence.

He nodded. "My sister was in a fine dander this morning and gave me barely a moment to sit, much less the opportunity to read the missive itself, before sending me on this errand. We depart tomorrow morning."

Caroline stared at him, then shook herself and managed to ask, "Has something happened to your father?"

She desperately hoped for a negative response, for it was too soon for the barony to transfer to Mr. Charlton. He had not yet proposed, and Caroline had no wish to compete for him with all the eager young ladies in Town.

"Good Lord, I should hope not, for then I would be required to take over his position," he said on a bitter laugh. Then he shrugged. "Lavinia says he is well but demands our presence. That is all I know."

"How odd," Rosemary said, again looking from Caroline to Mr. Charlton.

"When will you return to Kendal?" Caroline asked, and then, not liking the note of desperation in her voice, she cleared her throat and added, "For society will be quite tedious without your sister to lead us."

"I do not know when I shall return," Mr. Charlton, turning his dark eyes upon her, and Caroline wondered if they didn't hold a bit of longing. "But I do hope it will be soon, for there is much for me yet to do here."

Caroline felt her skin prickle a bit. What did this signify? She managed to hold his intense gaze for long moments until Rosemary shifted in her seat.

Then Caroline felt a sudden, strange lack of emotion. She was not embarrassed at having been caught staring at Mr. Charlton, sad that he was leaving, or entranced any longer by those dark eyes.

Mr. Charlton did not make his proposal that evening, but Caroline did not feel regret at all when he stood and took his leave of her, bowing deeply over her hand.

She maintained her odd emotionless state as she looked out the window and watched Mr. Charlton's carriage disappear down the drive.

"How odd," Rosemary said again. She had been standing silently next to Caroline at the window. "How very odd."

"You repeat yourself," Caroline replied without looking at her. "Why?"

Rosemary had been holding back one of the drapes to improve her view of the gentleman's departure, and she let it slip through her fingers. The fabric swayed in front of Caroline, briefly blocking her view of the drive.

"Do you not find it strange, Miss Bingley, that only this morning you went to Oak Park to solicit Mrs. Winton's aid in winning Mr. Charlton, and now they cannot leave Kendal quickly enough?"

Caroline's face jerked toward her companion's. "You were eavesdropping on our conversation, were you?" she demanded.

Caroline's sharp tone did not appear to unnerve Rosemary, who only said quietly, "You were speaking loudly enough to be heard in Bath."

Caroline could not deny that their conversation had grown in volume as it continued, but she had greatly hoped Rosemary had not overheard. She looked out the window and let the implications of her companion's words wash over her. Caroline's plan was no longer secret. Lavinia knew her desires, as did this woman, her paid companion.

"I am not your enemy, Miss Bingley," Rosemary said, as if she read her thoughts. "But I fear Mrs. Winton is."

Slowly, Caroline turned to look again at Rosemary. Her thoughts seemed to move so quickly that they blurred within her head.

What was this woman implying?

Lavinia was her friend, her dearest acquaintance.

"You mean…?" Caroline began, but she could not allow herself to name her fear.

"That Mrs. Winton objects to the idea of your marrying Mr. Charlton? Yes," Rosemary finished. "I am sorry to say it so plainly, but I fear it is so."

Caroline walked from the window and fell into a chair. She stared at the lace trim on her sleeve, willing the pattern to assemble itself into some sort of comprehensible structure, for like her thoughts, it blurred before her eyes.

No, it could not be possible.

Could it? Could Lavinia object to her marriage to Mr. Charlton?

No, it was a ridiculous thought indeed. They were friends, and Caroline said as much to Rosemary.

"Are you certain?" Rosemary asked in a gentle voice as she sat in a chair beside her mistress.

"Yes, I am certain," she said, though questions raced through her mind.

She did not relish being forced to doubt her situation.

"I speak only as a friend, Miss Bingley. I do not want to see you injured."

Caroline suddenly felt an emotion: anger. It coursed from her feet, through her body, to her face, and she could not contain herself as she spat, "You? A friend? No, you are a servant. Lavinia is my friend, my dearest friend, and she would never treat me in such a fashion."

What Caroline did not add was that she would never allow herself to be treated as she herself had treated Miss Jane Bennet. She would never play the role of innocent victim, to have her object removed from her. No, she would never permit herself to be so fooled.

Rosemary remained silent and composed as Caroline fumed and then began to pace the room, but the older woman's calm did nothing to soothe the younger, for her ire only rose, leaving her capable of speaking only in short sentences. "You have no grounds for such statements. Your observations are flawed, and you have misunderstood everyone! You are a mere servant in this household. You are no lady of status, even if every person here pretends you to be otherwise. You are certainly not my friend."

"Indeed, I am a servant, as you have twice reminded me," Rosemary affirmed with such irritating rationality that Caroline was tempted to shout at her. "I have contracted myself to your brother's employ, not yours, and I have promised to see to your care. As such, I shall have no compunction at proving Mrs. Winton's guilt to you."

"Ha! She is guilty of nothing," Caroline protested.

"As you have said, Miss Bingley," Rosemary said, "but mark me: after this is over, you will see Mrs. Winton for what she is, and you will realize that a mere servant is the best friend you could ever hope to have."

Caroline snorted and paced the room with added animation as she began to formulate a plan. "We shall see, Mrs. Pickersgill, who is my friend and who is not, for I shall devise a method for getting us to London and back into Mr. Charlton's company. Then," she said as she whirled on her companion, "we will know who is right!"

ꙮ Fourteen ꙮ

As it turns out, the formulation of a plan was ever so much easier than actually seeing it to completion.

Desperate as she was, Caroline could not bring herself to disappoint her mother by simply declaring her intentions to leave Kendal. No, she must engineer a method for departing for London without injuring Mrs. Newton, and that would be a difficult task indeed.

First, Caroline contemplated proposing a family voyage to Town under the pretense of enjoying the gaiety of the season, but she immediately discounted that as a possibility. Mrs. Newton despised travel and would not be induced to leave Kendal for something as superficial as balls and society. Why, she could not even be convinced to attend her son's wedding in Hertfordshire, so it was rather a useless attempt to woo her mother with tales of far-flung locales.

Second, Caroline considered the prospect of utter fibs. She could claim that Rosemary had received word from her relations that her presence was required in Town immediately and that she would accompany her companion to provide support during a difficult time. Upon reflection, Caroline realized that no one would believe such a tale. It was preposterous. No one would believe that Rosemary was important enough to be needed in Town or that Caroline would accompany a servant anywhere of her own will.

Third, and oh so very briefly, Caroline mulled over the idea of claiming desperation to see her brother. Instead of taking up residence again with Charles, which he would not accept until she made proper amends, she might stay in a reputable inn until Mr. Charlton's proposal could be secured. This, however, would not do either, for Charles would never allow it. One letter from Mama and Charles would ferret out Caroline, drag her back to Kendal, and reveal her misdeeds to her mother.

That would not do at all.

Caroline quite despaired of ever contriving a reason for following Mr. Charlton to Town, and she spent her days moping about Newton House under the watchful eye of Rosemary, who must suspect that Caroline had not lost her drive to chase Mr. Charlton and might do something rash if she were not careful.

A fortnight passed before opportunity found Caroline, and this sudden chance derived from the most unlikely avenue: Mr. Newton himself.

One morning at breakfast, he declared, "I fear, my dear Mrs. Newton, that it is time for Mr. Rushton and I to be away to London to see to the commencement of the Fairmont Bridge's construction."

Mrs. Newton immediately dropped the piece of toast onto which she had been applying a liberal amount of preserves and said, "Oh no! Already? It seems as though you just returned from your last journey."

Caroline too dropped her toast, but for an altogether different reason. She picked it up quickly and dipped her spoon in the preserves as she looked around to see if anyone had noticed her slip.

Curse it, they had!

Mr. Rushton and Rosemary were watching her much too closely.

Caroline met their eyes steadily, one at a time, as she listened to her mother try to talk Mr. Newton into remaining at home just a while longer.

"I fear, my dear," Mr. Newton replied, "that we must go to London, and we must leave before the month is out, for I have had it in a letter that construction is soon to begin, and you know that I cannot bear to sit alongside while other men have the fun of working with stone and mortar."

While Caroline managed to restrain her snort of derision, Mrs. Newton picked up her toast once again, but rather than spreading condiments upon it or consuming it, she began using it as a conversational aid. She pointed the toast at Mr. Rushton and asked, "And you must be away too?"

"I fear I must, madam, though I am grateful for your hospitality. I quite agree with Mr. Newton that a designer must be present for the production of that which he has created."

"But our household will be lost without you!" she cried, flinging the toast about as she gestured.

Mr. Newton reached across the table and rescued the crumbling bread. "My dear," he said as he patted her hand in consolation, "you are most welcome to accompany me, for it would make my time in London so much pleasanter." He looked at the whole company who sat around the table, and his sideburns widened as he smiled. "You are all most welcome to join us. We would, of course, not impose upon Mr. Rushton as I often do while in Town. We could take some rooms at a hotel or perhaps lease our own home for a time."

Mrs. Newton's face fell, and Caroline knew what was forthcoming. Her mother despised travel and would not leave Kendal without great inducement.

"But it seems as if Caroline has only just arrived," Mrs. Newton said. "I could not possibly leave her or demand that she embark on another voyage so soon."

Caroline used great restraint as she said, "I would not object to a trip to Town, Mama. You know I adore it so, and I could show you all its glories."

"You would undertake another coach ride so soon?" Mrs. Newton asked.

"Yes, indeed, Mama." Mrs. Newton appeared skeptical, so Caroline added, "As much as I despise bumping along in a coach, I have always found that the discomfort is quickly forgotten once the destination is reached."

"Does my daughter speak true, Mr. Rushton?" Mrs. Newton asked.

"She is mostly accurate," he conceded, "but there is no need to pass an uncomfortable journey. We may take just as much time as you please and view the sights as we go."

Mrs. Newton turned to her husband. "Is that so, my dear?"

"Why of course, Mrs. Newton. Why do you think so many people undertake such monstrous trips? It is enjoyable and quite a delight to see new places and meet new people."

Mrs. Newton began to look pensive, and Caroline was heartened, for a conversation of travel rarely reached this point with her.

Caroline added, "Besides, the occupants of Oak Park have been in London these two weeks, so our arrival would be more like a homecoming than a trip to a strange land. We would be reunited with friends."

Caroline glanced at Rosemary as she spoke the word "friends." Rosemary rolled her eyes but added, "For my part, I shall do as I am willed, but I must say that I have no objections to such a journey."

Caroline stared. No objections? Rosemary claimed to want to protect Caroline from Lavinia, but now she had no objections to going to Town, where they would again be in Lavina's sphere? What new game was this?

"Well," Mrs. Newton said, drawing out the word, "I suppose it is rather illogical for me to confine myself always to Kendal."

Her mother's voice sounded quite uncertain, so Caroline said, "Oh yes, Mama. You must travel or else you shall miss so much of the world."

Mr. Rushton cleared his throat. "But only if you are willing, Mrs. Newton."

"Yes, indeed," Mr. Newton added. "We shall see to your utmost comfort, shall we not?" He glanced around the table to see the affirmation in everyone's eyes.

"You already know my preference for a journey of moderate pace. It is easier on the horses," Mr. Rushton said.

Caroline scarcely stopped herself from rolling her eyes at him. Who gave a fig about horses? But she would say nothing to damage the look of acquiescence in her mother's eyes.

"We shall travel quite at our leisure," Mr. Newton said as he rounded the table and knelt before his wife. He took her hand in his and gave her a pleading look. "We shall see all the best views and rest only in the most comfortable inns."

Here, Mr. Rushton interjected, "And you are cordially invited to stay at my home while in London. I would not have you at a hotel when you can rest more comfortably with me."

Mr. Newton nodded his thanks and then returned his attention to his wife. From his position on the floor, he looked up, eyes imploring, and said, "Allow me to show you the world, my dear."

"Well," Mrs. Newton said again with a look around the table. The hopeful expressions of all gathered there must have solidified her tenuous decision, for she said, "I shall be very pleased to see the world if you will all be with me!"

And so Caroline got her wish. She was going to London.

·ଶ୧ ଦ୧·

Another fortnight passed before Mrs. Newton had managed to pack her necessities, and this only occurred under Caroline's constant reminder that the journey was indeed a splendid idea. After practicing continual persuasion for so many days, Caroline was quite shocked when at dawn on the day of their planned departure, it was Mrs. Newton who arrived first at the coach.

"Oh, I am so pleased that you have talked me into this voyage," she cried as the groggy travelers filed within: Mr. and Mrs. Newton on one bench and Rosemary and Caroline on the other. Mr. Rushton was astride his grey mare.

"I thought I would feel uneasy at the start of our trip," Mrs. Newton continued, "but I find myself ever so eager to be off now that the decision has been made!"

Caroline smiled at her mother, adjusting her position on the bench as the coach lurched to a start. "I too am pleased, Mama. Our journey will be full of beauty, and the weather will only warm as we head south."

"I cannot wait to feel the sun on my skin." Mrs. Newton grinned. "I am now most pleased to be traveling to London, for I have written to your brother to meet us there if he possibly can."

Caroline forced a smile. "Oh?" she asked. "I did not know you had contacted Charles. Has he responded?" She glanced quickly at Rosemary, who also appeared curious, and then looked deliberately out the coach window as her mother spoke so that no one might see her reaction.

"No, but I told him where we were to stay, and I am certain the letter will find him in his travels and he will come to see his mother."

Caroline nearly sighed in relief. The letter might take weeks to reach Charles, and then, it might take yet more weeks for him to travel to London. By then, Caroline would most certainly have won Mr. Charlton, for he seemed almost near to proposing on at least one occasion already, and now she had Lavinia's aid, despite Rosemary's contrary opinion.

Outside the coach, the sun slowly melted the dew from the grass, and Mr. Rushton rode beside them, looking very much pleased with himself. Caroline scowled as he tipped his hat to her in greeting.

"Why does he insist on riding horseback when there is a perfectly good coach?" Caroline asked.

Mr. Newton laughed. "He is a young fellow and ever in want of exercise and sun. He will join us inside only in the event of foul weather."

Under her breath, Caroline added, "Then I shall hope the sun remains for the duration of our trip."

⁂

This hope, of course, proved fruitless, for after nearly a week of blessedly dry weather, the Newtons' coach encountered precipitation: a soft spring rain accompanied by a moderation of temperature.

The rain began after their noontime stop for victuals and fresh horses, and Mrs. Newton become quite anxious for Mr. Rushton's health. She leaned out the carriage window and waved at him as he rode alongside.

"Mr. Rushton!" she called. "Do join us in the coach, for I fear you shall catch your death of cold out there in all that moisture."

Caroline watched as Mr. Rushton turned to respond. Though the rain appeared to be but a mist, he seemed quite damp indeed. His coat adhered closely to his upper body, revealing his outline in alarming detail. Caroline forced herself to look away from his broad chest and instead followed the line of his body to his head, discovering that even his hair was flattened to his forehead, and his hat appeared limp.

Mr. Rushton's face glistened with rainwater, but his eyes danced brightly.

"There is no need for fear, Mrs. Newton," he insisted. "I am quite well."

Mrs. Newton leaned back in the coach to appeal to Mr. Newton. "Do make him come inside! That rain is cold, and I would much rather have him snuggled inside with us."

Caroline winced. She did not relish the idea of a warm, wet Mr. Rushton snuggling amongst them.

But Mr. Newton did as his wife bade and leaned out the window. "Come, Rushton, do not be foolish. Join us before you become soaked through. There is adequate room, surely, for I purchased the largest coach available." He turned toward Mrs. Newton. "I knew the decision would prove fortuitous one day."

"I find myself quite comfortable," his wife said with a look around, "but I do worry about poor Mr. Rushton."

Caroline watched as poor Mr. Rushton's shoulders moved into a shrug and he relented, saying, "If you insist, I shall join you."

Mr. Newton rapped on the top of the coach to alert the driver to stop, and Caroline watched as Mr. Rushton reined in his horse and dismounted. He disappeared around the back of the coach, likely to tie up the great beast, and then reappeared at the door.

"Where shall I sit?" he asked, surveying the arrangement.

Rosemary, cursed woman, was asleep again, so she would not be moved from her place on the bench. Mr. and Mrs. Newton quite took up one full bench on their own, so there was only one spot available: between Rosemary and Caroline.

Caroline thought to poke her companion, for she suspected Rosemary was feigning slumber. Who could sleep through all that yelling and jostling as the coach ground to a halt? But Mrs. Newton pointed out, "There is adequate space there between Mrs. Pickersgill and Caroline."

And that is just where Mr. Rushton deposited himself.

Then he smiled at her, quite aware of her discomfort, she realized.

"Do slide to the right, Mr. Rushton," Caroline demanded. "I do not want my gown ruined by your damp clothing," she said as she pulled her lap robe higher.

But Mr. Rushton did not move.

৵৽ Fifteen ৵৽

"Miss Bingley."

The voice tickled her ear.

Caroline attempted to rub it away with her hand.

She heard a soft chuckle in response, but it faded so quickly into the pleasing sound of raindrops tapping on the roof that she wondered if she had imagined it. The gentle rocking of the coach lulled her, and slowly, all sound began to recede once more.

"Miss Bingley," the voice repeated, softer this time. "Wake up."

Caroline's eyes slowly slid open to find Mr. Rushton looking at her. She gazed back at him for long moments, enjoying his closeness before she realized she should be affronted by it.

Then she experienced a moment of horror at the thought that she might have fallen asleep on his shoulder, but as she took stock of the situation, she realized that she had been reclined against the side of the carriage. She righted herself and looked about her to discover that Rosemary, her mother, and Mr. Newton were asleep. The interior of the coach seemed muted, casting Mr. Rushton in softness, which must account for the fact that she had no urge to scoot away from him even though he was sitting so close that she could feel him along her whole side.

Slightly discomfited by his nearness, she turned her head and peeked out the window to find that the clouds had gathered so closely that they blocked out the sun, making it appear to be as dark as a moonless midnight though it was not yet suppertime.

Everything seemed calm, warm, and safe. The coach seemed to cocoon her.

Why, then, had Mr. Rushton awakened her?

"What?" Caroline demanded in a harsh whisper.

His eyes narrowed slightly. "I know I should have followed my own good judgment and allowed you to continue sleeping, but you were whimpering."

"Whimpering?" Caroline repeated, slightly louder than a whisper. "I was most certainly not whimpering. I do not whimper."

"Indeed, you were, and indeed, you do," he insisted.

Caroline crossed her arms in front of her.

Mr. Rushton smiled pleasantly as if she had just said something kind. "Were you dreaming?" he whispered.

Was I dreaming? Caroline wondered.

"I do not know," she whispered back.

Mr. Rushton watched her expectantly, and Caroline looked away as she tried to recall what she might have dreamt. She closed her eyes and attempted to forget Mr. Rushton's proximity as she focused on the sound of the wheels sliding across the muddy roads.

The wind gathered in intensity outside, and the images of her dream returned from somewhere within the confines of her mind. If it was true that she had been whimpering, then she expected the dream to have featured Mr. Darcy, but surprisingly, her brother's vexed face appeared in her mind. She could not hear his words, but he was making broad gestures with his hands, forcing her to walk backward, away from him. Suddenly, she was standing outside Pemberley with the door closed and locked solidly in front of her.

Caroline opened her eyes to discover Mr. Rushton still watching her.

"I cannot recall the dream," she lied. "And I most certainly did not whimper."

"Ah, now those are lies, Miss Bingley," he said in a disarmingly conversational tone. "Come, I have told you my secret. You must share yours. What has made you so sad?"

Caroline had not the least intention of telling him anything, but as she turned to rebuff him, his countenance was so sincere, the carriage so warm, and the rain so soft outside that she found herself saying more than she meant.

"I dreamed of my brother Charles," she confessed.

"Yes?"

"We argued."

"Ah."

"And he sent me away."

Mr. Rushton studied her for long moments as the carriage rocked them. "That was more than a mere dream, was it not? That is what truly occurred to bring you to Kendal?"

Caroline sighed and looked at her mother, who was still asleep on Mr. Newton's shoulder. "I told you once I came out of love for my mother, and I do love her, but yes, the truth is that I was forced to come."

"But why?"

"Charles and I argued."

He cocked his head sideways and waited for further explanation.

"I opposed Charles's choice of bride," she heard herself say. "Jane is a sweet girl, but a fortune hunter nonetheless."

Mr. Rushton considered her for a moment. "We are all fortune hunters, Miss Bingley, in our own way. Society tells us that marriage is the only way to gain or secure a fortune, but it is not true."

"Oh, but it is true!" Caroline whispered. "Though I have 20,000 pounds, I have nothing! I must follow my brother's wishes as he has control over my allowance. I must marry, but then my husband gains control of the whole." Caroline looked him directly in the eyes. "So you see, in order to have anything, Mr. Rushton, anything at all of my very own, I must marry. Only then will I have any sort of power over my life."

He did not speak but kept his eyes on her.

She sighed. "Miss Jane Bennet had nothing. No wealth, connections, or land. I knew precisely what she was about, and I only wanted to save Charles..." She thought of Mr. Darcy and her desire to marry him. "To save myself."

"That is perhaps the first honest remark you have made since arriving at Kendal, Miss Bingley," Mr. Rushton said with soft eyes. "I only wish it were the whole truth, but I shall forgive you for withholding, for it is clear that you are wracked with guilt."

"Guilt? No, I was innocent," she protested. "My attempt to separate them was just and fair. I was in the right."

Mr. Rushton's next words surprised her. "I believe you probably were, Miss Bingley, and your protest was meant to protect your brother, but your proclaimed innocence seems doubtful."

"You are speaking nonsense," she said, still in a whisper, as she leaned away to take in his full facial expression. "Whatever do you mean?"

"Take, for example, the charges against me. They were true. For a time, I was a fortune hunter."

"But you released your object when given the choice."

"Indeed I did, but until that very moment, I would have proceeded with the marriage. I was behaving as my father expected—even as society required. I was in the right, but still far from innocent."

Silence descended as Caroline contemplated his words. Their gazes met and the intimacy of the coach intensified. Around them, their companions slept on, and they did not witness the moment when Mr. Rushton's head leaned further toward her, their faces drawing very close, his lips a whisper away.

Caroline did not move. She could not, though she knew she should have. Instead, she closed her eyes, expecting any moment that his lips would touch hers.

So when his fingertips brushed her cheek, her eyes flew open.

Mr. Rushton remained as close as before, watching her carefully as his fingers trailed down the length of her neck. She sucked in a breath at the unexpected warmth that flooded her, and try as she might, she could not look away.

"No, not innocent," Mr. Rushton whispered. "We are, neither of us, innocent, are we?"

"No," Caroline breathed as his fingertips stroked the back of her neck and then disappeared back into his lap.

A protest rose within her, but not at his words. She had the oddest desire to object to the removal of his hand, the ending of the intimacy they had shared.

As if sensing her protest, he smiled. "Do not fear. I will hold you again once all your secrets are made plain to me, for I believe, Miss Bingley, that London shall reveal all."

৵৹৩ Sixteen ৩৹৵

Mr. Rushton's words had shattered the coach's intimacy and ended the odd détente between him and Caroline, and soon after, the coachman pulled into their final stop of the day.

As the carriage jarred to a halt, its occupants awakened to find Caroline's back turned as much as possible to Mr. Rushton, and so they perceived no change in the relationship between the two. And when Caroline elected to take dinner in her private chamber, no one found it out of character.

But now Caroline felt a spark between herself and Mr. Rushton, and she was not convinced that once ignited it would erupt into anger, as it should have, rather than into something altogether more terrifying. And that caused her great tribulation indeed. She could not experience romantic sentiments for a tradesman. No indeed!

Much to her relief, the sun soon returned, and with it Mr. Rushton had been restored to his saddle, so Caroline had been able to avoid him quite successfully for the remainder of their journey.

In a coach and four, the trip from Kendal to London should have endured six days, but with Mr. Newton's overly cautious care of his wife and Mr. Rushton's dislike of overtaxing horses, it took ten.

When at last they arrived in London and the coach halted in front of the town home Mr. Rushton owned in Grosvenor Street, Caroline was both overjoyed and overwhelmed.

She had not expected Grosvenor Street, one of London's finest. Indeed, the house's grand presence evoked awe and a bit of jealousy within her. An intricate pattern of cream-colored Portland stone and elegant sash windows graced its façade, and it seemed to tower above the adjoining homes. It made her sister Louisa's town house, which was no less charmingly designed of red brick, appear inconsequential in comparison.

Mr. Rushton was either wealthier than Caroline had believed or more deeply in debt. Either way, it mattered not to her, for he would always be a tradesman. She must remember that.

"Do come in," Mr. Rushton said as he bounded up the staircase to the front door. Caroline followed at a sedate pace and attempted to appear apathetic to the home's splendor.

Rosemary, who walked along beside her with her head down as if the steps might move beneath her feet, turned slightly to Caroline and whispered, "You did not tell me that Mr. Rushton's home was in this precise location."

Caroline's eyebrows lowered. "That is because I did not know its precise location. Why should it matter where the house is located?"

"I suppose it does not," Rosemary said in a halting tone. "It is only…well, this is Grosvenor Street!"

"Yes, one of the finest in London." Caroline turned to her. "I am shocked as well. I did not know they would allow tradesmen to lease on this street. I had expected to stay in Cheapside."

She regretted at once her mention of Cheapside. The very name called to mind Miss Jane Bennet, who had resided in that section of Town with her aunt and uncle when she came to London in pursuit of Charles.

She looked again to Rosemary and despised her for insinuating that her current situation held any similarity to Jane's. Lavinia had most certainly not removed Mr. Charlton to prevent a union, and her installation in Grosvenor Street must be a sign that her London excursion would not end as Jane's had. Caroline would win her object immediately and go about Town as the wife of a future baron. There would be no drama, no attempts at concealment. All would go smoothly.

She was about to speak again to Rosemary on the subject of fashionable addresses and her good fortune at staying on this street, but a maid appeared and escorted the group to their chambers.

Caroline followed the maid's precise footsteps up the house's main staircase and then to a fine guest chamber that overlooked the street. From her vantage point, Caroline could see Grosvenor Square and everyone who walked nearby. The chamber was ideal, for she would be able to accost Mr. Charlton whenever he happened by, and everyone came to Grosvenor Square eventually. Caroline would simply wait and seize upon him.

Rosemary was stationed across the hall, but she soon rapped on Caroline's door.

"Have you come to assist me with this gown?" Caroline asked upon Rosemary's entry.

Rosemary paused. "Yes, indeed I have."

Her companion crossed the room and began helping Caroline remove her dusty traveling attire. Her careful fingers worked the buttons and at length she said, "It is a lovely house."

"Yes," Caroline agreed on a sigh, "but I shall never comprehend how Mr. Rushton was able to purchase it. There must have been some error in drawing up the papers that allowed him to afford it."

"Hmm," Rosemary said. She was prevented from saying more until Caroline's dress had been removed and laid aside.

"Will you be much out in company while in London, Miss Bingley?" her companion asked as she slipped Caroline's wrapper onto her shoulders and then crossed the room to regard the trunks, which a manservant had delivered earlier.

"Of course! What is there to do in Town but be in company?"

"I see." Rosemary began to rearrange some items in one of Caroline's trunks. "And I shall be required to accompany you?"

Though she had no wish for the woman to follow her about Town, Caroline did not like the idea of a servant choosing her own duties. Rosemary was here to act as Caroline's companion after all. "Do you object to performing your duties in Town?" she asked.

"No indeed." Rosemary turned, faced her, and then lowered her eyes. She fidgeted with the hem of her sleeve and then said, "I do know now what I was thinking in coming here. I had hoped…. Miss Bingley, there is something I must confess."

"Oh?" Caroline sat on her bed, curious about what might cause the woman so much consternation. It could be nothing of true consequence, surely.

"I am known in Town," Rosemary said flatly.

"Known? Whatever do you mean?"

Rosemary raised her eyes and looked directly at Caroline. "I mean that people know me."

Caroline also raised an eyebrow and crossed her arms. "You have developed a reputation?"

"Yes, Miss Bingley. I have a reputation of sorts."

"Of what sort?" asked Caroline. Now she was imagining the worst. Had Charles hired a companion who was nothing more than a fallen woman of poor character?

"It is nothing as immoral or reprehensible as you must be imagining, but I thought it best to warn you that people may find my return to London rather interesting."

"Are you a fallen woman?" Caroline demanded.

"No, I am not wicked! I am merely known."

Caroline could not fathom what her companion was going on about, and she said, "Explain yourself clearly or leave me, for I am too tired to listen to more of this prattle tonight."

"I will tell you only that I am neither wicked nor dissolute, and that must provide enough comfort, for I shall only reveal my secrets if I am required to do so."

"And if I required you to speak?"

"You could not. Only my circumstances can induce me to speak."

Caroline could see very well that she would make no progress with Rosemary, and she was eager to rest, so she said, "Leave me, please."

Rosemary opened her mouth as if to protest, but then she obeyed her mistress and left the room without another word.

⚜ ⚜

Caroline awoke the next morning to the sound of iron horseshoes striking pavement.

After so many days of travel and so many nights in different coaching inns, for a moment Caroline could not remember where she was. She sat up, letting the bed linens fall away as she peeked out the window.

She was not in a coaching inn, but in London, in Grosvenor Street of all places, and now she must be about the business of discovering Mr. Charlton and Lavinia.

And so she passed a full week at her original plan of watching passersby as they visited Grosvenor Square. Neither Lavinia nor Mr. Charlton appeared, and on the first day of the second week, Caroline was forced to take more aggressive action.

She would have to go out and search for them herself.

On that morning, she rang for a breakfast of meats, bread, jam, and a small pot of chocolate, and after consuming her meal, she again rang the bell for assistance in dressing herself and coiffing her hair. Her appearance today was crucial. She could not meet Mr. Charlton without looking her very best.

As the maid went about her duties, Caroline found that she could not help but approve of the manner in which Mr. Rushton's household was being run. The servants obviously respected their master despite his acerbic wit and lackadaisical temperament, and they performed their assigned tasks without requiring much direction.

She had not expected Mr. Rushton to keep a respectable household.

Descending the stairs, Caroline steeled herself to encounter the gentleman in question, for she had not felt quite comfortable with him since their conversation in the coach. Still, she forced herself to smile as she entered the breakfast room with her reticule clutched tightly in her hand. "Good morning," Caroline said to the gathered party. "Please keep your seats."

Mr. Newton and Mr. Rushton, who stood despite her injunction against it, both bowed their greetings and then returned to their chairs.

"Will you not join us for breakfast, my dear?" Mrs. Newton asked. She seemed perfectly comfortable, even so far from Newton House and in the home of another, and Caroline could not help but be pleased. She had not expected her mother to fare so well in London.

"I have breakfasted in my chamber, and now that I am quite recovered from our long journey from the north, I find I am eager to walk about the streets as soon as Mrs. Pickersgill is ready. Mama, would you care to join us?"

"Mr. Newton, Mr. Rushton, and I are bound for Fairmont Bridge this morning," Mrs. Newton said. "We were hoping you would come along."

"Oh, it is a kind invitation, but you are well aware that I have little interest in bridges. I shall keep to my plans and have a nice walk about the city today, and perhaps I will visit some shops."

"Oh, well, I am disappointed, but I cannot chastise you, for we all have our own interests, do we not?" Mrs. Newton took a sip of her morning tea and gestured at a vacant chair with her cup. "Only do sit a moment and allow me to tell you my news."

Caroline did as she was bid, taking the empty chair beside Mr. Rushton, who smiled at her expectantly.

Feeling concern rise in her at Mr. Rushton's expression, she frowned back at him. He seemed to be taunting her without speaking. He knew something, and she did not like it. Deliberately turning away from his smirking face, she asked, "What news, Mama?"

"I have had a letter from your brother!"

"Oh?" Caroline asked, though she did not wish to hear what she knew must be forthcoming.

"He received my letter and is even now en route to London with his friends."

Caroline sat back in her chair as this news descended upon her. How had her mother's letter reached Charles so quickly? He was traveling she knew not where. It should have taken months for her mother's missive to find him.

Worse, his friends were coming with him. His friends!

Caroline forced a smile to her lips. "What friends?"

"Your former traveling companions save your sister and Mr. Hurst. They remain in Devonshire."

"I am sorry to hear that Louisa will not come," Caroline said and then, though it cost her, added, "but I am pleased that you will soon meet your new daughter."

"Oh yes!" Mrs. Newton said with a clap of her hands that fairly shook the dining table. "I long to meet our Jane!"

Mrs. Newton's eyes had filled with joyful tears. Her happiness was too pure to be trifled with, and so Caroline nodded in agreement. "She is sweet. You will approve Charles's choice."

"I am certain I shall!"

"Have you not forgotten something, my dear?" Mr. Newton prodded.

"Oh!" Mrs. Newton exclaimed as she picked up the letter that had been lying neglected on the table. "Charles included a letter to you, Caro."

Caroline watched not without trepidation as her mother removed a smaller letter from within the larger missive and passed it across the table to her.

Caroline looked at it, wishing very much not to read it in company, for she had a good notion of what it might contain. But everyone was regarding her, so she broke the seal and began to read silently. The words were scribed in her brother's nearly illegible handwriting.

Dear sister—

Please forgive the brevity of this letter, but I see little need in wasting ink when we are to be together soon. I do not know how you convinced Mama to leave Kendal, but as our party is traveling so near to Town on our return trip to Pemberley, I could not pass this opportunity to introduce her to my bride.

I dearly hope this visit will prove to be a harbinger of reconciliation for our family, but that joy, my dear sister, depends entirely upon you. I bring with me those with whom you currently claim an uneasy acquaintance, and I hope these relationships might be restored to their former states.

I hope you shall not force me to explain why you are no longer welcome amongst your former friends.

I trust Mrs. Pickersgill has been an adequate companion and that you are treating her with the respect she deserves.

Until we meet,
Your brother,
Charles Bingley

"Well?" Mrs. Newton asked, her eyes still bright. "What does he say?"

Tears clogged Caroline's throat. She refolded the letter and stuffed it into her reticule as if concealment of the object might also hide its message. Charles and his party were coming too soon!

None of Caroline's plans had been accomplished, and now she would be faced with the uneasy prospect of either winning Mr. Charlton very quickly indeed or making amends with Miss Elizabeth Bennet, for she refused to disappoint her mother by causing so much tension amongst her relations.

But oh how she detested the very idea of their arrival!

"Are you quite well, Caroline?" Mr. Rushton asked, leaning closer as if to measure her countenance.

Caroline looked directly at him. "Why would you ask such a thing?"

"Suddenly, you appear quite pale," he responded.

"Indeed, you do," Rosemary added. Her gaze was suspicious.

Caroline looked around the table to find Mr. and Mrs. Newton watching her expectantly.

"It is only that I am overjoyed at the news of his arrival," she managed to say. "Charles says," she cleared her throat, "that their party is on the way to Pemberley."

Pemberley! The symbol of all her hopes and dreams. If she did not do something very soon, she would be excluded from that great house again.

Rosemary pushed away from the table, and though Caroline could not quite say why, her companion had a definite air of determination about her. "I am prepared to go wherever you wish," she said.

Caroline also stood. Resolve, for she would not call it desperation, swelled within her. Today, she would find Mr. Charlton and extract a proposal at all costs.

As she and Rosemary said their goodbyes to the group assembled at the table, Caroline wondered how compliant her companion would be once she discovered where she planned to walk and with what purpose, but she did not speak of it yet. She only donned her finest bonnet and departed the house with her companion on her heels.

Once they were a good distance from Grosvenor Street, Rosemary asked, "Are we to call upon Mrs. Winton and Mr. Charlton then?"

Caroline gaped.

"Come, Miss Bingley. I may not yet have grasped all the particulars of your circumstances, but I do comprehend why we are here."

Caroline had not expected herself to be so easily readable, but she nodded. "I do intend to call on them, but first, we must discover their location."

"Ah, Mrs. Winton did not tell you where she was staying?" Rosemary's words were not exactly a question, even though her inflection implied it. They seemed more of an indictment against Lavinia.

"No," Caroline said, "but that signifies nothing."

"London is a large city, and we will likely spend days in search of them."

"You are mistaken, Mrs. Pickersgill, for the fashionable residents of London haunt only the most particular locales. We shall start with the shops and confectioners on Bond Street."

And so they walked in that direction, and after spending hours darting from one establishment to the next, Caroline finally settled into a dressmaker's shop, which she felt certain Lavinia would frequent.

Her friend would approve of this sort of enterprise, for it was the most elegant in town. The large main chamber featured high ceilings, and tall built-in cabinets of fabrics and other notions lined the walls. The main table displayed sumptuous silks and cottons, which were being perused by ladies in the most stylish dresses Caroline had seen since her arrival. Yes, it was a fine establishment.

Besides, she had the greatest need for a new gown for her time in London.

Ordinarily, Caroline would have relished a shopping venture in town and spent hours in thrall at the newest fashions of the season, but that day she took no pleasure in the atmosphere of excitement, and when she finally exited the shop, she was only slightly pleased with her purchase.

She had a fine gown on order, but her true object had not been accomplished: they had not discovered Lavinia.

Caroline decided to make one last attempt and led Rosemary down Bruton Street toward Berkeley Square, where she hoped to chance upon her friend.

When she and Rosemary arrived at their destination, however, they discovered not Lavinia but Mr. Charlton, the gentleman himself, leaning against the park square railing. He faced away, looking into the greenery beyond the railing, but she recognized his long, lean—almost thin—form and dark curls.

Upon seeing him lounging there, Caroline took a swift breath. The first encounter was crucial.

He must seem to have recognized Caroline first. It must not appear as though she sought him out, and he certainly must never know that she had undertaken this trip to London in order to find him.

But first, she must rid herself of Rosemary. She turned to her companion and said, "You will rest here for a quarter hour, Mrs. Pickersgill, while I speak with Mr. Charlton privately."

Rosemary looked beyond Caroline to observe Mr. Charlton at the railing. She narrowed her eyes. "I will do as you ask, Miss Bingley, but I do not trust him, and neither should you put your faith in him. He has too much of the upper-class disregard for morals."

Caroline glared. "You speak utter, utter nonsense. Besides, what care I for the opinion of a servant? I trust him, and that is all that matters." She gestured at a shady spot further down the railing. "Wait over there until I return."

Rosemary went, leaving Caroline to formulate her plan.

She would simply walk past, and certainly Mr. Charlton would notice her and turn.

She began to stride toward him, taking care to walk with grace and poise, but he neither noticed nor turned, so when she reached the end of the rail, she approached again, this time allowing her fingers to trail along the vacant rail until she neared him.

And again, Mr. Charlton did not offer her so much as a glance as she passed.

She sighed, turned, and repeated the process. Still, he refused to take note of her.

After several more failed attempts, Caroline decided to change tactics and take up a position at the rail a short distance away in the hopes that he still might notice her first.

She walked to the rail slowly with as much of a regal bearing as one who had just spent the past ten minutes walking back and forth in the same spot could possibly achieve.

She stood not ten feet away for another ten minutes without him so much as turning his head before she finally relented and said, "Oh! Mr. Charlton, whatever do you do here?"

Finally, the gentleman turned and looked at her. Recognition sparked in his eyes.

"Miss Bingley?" He walked closer and bowed to her deeply. "I am shocked! Shocked, but pleased to see you here. How is it that you have come to London?"

Caroline smiled and let her eyelashes flutter closed for a moment. "Did you not know that my family had planned a trip here?" she lied. "Mr. Newton and Mr. Rushton have some business or other in Town."

"Oh? I was unaware that you were to travel to this destination," he said with a bright smile. "I am so pleased, for Lavinia hauled us to Town so quickly, and matters between you and me remain unfinished, do they not?" he asked softly.

Caroline lowered her gaze demurely and did not respond. Caroline sensed that Mr. Charlton was tempted to take her hand; his fingers fairly twitched within his fine gloves. She watched him look about and knew the precise moment he saw Rosemary. His hands drew into fists.

"We are not alone, I see."

"No," Caroline said.

"I have had to elude my sister for a few moments' peace as well. She has been with me every moment since we left Kendal. It is most frustrating."

Caroline nodded in agreement.

"Then we must find a method of gaining some privacy," he said, "and the best technique, I have found, is to be in the largest crowd possible. My sister and I go to Vauxhall Gardens tomorrow."

"A pleasure garden?" Caroline asked, though she had not meant to. She had often been in company of the fashionable people who frequented such places, but Caroline had never lost her distaste for them. London was quite littered with such gardens, and though they all attracted a different sort of clientele, they had one commonality. All were known for their romantic assignations. In fact, she knew that private niches had been designed for the very purpose of encouraging such liberties to be taken. Vauxhall, though the most prestigious of these gardens, was also the most notorious, and Caroline had never had the least wish to venture within.

After hearing tales of young women quite ruining their reputations or, barring that, being snatched away from their companions and taken into the darkness to be molested by some gentleman or other, the very idea of such a place assaulted Caroline's sensibilities, leaving her rather aghast that a lady of any social class would frequent them.

"Indeed, Miss Bingley," Mr. Charlton said on a laugh. "A pleasure garden. Is not that the most wonderful invention?" He studied her and must have read the uncertainty in her countenance, for he added, "You will not allow your time in the country and its backward manners to restrain you, will you?"

Caroline set her jaw. No, she would not allow her past to determine her future. She would not permit anything to prevent her from a union with Mr. Charlton, especially now that her brother and Mr. Darcy were on the way to London.

"No," she said, "I shall not."

"Excellent!" cried Mr. Charlton. "Then join us tomorrow for supper, and perhaps we may sneak away for a few moments of privacy."

Before Caroline could officially accept or decline his invitation, he took his watch out of his fob pocket and sighed. "I must go. My sister will be waiting for me. I shall see you tomorrow at the Grove."

Caroline watched as he disappeared into the crowded street and wondered how she would ever manage to get away to Vauxhall, for her mother would most certainly not approve.

Well, Caroline thought as she turned back toward her companion, she would do it! Her object was so close. She would find a way, even if she had to go to the reprehensible Vauxhall and drag Rosemary with her.

Rosemary was currently resting where Caroline had commanded, but she was not alone. She had also encountered an acquaintance, a wealthy-looking woman with a regal bearing and a gown too fine to be worn for a day of idle shopping. Caroline quite envied that dress, and she was rather curious as to the woman's name and relation to her companion. Her mien and bearing were of polite society, and that was quite incongruous with Rosemary Pickersgill. How were they acquainted?

She must discover all.

Caroline approached them but remained on the periphery to feign a study of a shrub, as if she were suddenly entranced by the local flora.

"I must say I am all astonishment!" she heard the unknown woman say with a sly laugh.

Rosemary said not a word in response to the woman's remark, but her eyes flickered to Caroline, and she turned her body slightly to invite her into their circle.

"Oh, Miss Bingley," Rosemary said with a tight smile. Her tone was strained, and Caroline could not tell if she were adding to her companion's tension by joining the conversation or if she had relieved it. But tension or not, she was determined to discover the other woman's identity.

Rosemary looked back to her acquaintance and asked meekly, "Will you allow me to present my friend?"

The woman turned to Caroline, noticing her for the first time, and swept her from head to toe in one quick glance. Caroline raised her chin at this blatant assessment. Then the lady nodded once with great condescension, and Rosemary began her introduction, saying, "Viscountess Middlebury, may I present Miss Caroline Bingley."

Viscountess?

Now it was Caroline who was all astonishment. This woman was not the wife of a commoner or a lowly knight, baronet, or even baron. Rosemary was speaking with the wife of a viscount.

How utterly shocking.

After Rosemary completed the presentations, Lady Middlebury proceeded to ignore Caroline completely, and for her own part, Caroline barely prevented herself from looking between the other ladies in bewilderment. How had Rosemary become acquainted with the wife of a titled gentleman?

"Whatever do you do in Town?" Lady Middlebury said on a laugh of disbelief. "It is quite brave of you to appear. I had thought we would not see you here so soon given your predicament. I told Lord Middlebury that we should never think to see you again." The woman's tone was so haughty that even Caroline, who was used to consorting with the proudest and most arrogant in society, was momentarily taken aback. Her feelings were clear; she did not care for Rosemary Pickersgill.

Rosemary only managed a weak, "I..."

Rather startlingly, a new wave of emotion sneaked upon Caroline. She felt suddenly protective of her companion, and so without pondering the reasons for this, she lifted her chin and said, "You will pardon me, Lady Middlebury, for speaking out of turn, but Mrs. Pickersgill and I are due back on Grosvenor Street even now."

Lady Middlebury turned her proud face and hawkish eyes upon Caroline, who did not shrink back.

"Who are you?" Lady Middlebury asked with a wave of her hand. "I have already forgotten."

"Caroline Bingley, my lady."

"Ah. And who is your family?" she asked. Lady Middlebury inclined her head as if interested, but really, the posture was designed to intimidate. The feathers on her bonnet blew in the breeze and almost hit Caroline in the face.

"My brother, Charles Bingley, is the head of our family." Upon the shake of Lady Middlebury's head, Caroline added, "He travels often with Mr. Fitzwilliam Darcy of Pemberley."

"Ah! Yes, I have heard of Mr. Darcy of course. A fine family and so very rich—"

Caroline had not the patience to hear her next words. "You will excuse me," she interrupted, "but we must be off this minute."

"Of course, be off," the viscountess said and then turned to Rosemary to add, "I shall make your presence in Town known, my dear. There are some who will be rather anxious to find you."

Caroline took Rosemary's hand, and together they walked down Davies Street and turned onto Grosvenor Street before they broke their silence.

"Thank you, Miss Bingley," Rosemary whispered, though there was no one about to overhear her.

Caroline pulled her hand away and wheeled on her. "I do not know what I was thinking to adopt that tone with a viscount's wife! I should never have spoken as I did."

"Still, I thank you," Rosemary said softly. "You have no idea the embarrassment you saved me."

Caroline could also not guess the motivations for her own actions. She was no great friend of Rosemary, but seeing her thus abused had been too much! If anyone were to abuse her, by rights, it ought to be Caroline herself.

"What is this great embarrassment?" she demanded. "I must know."

Rosemary began to walk again, leaving Caroline to trail after her. "I would prefer not to say."

"I insist that you do, for I did not just insult a titled lady for no reason."

"I did not ask it of you, Miss Bingley; nor shall I share my secrets unless it is absolutely required. And it is not yet absolutely required."

Caroline stopped and stared after Rosemary, who continued to walk all the way to Mr. Rushton's house and disappeared within.

Caroline sat on a vacant bench and wondered at herself. Ever since her brother had banished her to Kendal, she had begun to say and do the oddest things. She had confessed part of her secret shame to a tradesman and defended her servant before a noble. It was as if she were suddenly possessed and unable to control her impulses. The Caroline of old would have ignored the tradesman and taken up the part of the titled lady, but she had done the opposite.

Caroline was quite put out to discover the resurgence of her country morals, especially the day before she was to visit Vauxhall Gardens with Mr. Charlton.

⊙ℛ Seventeen ℛ⊙

"Good morning, my dear," Mrs. Newton said as she entered Caroline's bedchamber the following morning, dismissed her maid, and took up the task of helping her daughter prepare for the day. "I am so very pleased that you insisted I come with you to London. Now that I have left Kendal, I am eager to see more of our fine country."

"I am so happy, Mama, that travel agrees with you."

"Tonight, Mr. Newton has promised to take me to the theater," she said as she added pearl-encrusted combs to Caroline's hair, "and though such entertainments have quite a reputation, he assures me I will be diverted. Will you not join us?"

"I fear I cannot, Mama, for Lavinia has asked me to dine with her this evening," Caroline said. It was not quite a lie, but also not the truth either. Undoubtedly, she would dine with Lavinia at Vauxhall, but Mr. Charlton had issued the invitation and not his sister.

"Oh?" Mrs. Newton smiled. "I did not know you had spoken with her since arriving in London. I am so pleased that you have found one another."

"We met yesterday at Berkeley Square," Caroline lied again.

"And Mrs. Pickersgill? Does she dine with you as well?"

Here was Caroline's opportunity to shed herself of her companion. It would be simple to tell her mother that the invitation had not been extended, but something within Caroline prevented her from saying so. And she despised that part of her—that country aspect—that niggled at her.

She had no wish to navigate Vauxhall, with all its dark walks and hideaways, on her own. It was all so distasteful, though she would never admit as much aloud.

Oh! She clenched her fists at her own turn of thought. How she wished to conform to polite society!

She simply could not manage it completely.

"Yes, Mama," Caroline said on a sigh of surrender, "she will dine with us as well."

"I am pleased to hear it, but…" Here Mrs. Newton trailed off and then began again. "Our Mrs. Pickersgill has seemed rather odd since our arrival in London, do you not think?"

Caroline pondered her mother's words as she stood to check the fall of her gown in the mirror. "Indeed, now that you mention it," she said, feigning indifference, "there have been some odd occurrences."

In truth, Caroline had not stopped wondering about the mystery surrounding Rosemary's exit from London.

Mrs. Newton patted Caroline's hand. "I do hope you will watch over our Mrs. Pickersgill and protect her, for she has been such a good friend."

Caroline wanted to protest the appellation of "friend," but she did not. She thought back to their encounter with Lady Middlebury at Berkeley Square. She had already defended Rosemary as only the most devoted friend might.

Beyond what most friends might do, in fact, but she would not tell her mother of her actions. It was all too embarrassing.

However, Caroline may as well admit to herself that she had developed a tenderness for the woman. She replied, "I will not allow any harm to befall her."

In actuality, Caroline feared that Rosemary might harm *her* when she discovered their destination for the evening, but her companion would relent and accompany her. She had no choice.

And that is precisely what happened.

As evening fell, Caroline ordered a servant to hire a hackney carriage to transport them from Grosvenor Street to Vauxhall.

"I do not like this," Rosemary said as the hackney whisked them southeast toward the Thames through the lingering evening heat.

Indeed, Caroline did not much approve of their destination either, but she would not fall prey to her country upbringing by agreeing. Instead, she said, "Oh, do not be so difficult, Mrs. Pickersgill. Vauxhall is a fashionable place. Why, the prince regent himself can often be found there."

Rosemary cut her eyes to Caroline. "That does not provide encouragement, Miss Bingley."

"Well, I do not care whether or not you are encouraged, for we are dining with Mrs. Winton and Mr. Charlton, and that is all there is to it."

Caroline's words were meant to reassure herself as well as Rosemary, and she could think of nothing more to say and only sat quietly as the hackney traversed the streets of London and then rumbled across the Vauxhall Bridge. As the wheels struck the stone, Mr. Rushton's face entered Caroline's mind, but she shoved the image of him aside. She must concentrate on her object: Mr. Charlton.

The hackney deposited its occupants at the entrance to the gardens, and the view within its walls quite took away Caroline's breath.

"It is lovely," she said as she peeked through the entrance. She had not expected it to appear so enchanting. Trees lined a long walkway, and lanterns dangled from their branches. Their light swayed with the breeze and cast a romantic, ever-moving glow across the walkers below.

"And crowded," Rosemary added.

Indeed, the garden teemed with people. The line to enter the garden was quite long and would take many minutes to navigate.

As they waited among the other would-be revelers, Rosemary stood with her head bent, again looking as though she thought the ground might suddenly shift beneath her feet. At length, they reached the front of the line, and Caroline paid the entry fee before proceeding along the tree-lined trail toward the Grove, which was located at the intersection of the four principal gravel pathways at Vauxhall. The garden was a blur of motion, glittering gowns, and dark gentlemen's attire. Around her, Caroline heard snippets of conversation and laughter, and she detected an orchestra tuning in the distance.

As Caroline navigated the path, she wondered at the multitude of people from all social classes mingling together and found herself quite certain she should never locate Mr. Charlton amongst them all, but she need not have worried, for Mr. Charlton found her.

"Miss Bingley," he cried from the path behind them. The ladies turned to see him already bowing low. "You have arrived at last. Come, Lavinia will be so pleased to see you."

He offered Caroline his arm, which she accepted, and the three of them walked toward the Grove, where the random sounds of the instruments became louder.

Mr. Charlton led them through the colonnade, where a hundred supper boxes had been arranged, and they followed as he wound deftly to the one they would fill that evening.

Lavinia noticed their approach, and a look of horror spread across her fine features, but it disappeared quickly, leaving Caroline confident that she had misinterpreted it. Her friend's face must have registered surprise only.

Lavinia swept forward to welcome them, but Caroline met her halfway and spoke first, as if she were the hostess of the event and not her friend.

"Ah, Lavinia," she said with a regal curtsey. "You may be certain of our pleasure at your invitation to join you for dinner here."

Lavinia curtseyed too, but she seemed a bit taken aback at Caroline's choice of greeting. When she spoke, however, her voice hinted at no discomfort or confusion. Her tone was regal as it ever was when she said, "Though I am quite shocked to find you in London, you are most welcome to dine here."

The party seated themselves around the table, and conversation flowed, albeit not freely, and Caroline could not tell whether the strain was due to

Lavinia's distant behavior or to the fact that the orchestra had begun to play, rendering hearing difficult.

Around dusk, a strangely minimal tray of victuals had been brought to the table. The cold ham, which was supposedly intended to feed four, would barely cover a piece of bread, and the chickens were the size of underfed pigeons. But Caroline could not be disappointed because she had become entranced by the orchestra.

The notes of George Frideric Handel danced around her, and Caroline had the greatest urge to put both elbows on the table, rest her chin in her hands, and listen the whole night through. But she sat bolt upright, allowing her pleasure to show only as she tapped her toes beneath the table linens.

Her enchantment endured until she chanced to see Lady Middlebury in a nearby box.

She leaned toward Rosemary. "Is not that the lady with whom you spoke at Berkeley Square yesterday?"

Rosemary looked and then winced. "It is."

"Oh dear," Caroline whispered, "I hope she does not spot us. After I behaved so rudely, she cannot help our situation."

"What are you speaking of?" demanded Lavinia. "I must know."

"Oh," Caroline hesitated and then chose to reveal the truth. Perhaps hinting at an association with a viscountess might spur Lavinia into more jovial conversation. "I was just pointing out to Mrs. Pickersgill a mutual acquaintance."

Lavinia looked around pointedly. "Who?"

"Lady Middlebury," Caroline responded.

"Well, how exceedingly interesting," Lavinia said as her eyes alighted on the woman herself.

Caroline could hardly guess why and was about to ask when Mr. Charlton stood. "Will you walk about with me, Miss Bingley?"

Taken slightly aback by the suddenness of his invitation, Caroline managed to smile and nod, but Lavinia said, "I do not think it wise, William."

"Oh come, sister, we shall keep to the lighted pathways. Rest here and our Mrs. Pickersgill will divert you."

And with that, Caroline found herself, quite without her companion, being escorted down the main path deeper into the garden and leaving a sputtering Lavinia behind.

Though she ought to be experiencing jubilation and triumph at this precise moment, Caroline felt only confusion.

This was the moment for which she had been waiting! She was on the arm of a soon-to-be titled, wealthy gentleman, and she was perched on the cusp of rising to the status of baroness, forever removing herself from the pall of her family history and never again being forced to depend on anyone else—not her brother, Mr. Darcy, Miss Elizabeth Bennet—to secure her place among the best society.

Yes, she must focus on that and not on the feeling of unease within her.

She forced herself to smile at Mr. Charlton.

"Vauxhall is lovely, is it not?" he asked.

She looked about her, noticing again how the lighted lanterns swayed among the tree branches, bathing the pathway in semi-light and moveable shadow.

"It is rather lovely," she agreed. The giggling walking parties and love-struck couples they passed along the path reminded her all too forcefully of its reputation.

Still, she allowed Mr. Charlton to lead her further into the garden, and as the sounds of Handel faded into the background, they met fewer groups of walkers. Soon, they encountered only couples, hanging upon each other in a manner that would be inappropriate in polite society.

Despite the idealistic setting, Caroline did not feel the thrill of her closeness to Mr. Charlton. Her hand rested along his forearm, but she felt only her glove beneath her fingertips. He elicited no response from her at all. She thought briefly of Mr. Rushton and of her reaction to him in the carriage, but she quickly removed him from her mind.

She ought to feel the same thing for Mr. Charlton, should she not?

Some sort of twinge in her heart? She had heard such sentiments described at boarding school, this feeling she should experience. It had always sounded a bit like indigestion, and that did not seem pleasing. But after her experience with Mr. Rushton, she had been forced to reconsider. This strange indigestion was rather pleasing. Still, she felt nothing in the vicinity of her heart when she looked to Mr. Charlton.

Caroline continued to examine her emotions as she looked up at him. He did not return her gaze, but only looked forward as he led her deeper into the shady hollow, and she studied him with immunity.

What was the matter with her?

He was handsome, well dressed, and rich. He had ancestors of note. He would be a baron.

Despite all these inducements, her heart was obstinately uninvolved.

Her mind, however, rejoiced over her position on the arm of the future baron. Yes, her plan was working itself out shockingly well, even if her heart seemed to be attempting a coup.

When Mr. Charlton stopped, they were standing alone at the edge of an even darker, more intimate section of garden.

"I confess," said Mr. Charlton, "that I could not listen to another note of that orchestra. Could you?"

"No indeed," Caroline lied.

"And I do have the greatest desire to speak privately with you, but I dare not drag you any farther into the dark. I do not want to ruin your reputation, Miss Bingley. Perhaps," he lowered his voice, "you could meet me at the ruins." He pointed down the dim pathway. "Just follow that corridor in a quarter hour or so and you shall find me."

With that, he dashed off, leaving Caroline quite alone among the trickle of visitors along the path.

Caroline looked around and then took a deep breath.

What could she be thinking?

Here she was in Vauxhall, preparing for her first assignation.

Well, not really her first assignation. She had allowed Mr. Rushton to touch her intimately in the carriage after all.

But this was her first moonlight assignation.

And it was with a future baron, not a tradesman.

It would mean the end to all her worries. She would never again fear that her past might be discovered, and she would no longer be required to apologize to Miss Elizabeth Bennet in order to return to the best society. Finally, she would be completely free of it all.

So Caroline waited fifteen minutes and then marched down the dark path to meet her future.

◦◦◦ ◦◦◦

The classical temple was composed of columns that supported a domed stone roof. Long drapes of a filmy material hung in the spaces between the columns and blew gently in the breeze. To the side of the temple stood a small flower garden, which was surrounded by a trellis of clinging vines that quite obscured the view within.

Caroline approached the structure but did not enter. Her determination had waned as she marched, then walked, and finally dawdled along the path toward the rendezvous point. Now, she found that she could only manage to look at the temple, and as her eyes adjusted to the muted light, she detected Mr. Charlton's figure behind the sheer fabric. He seemed to be speaking with someone.

Confused and thinking perhaps she had come upon the wrong ruins, Caroline edged closer, but by the time she drew near enough to hear the conversation, the pair had disappeared. And so she followed, quietly stepping into the temple.

She looked around the columned room and discovered that the attached trellis actually formed a sort of walled walkway, and she followed it, passing under the flowered vines that hung above her head. She was just about to round the corner to the entrance to a small interior garden when she heard a giggle.

A girlish giggle.

That was odd.

Then, even odder, she heard Mr. Charlton's voice. She could not decipher the words, but then there was another snigger.

Abruptly, Caroline realized what sort of scene she had come upon, and though she had no wish to see the particulars, she peeked around the corner. She could see nothing of the woman, however, without revealing her position in the garden.

But the scene was plain enough. Mr. Charlton was seated on a low stone bench, and the girl, whomever she was, was seated on Mr. Charlton.

Caroline shrunk back, horrified and enraged.

She had heard the rumors about Mr. Charlton and his habits; he had, in fact, confirmed them. But somehow, she had not believed him.

Of course, she was acquainted with the ways of polite society, but she had always been fortunate to remain in the company of those—her brother and Mr. Darcy—who had adopted a higher moral code and who would never lower themselves to such dissolute displays.

Now she was witnessing Mr. Charlton's debauchery for herself. It was true; he was fond of titillating maids.

Caroline's first instinct was to confront him, for fighting was part of her nature. He was supposed to be meeting her to propose marriage after all! She ought to be in the place of the dissolute woman!

She peeked again around the corner and very nearly stepped into the open, but then she thought the better of it.

Making a scene would benefit no one.

Besides, this behavior should neither shock nor offend her, for as she had so lately reminded herself, it was the way of their class, and if Caroline desired to fit in amongst them, she must learn to accept it.

As she turned and retraced her steps to the entrance of the ruins, Caroline felt the full force of her discovery. It was the strangest sensation. Here she was attempting to convince everyone—including herself—that she belonged as mistress of Oak Park and wife of a baron, but her soul cried out against the very thing her mind wanted.

Could she truly live with a gentleman who would behave in such a manner?

Or was her bourgeois upbringing causing her to view the situation in too moralistic a manner?

These morals were hallmarks of the middling classes, so was not her current state of mind to be blamed on her unfortunate background?

Caroline could no longer think. She simply crunched along the path back toward the Grove where she had left Rosemary. Her mind was in a whirl of emotions and thoughts, and she could not settle upon one or the other.

She simply continued to walk toward Rosemary, and when her companion saw her pale face and shocked expression, she asked, "Miss Bingley, are you well?"

"Oh yes," she said. "Why do you ask?"

"You look pale."

"Yes, you look dreadful, dear. Will you not sit?" Lavinia suggested, but she did not move to aid Caroline to a chair. Instead, she just stared at her.

"No," Caroline said. "I shall not sit. We must be away."

"What? So early?" Lavinia asked, sounding completely unconcerned.

"I am afraid I have had quite enough of Vauxhall for one evening."

"Yes?" Lavinia asked. "Well, I suppose my brother is still amongst the revelers."

It was more of a statement than a question, but Caroline responded anyway. "Indeed, he is."

ஐ Eighteen ஐ

Caroline and Rosemary rented another hackney and returned to Mr. Rushton's home in Grosvenor Street in silence. If in fact Rosemary had attempted to begin a conversation, Caroline had not noticed, for her mind was too full and confused to allow one more thought to enter.

She only wanted the forgetfulness of sleep to come and take away her tumultuous worries, and when Caroline's bedchamber door finally closed behind her, she sighed aloud. Although almost all the energy had drained from her body, she managed to walk across the room and sink onto the dressing table stool.

She looked at the mirror, but she did not see her own reflection. She only began removing the pins from her hair by rote, dropping them in a small pile on the table and then combing her hair absently until a knock at the door arrested her.

She decided to ignore the sound.

It came again.

"What?" Caroline asked. She had hoped to speak the word with a biting tone, but her voice came out weak and breathy.

"May I enter, Miss Bingley?" The voice that floated through the barrier of the closed door issued from Rosemary Pickersgill.

"No, you may not."

The pause was so long that Caroline thought—or rather hoped—that Rosemary had gone away, but then the door opened and her companion entered unbidden.

Caroline did not even bother to turn around when she said, "Did not you mark me? I said you may not enter."

"I apologize, Miss Bingley, but I felt the strongest urge to speak with you tonight."

Caroline glared at her in the mirror.

Rosemary continued, "Do not make me regret my decision."

"I find I do not have the vigor to protest. What is it you must say to me?"

Rosemary seated herself on the edge of the bed and looked at Caroline in the mirror. "What happened with Mr. Charlton this evening?"

"Nothing you ought to concern yourself with," Caroline said.

"He has not proposed?"

"No."

"I have already warned you that his sister may not be your ally, but—" she began.

"I will not hear such talk!" Caroline's fist descended on the dressing table, causing the hairpins to jump.

"—I ask because," Mrs. Pickersgill hesitated. "Because I do not want to see you suffer as I did."

"Do not compare yourself to me. We are nothing alike."

"We are more similar than you realize," Rosemary insisted as she rose to stand behind Caroline. "I too was raised in the arms of the middling classes—"

"I will not hear my family so degraded!"

Rosemary held up a hand and their eyes met in the mirror. "Allow me to finish, Miss Bingley, and then you may rail at me as much as you please."

Caroline crossed her arms before her and said, "Hmph." But she listened, eyes locked on Rosemary's reflection.

"I was once just as eager as you to rise in society, and one day, I caught the eye of a gentleman, a wealthy gentleman, and I believed all my tribulations were at an end. I married him, Miss Bingley, but as you see, it did not gain me one measure of enduring status, for here I stand, nothing more than a paid companion."

The two women stared at each other in the mirror's reflection, but Caroline had no will left in her to fight or even question the woman's story.

"Leave me," she begged.

"Yes, I shall leave you in a moment." A long pause ensued, but Rosemary did not depart. Finally, she said in a quieter voice, "Miss Bingley, you must understand this about me: I was not born to this station."

"Yes, yes, as you said."

"I was a gentleman's daughter and more."

"I hardly believe that," Caroline said. This woman could not possibly be what she claimed.

"I care not for your belief in my veracity, Miss Bingley, for your perception cannot alter the facts. I have experienced all that you fear and more. I have fallen in the eyes of society, and yet I live on, and I have even managed to be tolerably happy even if I have been reduced to being the companion of a pretentious young lady."

"Insolence!" Caroline said, though her voice lacked venom. "My brother will hear of this when he arrives."

"Your brother knows precisely what I am, Miss Bingley, and until this very day, I was willing to accept my fate. But you have taught me something valuable. Watching you persist no matter the obstacle, even when it was a foolish attempt, has shown me how easily I have given in to my circumstances. Well, no longer! Mark me. I will do anything to return to my station."

Rosemary turned on her heel, her strawberry blond hair shaking loose from its pins with the vehemence of her spin, and exited the chamber, leaving Caroline to stare at herself stupidly in the mirror.

Caroline knew not how long she remained in that position before lying down in an attempt to sleep, but she could not manage to drift off. She was angry, confused, and most of all hungry. The food at Vauxhall had not filled her.

She flung the bed linens from her, donned her wrapper, and stomped across the room toward the door. Here, she managed to mute her steps as she headed toward the kitchen in search of something to eat. She stole a slice of bread and a hunk of cheese, and for fear of encountering Mr. Rushton in another of his own midnight meals, she took her plate to the library, where the fire would likely still be smoldering and provide her enough light to read.

She opened the door and the voice she had hoped not to hear said, "Ah, Miss Bingley."

Caroline discovered Mr. Rushton lounging sideways on one of the Grecian sofas, his back propped against an armrest and a book splayed open across his chest. Such shocking posture! A gentleman ought not recline, but sit up straight.

His next words were also a shock. "How did you find Vauxhall this evening?" he asked.

She nearly dropped her food, but she managed to retain her hold and place her plate on the small table beside the unoccupied sofa as she forced herself to speak to him.

"Vauxhall?" she asked innocently. "Why would you think I went there?"

"My manservant hailed your hackney. Did you expect him to lie when I asked its destination?"

Caroline sighed, lowered herself to the sofa, and said, "Yes, I went to Vauxhall, and I did not enjoy myself if you must know."

"I suspected you would not, for though you claim no influence by your past, you will never be able to mount such a flagrant disregard for morals as does most of polite society."

Caroline selected a piece of bread, bit into it, and did not reply.

"And did Mr. Charlton make his proposal?" He asked this question in an altogether different tone. It was almost vulnerable, and so Caroline suspected immediately that he must be about some sort of trickery. "Do not bother asking how I discerned your desires in that direction, for you have hardly been subtle in your arts."

She thought to argue with him, but managed only to say, "How kind of you, Mr. Rushton."

But in truth, it was likely that only her trusting mother and Mr. Newton remained oblivious to her schemes, so she admitted, "No, he did not make an overture, but it is only a matter of time."

"You will be a fool indeed to accept him," he said.

"I thank you for opining on this topic, sir, but if you will forgive me, I will make my own decisions."

"I may forgive you, but will you forgive yourself? I thought you a great many things—foolish among them—but I dearly hope that you will not condemn yourself to the sort of life Mr. Charlton will offer."

She laughed. "He can provide all that I require."

"That is where you are wrong, Miss Bingley. He may cast an image of himself as a wealthy, carefree soul, but he is not unlike others of polite society who disregard their debt and gamble at every opportunity."

To Mr. Rushton's list of charges against Mr. Charlton, she could add dissolute debaucher, and he had confessed to being poor at money management, but she had heard nothing of his gambling. But what did that matter? It was entirely natural for the upper classes to behave that way, for they were born to their wealth and status and could not lose it. They could show no economy or moderation and indulge until their coffers emptied, and it was the duty and privilege of the lower classes to uphold them, was it not? After all, had not the landed gentry upheld them for years as tenant farmers?

It was only right, and it was the way of society.

But what of her father? He had earned his fortune with no aid from the titled landowners in the county. And the elder Mr. Rushton? He had lost his, and no amount of kindness on the part of his creditors had saved him.

It ought to be so simple. The titled were wealthy, and the poor were poor. That is how it used to be, but now trade and title were blurring, a most confounding condition. Caroline sighed. She simply could not understand the way of the world.

So instead of pondering that subject, she studied Mr. Rushton as she ate. He was still lying on the sofa opposite hers, and though his posture appeared relaxed, he radiated a sort of anxiety that Caroline could not comprehend.

Now finished with her small meal, Caroline stood. Hoping to intimidate him using the advantage of height, she loomed over him and said, "Your words do you no credit, sir, for I have heard nothing amiss about Mr. Charlton outside of what is expected of the aristocracy."

"Neither do your actions, Miss Bingley, do any credit to you." He looked at her with stern eyes. "I see you. I see exactly what you are thinking."

She shook her head, realizing that her hair fell loosely about her shoulders in a most improper manner. "You cannot presume to know my intentions, and moreover, you are very rude."

"I am well respected both in London and in the country, Miss Bingley, and that means I may be as rude as I desire and say whatever I choose, and still people defer to me and seek my good opinion. It is a most charming— and maddening—arrangement."

Caroline leaned down until she was much too close to him. "Charming or not," she whispered into his ear. "I would never seek your good opinion, so please do not endeavor to give it. And if you wish me to defer to you in any matter, you may as well abandon that hope immediately, for it shall never happen."

"Miss Bingley, you will fail in your quest."

Caroline blinked at him slowly as she formulated her retort. Finally, she said, "Indeed, I wish you would not think on my endeavors, Mr. Rushton, for it only leads to conversations of this nature. We are always at odds, and I fear you are not up to a true battle of wits."

"And you intend to supply these wits?" he snorted. "How amusing."

Caroline returned to her full height. "I wish I could say I found your behavior amusing, but alas, our reacquaintance has taught me to expect the contrary."

Upon those words, she spun on her heel, but before she could step out of his sphere, a hand grasped her wrist and prevented her from stalking away. Caroline whirled around prepared to spew angry words upon him and discovered that Mr. Rushton had risen from the sofa.

Worse, she found herself drawn even closer to him than she had ever been, even when he had caressed her face in the carriage. Now his eyelids were lowered in an expression she had only once seen on his face and still could not precisely identify.

Her face heated.

Traitorous blood, Caroline thought.

"If you find my behavior shocking, you would indeed be surprised, my dear Miss Bingley, if you could read my thoughts."

"I doubt very much that your thoughts would be appropriate for a lady to know," she whispered.

"You are correct." His voice had softened, and he released his grip on her arm and stepped back, but somehow, his presence still overwhelmed her. "It is best to keep my thoughts to myself, for you are too genteel to be acquainted with them." His words were laced with a particular sarcasm that told her he did not find her genteel at all.

Caroline stepped back too, eager to put more distance between them. His gaze was too intense. "Yes, it is best that you do not speak," she said. His intensity did not waver, and she added more weakly, "For you never speak a word of sense."

"Well, I will endeavor to do so for the first time now, Miss Bingley." His voice had returned to its normal tone, setting her at ease just a bit. "You must realize that Mr. Charlton is not suited to a woman of your ilk."

Caroline gawped at him, unsure whether he was complimenting or insulting her.

"Your marriage to him would be most unhappy."

"That is simply not true."

Mr. Rushton's face took on a sardonic bent. "So you desire a husband who, rather than admiring your impudent and independent spirit, would choose to take your inheritance and then ignore you?"

"Mr. Charlton would do no such thing," Caroline protested.

"I wager you would be living in separate abodes before the first year of your marriage concluded. He wants a wife who will bring him a fortune and then foolishly turn her back as he fritters it away at cards and women. You, Miss Bingley, while certainly wealthy and foolish, are something more." He gave Caroline the most intense look. "You are something more."

The combination of his countenance and his words caused Caroline to turn and flee to her bedchamber, where she passed a restless night in trying to discern his motives.

⎰⎱ Nineteen ⎰⎱

Caroline was quite shocked when upon rising late the following morning, taking a prolonged breakfast in her chamber, and finally descending the staircase of Mr. Rushton's town home well after noon, she discovered a red-faced Lavinia awaiting her.

She caught sight of Caroline as she descended the stairs and marched over to face her.

"Good God!" Caroline blurted, completely flummoxed by her friend's vexed demeanor, and then added more civilly, "I did not realize you were here."

The entirety of Lavinia's being radiated agitation. Even the feather in her hair seemed to quiver with anger. Lavinia, always calm and dignified, was more distraught than Caroline had ever observed her.

It was a fearsome sight to behold.

"My brother. He has not been here?" she demanded, her shrill voice echoing through the entryway.

Caroline's confusion deepened. "Mr. Charlton? No, we have not had the pleasure of seeing him since Mrs. Pickersgill and I were in your company last evening. Come," she said as she led her friend to the privacy of the sitting room, "we can speak in here."

"You saw him last at Vauxhall?" Lavinia demanded as she followed Caroline.

"Yes," Caroline said as she shut the door behind them. "At Vauxhall."

"After your assignation, no doubt?"

"What? No! I never encountered...."

Obviously not listening, Lavinia began to look around the room in anger, as if considering which decoration she ought to hurl into the fireplace. "Why did you come to London?" she demanded. "Why would you even think to? Are you that thoughtless and imprudent?"

Caroline stepped back at Lavinia's words. "You have me at a disadvantage," Caroline said, deliberately forcing her voice to project calm, as if she were dealing with a small child in the midst of a temper tantrum. "I cannot think of what has caused you to become so distressed. Do sit down and tell me what has happened."

"I shall not sit!" Lavinia said, and as if to punctuate those words, she began pacing the room with heavy steps. "My brother thinks to propose to you!"

"Of course, was this not the object all along?" Caroline asked, confused.

"No." Lavinia turned and looked at her with unapologetic directness, and then she spoke as if to herself, saying, "My plot to separate you has been a dismal failure. You have proved bolder and more cunning than I imagined."

Caroline took another step back. "What plot?" she whispered.

"Oh come. I contrived an occasion for us to come to our father in London so that William would not wed a woman as vulgar as you, *my dear Caroline.*"

The venom with which she unleashed her last phrase immobilized Caroline. Her friend had never spoken of her in such a way before.

But were these the words of a friend?

Caroline felt suddenly slow and dim. Could Rosemary have been correct? Was she now reliving the exact circumstances she herself had inflicted on Jane Bennet? Caroline thought back upon her interactions with Lavinia since her return to Kendal—the long wait for her first call, her initial seating arrangement at the Oak Park dinner party, her insistence on riding when she knew Caroline despised it, and apparently, her desire to remove her brother from her sphere. Were these the actions of a friend?

No indeed, Caroline realized as she looked upon Lavinia with a newness of understanding.

Dash it! Rosemary had been correct. Standing before her was the enemy.

Caroline's altercation with Mr. Rushton the night before had prepared her for battle, for though stunned and distressed, she straightened her back and took a few steps closer to Lavinia. Her friend did not back away, but her eyebrows drew down and her lips tightened. Anger in its purest form radiated from her countenance.

Caroline's astonishment at the unconcealed malevolence in her oldest friend was complete, and she would not allow it to remain unanswered. "You accuse me of vulgarity?" she said as she again stepped closer. "You invade this residence and then charge me with conduct in which no upstanding woman of quality, sense, education, and breeding would engage, and you expect me to accept your unfounded malice? It shall not be borne."

"Do you deny that you had hoped to entrap William into a marriage?" Lavinia demanded.

"I had no wish to entrap him. If I had intended to be subversive about the match, would I have come to you for assistance in bringing about the union? I hardly think so."

Lavinia's eyes had narrowed further and her lips drew into so tight a line that wrinkles formed at the corners of her mouth, but she did not speak. The two women eyed each other for long moments until finally Lavinia spun away.

Caroline was pleased to have set her down so completely, but her victory was not to be, for though her back was turned, Lavinia said to her quite clearly, "I may content myself, at least, with the knowledge that he has not succumbed to your machinations and eloped with you. That would have been the height of folly."

"Folly!" Caroline felt the burn of humiliation on the same scale that she had first experienced upon Mr. Darcy's wedding to Miss Elizabeth Bennet, but she used that fire to respond in kind. "Though your opinion of me in general is no longer a secret, your accusations are unjust. I would never lower myself by participating in an elopement. If Mr. Charlton ever disappears with a female, you ought to check within your own household, for he has a famous reputation for titillating the maids!"

Lavinia, purple with rage, whirled on her. "You cow!"

Caroline felt a slow smile spread across her face, for the use of derisive appellations was a sure sign of an opponent's defeat.

Lavinia gave one great tremble and then stamped a foot in impotent rage. "I will have nothing further to do with you, Miss Bingley. I will no longer recommend you to society or allow you to use my good name for your benefit. Our friendship, such as it was, is finished."

"Excellent," Caroline said in a shrill voice. "I have been desirous of ridding myself of you as well," she lied. Truly, she had no wish to lose an ally of the magnitude of Lavinia, and she would have much preferred to have succeeded in her plan to marry a baron, but one must retain one's dignity.

"Oh, do be honest, Caroline," Lavinia said. She seemed to have recovered her wits somewhat and now walked toward Caroline slowly. She spoke in a soft, patronizing tone that grated Caroline most thoroughly. "You can have no hopes for social improvement now. I know the genesis of your family's wealth, and I will not conceal my knowledge any longer." She completed her tirade by sighing and saying, "It shall be a relief to be shed of you, for I could hardly view you as more than a pet."

Caroline's mortification was complete. To be called a pet....

But still, Lavinia continued heaping hot coals upon her.

"For a time, I took a great deal of pleasure from introducing you into the finest society. I quite flattered myself that I was responsible for every positive change I perceived in your address and countenance after you had been in the company of acquaintances from my rank. It was a bit like teaching a mongrel a series of interesting tricks. The cur is appealing to watch, but when dinner is served and everyone is seated according to their rank, the dog, though he performed well, is still required to sit on the floor and scavenge the crumbs that might fall from the table."

Caroline felt tears leap to her eyes. Did they originate from anger or despair? She could not be certain. Nor could she allow those tears to fall.

Instead, she lashed her emotions tightly down into a small, dark place within her, and when she spoke again, she was satisfied with the modulation of her tone. "You were pleased for me to associate with your friends, but you balk at my association with your brother."

"Quite so, my dear," Lavinia said with disdain, "we have ever been unequal acquaintances. You must comprehend that I cannot allow you to have designs on my brother. It would sully the family name."

"I see," Caroline whispered, all the fight suddenly gone from her body. She desired nothing more than for Lavinia to leave her in peace to contemplate what had just occurred.

As if sensing her opponent's defeat, Lavinia came closer and sneered at her. "Oh," she said as she patted Caroline's hand in mock comfort. "Do not appear so injured. Even you have confessed to having attempted to remove an unworthy woman from your brother's realm. So I have only followed your lead, my dear."

Lavinia laughed and then exited the room in a swirl of skirts and superiority. All at once, realization struck Caroline. As she stared at Lavinia's retreating form, she observed what no amount of wealth, no quantity of the finest silk, and no title might conceal: the pure hatred of a shallow creature.

Dreadful as it was to see her former friend in this new manner, it was the next realization that struck her most forcefully.

Caroline had indeed done nothing less when she attempted to separate her brother from Miss Jane Bennet. She could not deny that she would do—and in fact had done—something very similar in the name of family protection.

She walked across the room and positioned herself in front of one of the large windows that lined the walls. Caroline stared blindly at her own reflection in the glass for some time, and when her eyes finally focused on it, she was shocked.

Before her was a frightened, powerless woman who, though financially stable, had managed to deny herself every other joy of society that was available to her sex.

A tear ran down one cheek, and though she quickly dashed it away with the back of her hand, she felt angry at her uncharacteristic lack of control.

But she could not blame herself, for it is difficult to ascertain one's true nature for the first time.

৵ও Twenty ৶ও

It was upon this very thought that Caroline heard her mother's voice say, "Your brother and his companions have arrived, my dear. Do come and greet them."

Good Lord, Caroline thought. How had they arrived in London so quickly? They must have been only a day's ride behind the mail coach! To be so soon in the company of Miss Elizabeth Bennet and Mr. Darcy and to know that her brother would be eyeing her closely, wondering if she would make amends, was simply too much. How would she survive the moments to come?

She could not fathom a method. She must simply endure it as best she could.

"Yes, Mama," Caroline called back in a controlled tone that contradicted the turmoil within her. She must take a bit of time to gather her scattered wits.

Caroline looked through the window, saw Mr. Darcy's carriage at the entrance, and wondered how she had managed to ignore its arrival. She had been so focused within that she had entirely missed the happenings in the world around her.

She took a deep breath and refocused on her reflection. She looked strained and bloodless. She pinched her cheeks and smoothed her hair, but it did little good.

Her jangled nerves nearly prevented her from turning and walking toward the entryway to greet the new arrivals, and she did not approve of this sensation at all. Nervous complaints were the hallmark of weak-willed, silly women everywhere, and Caroline had always been proud not to count herself among them. Now, here she was having some sort of apoplexy at the thought of encountering her own brother and a gentleman with whom she had traveled extensively.

But how could Caroline possibly face any of them now?

She was an abject failure.

Lavinia would see to it that she never met with Mr. Charlton again. He would not propose. She would not be the wife of a baron.

All hope of escaping her brother's injunction to make amends with Miss Elizabeth Bennet was now lost. If she wanted to escape the prison of the north, then she must depend on her brother. And now that she understood Lavinia's feelings toward her, she must not return to Kendal.

Ever again.

Resigned to her fate, Caroline entered an empty foyer. While she had been summoning her courage and contemplating her appearance, the guests had already been greeted and ushered into the drawing room, which had more seating than the small sitting room she and Lavinia had occupied, and by now, her mother was no doubt attempting to recount every happening in Kendal since the day Charles had left it all those years ago.

As Caroline drew nearer to the chamber, she saw that the double mahogany door was ajar, allowing her to distinguish the voices of the room's occupants from her position in the hallway.

Truly, she was preparing to make her entrance when she heard Mr. Darcy speak, and suddenly, she felt quite immobilized.

His voice had once been the audible symbol of all her hopes and dreams, and hearing it now in the wake of her greatest defeats was nearly more than she could bear. She could only stand and listen to its modulated tones and wish for what could not be.

With such strong emotions coursing through her, Caroline took the cowardly option and peeked through the open door instead of meeting her former companions with her usual boldness. They were all charmingly arranged about the room, but Caroline's eyes sought Mr. Darcy, and she discovered him standing behind the sofa. A deep brown coat covered his broad back, and he appeared to be quite at his leisure, for he leaned against the back of the sofa in a relaxed posture. When she observed that his hand was resting so that his fingertips could with great subtlety brush the shoulder of the woman—his wife, Miss Elizabeth Bennet, as Caroline would always think of her—who was seated before him, Caroline could not bear the unfairness. Miss Elizabeth Bennet had every tangible need met, and she had love as well.

On that thought, Caroline strode into the chamber prepared to be just as cold to Miss Elizabeth Bennet as ever and just as attentive to Mr. Darcy as propriety would allow.

The gentlemen all stood at her sudden entrance, and her mother was forced to break her litany of local news. "Oh Caroline, my dear, there you are. Do come and greet your brother, his wife, and their friends."

Caroline did as she was instructed only because it was precisely what she had intended to do.

"Charles," she said as she grasped his hand in both of hers. "How happy I am to see you looking so hale after your travels."

Her brother returned her greeting and gave her a searching look, as if attempting to gauge her intentions with one mere glance. Caroline offered him her boldest smile, which caused his eyebrows to draw down in confusion.

He may as well share in her perplexity, for she was acting without fully knowing her own aims.

She then smiled at Jane, who was eyeing her with a mixture of suspicion and openness. Jane's visage transformed into a look of honest pleasure that surprised Caroline.

After having just experienced the same suffering she had inflicted on Jane, Caroline could not imagine offering such an open expression to Lavinia Winton. No indeed.

But Jane had always been a kind-hearted girl, and now Caroline must admit that she was twice as good as herself.

"My dear sister," Caroline said. "I am also happy to see you here."

Jane smiled with ever-increasing openness. "Thank you. I am happy to be here."

Caroline then turned to Jane's sister Elizabeth, who was eyeing her with only suspicion and no openness at all. Caroline squinted at her, believing in her mien a certain level of suppressed anger. Possibly there was also a hint of superiority.

Caroline forced the smile to remain upon her lips, intent upon paying Miss Elizabeth Bennet every arrear at civility. "Mrs. Darcy, you are welcome too."

The woman only smiled and inclined her head.

Finally, Caroline looked to the gentleman who remained at her shoulder. "Mr. Darcy…" she began, and to her horror, she found that words failed her.

In the past, perhaps she would have uttered a caustic remark about the tedium of long journeys, but today, she could not think of a word to say.

Mr. Darcy bowed to her, looked away, and the moment was over.

The guests returned to their former positions, leaving Caroline in want of a chair.

She turned toward the fire, where she discovered Mr. Rushton lurking by the poker.

She looked to the pianoforte and considered seating herself upon the stool, but out of the corner of her eye, she saw Mr. Rushton gesture to the wooden chair beside him, clearly offering her a place.

She glared at him, unleashing upon him the venom she must conceal from others. What a blessing to have him here, for she could be just as rude to him as she liked. Yes, she would take the seat he offered.

Mr. Rushton had the audacity to smile as she approached, prompting her to say sotto voce, "Mr. Rushton, I did not realize you were to be a part of our family party."

"I might remind you that this is my house," he returned softly, "but I am certain you recall that already."

She glowered happily. She knew very well why he had installed himself in the chamber. He had come with the dual purposes of eating the food intended for their guests and of gathering information, for he must suspect that an explanation for her sudden arrival in Kendal would lie with her former traveling party.

"Yes," Mrs. Newton said, having not heard Mr. Rushton's reply. "We quite fancy Mr. Rushton a part of our family, and Mrs. Pickersgill as well, though she has been called away abruptly this afternoon. You will meet her soon, I am certain, for she is a dear friend of Caroline's."

Then she turned to her daughter and said, "My dear Caroline, do attempt to convince your brother to stay here in Mr. Rushton's home, for he has already issued the invitation." Caroline glared again at Mr. Rushton as her mother continued. "But Charles says they are to stay at a hotel. A hotel!"

Relief flooded Caroline. They would not stay at Grosvenor Street. Thank heaven. She did not think she could bear any further discomfort, but for her mother's benefit, she must attempt to persuade them.

"Mama," Charles protested, "it is a fine hotel: Grillon's."

"Well, it sounds very…French." Mrs. Newton turned to her daughter and said, "Caroline, convince him to stay here."

Caroline restrained a sigh. "Yes, Charles, do stay here if you possibly can and eat just as much of Mr. Rushton's food as you like." She glanced about the room to find everyone looking at her rather oddly. She must get control of her tongue and her emotions, for she was quite making herself appear the fool. "Mama has the greatest desire to acquaint herself with my new sister."

Caroline smiled at Jane, whose face brightened at the prospect of deepening her relationship with her new maternal figure.

"Indeed, I must become acquainted with my new daughter," Mrs. Newton said. "And Mr. and Mrs. Darcy as well, you must stay, for you are family too, are you not? I understand from Caroline that the two of you are sisters."

It was Mrs. Darcy who responded, saying, "Yes, Jane and I are indeed sisters, both in family lineage and in heart. So I suppose…" She looked at Caroline with a rather grim set to her mouth. "We are family."

"Then you must stay here so that we may all get to know one another, and I may as well begin now." She smiled broadly. "Jane, my dear, I do believe you have already brought goodness to my son's life."

"Oh, Mrs. Newton," Jane said as a blush graced her classical features, "it is kind of you to say, but quite unnecessary."

"Unnecessary? I think not. Only look at my Charles. He has quite come into his own since your marriage, I must say."

"I could not possibly claim credit for such a change," Jane demurred.

"I am as I always have been, Mama," Charles said, though he appeared a bit proud of himself.

"No, no, I sense a new confidence in you, Charles. Do not you agree, Caroline?"

She looked at her brother. In truth, she agreed wholeheartedly with the assessment, though he was exercising his new bravado in a most inappropriate way. Let him order about his servants, not his sister.

Caroline did not see, however, that such an admission in this company could do her any justice, so she said, "I sense in him only that he is a bit more thick-headed than usual."

"Oh, Caro!" Her mother laughed, and the rest of the room followed suit, albeit uneasily. "Do not tease your brother so. You must admit that he has chosen his wife wisely. He has not, like so many gentlemen these days, chosen his bride based on frivolity or greed. He has chosen from his heart, and that, I find, is the best way."

"I have indeed," Charles said, causing Jane to blush.

"And these are the things we must discuss," Mrs. Newton cried, "and why you must stay here."

"Mama," Charles said with great patience. "I believe we will all be more at ease if we stay at the hotel as planned." He turned to Mr. Rushton and said, "We will be pleased to accept your invitation to dine with you on Wednesday evening, however."

Wednesday evening?

That was a mere two days hence!

That gave her little time to....

To what?

What course of action was open to her now?

While Caroline was attempting to conceive a sensible reply, she was conscious of Mr. Rushton's movements on the periphery.

Caroline could think of nothing worse than to have to dine in company on Wednesday, for now she had no choice but to relent to her brother's desires. Her plans had all failed, and she may as well concede defeat. She was staring at the floor as if it might provide a polite response when a booted foot emerged in her field of vision. Then, a teacup appeared before her.

Reflexively, she took it and then looked to see who had carried it.

The hand was Mr. Rushton's.

Had he come to torment her from a closer distance?

No, his expression, instead of holding mockery, seemed to convey a sort of strength.

She decided she must have wished the expression onto his face out of her need for support, and so she sneered and attempted to return the cup and saucer to him. "I thank you, but I find that I am not thirsty."

He returned her sneer but did not retrieve the teacup, and he said quietly, "Take it anyway. Perhaps it will warm that chilly soul of yours."

Before Caroline could issue the appropriate response, her mother called, "What are you two talking of over there?"

Caroline rolled her eyes, but Mr. Rushton looked at her mother with a pleasant expression. "Why, we were merely discussing how warmth and comfort may often come from an unexpected source."

ළ ල

Caroline would never admit to experiencing comfort from Mr. Rushton, and she certainly received no reprieve from her own brother when he cornered her in the drawing room alone when the others had been preparing to see their guests to the carriage.

Charles approached her with caution, his questioning eyes immediately meeting hers as he glanced at the open door behind him.

She knew what he was about, but she would not aid him in his quest. She only sat silently and watched him pace the room.

Finally, he said, "Time has passed."

"Yes," she agreed. "Time has a way of doing just that."

He sighed in exasperation. "Time offers the chance of reflection."

Caroline must not seem to give in to him so easily, so she deliberately chose to misunderstand him. "Are you saying that, upon your own reflection, you see how wrong you were to insist on my guilt and removal? That you understand now how you have overreacted by insisting on having your will done?"

Charles turned around, eyes wide, saying, "What? No. I mean only...that...perhaps you had altered your opinion."

She remained seated like a queen on her throne, all the while feeling like a pauper in the gutter, and looked at Charles with feigned superiority. "My opinion remains unchanged, and as long as it remains thus, I shall never apologize," she bluffed.

He appeared surprised. "That certainly makes our visit here awkward." He paced a few steps. "Dash it, Caroline, this will be dismal if you do not relent."

"Well, that is your own fault. I did not ask you to bring the Darcys here, and as you cannot remove me from another gentleman's house, you shall have to suffer the consequences of your own choice."

Charles let out an exasperated sigh. "I had assumed you had seen reason."

"Reason?" Caroline asked a bit too loudly. "There is nothing reasonable about apologizing to someone whom I have not wronged!"

Indeed, Caroline would admit to having wronged Miss Jane Bennet egregiously, but Miss Elizabeth Bennet was another matter entirely. Here, Caroline was still in the right.

"Then I must appeal to your desire to restore family harmony if reason will not tempt you."

"I am not the person responsible for having destroyed family harmony; therefore, I cannot restore it through any action."

Charles shook his head. "That is utter nonsense, Caroline, as you are well aware."

"I am not aware of any such thing."

Tension lanced the air as brother and sister stared at each other.

Charles turned away, and when he spoke again, it was in a soft voice. "Caroline, be logical. Do you not want to retain your invitation to Pemberley?"

"You know I do," she whispered.

"And do you not want to continue traveling with your sister and me?"

"Nothing would provide greater pleasure."

"Then, can you not forget your pride and do what I ask, for my own sake if not for yours?"

"I do not know," she answered honestly.

Charles stood before her, his eyes holding a mixture of pity and indignation, and said, "I know how difficult this must be, Caroline, but it is difficult for me as well. And that is precisely why I must demand that you make your amends before our dinner Wednesday evening, or we will leave London, and your opportunity will have disappeared along with us."

Charles turned to leave the room, and out of desperation, Caroline leapt from her seat.

"Charles…please…wait," she pleaded, but his steps did not hesitate. He walked resolutely from the drawing room and toward the front door where the coach was already waiting.

Caroline yearned to follow her brother, to stop him from handing down such an ultimatum, but she knew it would do little good. His back was stiff and straight with determination as he bid their mother farewell. She would not convince him now.

In the entry hall, Caroline hesitated. Politeness required her to join Mr. and Mrs. Newton on the stairs of Mr. Rushton's house to bid adieu to her brother and his party, but she simply could not do it. Instead, upon exiting the drawing room, she turned in the opposite direction and fled upstairs to her bedchamber.

Finally, shutting the door solidly behind her, Caroline threw herself onto the bed and buried her face in the linens. She had expected to burst into tears the moment she gained some privacy, but she could not cry.

Her emotions had endured such wild changes that her body seemed no longer able to react properly. She had passed so quickly from anger to horror to sorrow and back again that she seemed to have run through all her reserves, leaving her completely and utterly numb.

As she lay with her face hidden against the soft bed coverings, she tried to take stock of her situation. Lavinia despised her, and Mr. Charlton would certainly not propose marriage now. Her brother had arrived and demanded her final decision regarding her apology to Miss Elizabeth Bennet. Her mother seemed suspicious, Rosemary was absent, and Mr. Rushton seemed to be enjoying her circumstances entirely too much.

After enduring the day's events, Caroline felt as if she really ought to be suffering from nervous complaints and demanding smelling salts, but she felt nothing. In the space of one day, the entire world had crashed around her, and yet she was a void. Her only concern now was to think of what must be done in order to extricate herself from the rubble and debris.

But what could be done to remove herself from the wreckage of her own life?

She knew very well that nothing could be done.

Lavinia would never allow her into Mr. Charlton's sphere again. Caroline had not the least hope of becoming the wife of a baron, thereby raising herself out of the mire of trade and into the glory of polite society by her own actions.

She must again depend on others.

She turned her head and sighed. She was glad that Rosemary was not at home, for this was just the sort of time when the woman would appear and moralize over the situation. She would gloat about having accurately assessed Lavinia's motives in taking her brother to London, and she would remind Caroline that her current circumstances were entirely of her own making.

She did not need to be reminded of these truths, for she was all too aware of them as it was.

Now, the prospect of returning to Kendal loomed before her. Once the Fairmont Bridge was comfortably in progress and their sojourn in London ended, her exile in the north would continue indefinitely.

But upon her return, her situation would be altered. Lavinia would ensure that she was no longer welcomed into good society there, and Caroline would be forced to explain matters to her mother, which she could not bear.

She could not admit her failures—either of action or of character—to her mother. She would not. She did not want to see the shame and sorrow in her mother's eyes when she discovered that Caroline had been the cause of the split between all her children. She, who saw no real value in associating with the wealthy and titled, would look upon her daughter with new eyes. She would see Caroline for who she was.

Yes, Caroline could admit it. She always wanted to be seen as better than she was.

It was a failing indeed.

This was too much. Truly, Caroline ought to be shaking or crying or screaming.

But she was just lying on the bed. Her body had given up, and now her mind was beginning to yield as well.

She may as well face the painful truth of her circumstances and concede defeat. It was time for her to surrender. Her desires in the matter were irrelevant. Whether or not she believed in her own guilt, she must now capitulate. She had no choice.

Tomorrow, she must make amends with Miss Elizabeth Bennet.

Twenty-one

Caroline repeated this truth to herself as she fell into a fitful sleep, and when she awoke, they were the first words that entered her mind.

Today, she must make amends with Miss Elizabeth Bennet.

Yes, it had to be done.

Caroline sat up slowly, feeling unbalanced, and attempted to orient herself. She had dozed off precisely where she had thrown herself the night before and had not bothered either to position herself correctly on the bed or pull back the linens. She lay exactly as she had fallen.

She managed to stand and look about her. The curtains had not been drawn, and light streamed into the room. It was later than she had expected, probably well after noon.

Caroline sighed and turned from the window only to be faced with her own reflection in the mirror. Her hair, which she had not bothered to take down or brush, resembled a bird's nest, and wrinkles marred the fabric of her dress.

She ran her hands down the front of her skirt, but her efforts were to no avail. She shook her head, ashamed at herself for having fallen asleep in the clothing she had worn the night before.

What was becoming of her?

Caroline supposed that this is what happened to women once they reached such a hopeless state. They simply fell apart.

Well, she may have no hope of rising in society or of ever attaining any control over her own life and fortune, but she would go into her hopelessness with as much pride as possible.

She would go to Grillon's and be done with her apology, but she would do so looking like a queen.

Caroline rang the bell, first for nourishment and then again for assistance in her preparations for the day.

As the maid arranged her hair, she sat listlessly at her dressing table and attempted to compose her speech to Miss Elizabeth Bennet, but the words simply would not arrange themselves.

What could she say?

Yes, I attempted to separate your sister from my brother, but they are now married and I must accept her as one of my family. That at least was the truth.

Yes, I disliked you, but it is all over now. That was less true.

Yes, I wanted your husband and his home for myself. That was true, but far too humiliating to admit.

Caroline sighed aloud and realized that the maid had completed her coiffure and left the room while she had been engaged in her own thoughts.

Well, she may not know how precisely she would issue the apology, but she may as well go and be done with it.

She stood, opened her bedchamber door, and crept down the hall. She felt quite foolish creeping about during the daytime hours, but she greatly hoped to sneak out of the house and complete her errand with no one, especially her mother, the wiser.

Caroline met no one in the hall or on the stairs, and she had the front door within her sights. She must only walk a few more paces to be out of Mr. Rushton's home and into the anonymity of London's streets.

"Miss Bingley," a male voice said.

Curse it! She had been caught.

Thoroughly embarrassed, Caroline turned slowly to discover Mr. Rushton's butler standing at the foot of the stairs regarding her with scarcely concealed curiosity.

"Yes?" she demanded in her haughtiest tone. "What is it?"

"A letter, miss," he responded.

"Well, bring it to me."

He crossed the room and handed her the letter. Caroline did not thank him, but simply snatched the folded paper from the silver tray he held and disappeared into the sitting room, shutting the door behind her.

Out of habit, Caroline crossed to stand beside the escritoire as she stared at the unfamiliar handwriting and wondered who could have possibly written. The lettering was bold and neat, but she could not place it. She tore open the seal and began to read.

My dear Caroline,

Long hours did I await you in the ruins that night at Vauxhall. Did you become lost? Or did you meet another gentleman instead?

It matters not, for nothing could prevent me from composing this letter to you, my darling, not even my sister's ire. I refuse to concede to her wishes, for my desire for you overwhelms me and I cannot restrain myself from speaking. Will you marry me, my dear, and run Oak Park?

If you wish to make me the happiest of gentlemen and answer in the affirmative, then you must come away with me immediately. Meet me at dusk where first we encountered each other in London

All my affection,
William Charlton

Caroline plunked down onto the wooden chair beside the writing desk. Her breath was coming short and quick, and for a moment she thought she might swoon.

Laughter bubbled within her, and though Caroline covered her lips with her hand, a giggle escaped.

Mr. Charlton had proposed!

Last night, Caroline had lost all hope, and suddenly, with the dawning of a new day—or at least with the noontime sun—her dreams and schemes had come to fruition.

Here was her salvation, and it came at the last possible moment. No longer would she be required to apologize to Miss Elizabeth Bennet in order to rise in society. She could ascend on her own and under her own power.

Caroline sat for a moment, basking in this sudden turn of events.

Of course, there was the question of Charles. He would be angry at her disappearance, but eventually, he would relent and welcome her again into his company. And if he did not, she would at least gain her own place in society.

Caroline smiled at her next thought: she would have the additional benefit of evicting Lavinia from Oak Park.

The laughter suddenly died on her lips.

If she married Mr. Charlton, she would have all these things, but at what cost?

Her husband would be unfaithful always.

Proper society would look away, but could Caroline?

And she would run Oak Park, but Mr. Rushton had hinted that he gambled as well. Was she capable of risking her only power, her money?

But finally, she would have a home of her own.

She would always have her own place.

She did not know how long she sat at the writing desk contemplating her situation before she heard the door to the sitting room open.

Caroline glanced over her shoulder at the new arrival.

Rosemary Pickersgill.

If she were to succeed in sneaking away to Mr. Charlton, Caroline must not allow Rosemary to discover the proposal. She turned her back to her companion, intent on concealing the letter as quickly as possible.

"Mrs. Pickersgill," she said as she folded the paper with silent fingers and then slid it under the desk blotter. "I have not seen you since yesterday. Wherever have you been?"

"That is a fine greeting, Miss Bingley, but there is nothing you may say to me today to ruin my spirits."

"Oh?" Caroline asked as she thought of the marriage proposal hidden beneath the blotter. That might shake Rosemary's joy, but Caroline would not speak a word of it.

She turned to face her companion more fully. Yes, she did appear nearly overcome with joy. Her eyes fairly shone with vigor, and she seemed years younger somehow.

"Tell me," Caroline encouraged as she moved to join Rosemary on the sofa, "what has brought you such joy."

"I have just had a most successful meeting with my solicitor."

Caroline could not conceal her shock. "Your solicitor?" She laughed. "Why would you have need of a solicitor?"

Rosemary did not seem at all affronted by Caroline's mocking laughter. She only said, "You recall, Miss Bingley, that I once told you I would share my secrets at the proper moment."

Caroline nodded slowly, unsure whether to continue laughing or give way to the feeling of unease that rose within her.

"This is the proper moment, for Lady Middlebury has spread the news of my arrival and my name will soon be gracing the gossip columns, I fear."

"Tell me then, Mrs. Pickersgill," Caroline said, still unable to believe that anything this woman might say would be worthy of such anticipation.

"I do not mean to shock you, Miss Bingley, but I fear we have not been properly introduced."

"Have we not?"

"No, for before you, you see Rosemary Pickersgill, paid companion and thorn in your side. But not so long ago I was Lady Braye, wife of Mr. John Pickersgill or Baron Braye."

Caroline's eyebrows dropped in confusion. "I do not comprehend..." Her voice trailed off as she stared at Rosemary. Sitting before her, apparently, was the Dowager Lady Braye. She ought to be tucked away in a secure country estate and consuming chocolates, but she was here in London acting as a mere servant. "You? The wife of a baron?"

Caroline meant the question as an insult, but somehow it fell flat.

"Indeed, Miss Bingley, close your mouth. Do not appear so shocked."

"But..."

"How did I come to be your companion?"

Caroline nodded.

"My husband John died two summers ago." A shadow passed over Rosemary's features. "I was devastated, for I truly loved him. He was the kindest and best of men, and he also loved me. You see, Miss Bingley, he married me, the daughter of a country gentleman without a great dowry, land, or any relations of consequence.

"As you might imagine, I was thrown into an utterly new society when I came with him to London those first years, and John was generous both with my inheritance and my allowance. I admit to having indulged more than I ought to have. I had the finest gowns and attended the grandest balls. I had attained the pinnacle of social delights and I reveled in it. Until John died."

"But your inheritance?" Caroline demanded. "What of that?"

"Patience, Miss Bingley." She paused to clear her throat. "We had no children and thus no heirs upon whom to bestow the title after John died, so the barony passed to his brother James. At first, James invited me to remain in his household and was generous with my treatment, but I fear his wife had no wish to share her home with a dowager, and so she used her influence to remove me, inch by inch, from her sphere." Rosemary shook her head sadly. "I feel rather foolish. I trusted them and did not realize what was occurring until I had lost everything."

Caroline could hardly think how to react, and her mind seemed stuck on Rosemary's true identity. It made no sense. How could this woman be the Dowager Lady Braye? How had she lost her fortune and come to this place? And how could Caroline have not recognized a lady of quality in her own household?

Rosemary continued, "James, the new Lord Braye, became quite intoxicated by his power and position—an easy transformation, I can assure you—and his wife preyed upon this weakness. She convinced him that I was a drain on their household and, in fact, that I had extorted John into marriage in order to gain his fortune. Then, through some legal machinations and deceit, I was out."

"Out?" Caroline repeated.

"Yes, all that was rightfully mine was removed, and I was quite alone and poor. Rumor circulated through London that I had been declared a fortune hunter, and as such, I had been legally disinherited. It was quite a scandal."

"But surely you had friends or relations who would come to your aid, despite the lies?" Caroline demanded.

Rosemary's face softened and then transformed into regret. "I did, but after a time, I began to recognize that my dependency on them could not last, and that was when Charles mentioned his need to find a companion for you."

"Charles knowingly sent the widow of a baron to be my paid companion?" Caroline could hardly believe her brother would be so foolhardy.

"He thought it would appeal to you to have a former baroness in your entourage." Rosemary offered a hesitant smile. "And I needed employment. Truly, I had no other option. John's family would have no part of me, and it was not in my nature to rely forever on my friends."

"And why tell me this now?" Caroline asked. "Has something altered?"

"Do you recall the tears I shed that evening you entered my chamber at Newton House?"

Caroline nodded.

"I had recently received a letter disclosing all the rumors that had been circulating about me in Town. I was a fortune hunter and extortionist, and my marriage was a fraud. This news quite broke my heart, for John and I loved one another. I did not want my marriage to be so abused."

"And so you hired a solicitor?"

"Yes." Rosemary looked at her directly. "Thanks to you, Miss Bingley."

Confused, Caroline only stared at her.

"Watching you fight these past months to attain your own goals—no matter the cost to you—has inspired me to fight for mine," Rosemary explained. "I have returned to my solicitor and am attempting to reverse the decision against me. Their charge against me—that I coerced John into marriage in order to gain his fortune—is unfounded. Such an accusation only has legal merits if the gentleman in question is a youth. There is no legal precedent for me to be disinherited for that reason."

"And you expect to win?"

"Indeed I do."

Suddenly, matters became very clear to Caroline. Rosemary had always displayed a comprehension of manners and etiquette beyond the station she was presumed to hold. She had also shown a great deal of dignity in her bearing.

Though Caroline had not been able to see it until now, Rosemary had always shown herself to be a lady of class and distinction.

The truth was that everyone else—her mother, the occupants of Oak Park, and even Mr. Rushton—seemed to have suspected something of Rosemary's history based on her comportment alone.

Only Caroline had remained oblivious. She felt like an utter fool. She had mocked, insulted, and tortured this woman, who ought to be inflicting the same kind of pain upon women of Caroline's class.

Why had Rosemary allowed it? Why had she concealed her identity?

"I see the questions in your eyes, Miss Bingley. You feel I betrayed you by not sharing my past, but I did not. I am no longer of the titled class, and so my status could have no bearing upon you." Caroline was about to protest when Rosemary continued. "Besides, you shared nothing of your own past with me."

Caroline was silent.

"Mr. Bingley summarized your actions and his reasons for sending you away, and I admit that I quite agreed with his decision. I had once been in Mrs. Bingley's position, after all, and as such, I had no great fondness for you."

"I do not see how this conversation is helpful," Caroline said.

"Do you not? Well, allow me to continue." Rosemary's tone was airy and light, but her next words were harsh. "Though you have done little to endear yourself to me, I believe I have been enough in your company to see that Mr. Bingley has overreacted. He has overlooked two crucial aspects of your character: fear and misunderstanding."

Embarrassed and angry at Rosemary's words, Caroline snapped, "You take upon yourself too much power, Mrs. Pickersgill, for you are still in my family's employ and thus dependent on me, no matter who you used to be."

"That is not precisely true, as I shall later explain, but allow me to finish my speech, for this is something you ought to hear." Rosemary did not await Caroline's permission. "You fear that one day you will be in my situation. You will be exposed as the daughter of a tradesman and a social climber, and you will do anything if you believe it will ensure your safety, including the pursuit of men who would never truly show you love. But the worst of it is, Miss Bingley, that you misunderstand the ways of the world."

"Indeed I do not!"

"You believe that a marriage to a man of fortune or title will ensure your entire future happiness, but as you see in the example before you, that is not necessarily the case!"

Upon this pronouncement, Rosemary seemed quite content to leave Caroline to her contemplation. In fact, Caroline was so lost in her own thoughts that she hardly recognized the moment when her companion left the room.

Could this be true? Had Caroline been searching for her future happiness and security in vain? Would a marriage to Mr. Charlton prove so fruitless?

ঔ৩ Twenty-two ৩ঔ

No, Caroline thought, she could not be so utterly incorrect!

All her experiences told her that money, title, and land were her best opportunities at protection and status. It was the way of society, and society could not be argued with, could it?

No indeed, it could not.

She leapt from the writing desk, determined to find Rosemary and demand further explanation of her meaning when she chanced to look out the window and notice that dusk had already begun to fall.

Dusk!

How could she possibly have remained so long in the sitting room? She had not even had the opportunity to pack a trunk for her elopement, and yet the time was upon her to meet Mr. Charlton. She must be at Berkeley Square even now.

Briefly, she considered dashing upstairs and throwing some necessities into a small bag, but she decided against it.

Impractical, unwise, foolish: they described her decision with accuracy, but time had quite run out.

She must forget all practical questions and act. No bag, no note, no goodbyes. She must leave before someone caught her and attempted to talk her out of the decision.

Besides, Mr. Charlton was wealthy and would purchase any article she required. Yes, all would be well once she met with him.

Caroline had left Mr. Rushton's house before she remembered the proposal letter, which was still hidden under the blotter.

Well, no matter. By the time anyone discovered it, she would be safely wed to her baron.

No one—not Charles, Mr. Darcy, Miss Elizabeth Bennet, and certainly not Rosemary Pickersgill and her cautionary tale—would be able to stop Caroline from finally removing from herself the stench of trade and freeing herself from following the whims of others. She would be Lady Charlton, and as such, she could do just as she pleased.

Lady Charlton. Caroline repeated the name as she traversed the streets toward Berkeley Square in the day's waning light.

As she walked with determined steps onto Davies Street, Caroline contemplated her first acts as Lady Charlton.

She would announce the marriage to her brother, officially removing herself and her fortune from his control. No longer would Charles be able to insist she take any action against her will.

Though Caroline would do her best to repair matters with Jane, who was now family, she would have no need to make amends with Miss Elizabeth Bennet, for Pemberley would no longer mean a thing to her. She would have her home and her fortune at Oak Park, and she would never again have to rely on Mr. Darcy to bring her into society. She would be a baron's wife!

And Caroline would delight in throwing Lavinia out of Oak Park on her ear. She laughed aloud and then sobered.

Lavinia.

And her son. The next in line for the barony.

The woman despised her. What would happen to Caroline if Mr. Charlton were to die before an heir could be produced?

Lavinia's son would become the baron, and Lavinia herself would certainly have no pity on Caroline.

Would Lavinia, like Rosemary's relations, remove and disinherit Caroline?

Would she marry a baron only to end a paid companion?

Caroline's steps slowed as she neared Berkeley Square.

What if she had misunderstood Mr. Charlton as she had Lavinia and Rosemary?

She must know the truth.

With renewed purpose, Caroline completed her trek to the square and spotted Mr. Charlton leaning against the rail precisely where she had first seen him.

Only this time, he saw her when she first approached.

"Miss Bingley," he whispered. "You are here."

"Yes," she agreed. "I am here."

"Come," he said, as he attempted to lead her along the rail. "My carriage waits for us at the street." He glanced at her, confused. "Have you a bag?"

"Wait," Caroline said. She refused to take another step though he pulled at her arm.

"We ought to be away, for my sister may discover my absence."

"Yes, we ought to discuss your sister," she said as she extracted herself from his grasp.

"I wish you would not think of her!"

"She despises me and would object to this union if she knew of it."

He sighed. "Yes."

"And yet you still wish to marry me." She narrowed her eyes at him. "And because you have always spoken so very plainly about your inheritance and even your faults, you must also speak plainly now. Tell me why."

He hesitated, looked at the ground beneath his feet, and said, "Because I love you."

Caroline laughed and Mr. Charlton's head snapped up.

"That is not the truth, is it?" she demanded. "Before I step foot into your carriage, Mr. Charlton, I demand to know your motives. Do you seek revenge on your sister?"

"No," he said quickly and then added, "Yes. Well, somewhat."

"Explain."

He exhaled and then his words came: "You know how much I hate this barony nonsense. I am terrible at managing my own finances much less those of an entire estate or country! I have lost quite a bit of money already, and I cannot allow Lavinia or my father to learn of my folly. I must pay my debts quickly and quietly, and then I must find someone to keep Oak Park from falling into shambles."

Caroline sighed. So it was her fortune that attracted him. Only a few weeks ago, that fact would not have seemed half as reprehensible to Caroline as it did now.

She would marry him, and in the process lose her money and the only small shreds of power she had.

"It is a good plan, is it not?" Mr. Charlton asked, his voice shockingly logical. "You will have Oak Park and a title, and I shall wipe the slate clean and remove my sister from her place in the household. You shall manage the house and keep me from complete ruination. It could not be more agreeable to either of us."

Caroline eyed him. "And if you were to die, I would be left with nothing. No money, and Lavinia would throw me out and install her son in Oak Park as baron."

He looked at his boot. "It would not happen that way."

"How can you be certain?" she asked.

He seemed to have no answer.

Caroline sighed, and, suddenly tired of the nonsense, she spoke with utter candor and no rancor at all. "You are wrong, Mr. Charlton, for I object to the very idea. I fear you will have to marry someone else in order to accomplish all you desire. Though I harbor you no ill will, for only recently I would have believed this the ideal solution for both of us, I cannot marry you."

The couple looked at each other for long moments, assessing.

"I am sorry to hear that, Miss Bingley." He sighed too. "Now I must find another wealthy young woman with whom to elope in order to save my family."

"I wish you luck, Mr. Charlton, and you must do the same for me, for I must now lower myself by apologizing for a crime I did not commit and thus save my own family."

৵৽ Twenty-three ৽৵

Grillon's Hotel stood only two streets over from Berkeley Square, and Caroline resolved to walk the distance as quickly as possible before reality intruded upon her and she realized what she had done and what she must do.

The hotel was large and grand, but beyond its size and scale, Caroline hardly noticed it. She simply forced herself up the stairs and into the building, past the plush rugs and wall hangings to the first liveried servant she saw.

"Mrs. Darcy," she demanded. "I must speak with her immediately."

The servant did not appear shocked by her rudeness but only said, "She is in a private sitting room, miss. Do follow me."

Too soon Caroline was announced and ushered into the presence of the lady herself.

There, reclining on a sofa, was Mrs. Darcy. Charles, Jane, and Mr. Darcy were nowhere to be seen.

Elizabeth stood abruptly, and Caroline thought she saw her wince ever so slightly at discovering the identity of her guest. Then she recovered herself enough to say, "Miss Bingley, you must be in search of your brother. He is above stairs, I believe."

Caroline hesitated only a moment in the doorway before steeling herself to do what she must do.

"No, I come in search of you, my dear Mrs. Darcy," she said as she walked farther into the room and heard the servant close the door behind her. Even to her own ears, her voice sounded contrived and awkward. "You are alone, I see."

Elizabeth returned to her seat and picked up the book she had been reading. Then she smiled. "Yes, Miss Bingley, as you see, you have caught me quite alone here."

Caroline advanced further. "You are reading."

"Yes," Elizabeth said with another rather smug smile. "Jane and I are reading this book of poems upon my sister Kitty's suggestion."

"Ah. How does your younger sister do?" Caroline asked, though she could not remember if Kitty was the moralizing Bennet sister or the giddy, silly sister.

"My sister is well, thank you, Miss Bingley, but I do not think you came here to speak of my relations."

"No," Caroline agreed. There was a long pause as she mustered her waning resolve. Finally, after two aborted attempts, Caroline managed to say, "I find I owe...."

There, she had begun the apology, but it died suddenly on her lips.

Caroline had been quite determined to get the apology done with, but now, she was experiencing a nagging feeling of her own conscience. An apology would remedy all her problems, save one: she could not live with herself if she made it.

She simply could not do it.

Caroline could not apologize for something any woman—and indeed Miss Elizabeth Bennet herself—might have undertaken in her situation.

"Oh, I simply cannot do it." Caroline sat down across from Elizabeth. "I must speak frankly, Mrs. Darcy."

Mrs. Darcy raised a suspicious eyebrow. "Must you?"

Caroline continued with all honesty. "My brother is quite anxious that I conceive a way of making amends with you. He has suggested an apology, but I find it a pointless endeavor."

Elizabeth appeared amused, and her eyes brightened as if she had heard a diverting joke. "Do you?"

Caroline felt Elizabeth's amusement as if someone had boxed her ears. She did not appreciate her obvious display of pleasure, but she forced herself to continue. "You cannot be unaware of the reasons for my actions all those months ago regarding your sister and my brother."

Elizabeth nodded. "I believe I have a full understanding of what transpired."

"And you also must know that your husband was the chief instigator in separating them."

Again, she agreed. "Mr. Darcy has confessed as much and asked forgiveness."

Caroline leaned forward, desperate for Elizabeth to comprehend her. "But as a devoted sister yourself, you must understand why I cannot make apologies as Mr. Darcy has."

Elizabeth's amusement did not seem to wane at all as she laughed a bit and said, "I have always believed that one might make an apology whenever one has committed a wrong."

"And that is precisely why you will understand my refusal to apologize." She looked Elizabeth full in the eye. "I have done nothing wrong."

Annoyance briefly crossed Elizabeth's features before amusement seemed to claim the victory. "Have you not?" she asked, smirking.

"Consider, Mrs. Darcy," Caroline said with all seriousness, "your own actions regarding your sister Miss Lydia."

Elizabeth's amused expression faded. "I caution you not to speak ill of her in my presence."

"My intention is quite the contrary, I assure you. Though I know not all the particulars of what transpired, one thing is perfectly clear to me: you believed your sister to be in danger, and you would have undertaken any action to save her."

Elizabeth studied her for a moment, her face completely devoid of emotion. "Miss Bingley, I do not comprehend what you expect this line of discussion to gain for you. I—"

"I only refer to this uncomfortable matter to remind you of your own sentiments for your family. You would have done all that was necessary to save Miss Lydia, and that is all I did. Only I did not fully realize my brother's love for your sister, and I am pleased for him now."

"You admit you were in the wrong?" Elizabeth asked, eyes wide.

Caroline hedged. "I admit that he loves her, and he has married her. Now my objections are at an end. She is my family now."

Elizabeth continued to look at her with a level gaze. Caroline returned it.

"I do not know how you view Mr. Wickham now that he and Lydia are married, but I hold your elder sister in highest regard. Truly, I do." And Caroline's words actually were true. She did like Jane.

Elizabeth watched her in silence as if deciding whether or not to argue some salient point.

But Caroline pressed onward. "That is but one half of the issues that must be addressed, for there are other impediments to our ever being friends, as you well know."

The ladies regarded each other carefully before Elizabeth said with all frankness, "Yes, you desired my husband for yourself."

Elizabeth's forthrightness startled Caroline, and she knew not how to respond.

After a moment's thought, she said just as bluntly, "In this circumstance, you cannot expect me to own such a thing aloud. No woman would."

More hesitation.

"No," Elizabeth agreed. "I suppose you are correct."

"And," Caroline said, "you are too astute not to realize that we shall never be friends, apology or not."

Elizabeth nodded slowly. "Such a thing would be well nigh impossible."

"And if I were to venture an apology," Caroline added, "you would not believe me."

"No, indeed," Elizabeth said. "If you were to make your apologies, you would certainly not mean it."

"No, indeed, I would not."

"Then we are at an impasse."

Caroline shook her head. "This, Mrs. Darcy, is my proposal. For the sake of family harmony, we may as well agree to become indifferent acquaintances."

Elizabeth appeared to consider her words and then said hesitantly, "It would be folly to attempt friendship."

Caroline nodded with vigor. "Indeed."

Elizabeth indulged in a few more moments of thought before saying, "I do not like to disappoint Mr. Bingley, for he is the best of men, and it would be so much easier on your brother and my sister if we appeared to have put aside our grievances."

"Yes, I do not like to disappoint my brother either, and as I said, I have already made amends with your sister."

The two women sat in mutual silent contemplation before Elizabeth finally said, "Then, Miss Bingley, for the sake of our families, I believe we have struck an agreement."

The tension Caroline had been carrying about her shoulders and neck suddenly dissipated. This unpleasant situation might actually resolve itself to everyone's satisfaction.

"Yes," Caroline said. "I will treat you with courtesy and respect."

"And I shall do the same."

"For the sake of harmony, we will tell Charles that all is well between us…"

"…but we will not push the endeavor to friendship," Elizabeth supplied.

"No, indeed."

Elizabeth smiled.

Caroline returned it.

There, the matter was settled.

Family harmony was restored.

~ Twenty-four ~

Caroline returned to Grosvenor Street while the household was at dinner, but she could not bring herself to join them. Instead, she meandered without definite purpose to the pianoforte in the drawing room and settled herself on the stool.

After leaving Grillon's, Caroline had spent the whole evening in contemplation, and now her mind felt sluggish. All her plans had been overturned and all her hopes dashed. She had lost two gentlemen—both Mr. Darcy and Mr. Charlton—and had come to see the painful truth of her friendship with Lavinia Winton.

In the past year, she had lost quite a great deal indeed.

But she had, at the very least, the comfort of having regained her family. She realized now, however, that she must resign herself to spinsterhood and to being without any control over her own future. Evidence showed that she was not the sort of woman with whom gentlemen fell in love, so she ought to face the prospect of never having a home of her own or of enjoying the benefits of her fortune on her own terms.

Why, she may as well return to her mother's home and live there for the rest of her days. She would at least enjoy observing Lavinia's daily horror at hearing whatever chit Mr. Charlton married addressed as Lady Charlton.

That would be some consolation.

Caroline could not say she felt either pain or pleasure at her future prospects. She felt precisely nothing. Perhaps she was still overwhelmed.

And that is why she went to the pianoforte. It seemed to calm her as her fingers stroked the keys. She was in the midst of a lovely, soft piece, and her mind felt peaceful and serene as a result, when she heard a voice behind her.

"Miss Bingley." The voice was warm, but still it startled her, and she craned her neck to see who had entered.

Mr. Rushton stood in the doorway, smiling as if he understood something secret about her. Slowly, he approached, his eyes focused on her.

Caroline managed to pull her hands from the keys and then sat on the stool completely immobile.

"Caroline," he said. His eyes suddenly seemed hooded and more intense than she had ever seen them appear.

She clasped her hands in her lap and forced herself to maintain eye contact.

"I…" he began, stopped, and surveyed her from head to foot.

Caroline stifled the urge to check herself for wrinkles or to straighten her hair. No, she would not allow him to disconcert her with his boldness. Instead, she crossed her arms over her chest and raked over his appearance with equal boldness.

"You are not dressed for dinner," Caroline said.

"No, I was out."

"Ah," she said, not knowing how else to respond.

"I was searching for you."

Caroline's eyebrows drew down in confusion, and there was a long pause as the two looked at each other.

"I found this…." Mr. Rushton's voice trailed into silence as he pulled a folded sheet of writing paper from his coat pocket. "Under the blotter."

"Oh," she said, "I had forgotten about that."

Caroline watched as he refolded the note and returned it to his pocket. Then he gestured toward the pianoforte.

"That was," he said, as he came ever closer, "the most unguarded moment I have ever witnessed."

Caroline looked into Mr. Rushton's face, and then she heard herself saying, "I do not take your meaning, sir."

"Of course, you do not take my meaning, for no one has ever complimented you on your honesty and vulnerability."

"Can vulnerability be an asset?" she whispered.

"Asset or not, no person is without it."

"Even you, Mr. Rushton?"

Here, Mr. Rushton came around the pianoforte and positioned himself beside Caroline's stool.

Out of sheer habit, she turned to face him fully. He hovered above her, and although he was not so close as to make it feasible, Caroline imagined that she could feel the heat of his skin and the stirring of his breath as he said, "Even me."

His expression was rife with meaning, but still, Caroline could not comprehend it.

An unfamiliar—and not altogether uncomfortable—sensation ripped through her body as the focus of his gaze lowered from her eyes to her lips.

She licked them, but she had not meant to do so.

Heat flooded her face, and, embarrassed at her reaction to a gentleman such as Mr. Rushton, whose family had been brought low, Caroline shot to her feet.

Too late, she realized that a standing position only brought her closer to him. Now she actually could feel the warmth of his skin and the stirring of his breath.

They stood still, their bodies close and their gazes locked together.

And with shocking suddenness, Caroline comprehended the absolute truth of her vulnerability as she faced the full level of her attraction for him for the first time.

Somehow, his proximity had done queer things to the dimensions of the chamber, for it seemed much smaller. Not only had it diminished in size, but it had also warmed considerably.

"But tell me, you have not eloped with Charlton, have you?"

"What?" Caroline stared at him. "Eloped?"

"Yes, eloped. Have you?"

"You ought to know that I would never consent to such a method of matrimony! Besides, there was not time for an elopement."

He shook his head as if attempting to understand her. "So you are not married?"

"No, indeed," Caroline said, her voice suddenly gone soft.

Mr. Rushton took a step closer, and all the noise from the busy street vanished into sheer silence.

"Come," he said, "you must admit that you do—or did—have designs on that gentleman."

Caroline would not deign to answer. She would not even look at him, for such a task seemed far too difficult in this small, warm, intimate room.

In response to her obstinate silence, Mr. Rushton lifted her chin with his forefinger. Their eyes met, and she knew that there was no concealment deep enough to obscure her true motives from him.

"Quite so," he said, with a shake of his head. "I have no need of your reply, for I see very plainly that my supposition is true. But Miss Bingley, you must see that Mr. Charlton is a man who is ruled by something other than sentiment. He has other motives."

Caroline sighed. "What does it matter? No gentleman would fall in love with me."

"No, my dear Miss Bingley, that is not the case. I am certain that some unlucky man will offer you his heart, and for his sake, I do hope that you will be generous with it."

"I am not generous, as you well know."

"Indeed, therefore it is fortunate that you are not the type of woman with whom such men fall in love. Your attempts at pretense and accomplishments are so very blatant. Your machinations so transparent. Most gentlemen would be put off by you and lured by a woman of more subtle arts."

She glared.

"I see you are more hurt that your machinations are so obvious than you are distressed that this gentleman will never love you. You do not love him."

Caroline blushed, but she did not demur. "No, I do not love him."

Mr. Rushton's hand was still on Caroline's chin, but she did not feel trapped. She felt strange, almost immobilized by his touch. "And you did not love Mr. Darcy either."

"No," she said, speaking the truth aloud—and perhaps truly realizing it—for the first time. "I did not love him."

Mr. Rushton was looking at her so intensely that she let her lashes flutter lower in an attempt to avoid his searching gaze.

"Caroline," he said. "Look at me."

She found she could not.

"If you will not look at me, then…" He paused and slipped his hand to the nape of her neck. "You must allow me to experiment…"

Caroline looked at him then.

His face had drawn very near to hers, and the unfamiliar sensation intensified.

Perhaps it was the intimacy of their location in that empty room that was affecting her good judgment, but she did not pull away or attempt to rebuke him verbally. No, she stood quietly and watched through lowered lashes as he came ever closer.

She felt his breath stir the loose hair at her temples as he said, "Be still, Caroline, and allow me to…"

He had not needed to say it. She could not move.

She felt his left hand come to rest on her hip.

When Mr. Rushton's lips brushed hers, a frisson of incomprehensible feeling skittered through her, and without realizing precisely what she was doing, her hands came to grasp at his coat.

He pulled away with the apparent intent to gauge her reaction—to discover the results of his experiment—but Caroline was in no humor to be studied or gauged.

She pulled back, and he let his hand slip down Caroline's arm, but he did not let her break their contact completely. "Caroline, you must marry me."

Had he not maintained a firm grip on her fingertips, Caroline would have retreated as far as was possible within the confines of the chamber.

"No," she said flatly.

"Do not be absurd, woman. You know very well that we are perfectly suited for each other."

She jerked her hand away from his grasp. "I know no such thing."

Tears had sprung to her eyes, but through sheer force of will, she did not allow them to fall. Truly, she had never experienced the level of emotion she had felt with Mr. Rushton, but she could not bear to fail to follow her father's wish that she—and all his children—marry people of status.

"I have understood you as I have understood no other woman, and, I believe, you comprehend me better than any woman of my acquaintance. We, neither of us, play at false modesty or hide our true motives."

"If you are aware of my true motives, you know that I will never marry you."

"No, I know no such thing, for if you would but allow yourself to be influenced by something other than your fear, then you may just find that your material concerns will be taken care of."

As he spoke, he had been approaching slowly, and now he was again upon her. Her calves were pressed against the stool, and she could not retreat further.

In truth, she did not want to.

She desperately wanted to allow her feelings to guide her, perhaps only this one time, so she abandoned herself to her sentiments.

When she kissed him, it was not tentative or experimental, but desperate and full of passion. The kiss encompassed her embarrassment at being rejected, her fear of being alone, her rage at society's strictures, and her despair at the knowledge that, no matter what, she must not marry beneath her intended status. Yet, the kiss was something more. It was rife with long-concealed anxiety and unattainable hope.

And it was the first moment of uncensored emotion she had ever experienced.

But it was not to last.

"Caroline!"

The word barely registered upon her first hearing it, and only upon its second pronunciation did Caroline tear herself away from Mr. Rushton.

In the open doorway stood her mother, staring at her with a completely incomprehensible expression.

Caroline could only watch as her mother closed the door with measured control.

"I would ask what you are about in the drawing room," Mrs. Newton said as she approached the couple. "But it is quite apparent."

"No!" Caroline fairly shouted in protest at the whole situation. Her cheeks were hot as a newly stoked fire, and she stepped forward, though not quite certain whether she ought to attack Mr. Rushton for putting her in this circumstance or object to her mother's catching them.

Mrs. Newton spoke to Mr. Rushton, who was standing close behind Caroline. "You do realize the predicament you are in, sir."

"I fear that I do." Caroline turned to glare at him as he ran a hand through his blond hair. "And yet it is worse than you know, Mrs. Newton."

Mrs. Newton turned to her daughter. "What have you done to him, Caroline?"

Caroline sputtered. "What have *I* done to him? Mama! How can you ask me such a question? I have done nothing. Nothing!"

Her mother smiled oddly, but said not a word.

Caroline continued, "Mr. Rushton has taken advantage of me. Your daughter!"

Mrs. Newton looked at Mr. Rushton. "Is that true? Have you taken advantage of my girl?"

"No indeed," he said with shocking frankness. "She has taken advantage of me."

Caroline gasped. "What?"

"But it is worse than that. I am in love with her."

"Oh good God!" Caroline said with a horrified glance at her mother's pleased expression. "This is not to be borne!"

Mrs. Newton looked between Mr. Rushton and Caroline, and her face transformed from pleased to exultant as a wide smile spread across her face.

"I comprehend very well," she said to Mr. Rushton. "My daughter will never admit to her true feelings, and based on the circumstances in which I found you, she certainly has them."

Mr. Rushton looked sidelong at Caroline and replied, "Yes. She has them."

"The two of you ought not to presume to tell me what I do and do not feel," Caroline said. She took a few steps toward her mother, hands outstretched. "I certainly experience no sympathetic emotions for this person."

"Poor Caroline," Mrs. Newton said, taking both her hands. "She has spent her whole life searching for home and she does not recognize it when it is standing before her."

"I do not understand," Caroline whispered.

"Then allow me to speak plainly. You are violently in love with Mr. Rushton."

"No," Caroline whispered. "I most certainly am not."

"But you realize, of course, Mrs. Newton, that it is hopeless," Mr. Rushton said in a tone of irritating practicality. "She will marry only a gentleman of large fortune, a title, or both. And as far as she knows, I have none of these attributes."

"You speak as if I would marry you, even with those enticements," Caroline spat.

"Ah, but you shall marry him, Caroline," Mrs. Newton said. Her face held the strangest combination of seriousness and glee.

"I shall not." Caroline's anger burned and she thought to walk out, but her mother's expression alone seemed to block her way. "Only I may decide what is for my own benefit, and I can say with utmost certainty that Mr. Rushton can have no worthwhile influence on my opinions."

"And that is precisely the problem," Mrs. Newton said. "You allow the wrong people to influence your opinions: Mr. Charlton, Lavinia, even to an extent your dear father. I have seen you work to please those who care not a fig for you and conceal your heart from those who love you."

Caroline had not realized the depth of her mother's understanding of what had transpired between herself and Lavinia and Mr. Charlton.

"Yes, I know everything. I surmised that something was amiss when Lavinia and Mr. Charlton left Kendal, and that alone persuaded me to take this trip to London. I knew you would find a way to Mr. Charlton, and this seemed the best method to ensure your safety while you saw for yourself what he is. But now, I have watched you suffer enough." Mrs. Newton held up a hand to prevent Caroline from protesting again. "I am afraid you have compromised yourself with Mr. Rushton, Caroline, and I shall not conceal that fact from anyone."

"Mama! You know very well that Mr. Rushton is at fault…." Caroline allowed her voice to trail into silence. Only to herself did Caroline acknowledge the lie. She could have forced Mr. Rushton to leave, but she had not wanted him to go.

Though Caroline had not spoken aloud, Mrs. Newton looked at her as if he could see into her heart and mind. It was so disturbing that Caroline was forced to avert her eyes. She was a wanton hussy, and everyone in the room—including her own mother—knew it.

Lord! Whatever had she been thinking to allow a gentleman to embrace her like that? Worse, she had craved it. She had thrown herself back at him.

Now, she must arrange matters so that she could escape unscathed.

She mustered all her strength and willed her voice to be forceful and authoritative. When she finally spoke, she was the Caroline of old, the Caroline of twenty minutes ago, before she had allowed Mr. Rushton's advances. She rose to her full height, and her voice was terrifying, even to her, when she said, "I shall not be forced into a marriage to *him*." She jerked her hand toward Mr. Rushton.

Here, Mrs. Newton approached and took Caroline's hand in her own. "What I am about to say, I say for your own benefit and because I love you."

Caroline could not fathom what might next spring from her mother's traitorous lips, and she was truly shocked to hear her words. "You are ruined, my dear girl. You have been glimpsed in an intimate posture with a gentleman in an empty chamber. Now, you must either face life as a ruined woman or marry the man with whom you committed the indiscretion."

⚬⚬ Twenty-five ⚬⚬

Caroline did not dare to speak at that precise moment, for her rage and embarrassment were burning too brightly within her. She had disappointed herself and her entire family in indulging in such an emotional display with Mr. Rushton, and now she was being maneuvered into a marriage to a gentleman of whom she could not approve.

Caroline had nothing left within her but a broken spirit and a heart of dashed hopes. It was time to admit the truth.

Gathering herself, Caroline spoke in a painfully modulated voice. "I admit to having failed to attain all I have attempted. It seems I have taken the wrong path at every turn, and the best I can say for myself is that I was only hoping to gain that which every other woman attempts to achieve."

Caroline looked to Mr. Rushton, realizing she may as well accede to the wishes of her heart, and said, "Please leave us, Mama."

There was a pause and then her mother smiled, causing Caroline to stare in disbelief.

"You must be aware, Caro, that my departure will only solidify your ruin."

"I understand, Mama. My decision is made."

Mrs. Newton smiled again and then grasped Mr. Rushton's hand as if welcoming him to the family. "Ten minutes," she said as she turned and left the chamber.

Caroline waited until she heard the door shut behind her mother and then she spoke. "Mr. Rushton, it appears I have no choice but to accept your proposal."

She turned to face him again, but found that she could not read his expression at all well. His next words surprised her.

"That is not precisely true, Miss Bingley," he said, but he stepped closer. "For those who are truly motivated, there is always a method of escape."

"Oh?" she asked with feigned innocence as she reached out tentatively to touch his sleeve. "And what method would you propose?"

"Your mother has concocted this scheme for your own benefit, and if you truly do not wish to accept my proposal, she will not speak ill of us, no matter how deeply we deserve it. Mrs. Newton hopes only to give you ample excuse for doing something that heretofore your pride would not allow."

How accurately he summarized her, except on one score.

"It is not solely pride that has been the root of my actions, Mr. Rushton. It is also fear, as you are well aware. Have you not told me as much on numerous occasions?"

"I confess I was not aware that you marked me."

"You may rest easy in your comprehension of me, for at first, I did not listen. I believed you to be utterly incorrect," Caroline admitted.

"And now?"

"Now, a fearsome prospect is before me," she said as she ran her hand up his coat sleeve to his shoulder. "I have entangled myself with a gentleman who is quite opposite of the husband my father envisioned for me and whom I imagined for myself. I will fail at raising my family's status."

"But you shall have all the benefits of my fortune, ill gained though it may be." He paused to wrap an arm around Caroline's waist. "And you will have love."

"Yes, and that, Mr. Rushton, is my greatest fear."

His eyebrows met in confusion. "I do not believe I comprehend you."

"I will be required to open myself to you, to become vulnerable to your searching gazes, to admit the abject failure of all my schemes. I do not know if I could bear such an admission."

"Your schemes have already failed. Your admission changes nothing."

"But worse, I must become a love-struck puppy. I must laugh at your every joke, hang upon your every word, and spend my days in thrall of your wit. I do not believe I could bear the lies. As you are aware, my life has been built upon them, and I find it quite tiresome to uphold them any longer."

Mr. Rushton smiled.

He comprehended her.

Yes, he understood.

"Caroline, you harpy, I know very well that your personality has no chance of improvement, and I fully expect you to pick and prod at me for all the days of my life."

"But it is too late for you, for you have already confessed your love, have you not?"

"I fear I have."

"And I must confess as well," she said with a sly smile. "I despise you." Caroline knew quite well that her face revealed the truth of her feelings. Her cheeks were rosy, and her eyes were moist with unshed tears. Here was a gentleman who understood her. A gentleman she truly loved.

His arms came around her waist, and when he spoke again his voice was soft. "I despise you too."

༄ Epilogue ༄

Caroline's return to Kendal led to the revelation of secrets she had not realized the sleepy little hamlet held.

Mr. Charlton, as it turned out, had indeed eloped, but his partner was Miss Brodrick, the daughter of a local pencil manufacturer. On a purely practical level, Caroline could not disapprove of his choice. Perhaps the sensible young lady could manage to rein in her new husband and prevent him from depleting his family's fortune.

On a more wicked level, the marriage had provided great joy to Caroline, who felt no compunction whatsoever at her pleasure over Lavinia's embarrassment. Yes, she could just imagine her former friend's expression when she discovered the truth of the matter: her brother had eloped with someone even lower on the social scale than Caroline Bingley!

And upon her brother's inheritance of the barony, Lavinia would be required to hear Miss Brodrick called Lady Charlton.

Caroline's amusement over Lavinia's condition was tempered, however, when she discovered the truth of her friend's situation.

Her husband, Mr. Ralph Winton, was not the genial, selfless gentleman who had sacrificed to allow his wife to return to Kendal to help during her family's time of crisis.

No, indeed.

Mr. Winton was happy to see her go.

Her absence gave him complete discretion in pursuing his own dissolution. He had already gambled away their fortune, given his mind in exchange for the dubious pleasures of whiskey, and traded his marriage vows for the comforts of a mistress.

Had Harold Charlton not had the courtesy to die of consumption when he had, Lavinia would have been required to return home in disgrace, as just another victim of a dissipated, purposeless man. As it was, she had been able to claim a nobler motive than merely escaping a wretched husband.

Mrs. Pickersgill was making successful strides in her legal battle with her husband's heirs and had left the matter entirely in the hands of her solicitor in order to return to Kendal for Caroline's wedding.

Days before the ceremony took place, she received a letter from her solicitor that indicated that documents were being drawn up to finalize the return of her jointure, including her monetary inheritance and her retention of her late husband's small town home, which he had always intended for her. She would be able to return to London in triumph due to her willingness to fight her own family.

A new understanding had built between Caroline and Rosemary, and their friendship was growing stronger as her former companion helped her prepare for her wedding to Mr. Rushton. For the first time in her life, Caroline knew what it was to have a true friend, one who was not interested in gaining anything from an association with her and from whom she did not hope to gain anything in return.

Caroline's agreement with Mrs. Darcy had pleased Charles greatly, and he promptly invited her to rejoin his traveling party, which was bound for Mr. Darcy's home in Derbyshire. Though pleased to return to her brother's good graces and to have retained her welcome at Pemberley, Caroline declined his invitation and instead requested his presence at her wedding, which was to take place upon their return to the north some weeks hence.

⁂

Upon the eve of Caroline's wedding, she received a letter borne by courier and carrying an unfamiliar seal.

She had almost chosen not to open it, believing it could contain nothing that needed to be read at such a moment, but upon Mr. and Mrs. Newton's prompting, she did so.

The seal belonged to a solicitor in London, and Caroline scanned the document from top to bottom. Her eyes landed upon Mr. Rushton's signature and beside it, her brother's. She looked to Mr. Newton for clarification.

"What is this?"

"Mr. Rushton and your brother completed the matter of your marriage settlement, I presume," he said with a broad smile.

Caroline sat down and read the document once and then again.

"The money Father left me." She looked at Mr. and Mrs. Newton with wide eyes. "He has allowed me control of it all, from the first moment of our marriage."

"Yes," Mr. Newton said. "Mr. Rushton spoke of it to me. I knew you would be pleased. Does she not seem pleased, my dear?" he asked his wife.

Mrs. Newton nodded. "I believe pleased and shocked." She turned to Caroline. "He is a good man."

Caroline looked away from her mother to regard the letter again. It made no sense. Who but a fool refused a fortune of 20,000 pounds? She greatly hoped that she was not engaged to a fool.

"But why?" Caroline asked.

Mrs. Newton smiled. "He has no need for it, dear. I think he wanted you to understand that his proposal was about something more than your fortune."

Caroline stared down at the letter.

Upon their nuptials, her fortune should, by all rights, become legally his. He should control it and, thereby, control Caroline as well.

And at that thought, Caroline understood him perfectly.

His wedding gift to her was the very thing around which all her striving had been centered. He was giving her lasting security by eschewing his legal right to her fortune.

No longer would she have to scramble up the social ladder, for even in the event of her husband's death—when most women, even Mrs. Pickersgill, were vulnerable to being left penniless and thus falling upon the mercy of relations or friends—Caroline would never find herself in that predicament. She was no longer slave to appearances or social whims or gossip. She depended on no one for her future security.

Caroline Bingley was finally her own mistress.

And that meant that she could finally give herself wholly to Mr. Rushton, the only gentleman she had ever loved.

❧ ❧

The barouche carried Mr. and Mrs. Patrick Rushton with inexorable swiftness toward Rushton House, and within its confines, its occupants sat rather stiffly for a bride and groom on their way home from their wedding breakfast.

Having not found an opportune moment to mention her inheritance all morning, Caroline now could not seem to find the words to express her feelings on the subject, or on any subject at all.

She found only the courage to make furtive glances at her husband, who, she must admit, looked handsome indeed in his fine black suit. She could not manage to meet his eyes, but looked at Mr. Rushton whenever she believed him to be focused elsewhere. When their gazes did chance to meet, she felt heat rise to her face and a flutter building in her chest.

Caroline blamed this odd behavior for the feeling of tension mounting within her.

She clasped her hands in her lap, willing them to remain still, but she jerked visibly when Mr. Rushton finally broke his silence, saying, "There is no need to conceal your anxiety, Caro, for I know very well that you must feel it."

Caroline faced her husband, but she could not yet admit her feelings aloud, so she responded with her usual sarcasm. "What can you possibly mean, sir? What cause have I to experience anxiety?"

"Come," he said. His blue eyes showed some internal pain. "You are aware of my family's fall from fortune. Though you have seen my home in town, you must harbor some fear regarding the condition of my ancestral estate."

Caroline looked at him for a long moment, and then, over his shoulder. They were coming upon the stream that she knew formed the boundary to his property, or had at one point.

"How far are we from the house?" she asked.

"What?" he replied, confused.

"The house: how close is it?"

Mr. Rushton lowered his eyebrows at her but then looked outside to discover where they were. "Not a quarter mile."

"Excellent, have the coachman stop the carriage," Caroline said, delighted at the confusion on his face. "I should like to walk."

His blond eyebrows dipped even lower. "But you despise walking."

"Yes, but if I am entering a new life, I intend to do so of my own volition and under my own momentum."

Mr. Rushton nodded, did as she bid him, and stopped the carriage. He assisted her to the ground and sent the driver on.

They stood together in the grass as the cloud of dust dissipated in the wake of the barouche's disappearance. Their eyes were locked, as if each were trying to read the other's thoughts, and then Mr. Rushton offered his arm.

She took it, and they walked slowly toward the stream.

"I suppose it is natural for you to desire to meet your future on your own terms and under your own power. You had little choice in the decisions that led to this point."

Here, Caroline laughed aloud. "Little choice? What can you mean?"

Mr. Rushton looked upon her as one might regard a lunatic.

"Oh, you refer to the circumstances of our engagement," she said.

"Indeed."

"Well, you may cease being concerned about them, for I can assure you that nothing has occurred that I did not truly desire in my heart, though I hesitate in sharing that truth with anyone, especially you, husband, for you shall undoubtedly enjoy wielding this new power over me."

He smiled broadly at her and then sobered. "I should think you understand by now that I love you. And it should be abundantly clear that I have no desire for power over you." He referred to the solicitor's letter, Caroline knew.

She desired to speak, but she had never been easily able to understand her own heart, much less share its content with others.

So the couple walked on through the summer green grass as far as the bridge across the stream.

Finally, Caroline stopped. "I know that you do not act for dreams of power. Your actions—your repudiation of my fortune—revealed to me your love in a way that your words may never have."

"I wanted you to understand that my motives were not the same as other gentlemen's may have been."

"All my life, I have labored under the misapprehension that society's values were correct. That a person ought to be born to his position and inherit his fortune, but Mr. Newton, my own father, and even you have shown me that perhaps English society is changing."

He offered her a look of mock shock. "Do I understand you correctly? Have you finally abandoned your preoccupation with society and its whims?"

Caroline laughed again. "No indeed! I shall always seek the best company and purchase the finest of every item available, but I shall no longer be ashamed of my past. I will not make my every decision based on my fear of its discovery, and I shall never look down upon tradesmen again."

"Never?" Mr. Rushton asked, clearly dubious.

"Well," she hesitated. "I shall not look down upon them overmuch as long as they behave with civility."

"So have you changed at all?"

Had she?

No, Caroline thought not. She was still the same woman who enjoyed music, good company, and society parties. She would never be a soft, submissive creature, and she would speak her mind at every opportunity. No, that much remained the same.

Still, she had indeed learned something from the events of the past year.

"I have said only that I realize that society may be changing. It would be foolish—would it not?—to deny that fact, to refuse to understand it. And so, you must tell me," Caroline said, gesturing toward the bridge at their feet, "about this structure before me. Mr. Newton informed me that it was one of your early designs. And it appears more complicated than throwing some logs across a stream as I previously believed."

Mr. Rushton gave her a smile, but he did not respond to her invitation to explain its design and construction; instead, he only took her hand in his and led her across it.

Still, she understood his meaning. The bridge served its purpose, and it was a thing of beauty to behold as its stone slabs sparkled in the afternoon sun. This bridge was a product of his mind as well as his hands, and it had saved his whole family from poverty. For Mr. Rushton, it was an object of pride, not shame.

And it ought to be for her as well.

She looked at this man—her husband—beside her. He was smirking. "So tell me, Caro, for we have danced about this subject, do you think you shall ever admit how desperately you love me?"

She returned his smirk. "I had not thought I was required to speak those words to you, husband, for my actions revealed the truth, even before I realized it myself. Did not I allow you to take advantage of me and compromise my reputation?" Caroline felt herself blush, but she continued. "Did not I throw myself into your arms like a wanton woman?"

He turned so that they were facing each other, their hands still joined between them. His blue eyes were wide and clear, and in their expression, she was surprised to observe what in any other gentleman she might have described as uncertainty. But that could not be, for Mr. Rushton was perhaps the surest individual she had ever encountered.

"Yes, but did you not know that a gentleman likes to be assured of the love of his wife?" he asked. "He does not care to speak his feelings aloud if hers remain hidden. So you must speak."

"You ought to realize early in our marriage, husband, that I have no interest in doing as I am told." Her lips stretched slowly into a smile as she stepped closer until their bodies were very nearly touching. "If I choose to let my actions speak for me, then you shall have to learn to accept it."

Caroline raised her free hand to her husband's neck and allowed her fingers to trail toward his collar. His expression had turned hungry, and it seemed he could remain still no longer. Mr. Rushton pulled her flush against his body, causing a little gasp to escape from her lips. Pressed against him in the middle of the road to Rushton House, Caroline felt as if she had finally found her home, and it was not in the house that awaited them at the end of the drive. No, it existed in something else entirely.

Caroline realized in that moment that she could not date her falling in love with Mr. Rushton upon her first sight of his beautiful grounds at Rushton House—although they turned out to be lovely indeed—but upon her understanding of the depth of his character and upon her comprehension of her own heart.

⋙ ⋘

❧ Author's Note ❧

I am most indebted to Jane Austen for her creation of the wonderful world and characters of *Pride and Prejudice*. I would also like to thank my family and friends who contributed to this book and to my life in general: Bert Becton, Marilyn and Robert Whiteley, and Octavia and Ed Becton. I am grateful to my editorial team Beverle Graves Myers and Kelley Fuller Land, both excellent editors and writers. Though any errors within this text belong solely to me, I will—as usual—do my best to foist them upon someone else.

❧ ❧

❧ About the Author ☙

Jennifer Becton has worked for more than twelve years in the traditional publishing industry as a freelance writer, editor, and proofreader. Upon discovering the possibilities of the expanding eBook market, she created Whiteley Press, an independent publishing house, and *Charlotte Collins: A Continuation of Jane Austen's* Pride and Prejudice, her first historical fiction novel, was published in 2010 with great success.

She also writes thrillers under the pseudo-pseudonym J. W. Becton. *Absolute Liability*, the first in the six-book Southern Fraud Thriller series, became an Amazon Kindle Best Seller, and *Death Benefits* (Southern Fraud 2) will be out in early 2012.

❧ ☙

Connect with Jennifer Online
Blog: http://www.bectonliterary.com

Facebook: http://www.facebook.com/JenniferBectonWriter

Twitter: http://twitter.com/JenniferBecton

Southern Fraud Thriller Series: http://www.jwbecton.com

❧ ☙

www.ingramcontent.com/pod-product-compliance
Lightning Source LLC
Chambersburg PA
CBHW030029030726
47500CB00001B/27